POWER OF PINJARRA

SANDY DENGLER

BETHANY HOUSE PUBLISHERS
MINNEAPOLIS, MINNESOTA 55438
A Division of Bethany Fellowship, Inc.

Cover illustration by Dan Thornberg,
Bethany House Publishers staff artist.

Published by Bethany House Publishers
A Division of Bethany Fellowship, Inc.
6820 Auto Club Road, Minneapolis, Minnesota 55438

Printed in the United States of America

Library of Congress Cataloging-in-Publication Data

Dengler, Sandy.
The power of Pinjarra / Sandy Dengler.
p. cm. — (Australian destiny ; 2)
I. Title. II. Series: Dengler, Sandy. Australian destiny ; 2.
PS3554.E524P69 1989
813'.54—dc19 88–32756
ISBN 1-55661-057-2 CIP

SANDY DENGLER is a freelance writer whose wide range of books has a strong record in the Christian bookselling market. Twenty-six published books over the last nine years include juvenile historical novels, biographies, and adult historical romances. She has a master's degree in natural sciences and her husband is a national park ranger. They make their home in Ashford, Washington, and their family includes two grown daughters.

AUSTRALIAN DESTINY SERIES

Code of Honor
Power of Pinjarra
Taste of Victory

CONTENTS

CHAPTER ONE

IN THE WAKE OF HARRY READFORD

1891

"Mirram and Wareen were hunters, and they were friends. They ranged together through the hills to the west of the sacred Oobi Oobi Mountain where hunting is good. Each evening, when the sun woman left the sky, they would sit before their fire and tell each other all they had done that day. Each was thus as wise as the other, and each was thus as foolish."

The world around Indirri, every bit and piece, lent itself to the haunting mystery of the Storyteller's tale. There is an end to the earth, and an edge to the world, where the sun woman lives; everyone knew that. But you'd never guess it now, for each night darkness spread out into thicker darkness, above and below and all around. No beginning. No end. The stars kept measured pace with the seasons as they always had. Nothing changed, yet all things changed.

It was logical that the sun woman was also the keeper of fire, for she was powerful among the people of the Dreamtime, and fire is power. Tonight, as every night, three tiny yellow dots of daytime flickered in the constant darkness. The Storyteller's little fire drew the uninitiated young men. Farther on, the initiated men huddled around their own bit of daytime. A ways off, by a gum tree, the women sat around their own fire burning off the hair of a wallaby. Obviously, women made practical use of that which fueled men's dreams, for was not fire the essence of power?

The Storyteller rumbled on. "At night Wareen would find his bed among the rocks because he was one to sleep under the protection of the earth. Mirram would make his place in the open because he was one to sleep under the stars.

"One night it rained fiercely. Mirram climbed into the rocks and beseeched his friend, 'Let me join you.'

" 'No. For you are too wet.'

" 'Let me join you. The rain is fierce.'

" 'No. For you were foolish to sleep out there.'

" 'Let me join you. The sky lights are gone. It is dark.'

" 'No. You did not honor the earth by entering her embrace before; now when your lights are gone, you must live with that.'

"Mirram became exceedingly angry, all the more because he was very wet. His anger made Wareen exceedingly angry, all the more because he was very sleepy. They argued, and then they fought. Mirram seized a great rock and smashed Wareen's face with it. But Wareen threw his spear. It stuck fast in Mirram's spine—at the end of his spine—right here; see?

"And so it was that Mirram became the first of all the kangaroos, with a great, bounding tail. And Wareen became the first of all the wombats, with his flat, pushed-in face."

Fingerlike tendrils of orange and red laced themselves through the few coals left of the night's fire. They splashed yellow flickers across the Storyteller's whole body, and made subtle changes in the colors of his paint.

Indirri sat silently beside his respected teacher, running the story through his mind twice more. He might not hear it ever again, and yet he must know it word for word. Someday he would become an elder and then he would be called upon to tell the clan's children how the kangaroo and the wombat came to be.

Mungkala spoke up. "Where exactly are the hills?"

"By and by I'll show you, sometime when we pass near."

Mungkala frowned. "It is wrong for friends to argue and fight, true?"

"True."

"But if Wareen and Mirram had not fought, we would have no kangaroos and wombats. Kangaroos and wombats are very good. So good came from the fight that was wrong."

Surely the Storyteller would be angry with this upstart. It was a child's place to listen, not to argue. If Indirri knew that, certainly the Storyteller did.

But the Storyteller was grinning, and his grin spread into a sparkling smile, his big bright teeth only slightly yellowed by the firelight. "So. A puzzle. And what is the answer?"

Mungkala shrugged. "Maybe there isn't any."

"Every puzzle has an answer waiting somewhere. Hiding. Not always can men find it, but it's there. Think."

Mungkala was always quick to question, but he was not one to dwell long on a thought. A fly wouldn't have time to buzz before Indirri's younger cousin quit thinking. "Do you know the answer?"

"To this puzzle, yes. Indirri, do you know?"

Indirri shook his head, suddenly embarrassed to have been singled out from among the four youngsters.

The Storyteller straightened; story time was over. "You—all of you—spend a little time seeking. Perhaps you can come to me tomorrow with the answer." He rose in one fluid movement and strode off through the darkness to the men's fire.

Mungkala studied the flickering coals. "What if he doesn't know the answer? What if he's just trying to get us to find his answer for him?"

Maybe the Storyteller wasn't angry at Mungkala's insolence, but Indirri was getting tired of it. "What if you bring him the wrong answer and he laughs at you? You'd deserve it, that's what. He's the oldest in our clan. He's even older than my great-uncle. Of course he has the answer. He knows everything."

Mungkala stood up and stretched. "Know what's wrong with you? Your head never asks any questions. You might as well be a lubra. You think like one—I mean, you don't think like one!" And he ambled off toward his sister's humpy, probably to try to cadge some little snack before sleep.

So he thought Indirri was a silly old girl, huh? Inside his head Indirri threw sand onto the rising fire of his own anger. Friends and clansmen must not fight. It is wrong to fight.

But then, how did kangaroos and wombats get to be?

Marty had a reputation for good night vision. But in this star-studded darkness he had to depend on his nose and ears to tell what was happening. Three horses plodded heavily through the unseen Queensland dust.

"How far are we from camp, Uncle Martin?" Jase's raspy twelve-year-old voice asked.

"Five, maybe six miles yet. Two hours."

"That far?" Jase wiggled in his saddle; Marty could hear it creak. How did the horses make their way so easily in this blackness?

Jase pointed off to the west. "What're those three fires way out there, then—blackfellers?"

"Likely. No drovers out this way."

Marty shifted in his saddle. He had been riding almost constantly for the last twelve hours, not counting half an hour for supper. At thirteen he was as tough as any grown man on the station. He had prided himself on that—until now. He was aching all over from all this saddle pounding. "Know how you can tell they're blackfellers? Three fires instead of one big one. For people without matches, they sure like their fires."

Beside him his father snickered. "Ever heard of Goolagaya?"

Jase's saddle creaked again. Jase must be stiffer than Marty; he was almost a full year younger and he'd been on the station only a couple weeks so far. "Who's he? One of those blackfeller things?"

"*She*. An ugly old hag. Lurks in the dark, grabs and eats any little tad who wanders away from the safety of the firelight. She's one of the big reasons blackfellers are so scared of the dark."

"She doesn't grab whitefeller kids though. Right?" Jase's saddle creaked again.

Marty laughed. "Jase, you're 'most grown up. You don't believe that stuff, do you?"

Pop chuckled in the darkness. "Never can tell. Maybe you two boys better stay close to me."

Marty forced his mind off ugly old crones and onto better things. "Bet that's why Turk Moran always has a cigarette lit. Little red dot in the darkness—you know it's Turk. He's keeping the old Goolagaya away."

"Sure," Jase cackled—his version of giggling. "Turk's old, but he ain't much bigger than a kid. Like Uncle Martin says, you never can tell."

Pop's voice sobered in the darkness. "Jason, I sure hate to see you come along on this, but there's just no way around it. Too far from home to take you back. It's going to be some hard riding. Might even get dangerous; Turk's armed. Don't know how I'd tell your mum, if something happened."

"I'll be fine, Uncle Martin, really!"

"You being my nephew, I feel even more responsible than if you were my son. So you stay low. And remember, the ratbag's no hero, and he's likely not gonna give up peacefully. You stay clear out of the way."

Pop was about right on the distance. Marty couldn't tell time as well with stars as with the sun, but they rode for hours across the empty flatness. Now and then he would draw his knees up on his saddle pommel trying to get more comfortable. But there was no place—not one place—comfortable on this rock-hard horse furniture. How could Turk Moran even think of doing what he was doing? Crazy Turk!

The campfire loomed on the horizon nearly an hour before they reached it. Marty slid from his saddle with deep, warm gratitude. Picketing his mare beside Pop's, he unsaddled her and hurried over to the fire hard on Pop's heels.

Nearly two dozen men were gathered round the campfire in the flat darkness, their fronts red-orange and their backs black. A few stood leaning against the water wagon while others sat or leaned on a hayrick parked at the edge of the circle.

Pop shook hands with a tall, thin man with a marvelous, droopy handlebar mustache. "Good to see you. This here's my nephew, Jason James, and you know Marty, of course. Jason, Cyrus Bickett. Cy, you musta put the hard word on every station in the district."

Cy Bickett grinned. (Anyway, Marty thought the man grinned; the corners of his mouth were buried behind the mustache; you could never really tell with Cy.) "And why not? That bloody galah's got at least a few cattle off every station round. Here, you three. There's lashings yet, and it's extra grouse. Dig in."

Jase shoved in close to Marty and glanced at him. The big round eyes spoke questions.

Marty translated. "There's lots of good food, so help yourself." It was an invitation Marty had been dreaming about for five hours. He snatched the top tin plate off the stack. It had been used, so he grabbed a handful of sand and polished it clean. A gentleman with a bushy white beard ladled him a big plateful of kangaroo stew and poured him a tin cup of tea from a billy in the coals.

Balancing his plate, Pop sat hunkered down by Mr. Bickett and two others, so Marty parked cross-legged beside him and picked the potato chunks out of his stew. He always ate the potatoes first.

"Martin, we figure Moran's gunner take about the same route Readford did. He's got no more than two days on us. If we push hard we should catch up to him not long after he crosses the Barcoo. His cows will only walk so fast."

Pop smiled. "*His* cows, huh?"

An expletive burst forth and Mr. Bickett glanced guiltily at Jason. "He's such a flootin' charmer; he does that to you. Gets you thinking his way." He wagged his head and the ends of his long mustache swayed. "Can't be—what?—five-six tall at the most; about the size of this nipper here," and he nodded toward Jason again. "Weighs less'n a dingo; and there he's shoving a thousand head of cattle ahead of him. Don't charm just people; he charms cows, too, to get 'em doing what he wants like that."

"Got two helpers with him, don't forget. Just like before."

"Sir? 'Scuse me." For the first time since sitting down, Jase raised his head from his plate. "I don't understand. Did Mr. Moran try this once before, do you mean?"

Marty finished his potatoes and started on the carrot chunks. He always ate carrots next, unless there were turnips.

Mr. Bickett slurped his tea. "You ever meet Turk Moran?"

"Yes, sir. Last time I visited Uncle Martin."

"Then you know how he's always yarning. Lot of his yabba comes out of books and magazines. The way we figure it, he read a *Bulletin* story about how a Harry Readford stole near a thousand head of bullocks, including a white bull, and overlanded them nine hundred miles with the help of two drovers. That was in 1870—'zactly twenty years ago. We suspect now Turk's got it in his head he's going to recreate the event and maybe make a quid or two on the deal. Relive the glory days, you might say. Bushrangers and duffers. All that."

"But now's different since we have the railhead over in Barcaldine. Wouldn't it make more sense to drive his mob the sixty miles to the railroad, sell them and get away quick?"

"To you and me it would, but not to Turk, I don't think." Mr. Bickett poured himself another cup of tea.

Jase wagged his head. "Sure to get caught and hanged. What a nong idea."

"Readford was acquitted. Set free."

Marty now had the onions out of the way. At last he was ready to eat the good part—the meat. His Pop grinned. "Readford hid his cows out in that ravine by Eagle Station, then headed south. The men chasing him twenty years ago didn't know where he was or which way he was going. But we know 'cuz we read the article, too."

All at once Jase jumped and sucked in air. What scared him? Marty, sitting beside him, glanced up and almost jumped, too.

The aborigine before him probably wasn't much older than Marty. Marty was small for his age—hadn't gotten his growth yet, Mum said. But this young man would probably be slim and wiry forever. He wore absolutely nothing except for some dots and streaks of white paint. In silence he had popped *poit* out of nowhere. Now he stood in that same cloaking silence before Pop and Mr. Bickett.

Ross Sheldon, the hulking pastoralist with the run above Barcaldine, moved into the firelight from behind the hay wagon. Marty didn't much like Mr. Sheldon, but he couldn't tell why. The man was powerful, he had money, he was well enough respected. No reason not to like him, as Pop said. On the other hand, the fellow wore these bright brocade vests and waistcoats everywhere, even out here in the flies and bulldust. Marty didn't much like pompous people who put on fancy airs.

Mr. Sheldon waved a hand impatiently. "This is Gimpy Jack. Walks with a bad limp, but Syd says it doesn't slow the boy down any and we should use him. He'll be tracking for us. Syd says Gimpy can look at a toe print and tell you what the fellow had for breakfast."

"Ross," said Pop patiently, and he sounded bemused, "even Marty here can track a mob a thousand strong."

Mr. Bickett set his tin cup aside. "Well, there's a bit of a problem, Martin. Ross and a couple others mustered some fairly big mobs down south of here. Assuming Turk is taking the same general direction as his hero, he'll be driving right through there. We want to make sure we stay with his mob and not get off onto someone else's."

"And this blackfeller's going to track one bunch out of many?"

"Let's hope so."

The next morning Marty was definitely not ready to climb back in a saddle, and he knew Jase's backside was in even worse shape. Yet, before dawn they were on their way.

There was a weirdness to all this, an unreality. A score of riders strung themselves out across a ragged line, side by side, so that no man need eat the others' dust. Still, the pervasive, penetrating bulldust coated them all in a uniform red-beige. They rode on in grim silence—these color-muted men.

Just being here was strange to both Marty and Jason. These young boys, though companionable, would never be alike. Jase was small like his mum, and skinny, with shiny dark hair and black, black eyes. He looked like a little kid among big, serious men. And Marty, though bigger than Jase, knew he too looked like a nipper.

It was the weirdness of Turk Moran himself that started all this; Marty knew that much. Turk was small and wiry and wore spectacles halfway down his hawk-beak nose. No matter what the subject, Turk knew more about it than anyone else. Turk was the greatest drover, the greatest gambler, the greatest beer drinker; and yet, Marty had not once seen Turk do any of those things. It was strange the way Turk was always big-noting himself; you couldn't tell if it was true or false.

And now Turk had gone and stolen a thousand cattle. Marty remembered one of the psalms his mum read out of the Bible—about God owning all the cattle on a thousand hills. What if Turk had gotten some of God's cattle mixed in with Cy Bickett's and Pop's and the others'? If God were even an eighth as angry as these men . . . Would a man like Turk ever consider the wrath of God?

The sun with all its vivid, intense heat beat upon Marty's hat and shoulders. It burned his eyes and forced them almost shut. He had grown up in this. He should be used to the heat. That was another part of the weirdness; how heavily the sun and the shimmering open spaces were making his senses reel.

Cy Bickett pulled his horse back from the line and jogged over to Marty. He slipped in beside Marty's horse. "Yon Jason there's too young, but you ain't. Your father says you're pretty good with a .22."

"Guess so, kinda."

Mr. Bickett pulled a long-barreled pistol out of his belt. "I don't want you using this unless there's no way not to. You don't ever point it toward one of us, even for an instant. And you don't ever leave it unloaded. It's the unloaded guns that kill people. And you don't for a second forget that there's death in the other end of it."

Marty's heart went thump. The cool, heavy, ungainly pistol was suddenly in his hand instead of Mr. Bickett's. He stammered. "I don't think, uh . . . Mr. Bickett, I mean I don't really think I oughta—"

"If Moran gets trapped like we plan, he's gunner start looking for the weak link in the net; and that might be you boys. I want you to be able to protect yourself if you have to."

"What's Pop . . . ? I mean, doesn't Pop think I oughta—"

"Your papa agrees you're close enough to man-sized. Oh, one other thing. Don't go blowing the ears off your horse there."

"Ears. Right. Uh, wait; don't you think I oughta—"

He was gone. Mr. Bickett had ridden off to talk to someone else, leaving Marty to ponder the horrid gravity of growing up.

Beside him, Jase murmured, "Whacko! Sure wish he'd do the same for me."

"Your horse'd never hear again."

They crossed the Barcoo an hour past lunch, and Marty thought of other rivers he'd heard of, rivers you need a boat to cross. The Murray was one such, and the Darling—rivers with water in them most of the time. At this particular "ford" the Barcoo consisted of soft sand half a mile wide. A thick green row of acacias lined its southeast bank. A quarter mile upstream, a wallow of caked clay marked, like a gravestone, the dead remains of a dried-up billabong.

All of a sudden they were on him! Ahead lay a stretch of low, casual, rounded rises, not really undulant enough to be called hills. And from among them rose the dust of a thousand cattle. Turk was driving his stolen mob in the heat of day. Even Marty knew that if Turk was keeping his cattle on their feet and moving when they wanted to loaf, he must have caught wind of his pursuers.

The line of irate stockmen spread thinner, grew ragged, as they *spurred* their horses forward . . .

. . . and the chase was on!

Stiffness and saddle sores faded to nothing. Marty's gelding plunged forward, caught up like Marty in the heady thrill of this wild ride. The gelding's strong, rhythmic strides jolted and faltered as they swooped up the first rise. He dodged boulders and jumped the craggy little outcrops as Marty mostly just stayed on top. When the horse's big feet nearly tangled in a clump of grass, Marty was sure they'd both go crashing down, but he recovered his stride. Somewhere among the low trees to the right, Jase whooped like a jubilant banshee.

Within minutes they were in a sea of cattle, a million cattle, and Marty remembered how many a thousand cows really is. The mob was rushing, breaking, scattering amid a dense and gritty pall of bulldust. Marty couldn't see; he couldn't breathe; he didn't know where he was, let alone where anyone else might be. He could hear the gunshots, though. A dozen of them crackled and roared above the thunder. A voice cried, "Over that way!"

Lovely! *What way?*

The universe was full of bawling cows and horns and hooves and dust. The world churned along at the speed of Marty's running horse. Straggly trees reached out and grabbed at him as he brushed past; a branch nearly pulled him off. His horse stumbled on the uneven ground. Where was Jase? Jase couldn't ride as well as Marty, and Marty was having trouble enough. What if Jase . . .?

He was over there, a bit ahead, a hazy gray phantasm looming above the maelstrom of horns and razorbacks. Marty jerked his gelding's head aside and forced him off toward Jase. The most dangerous thing in the world is to lose your horse from under you in the rush of a panicked mob. He must stay close to Jase, just in case the boy fell. What could Marty do if the worst happened? Who knows? He knew only that he must not lose his cousin in this chaos.

The rider ahead dropped from sight as big bay hindquarters came flying up through the dust and tumbled forward. Not only was Jase down, he might be crushed beneath his horse! Moments ago they had been in the thick of the mob;

now they seemed to be more in the thin of it.

Without really thinking, Marty jerked his horse to enough of a stop that he could jump off beside the fallen bay. Still without thinking, he pulled that clumsy pistol out of his belt. He would try to drop any cow bearing down on Jase; one or two carcasses piling up might be enough of a barrier to keep Jase from being trampled.

He had slaughtered many a bullock—put the bullet just so in the curl of hair on the forehead. But those cattle had been standing docile in a feedlot. These were coming at him at that bounding, jerky cow canter. He tried to steady his shaking hands. How could he hit one little spot on—?

"Noooo!" a man's voice shrieked beside him, wailing to heaven itself.

Marty wheeled as a wild-eyed cow thundered past. Through the choking, obscuring dust, he saw a blood-soaked shirt.

Turk Moran! It wasn't Jase at all! As his horse struggled upright and ran off, Turk pulled himself reeling to his knees. Screaming blasphemies, he twisted, swaying, to face Marty, and with him came the muzzle of a shotgun.

In defense, without thinking, Marty swung the gun in his hands toward the drover he'd known for years.

Never in his whole life to come would Marty ever be able to remember which of those two horrible roaring guns fired first.

CHAPTER TWO

THE WHITE KNIGHT OF BARCALDINE

Pearl, at thirteen, was three years older than her sister Enid. She was bigger, wittier, prettier. Her dark blond hair curled and Enid's brown mop didn't. So why were people always passing Pearl by in order to make a fuss over Enid? There they were doing it again. Half a dozen church elders mobbed around Papa and Enid, and here stood Pearl alone on the church steps.

"So, young lady, and what do you think of the events this morning? Glorious, isn't it?"

"Yes, sir. Absolutely." Glorious. Hmph. If you believed this hubbub, when Papa brought Pearl and Enid to church this morning they were all pagans. *Your father and sister are brand-new Christians! Isn't that wonderful?* And what did that make Pearl and Mum—Hottentots? Ragged old Christians? Aborigines were pagans. So were the thousands upon thousands of Chinese who swarmed across the goldfields to the west. Pearl was a Christian, born to it, baptized, raised in the church. So were Papa and Enid and Mum. And now look at all this.

Elder Babbitts' crooked yellow teeth were smiling so Pearl smiled also. The elder's smile disappeared, replaced by his usual stern now-this-is-serious stare. "Do you understand exactly what happened this morning, Paula?"

"Pearl." She corrected, then added a hasty, "By your leave, sir."

"Pearl, of course. Do you understand that by confessing their sins, and by openly committing their souls to Jesus Christ and acknowledging their faith in Him as their Savior, your father and sister have passed from death into life?"

"Yes, sir." Certainly she understood, from catechisms and Sunday school verses memorized years ago. You confess your sins every Sunday; it's written right into the service. Jesus is life, and Pearl was born into life, no less than Papa and Enid.

"Now, dear Paula, have you made that same confession?" Elder Babbitts' tone of voice assured her he was certain she was hell-bound.

"Yes, sir." She glanced around, desperate for a way out. She could see none.

Undaunted by the positive reply, Elder Babbitts treated it like a negative and launched into a rehearsal of the morning's sermon.

"Pearl! Come!" Papa was calling her at long, long last. Relief flooded her and she excused herself from Elder Babbitts' monologue and rushed down the steps. She latched onto Papa's right arm, and Enid took his left and they headed home, walking the way they always did from church—arm in arm.

Papa was a handsome man indeed, with his craggy face, sparkling blue eyes and wavy golden hair. Pearl took a great deal of pride in being his daughter, in walking beside him so elegantly. Elegantly. Yes, indeed, the Fowkeses were elegant. What a far cry from the past.

Papa's father and Mum's too had both been deported convicts. Ah, the blood-curdling stories of deprivation and horror Grandpa Fowkes told, stories about the voyage in chains from England, stories of hardship as he served out his sentence in the world's ultimate penal colony. He especially loved to describe the shame and prejudice free landholders were so quick to heap upon ex-convicts, denying them everything from a full political voice to the best of the farming land. And now here was Pearl Fowkes, his granddaughter, enjoying every advantage of modern civilization.

Pearl dragged them to a halt before the window of a little millinery shop in Wharf Street. Papa tugged her into motion again and they angled up into St. Paul's Terrace. Mum was dressed and waiting for them, as always, when they walked in the door. Mum worked hard six days a week and claimed the Sabbath as her personal day of rest. Pearl couldn't wait until she had a full-time job so she could rest on Sunday also.

Mum complained bitterly about the lack of domestic help and the high cost of a simple maid as she set out the Sunday dinner single-handedly. Papa and Enid glanced at each other now and then, smugly, as if their non-news were the greatest news in the world. The family sat down at the little mahogany dining table just as always, with Papa offering the blessing first, then the bowls of food passing around from left to right.

After a few moments Papa cleared his throat. "Maisie," he began, "this morning Enid and I made the most important decision that is possible to make. We confessed our faith and committed our lives to Jesus Christ."

Mum eyed him with the same *and so . . . ?* look that Pearl felt. "I always rather thought you were religious enough already."

"In the past I was searching. Today I found." Papa laid his fork down. "There is more news. The church is building a mission church—a branch, if you will—in Barcaldine. I shall accompany the minister as his assistant."

Mum dropped her fork and stared. "You're leaving home? Leaving Brisbane?"

"We all are. We're moving to Barcaldine. Should be there soon after Christmas—by the end of summer perhaps, or February at the latest."

"But your job—you're just beginning to make good money. And my job . . . It took me years to build up a very exclusive clientele. No. It's nonsense. Rubbish. I won't hear it!" She retrieved her fork and viciously attacked the roast lamb on her plate. "No."

Papa waited patiently until the silence was unbearable. "It is a call to service I will not ignore," he continued. "The church will pay us a hundred pounds a year, and you can take up your laundry business there as you are doing here. The girls will be educated in the local church school. I understand there are several fine schools. As for Pearl, I am sure she will be able to find work as well; she's old enough. She can help out."

Mum raised her fork in defiance. "I am exclusive laundress to the families of the lieutenant governor, the chief of police, the director of the Royal Botanical Gardens, to name a few. Do you realize what it took to establish myself thus? They enjoy position, Herbert, and they *pay*. In this Barky Dean—whatever you call it—who is going to pay what my services are worth? Who has position? No one, I guarantee you. Aborigines and a few smelly shepherds. Not a soul of consequence. You ask me to leave all this—for that. Bah!"

"I'm not asking you, Maisie," Papa said quietly. "I'm telling you."

Pearl's heart sank heavily. When Papa assumed his low-pitched, this-is-the-way-it-is voice, there was no arguing. Pearl couldn't imagine moving away from the city. She still vividly remembered leaving Parramatta, the small town of her birth, to live in Sydney, and how Sydney spoke to her instantly: "I am your home. I am in you." Brisbane, while not so large or urbane as Sydney, was still a city of some substance, with darling shops and busy ways. And now they were on the move again.

To nowhere. Pearl was bound to nowhere. The lamb turned dry in her mouth; the potatoes choked her. Nowhere! And all because Papa's overdeveloped religious fervor was soaring to new heights—soaring out of control, obviously. But Mum would be the first to agree; Pearl could see it now in her mother's stricken face, pale in contrast to her dark hair. Her plump face was so tightly drawn that it seemed to lose its plumpness instantly.

The only person enthusiastic about the idea was Enid. But then, of course she would. Enid knew exactly how to play upon adults' emotions, Papa's especially, saying precisely the right thing at the right time in order to have her way and garner favorable attention. *Bitter. Life was so bitter!*

Bitter? The journey to Barcaldine stretched the word to new horizons even before they left. Ever since they had moved here to Brisbane, Mum had spent every shilling she could touch to make their home truly elegant, the way her clientele's homes looked—carpets, draperies, furnishings. Now she had to sell nearly everything—and at a loss, too, because times were hard and few people in these trying days could afford pretty things.

But it wasn't just the home and its furnishings. It obviously hurt Mum very much to leave the important Brisbane citizens she had served these years; you could tell it in her sad eyes and tearful evenings. Pearl, much like her mum, felt the loss too. She had to give up all her school friends, whom she would never see again. How sorrowful. True, most of them had been stuck-up snoots who treated her like a lesser person, but they were her friends and they were moneyed.

Papa hinted that Pearl could take only one trunk. "Rubbish!" muttered her mum. But even two trunks and a band box would not hold all Pearl's clothes and mementos. She had to leave behind some of her dearest possessions, including a bisque china doll that (she learned months later) fell into the hands of a very common and poor girl who lived down the street. It didn't ease the pain in the least that Pearl hadn't looked at that doll in years.

Bitterest of all was the actual journey to nowhere. Papa and his family, Barcaldine's new minister and his family and a half-caste helper named Toby were to travel as a company. Pearl didn't much like the minister's mousy little wife, their young children were annoyingly rambunctious, and she never knew what, if anything, to say to Toby. And that was what it was like all the way up the coast railway from Brisbane to Rockhampton.

At Rockhampton the party unloaded all their belongings on the railway platform, and then reloaded onto another train. The trip was hardly half over and already Pearl was intensely weary of travel. After much hissing and tooting and ringing of bells, the train began to lurch forward, spraying soot on everyone as it rolled.

As they moved slowly out of Rockhampton, Pearl noted the contrast to Sydney and Brisbane. Those were cities of commerce, with busy quays and many important bank and office buildings. Rockhampton, though, was a working city, a mining town, and it swarmed across its ragged hills like no city Pearl had ever known. Smokestacks from a dozen mills belched more black smoke than the train did. Even from inside her railway car, she could hear the noise and feel the thudding vibrations of a stamp mill by the tracks. What must it be like to live in this noisy, dirty town? She caught sight of a mob of happy children, laughing and playing tag on a slag heap. They didn't seem to mind the noise and dirt a bit. But then, children usually don't.

Beyond Rockhampton, Pearl somehow lost track of time. Not for the life of her could she recall the date exactly, nor could she remember how many days they had been in transit.

But there was one thing she couldn't forget—the stifling heat. Relentless summer sun made the rolling countryside glow and shimmer. Passengers opened their windows as wide as possible, with only a few stuck closed. Even so, the cars felt like ovens, heated not just from above but pouring in on all sides. Only when the train was ripping along at top speed (not all that frequently) did any kind of breeze stir inside.

At a barren little stop called Anakie a woman came aboard with a small chest slung on a strap around her neck. She moved from car to car, opening the little drawers in the chest to show her wares—gemstones from the mines of Anakie. To hear her talk, Anakie was the gem capital of the world. Capital? All Pearl had seen there was a few shacks and tents.

Indeed, all Pearl was seeing anywhere was shacks and tents and a few weather-beaten buildings with unpainted wooden sides and galvanized metal roofs. Her father wasn't dragging her off to nowhere. They were way beyond nowhere.

"Pearl, dear, wake up. We're there. We have to get off the train now. Pearl?" Mum was shaking her shoulder, tapping her cheek.

Groggy, Pearl lifted her head from Mum's lap. Darkness. They *would* have to arrive in the middle of the night! She struggled to sit up. Enid was stretching, just as droopy-eyed. Pearl felt like something the cat had dragged in as she stumbled out onto Barcaldine's rough-hewn railway platform. Papa arranged something with Toby and herded his family down into the street.

"Keep up!" Papa kept saying, but keeping up was the last thing on Pearl's mind. This was obviously the season referred to as "wet." Dark, heavy mud clung so thick to the sides of her shoes that her feet got heavy. She tried to keep her skirts high and out of the glop. No such luck. She watched the ground, picking her way carefully, but she couldn't avoid the constant puddles and mires. At least this town had some proper wooden buildings. It was still out beyond nowhere, though. Such a primitive, unappealing place! Whatever could Papa have been thinking of to consent to this?

Pearl stopped cold. She was standing beside a high galvanized metal fence in nearly complete darkness. She saw only one color—black; only one thing—nothing. Where were her . . . ? Panic seized her. Papa! Did she dare cry out? No! Heaven knows what sorts of black and hideous native murderers her voice would attract. A town this crude and uncivilized was sure to abound in ruffians and scoundrels, maybe even heathen Chinese. She must not draw attention to herself.

The main street! She'd find that. Surely her family would be there. At the very least, she'd meet a constable or some kind-looking person in a proper business suit. She groped along the tin fence for a ways, then cried out in pain as she ripped the palm of her hand on a loose nail. Her hand hurt. Her shoes, soaked through, were mudcaked. Her hair was in disarray from sleeping on Mum's lap. She dreaded to think what her dress must look like. She couldn't be seen in the darkness, but then, neither could she see. In the blackness, foreign smells and alien sounds descended upon her from mysterious nowheres. What a horrid mess! What a horrid, horrid mess!

Suddenly she saw a light. There was a light beyond that building; she couldn't see the lamp itself, but she discerned a faint glow in the air. She walked faster. Hope!

Whonk! She fell flat on her face, her shin throbbing with pain. She sat up and groped around her feet until her hand touched a metal object. She had stumbled over an iron something lying right out in the middle of the way! She rubbed her burning, aching shin with her left hand because her right hand still stung from the wound in her palm.

Her nose began to run and her eyes brimmed over. She sobbed. Oh, bother! Now her face was going to get all red and puffy; she'd be the ugliest thing in Barcaldine, and obviously that is very, very ugly indeed! Terrible settlement. Worthless town. The sobs forced themselves upon her with shuddering regularity.

Whddddddddd—a horse sneezed not ten feet away. Unbidden, Pearl's voice made a strangled little noise she'd never heard before. She bolted to her feet as she clamped her good hand over her mouth. *Don't let anyone know you're hiding here!*

"'Scuse me, mum. Can I help?" The voice sounded young, like a boy. It was a smooth, warm voice, heavy with the northern drawl.

"Thank you, but I'm quite fine. And my father will be along any moment. Thank you anyway. Papa will be here momentarily." She saw a light mark in the darkness before her and realized it was the blaze on a horse's face.

The blaze bobbed as the young man dismounted. Pearl could just barely make out his general form in the blackness. "Your father's got business way out here at this hour? I thought when I heard you yelp and watched you walking out the alley that you might be lost."

"Who are you?"

"I'm sorry. Shoulda introduced myself first. Marty Frobel. Martin Junior. We have a run up north a way." He shifted nervously in front of her. She thought perhaps he was holding out a hand to shake hands, but she couldn't possibly, not with the painful tear in her palm. The rich, gentle voice continued. "We're staying at the Commercial Hotel, Pop and me and my cousin and the station manager. I just been out to the yards to check our horses. You sure you aren't lost?"

She let one last shuddering sob escape. "Yes, I am. Lost, I mean."

"Where do you think you ought to be?"

"I don't know. We just got off the train. Papa was taking us to a hotel, but I don't know which one. I don't think he knew. Just . . . just a hotel. Somewhere. I don't know where he plans to go or where they are or even where the railway station is anymore. I don't . . ." She finally gave up trying to explain, overwhelmed by the enormity of it all.

An awkward silence fell between them. "Well, let's see. From the railway they'd likely go to the Shakspeare, the Commercial, or the Grazier's, depending whether you went down Willow or Beech. Remember the street?"

"No."

"Let's check Ash Street first. Ask around. Town's not that big. Careful of the axle there; don't trip again."

He stepped in beside her and started to move so she walked as well, back the way she had come. "How can you see in this darkness?"

"Don' know. Always could pretty good. Pop says I got owl vision. That's why he sent me out to check the horses. Besides that he didn't feel like going, of course." The mellow voice reassured her. It sounded very mature for a boy. Maybe he was older than she first guessed.

"I hope you can't see *too* well because I must really look a sight. This mud—"

"This mud's nothing. You shoulda seen it January a year ago. Worst rains in years. Everything bogged. Two feet of running water in front of the railway station where you got off. We thought we might not get the flocks shorn at all, it was so bad. Couldn't muster 'em, couldn't get the shearers into the stations. Did it rain where you came from?"

"Last summer? Yes. But then, in Brisbane it's fairly regular. The rain is, I mean."

They stepped from darkness into sudden light. However

dull, the feeble orange glow seemed heaven-sent.

Marty stopped. "You got blood on your dress. And your hand there. Here, lemme see."

Why did she so willingly let him look at her hand? She felt safe with him that's why—safe and comfortable. Like Papa he seemed—well, he himself seemed so safe and comfortable. His work clothes—drill pants and a cotton shirt—appeared well worn but not ragged. His droopy hat, the same kind of hat she'd already seen on hundreds of men and boys out in this wasteland, hid most of his brown hair, but it couldn't mask the gentle, deep-set eyes. And he was older than she'd first guessed. He had to be her age or a little more.

He yanked out his handkerchief to bind her hand. "Now if you were a horse, I'd know just what to do. Paint it with pine tar and turn you out into the paddock for a week or two." He wound the handkerchief around her palm. "I'm lots better with horses than I am with people. My cousin Jase won't let me touch him—'specially since last winter when he broke his leg and I suggested shooting him. There. Prob'ly won't do much for it, but it'll look a little better as you're walking down the street."

She realized she was smiling. In the middle of all this terrible circumstance, she was grinning like a brainless little schoolgirl.

"Eh, lad! Got a girlfriend, I see." From over in the shadows by an unmarked building, three leering men loitered.

"Union men. Strangers in town. Don't let 'em bother you." Young Marty led her off upstreet. "Town's full of union men right now; planning something, Pop says." Marty grunted. "You know, your Papa might have trouble finding hotel rooms. Besides the union people, most of the pastoralists, like us, are in from outback."

"Your father owns a station? Sheep station?"

"Sheep, cattle, horses. Up north a ways on Torrens Creek." He sounded so casual, but she got the distinct impression that there was far more to his father's holdings than a few head of livestock.

Were fifes and drums approaching? It certainly sounded

so. From around the corner came a parade, and Pearl had never seen one like it. The musicians led. Behind them, singing, shouting, roaring men waved torches and flags aloft. There had to be a hundred people. The inevitable happened: one of the flags ignited. It flickered and blazed a moment until its carrier hauled it down and snuffed it.

Marty hazed her off to the left, crowded close to the buildings, and brought his nervous horse up alongside as a sort of prancing, shying wall. The parade drew abreast and passed.

Without really thinking, Pearl pressed against Marty. This unwashed mob of scraggly, booze-ridden noise-makers frightened her. "More union men?"

"Too right. They hold parades 'most every night, just to keep their spirits up, I guess. Shearers mainly, with some waggoners and such. Railway workers. Union headquarters are right here in Ash Street. The laborers live in a tent camp outside town here; gathered from all over Queensland and some up from the south, I hear. Gonna be a bloody fight with the pastoralists come shearing time. Pop says that there's trouble on the hoof." He paused. "Your Papa on one side or the other?"

"No. He's here to help set up a church."

"Um. The unions don't have enough power to really do anything that will make a difference. Just make trouble, is all."

She twisted to watch the last of the parade howl by. "They look quite powerful enough to me. A fight? You mean like a real war?"

"Maybe. Pastoralists drew up some papers for shearers to sign; they refused and Syd Sharwood says he doesn't think they'll ever consent to. The graziers want to hire anyone they feel like hiring, and the shearers want us to hire only union people. They think their union people are worth a quid or two more than ordinary folks. It's a money thing. Eh, yair, it could come to shooting."

"But not your father. Or you. Shooting, I mean."

And Marty Frobel turned ice cold, just like that—cold and

hard. He didn't say a word, but the warm and gentle good humor vanished into the murky night.

They walked in silence to a brightly lighted doorway, a hotel lobby. "We'll try this one first; it's the likeliest place your father'd come to." Marty left his horse at the rail and piloted her in through the door.

Suddenly Marty was slamming into her; then he seemed taller. A big man in a gaudy brocade waistcoat had grabbed him by his arm—half wrenched the arm out of its socket, it looked like.

"What are you doing with her?" The man's voice sounded far harsher and more accusing than anything old Elder Babbitt could have mustered.

Pearl could feel the anger boil up in this Marty Frobel and she didn't blame him a bit. He stammered and started over. "Helping her find her pop."

"Don't you lie to me, boy. Look at her! Mud, front and back. What'd you do to her?"

Now the anger was boiling just as hot in Pearl. "Marty, is this your father?"

The big man snarled, "I didn't ask you to speak, girl. Answer me, boy!"

And that did it. She no longer cared whether this were young Marty's father or not. She didn't even care if he were an elder or something. "Sir!" She barked it so loudly the man paused, gaping at her. "This young man helped me most honorably, acting the perfect gentleman. And I am a lady. You'll not address either one of us in that tone of voice."

From over by the hotel desk rose a howl of laughter. The clerk was grinning. "Careful who ye chuck a charly in front of, Sheldon! That there's a *lye*-dee! Here, Missy. Your father's out looking for you and the rest of your party's up on the first floor. Room nineteen."

Another voice spoke. "Come on, Ross. You know young Frobel here's dinkum, same as his old man." Obviously, this was a small town where everyone knew everyone else.

Marty licked his lips. "I'll, uh, put the word around here and there on my way back to the Commercial, so your Papa will know you're safe. G'night, Mum." He stared at that Mr. Sheldon and the big man reluctantly let go. Then just like that he was gone into the night.

Pearl watched him disappear into the darkness outside before she could command her mouth to frame the properly polite words of extreme thanks. How could she just let him go without thanking him? Because he left so fast. Because this rude incountry drongo interfered. She glared at Mr. Big Brocade and flounced off to the staircase. She was so mad she almost forgot what a pitiful sight she must be with the mud and slop and daub of blood.

That Marty was a gentleman indeed, the very nicest of gentlemen, even if he was a backblocker. Like a true white knight he rescued her without expectation of anything in return.

And the loudmouthed fellow was a boor, no matter how costly the clothes he wore. Her feet paused on the stairs when the thought struck her: so wrapped up had she been in her own travails, she had never told Marty Frobel her name.

Chapter Three

All for a Lack of Lubras

In the very beginning, as the tribes were just starting out on their journeys, the mountain travelers got very thirsty. In their distress, they called out to Euro Man. So Euro Man went ahead of them, digging water holes along the way. Even today, the euro's trail will lead a man to water.

To the casual eye, this particular euro's trail led nowhere. After randomly zig-zagging across a grass hummock, it disappeared into the rocks. Indirri's was not a casual eye, however; nor was it an untrained one. Although the wise old Storyteller liked to tease Indirri about the changes in his body that announced his approaching manhood, he often boasted that Indirri possessed hunting skills far beyond his years. His tracking skills had been honed so now his eye could follow the faintest signs indicating where the euro had gone. His mind pictured the euro and his movements written in the script of that faint track.

Indirri readied his spear. Soon. Now he must keep one eye to the track and the other to the rocks above, for any moment the little gray kangaroo would come bursting out of its hiding place. *Be patient. Be silent.* Half a spear length away a carpet python recoiled with a jerk and poured itself back into the safety of the rocks. Indirri made mental note of its position and kept to the task at hand.

There was the water hole—a slimy, stinking little green dish in the rocks two spear-throws distant—buzzing with flies. Euro trails always led to water. The euro leaped up and out even as Indirri's arm moved—a spear cast that reflected more reflex than strategy. His spear penetrated the side of the animal's belly, its shaft clanging and bumping on the rocks as the euro bounded wide-eyed from boulder to boulder. The spear dropped out. The little kangaroo tired quickly, though, and within a quarter mile Indirri had caught up, seized it and broken its neck.

Indirri explained patiently to Euro Man how necessary it was that he kill this creature, for his clan needed the meat. That carpet python would not have been enough. Spear in hand and the euro balanced on his head, he walked back and dug out the snake. He killed it by biting it behind its neck, then, satisfied, headed south to join Mungkala and return to camp.

Was Indirri more than just a little bit proud? At not-quite-fourteen wets, he was the only man to bring in meat that day. He had every right to some smug self-satisfaction, particularly when his aunt's moiety arrived unexpectedly near sunset, and her party brought no meat at all.

In spite of his prowess, Indirri couldn't join the men at their fire that night; he hadn't yet been initiated into manhood. From a distance he watched the men of both moieties absorbed in earnest discussion. He yearned for manhood, yet he dreaded it. From the whispered tales he had heard of the initiation, he didn't understand how any man survived the rite, let alone how he fathered children after submitting to it. Great power flows from great suffering, so you really didn't want to be let off too easily. Still . . .

The Storyteller was drawing maps in the dust and Indirri's uncle was looking straight at Indirri as the old man spoke. They were talking about him; or were they talking about all the older boys? The men were nodding. Two of them tapped with fingers on the Storyteller's map. Something important was happening. Now Mother's cousin walked over to the women's fire to tell them something . . . and here came the Storyteller.

Sitting down beside Mungkala, the old man looked at Indirri. "So. A euro today, eh? Big man. All you, big men."

What was coming? Mungkala bit his lower lip nervously.

The Storyteller sketched in the orange dirt beside the fire. "Three generations ago in the south lived the Iningai—a mighty people, tall as a brigalow tree and strong as the Old Man Kangaroo. They were so strong, they lived two lifetimes long. But they were not strong enough. Last trade journey, thirteen wets ago, only one of five still survived. Much sickness, deaths from the whitefellers, no babies." He added two circles to the rough map and pointed to it with a dusty forefinger as he spoke. "Barcoo River here; south here; they lived here and here."

This meant nothing to Indirri; he'd never been there.

The Storyteller rocked back on his heels and studied the fire. "Head man for the other clan there, he says he hears that the Iningai—what's left—have some young women, not many young men. Look at us; we have young men, but no young women. So, for the first time in many wets we will take up raiding again."

Raiding. Warfare!

Indirri stared not at the Storyteller but at Mungkala. Mungkala was absolutely glowing with anticipation. "Raiding! To steal lubras for us?"

"And why not? Strong young women. Tall. Give you strong children. Raiding is honorable. Long ago it was the custom until we became so few and whitefellers became so many."

"Why not just bargain for some women?"

"Bargain with what?"

And there the Storyteller had him. Their clan's power was dissipating; everyone knew it, though no one said it aloud. They had nothing to offer a people superior in form and lifespan. Raiding. That night Indirri felt so churned up inside he could hardly sleep.

Raiding, however, must wait; the aunt's clan was here to trade. The next morning, business began. Indirri had heard stories of massive trading ceremonies in the past when great baskets and dilly bags of goods were exchanged—wonderful goods from far, far away. This would be a very small trade by comparison. Still, formalities must be observed.

As the sun moved higher, the men of the clans lined up facing each other. A man on Indirri's side shouted to the other side, complaining loudly of a slight made him. A man in a grey beard returned from the other side about an ugly incident from long ago in which he had been the victim. Indirri was shocked at the nature of it. For some time the accusations flew, becoming more heated.

Now the boomerang clubs, the murrawirri, were coming out. The men fell upon each other shouting and flailing. Indirri knew this was a mock battle, a simple clearing of the air. Even so, it scared him deep in his stomach. He tried to imagine fighting a real battle, with true war clubs, lethal boomerangs, real blood shed. And if they engaged the Iningai, it would soon be happening!

The battle ebbed. Calm prevailed. All animosities had been dealt with, all wrongs expunged. Finally the trading could begin, with pure, unsullied amity and good faith.

Again the sides lined up, each man with his trade goods at his feet. A very old man in the aunt's moiety stood amid several lethal-looking clubs and non-returning boomerangs. Indirri's people offered cunningly made spear throwers, piti bowls, and dilly bags in exchange. The Storyteller clustered little bags of pituri around his feet; he was known far and wide for the high quality of his medicine. Mungkala's great-uncle had pearl shell from up north; the other group did not. Ah, but the other side brought out several big round cakes of ground red ocher. Indirri's mother had been complaining bitterly that the last of her ocher was gone.

"I wish, please, a bag of pituri," called one of the other men. Storyteller threw his choicest bag across to the fellow. Because he had given, Storyteller now had the right of request. "I wish, please, that fine kanilpya there." It was thrown to him.

The former owner of the kanilpya bowl now had the right of request. And so it went, back and forth, as the summer sun climbed higher and ever hotter. Goods seemed to fly from side to side willy-nilly; sometimes the same item returned to its original owner more than once as the other side bartered for a better exchange. And yet there was a grand order to it all. By the time trading was over, hardly any man possessed anything with which he had begun.

And, courtesy of Uncle, Mother had her red ocher.

The excitement was over. The two clans would drift apart now, the aunt's moiety to the northwest on the next leg of its trading expedition, and Indirri's clan . . .

. . . to war. He still couldn't believe it.

Through the next full moon the clan moved along an unfamiliar route as the women and children stayed within sight of each other, and the men and young men kept watch on the periphery. The men did less hunting now, more patrolling. A man's most pressing responsibility is to protect the women, and they were entering dangerous territory.

Indirri had never seen this country before, although he did his best to memorize the subtle changes in this nearly faceless plain that would show him the way next time he passed. The lines the Storyteller had drawn in the dirt that morning came to life in this land, which had features uniquely its own.

They passed within sight of a whitefeller's camp, its tin roofs glowing like the sun. They passed within a mile of a flock of sheep. Indirri knew better than to go near them, let alone to spear them; whitefellers were extremely possessive about their animals. The clan crossed a strange see-through wall made out of a mesh of thin, stiff metal cord. It stretched for miles in both directions; Storyteller called it by its whitefeller name, "fence." Indirri could not imagine how many lubras it would take to weave all those miles of metal mesh.

By the second new moon they were deep within Iningai territory, but it looked deserted. Indirri saw plenty signs of whitefeller, and plenty of sheep, horse and cattle tracks. On one occasion he encountered the trace of huge padded feet with ungainly toes. Camels. More whitefeller animals. But where were the blackfellers?

Again the men clustered around a late-night fire, heads

together. Indirri and Mungkala, along with the two boys of ten wets, patrolled the perimeters of camp, for they could take no chances. Iningai were a mighty people—wherever they were. Indirri was very good at smelling danger—better than Mungkala, though not as perceptive as his uncle. Neither he nor his uncle sensed fear or danger in this territory. All he could smell was nothing. Emptiness.

The next morning Indirri's uncle made a general announcement. "Our enemies are gone, and their women with them. No sign, no tracks—very bad. Some have said go back to the land we know. Others have said we must not quit. They want to continue to seek out our enemies, to persist. They say if these people are as few as it seems, we might all consent to join together, their young and our young. No raiding. No warfare.

"And some have said stay here. This land has better hunting than ours; the grass is rich. Look at how much our women and children gather without roaming widely. The signs of seasons are true here just as they are back home. We can use everything we already know, but we will eat better."

Three options from only four initiated men. Indirri got a strong feeling that no one had any clear notion of what to do next. What was the big thing about young women anyway? True, the clan would not survive without children. But surely child-bearing women were not so scarce but that with a little concerted effort they could raise the birth rate. Either the initiated men were so impatient for the excitement of a raid that they would not be put off, or there was something about this situation Indirri was not aware of.

A flight of doves steered them in the direction of a water hole, and a helix of spiraling eagle-hawks told them a dead animal lay to the southeast. The women hefted their dilly bags and digging sticks. Indirri gathered up his spear, spear thrower and boomerang. They were on their way.

The water was a muddy little billabong in a side channel, which provided enough water for the day, and some to spare. They weren't so lucky at finding food, however. The dead animal was a whitefeller's cow, so they gave the carcass a wide berth. No matter how bloated and sun-rotted it might be, any whitefellers catching them near the carcass would assume they had speared it. Blackfellers had been shot for less.

Indirri lagged behind at the tail end, thinking about his initiation. It would be soon. Although he did not in the least relish the thought of all the scars, or the circumcision, or the pain that was associated with the process, he would submit because he wanted the power that came with it. Power to dream, to help determine the clan's movements and future. Power and wisdom to absorb the clan's past and to deliver that past to other generations. The stories he had heard already were only the barest surface of the dreaming, like an echidna burrowed in the dirt—a few of its prickly spines sticking out to be seen and felt, leaving most of the animal still hidden underground. The Storyteller had told him of the few visible spines. But the heart and soul of the dreaming were buried yet; only venturing into manhood would allow him to dig them out, to capture the magnificent whole of it. A thousand generations of wisdom waited for Indirri, waited for him to become fully a man at last.

The clan paused on the edge of a thicket while the men read the ground ahead carefully. The earth told of plenty of whitefellers and their animals, but no blackfellers at all. Cautiously they moved out into the brilliant vastness of a broad, treeless plain. Indirri would have preferred that they stay near the shelter of the brigalow thickets, but the roots the women wanted grew out in the open. Besides, nobody cared what Indirri preferred. He had no voice yet.

A whistle, urgently high-pitched, suddenly shook Indirri from his reverie. Danger. Dropping low, he skittered in closer toward the women and children. He knew exactly where they were, though they had disappeared from view, hiding flat in the rough grass and bush. He flattened himself, attuning ears and nose to the faint breeze.

Horses approached at a rapid clip; Indirri could feel the vibrations and hear the hooves. A male whitefeller voice in the distance called *thairthayahr*. A gunshot made every nerve and muscle in Indirri's body leap. Another. His mother screamed and he recklessly raised his head.

One of the whitefellers had Mungkala's sister by the hair. He raised a weapon in his hand and struck her head. She melted, hung lifeless, and he dropped her. At the far rear, Mungkala came running forward shrieking. He paused and arched, his spear poised beside his ear.

Foolish Mungkala! He was much too far away, his quarry well beyond spear range. But the whitefellers did not know that—and did not care. From the horse nearest Indirri, a whitefeller swung his gun weapon toward Mungkala; it roared and spit smoke. Mungkala jerked, his body lifted into the air before it slammed backward into the grass. His spear and spear thrower dropped out of sight, useless, beside him.

One of the whitefeller horsemen had found Indirri's mother. He pointed his weapon at her. It was a short weapon, less than the length of a man's forearm, but Indirri knew it was as deadly as the longer ones he had seen. Never in his life had Indirri felt so helpless; he should be on his feet now, protecting his mother. But if he stood up, they'd kill him as they had killed Mungkala; he was too far away to hit them with a spear, too close to avoid being hit by their gun weapons. What could he do? He must do something!

In a flash the Storyteller materialized, popping out of nowhere less than four spear lengths beyond Indirri's mother. Instantly the Storyteller's spear drove true and straight through the middle of the whitefeller who would dare shoot a lubra. Not even Indirri's eye could follow the action, so swift and sure was the old sage.

The murderous whitefellers cloaked themselves in a blue-gray cloud of deafening noise. Indirri flattened his head against the ground and waited, horrified.

In a blaze of thunder and smoke, the whitefellers snuffed out a thousand generations of wisdom.

Lying still as a stone on the ground, Indirri struggled to keep his wits about him. He must not leap up too fast—not yet. With his head pressed against the ground, his ear told him precisely where each of the five horses was. These enemies were not yet close enough—he and his spear were as one, and he knew his weapon's range and limitations.

At the cost of his own life—there were too many gun weapons to defeat—Indirri would rise up and destroy the leader of these murderers. Obviously it was the big man who wore a vivid chest cover that seemed to glow in the sun. In Indirri's mind's eye, he planned every detail of his revenge. That bright chest cover might hold magical properties to protect him, so Indirri must drive his spear home just below it.

Death hovered very close, yet he did not fear it. He was ready. Rage had driven all fear away.

Four spear lengths was the farthest he could throw with enough strength and accuracy to ensure his revenge. He waited. The leader's horse danced about, not ten spear lengths ahead. Nine. Seven. Soon. Six. Ready . . . Five . . .

"Heeze blee dnbahd!" cried the leader. "Bahkdih thistyshin!" The horses were bolting, churning. They were leaving!

Indirri lifted his head that his eyes might confirm what his ear had already told him. They were all in rapid retreat. One horse ran free and another carried two men—the man the Storyteller had speared and another who supported him. Ten spear lengths, then twenty, then more—and they were gone, far beyond range.

Indirri called. Silence was his only answer. His mind as cold and black and numb as a winter night, he moved from here to there among the tufts of grass and the sun-dried weeds, to the places where his clansmen had hidden. First he found his mother. Dead. Uncle. Both boys. Mungkala's sister. All gone.

And then Indirri's worst fears were confirmed. The Storyteller, his unseeing eyes still open, lay twisted on the ground where he had fallen. All his knowledge and love and humor gone back to where it had come from. No need now for Indirri to undertake the rites of manhood—the old man had taken his lore with him, and with him, Indirri's future as an elder and sage.

His clan had done nothing to whitefellers to deserve this. They had purposely avoided the whitefellers and their animals. In return, the whitefellers had stolen his birthright and stripped him of his future. And now they had destroyed everyone he loved.

But wait . . . where was Mungkala? Like a kangaroo speared in the belly, Indirri plodded listlessly to where his friend had fallen. Mungkala was still alive, but his right arm was mutilated, his right side torn and bleeding. His blood, so much blood, soaked the ground. Probably Mungkala would die soon, like the others.

Heavily he sat down at Mungkala's side and drew his knees up. He crossed his arms over his knees to rest his churning head and stunned heart.

In a few senseless moments, whitefellers had robbed him of everything, including the spiritual power he might have gained when he reached manhood. Now they had earned his undying hatred. Hatred has a power all its own.

CHAPTER FOUR

A PACK OF DINGOES

Ask city slickers what they think of when they hear the words *outback*, *backblock*, and *squatter*. They'll probably say: *crude, wild colonial boys, ruffians, unpolished*. They'll tell you how unrefined anyone is who lives out back of beyond.

But they'll be wrong.

There stood Marty's mum, glowing just a little bit pink, mildly embarrassed but pleased by all the attention. She looked elegant in the latest wasp-waist style from Melbourne, her hair done up softly. And Pop! In his perfectly pressed wool serge suit and tie, he looked as grand as any Sydney banker. He stood beside his lady with a regal air—proud, quiet, gentle.

Ross Sheldon was wearing that brocade waistcoat with the gold thread embroidery, so you knew he considered the occasion momentous. He raised his glass. "To the newlyweds of a quarter century. Frobel, twenty-five years with one woman says something for you. Says even more for her. Our congratulations."

A pubful of celebrants hoisted glasses and cheered boisterously. Acknowledging the toast, Pop raised his glass. "I spent the best quarter century of my life right here between the Barcoo and the Creek. Here's to the lady who made it the best."

Mum's cheeks blushed scarlet. She glanced nervously across the crowded room to Marty. From his perch on the upstairs bannister he grinned and waved.

They were all right, these backblock people; Marty felt proud of them as they toasted his parents.

"Ain't right. Not right atall." A small, thin, sour-looking man leaned against the staircase and scowled at the proceedings.

"What's not right?" Marty thought the fellow might be one of Sheldon's drovers, but he wasn't certain.

"Hosie been dead less'n a week and look at these people. Supposed to be Hosie's mates, and they're carrying on like it's Christmas. Like nothing ever happened."

"Hosie. Oh—you mean Mr. Hosteen, the man who got killed when the aborigines attacked Mr. Sheldon's party."

"Worse'n a pack of dingoes, them abos. Less'n animals." He paused for a swill of grog. "Speared right through the middle, he was. Didn't die till the next day, all tied up in a proper knot, he hurt so. Hideous way to pass in his marble, and here's all his mates making merry. A week. Ain't right."

What could he say? So Marty said nothing. He shuddered to think of all the times he rode out across the paddocks alone, never suspecting that there might be the danger of an aboriginal attack. To think that a war party fell upon Mr. Sheldon's group—in broad daylight! Scary.

Beside him, Jase leaned on the bannister. "I'm going over to the railway station to see if I can pick up some casual work hauling. Come along?"

Marty didn't have to think about it for very long—he could hover on the edge of the crowd in this stuffy pub or make some quick money for himself driving someone's wagon. "Yair, I guess." He hopped down off the bannister and began jostling and shoving his way through the mob of pastoralists and drovers.

Fresh air. Marty always forgot how much he hated crowds until he'd been in one for a short time.

Jase jabbed his arm. "Over 'cross the street there; that Fowkes girl's looking at you. What's her name?"

"Pearl. At least, that's what Mr. Sealy says. Knows her father."

Jase cackled. "See 'er looking? She's sweet on you, Cuz."

"Right." Marty feigned indifference, but couldn't resist a peek anyway. Jase was right. She *was* looking at him, and it gave him a funny feeling, like getting all queasy or just winning some big, important race.

She was charming. Her golden hair was pulled back and up, the ends of it clustered in little ringlets beneath her hat. It was April, and the autumn sun was not nearly so intense; but she toyed with an opened parasol anyway, and sometimes even used it to shade her face. She was strolling north on Maple and Jase was kind of shoving Marty out into the intersection, so they all sort of drifted together.

She dipped her head, very ladylike. "Mr. Frobel. Mr. James."

"Miss Fowkes." Marty tipped his hat. She continued north, and since Jase and he were going that way, Marty fell in beside her. "How's your hand doing?"

"All better, thank you. After all, that was a month ago."

"Yair. Time goes fast."

A heavy silence fell on the trio. Marty could talk easily with any of the drovers, but how did one make polite conversation—*really* polite conversation—the way this city girl was used to? Especially with one's younger cousin tittering along beside you?

"Getting settled in now, I trust?" There, that sounded cultured. Marty felt just a little smug.

"Thank you, yes."

More silence. It was she who broke it this time. "My father went calling on the strikers' camps yesterday, and so I went along."

"Hope your father told you to never go out there alone."

He must have, because she ignored the warning. "What an amazing place," she said. "Hundreds and hundreds of tents. The union strikers' tents are all ajumble and hodge-podge. But at the army camp, their tents are so very orderly. I suppose that says something about the men who live in them."

"The strikers set up a library in one of their hodge-podge

tents. That says something about them, too, I think," he replied.

She stopped and studied him. "Your father's a pastoralist—a stockman and station owner. The union's his enemy. And here you're speaking kind words about the shearers and their union."

"Not about the union. Just the shearers. Pop says the shearers aren't a bad sort when you take 'em one by one. It's when those outsiders talk union and get 'em all together, they're trash. Look at the mess! Five hundred soldiers and all their officers and medical corps people, and the newspaper reporters from all over the colonies. And when we ought to be out in the paddocks tending to business, all the pastoralists have to be here in town trying to keep a lid on trouble and dealing with the shearers.

"Pop says he read in the *Western Champion* last week that there's forty-five hundred people in town here. And all because of this labor strike business." He stopped. He was spouting off too much. That sure wasn't very clever of him.

Still, she seemed to accept his opinion as gospel truth. She wagged her golden head and continued the drift north. "I agree, it is a mess. Papa says the strikers' camp is a vermin-filled hotbed of drunkenness and disease. Papa preached there last Sunday. Told them all they have to repent."

"Mmm. Think any of them repented?"

"When they found out he wasn't ordained, they threw bottles at him. Papa says he doubts the depth of their commitment to the faith."

"No need to doubt the depth of their commitment to the bottles."

She giggled, and it tinkled like music.

Suddenly making money was not high on Marty's list of priorities; getting rid of his cousin was. Let Jase find pick-up work hauling. Marty would make certain that Miss Fowkes enjoyed a safe afternoon stroll, for the streets here near the railroad yard swarmed with strikers.

Jase darted ahead. "Mr. Miles! Mr. Miles!"

"Mr. Miles owns a carting company," Marty explained. She

probably already knew that, but just in case. "Has half a dozen bullock carts and horse drays. Jase and I drive for him now and again."

Those incredible creamy-blue eyes flicked toward him. "You drive those big bullock carts?"

"Yair, well, uh," he stammered, "I, uh, don't use some of the words the older drivers use—not often, anyway. Uh . . ."

Fortunately, Jase and Mr. Miles were now so close he could drop that subject. "Mr. Miles, may I present Miss Pearl Fowkes. Miss Fowkes, August Miles."

They exchanged pleasantries as Marty's mind raced, darting from nook to nook among his memories in search of something to talk about. His mind was distressingly blank.

Jase was whining, "No hauling atall?"

Mr. Miles shrugged. "Way it is, lad. No trading, no merchandise. Stores stocked up a month ago, anticipating this. That's why hauling was so good then. Now Barcaldine's just one big fortified camp, holding its breath and waiting for trouble."

Marty's heart gave a disappointed lurch. With no work to do, Jase would be at his elbow the whole blessed day.

Mr. Miles kept talking. "Besides, I had to promise to use only union haulers, and they're striking in sympathy with the shearers, same as the railway workers. So I couldn't hire you boys even if I had something to cart." He paused and frowned. "Yer know, though—yer might go ask Henry Sealy. He's taking a string of bullock wagons out next week or so. He has his own private carts, so there's no union involved. He might be able to use you."

Next week. He was stuck with Jase clear till next week!

"Uh, yair, well—thank you, sir." Marty nodded and started to move off. Two other haulers worked out of the railway station. Maybe one of them . . .

Mr. Miles nodded toward the station. "Might steer Miss Fowkes away from here, Marty. The army's bringing some arrested strike leaders in from Clermont and it'll get ugly when they arrive. Not something for a young lady, eh?"

"Too right, sir!" A train carrying prisoners and guards,

eh? Interesting. If it came through soon, it would pass them on its way to the station. That explained why so many strikers and hangers-on milled about the railway yard. Marty's chest swelled with importance as he undertook what seemed to him to be a most noble task, protecting this young lady—cousin or no cousin. It was far more than he had dared hope for! Clearing his throat, he nonchalantly asked her, "Anyplace you'd like to see?"

"Well . . ." For a moment she considered the offer, her soft brow delicately knit. "Though I've been in this town only a month, already I've noticed how important sheep and cattle seem to be here—and I know so little about what one does with them."

"Good-oh. Let's see. McLaughlin's wool scour isn't too far away. Let's start there." Marty grinned and started off at a leisurely pace along the trackside. He'd stay close to the railway, just in case there might be something to see. "Jase? Try Harry Cleave. Maybe he has some work for you."

"You heard old Miles. Union only and nothing moving. I'll come along and remind you all the stuff you forget." He cackled and pranced ahead. The drongo.

"Where did you say we're going?" Her voice was so soft.

"Wool scour. That's a shed where they clean up the wool. Wash it. There's a shearing shed not far beyond. We can stop there, too."

A million horses—well, more like a dozen—came clattering by. Army troops. The leader of the mounted unit tipped his hat toward Pearl. "Good afternoon, Miss Fowkes."

She smiled and nodded, the soul of propriety. "Major Paterson. Good day."

And the unit clattered on.

"You know him?" Marty tried to wave away some of the bulldust the horses were raising.

"When Papa visits the army camp I usually go along, so I know most of the officers. They invite us to tea."

"Mmm." Marty had never been invited to tea, not even by Mum. Then again, he had never wanted to be, until now. "Wonder where . . . uh oh!"

From where they stood they could see the tin roof of McLaughlin's shed flashing in the sun. A train had stopped right in front of the shed, gray smoke boiling out its stack. The trouble Mr. Miles was expecting at the station had instead de-trained right here, at McLaughlin's wool scour.

Guards with rifles and bayonets lined up beside the railway car as the arrested strikers from Clermont stumbled off the train, bumping into each other. They were manacled in pairs along a heavy chain, a clumsy parody of a twenty-bullock team.

From all directions strikers came running and yelling. Unloading the prisoners away from the station hadn't put the strikers off in the least. Major Paterson's regulars fell in beside and behind the chain of misery, and the major himself led the way. Here they came, straight toward Marty.

"Perhaps it would be better to examine the wool scour some other time," Miss Fowkes suggested.

The chaotic, noisy procession moved along—guards shouting, horses clattering and prisoners clanking their chains of woe. All around them the hostile strikers churned angrily.

"Jase! Help me shove a path through; straight south looks like the safest way to go." Marty wrapped an arm across Miss Fowkes's shoulders to pilot her toward safety.

"Just a minute. Somebody's bound to bung on a blue any minute. It's gunner get exciting in a hurry!" He disappeared into the crowd.

"*Jase!*"

Half the mounted unit pressed their way forward, flanking the major and forcing the crowd to make way. As guards waved their bayonets high, the phalanx of nervous, sweaty horses plowed a furrow through the milling mob. And Marty was in the middle of it all.

A tree. Gotta find a tree, Marty thought frantically. A good, solid tree would offer some protection, but the only trees along the railway were a few scrubby acacias. The shouting intensified as someone in the mass hit a soldier with a rock.

These army mounts were local squatters' horses; they

could handle the confusion of a mob of cattle or sheep, but not this screaming melee. With flaring nostrils the horses danced, their eyes rolled back in fear. One of them, panic-stricken, bolted into the crowd.

Suddenly a man in a dark coat slapped his hat against the face of Major Paterson's bay. The horse lunged straight up, terrified, and nearly rolled backward. Marty watched as the dark coat pushed through the throng and disappeared as the crowd parted, closing the gap behind him.

From somewhere within the line a rifle went off; the bittersweet blue gun smoke dissipated itself in the roiling clouds of dust. Marty's nerves, like the horses', could take no more. He flung Miss Fowkes down against the trunk of a puny acacia and huddled over her, protecting her as best he could. Jase was gone, but Marty could not think of him now. He was painfully aware that their sole protection in this din was a soft lacy openwork of frail branches. Another gunshot exploded in the air. Marty held on to the tree—and Miss Fowkes—for dear life, waiting for it all to be over.

For what seemed like centuries the horror whipped and whirled about them. Miss Fowkes coughed and choked on the dust. So did Marty. The chains jingled more faintly. The shouting grew less intense as the strikers swept along beside the prisoners. Still, Marty waited a good long time before he raised his head.

He was handing Miss Fowkes to her feet when Jase came along, wound up like a two-penny clock. Grabbing Marty, he yelled, "What a blooming coward, lying there in the bulldust! That big galah nearly dumped the major! Lucky that last bloke nabbed him 'fore he got away!"

Marty started to stutter something, but Miss Fowkes didn't give him a chance. She berated Jase soundly for calling her protector a coward. She got on Jase's back so stridently that Marty almost believed her. He hadn't really lost his nerve; Miss Fowkes's safety was his first responsibility, and he had discharged that duty well.

Yet every morning for days afterward Marty awoke in a cold sweat. The vivid nightmares ducked in and out through the corridors of his mind, evading remembrance.

Mr. Miles had been right. Henry Sealy, the manager of Barcaldine Downs, had built a string of bullock carts to drive west. Pop overruled Mum's objections and gave Marty permission to sign on as a driver. But not Jase. Jase was still a bit young to handle five yoke of bullocks, said Pop.

Marty enjoyed the life of a bullocky. You were your own man. You felt a wonderful sense of power, being in control of ten strong, massive beasts. Of course, on this trip Mr. Sealy put only four bullocks to a cart and didn't even use his big table-top wagons. Besides, it was hard to feel very strong and powerful when you were soaked to the skin, which was often because it rained frequently, and Marty was usually the last wagon in line. The carts ahead of him would churn the track into deep, gooey ruts, making progress difficult as well as messy. He found himself caked with mud more often than he cared to think of.

Mr. Sealy led on his sorrel mare and a half dozen outriders rode among the bullock carts. They all carried rifles or shotguns in dark shiny-wet scabbards. *Were these men expecting trouble or simply being cautious in light of the labor unrest?* Marty was sorry he had not asked Mr. Sealy. Another thing, why was he taking this route?

They followed the railway, sometimes using the side path the track-layers had forged, and sometimes blazing their own way through the brigalow. Marty fell easily into the slow and steady splock-splock rhythm of all those cloven feet. The railway trestled across a slight, gentle dip. The bullock carts lurched down the dip and slipped and slid up the other side. Marty had to prod his oxen hard to get them out of the dip. If Miss Fowkes could only see him now, Marty smiled to himself.

They were maybe three miles out when they heard the distant hooting of a train whistle. As his sorrel mare waltzed excitedly in place, Mr. Sealy flagged the train with his hat. The locomotive huffed and puffed, then finally squealed to an impatient halt. Rain sizzled and steamed on its shiny black boiler. Marty brought his bullocks to a stop, then applied most of his attention to the train. Magnificent. You'd almost think it was alive!

A motley assortment of men poured out of a car, each with his bundle of belongings. Some were half- or quarter-castes; some were old; some nearly as young as Marty. Their swags bulged. Obviously these men planned to be on the road a long time.

Suddenly it dawned on Marty. Shearers. These men were free shearers, nonunion workers brought in to break the strike and get the shearing started. Mr. Sealy had contracted with these outsiders and now he wanted to cart them to his station with a minimum of fuss and danger. Had Pop known this, would he have let Marty come? But then, surely Mr. Sealy would have mentioned to Pop and the others that they might make use of the free labor as well. Bantering and swapping insults in strange accents, the men clambered aboard Marty's bullock cart.

"Bit small to be driving bullocks, ain't you?"

"Picked before he was ripe, eh?"

Marty was used to allusions about his small size. He shot a grin over his shoulder. "I can stop 'em if you'd rather walk."

"Break it down, mates. He's a good sort."

The horsemen drew their rifles and shotguns, balancing them lightly across their pommels. They were watching everywhere.

Mr. Sealy led off, south and away from the railway. Instantly the going got a lot easier. In a wet year like this, grass grew practically everywhere, binding the dirt. Cloven hooves that would cut bare mud into a churned morass hardly dented grass at all. Frequently the bullocks slid and staggered on the slippery wet tufts, but that was a minor price to pay. Marty turned his cart a little aside so that his bullocks weren't following right in the others' softened tracks. His oxen wound through the scraggly forest with a decidedly springier step. They seemed to know they were heading home.

Someone shouted beyond the trees to the east. Marty

heard horses approaching. Many horses. A score of riders burst out of the bush. Union men! Another group crashed through the brigalow beyond them. Still more mounted riders thundered toward them from the railway. A hundred of them, at the very least! The unionists had heard rumors about Mr. Sealy's free help—and they were here to stop the scabs before they could start!

A shotgun roared. More infernal shouting. Another gunshot. Marty left his bullocks in the capable hands of God and started running. Where to? He didn't know. He didn't care.

Three strides later he slid in the wet grass. His right foot zipped out from under him and he slammed down on his hip and right arm. The pain in his right shoulder slashed through his whole body, snatching his breath away. Panic seized his pounding heart.

Numbed by terror, he curled up in a tight little wad in the cold, rough grass. The solid hooves of horses shook the ground. Guns roared all around him. *Why me? Why always me?* He had no idea how much time had passed. He hadn't the slightest notion who—if anyone—was winning. He didn't care. The guns blasted his nerves and made his rigid body shake. His mind imagined blood flowing and men falling that his eyes, pressed tightly shut, could not see.

Shouts of war turned into shouts of jubilation. Men were laughing and crowing; horses pounded a retreat. No more guns. It was over, but he could not unlock his muscles; they had petrified. His body had stopped shaking, but he couldn't make it move.

Warm, rough hands unfolded him, checked for injuries, and sat him up. Mr. Sealy continued to probe about a bit, announced his shoulder had probably popped out of joint but it was all right now, and bound his arm tightly against his body with kerchiefs. Amidst jolly yabba, the horsemen and the shearers congratulated each other on the victory. They gave Marty a leg up behind Mr. Sealy and he rode double-dink on the sorrel mare all the way to Barcaldine Downs.

Only Mr. Sealy, it seemed, failed to enter into the heady joy of victory. Grumbling more to himself than to Marty, he spent most of the ride home reviling union men and their violent ways in the bitterest of terms. "Brainless animals," he'd mumble. "Coulda got someone killed. Not worth a brass razoo, the whole mob of them. Worse'n a pack of dingoes."

CHAPTER FIVE

DREAMS OF OTHER PLACES

Somewhere in the last rains of the autumn wet, everything turned around. All the union leaders that had been transported from Clermont stood trial, first in Barcaldine and then in Rockhampton. They were convicted. The union movement scurried about like a chicken with its head lopped off to keep the effort going. But deprived of their driving force—the leadership—they accomplished nothing. Constant rain reduced the tent camps to slurpy, slogging misery. Dysentery and fever sapped men's physical strength. The carters began carting again, and the railway workers started once more to lay track westward. Most of the newspapermen went home. The world had lost interest in Barcaldine.

On June 14 the union held its last parade. From the nearly abandoned tent camp to the union office on Ash Street marched a sad and sorry crowd as the fife and drums played Auld Lang Syne. It was over. The pastoralists had won.

From the balcony of the Shakspeare, Pearl watched the street below as the silenced fife and drums disappeared into the dark building. Why did she feel these men's sadness so strongly? They hardly deserved sympathy; they were rabble, cursed by sin and strong drink. They had opposed Marty's father and his associates—all prominent and influential men, men of wealth and high regard.

Papa moved through the dejected, milling mob, shaking hands, speaking to this man and that. Obviously, Papa was in his element. Pearl was not. Already she was becoming terribly bored with Barcaldine, and she had been here only a few short months. When the months stretched into years, how would she be able to stand it?

And as months always do, they did indeed stretch into years. The labor problem pretty much resolved, the Frobels never came to Barcaldine anymore, especially after the railway was extended to Longreach the next year. Pearl longed for the genteel company of the powerful squatters, men with money. When Papa brought home dinner guests, which he often did, they were always such common people.

Pearl completed schooling and was more than happy to put education behind her. The schoolroom had been dark, cramped, and overcrowded. Soon Pearl obtained employment at the new soap factory, owned by a friend of Papa's. Pearl was glad to have a job, even if it was making the soap her mother used in her laundry business. However, she eventually became disgruntled, noting that there is absolutely no pleasure to be found in sheep grease and lye.

Desperate to smell like something better than cooked fat, Pearl tried the boot factory. It was a good job, sewing together leather uppers. She could get shoes for her father at great discount, and sometimes they made a women's style that she and Mum could tolerate. But when she ran the sewing machine needle through her thumb, nail and all, she decided it was time to find a new job.

Finally, she applied for and was accepted to work at the local hospital, but her joy was short-lived. Early on the morning of the day she was supposed to report for work, the hospital burned to the ground.

Thinking her job had gone up in smoke too, she didn't report for work. And since she was the only unemployed family member, she became the official lunch-maker. Sitting in the kitchen, mulling over her misfortune, Pearl hadn't started the lunch for the day yet. It was too hot for soup, and the bread wouldn't arrive at the grocer's for another hour. Their only chunk of cheese had turned hard and unappetizing in the midsummer heat. The last of the mutton roast had been used yesterday for sandwiches. There was nothing left—

just like her life: it added up to zero.

Suddenly Enid came bursting through the back door. She was almost sixteen now, but the years hadn't done a thing for her hair. It was still straight, still that same color of brown. She drew it up and back in a fashionable bun, as did most women, but little ends and wisps constantly fell down around her ears, neck, and in her eyes. Enid would never be as elegant as her sister.

She frowned at Pearl. "Why aren't you at work?"

"Because my place of employment is a heap of smoldering ashes."

Enid put on that maddening air of false patience. "Pearl! People do not instantly become well and walk out of a hospital simply because the building burned down. Dr. Symes is angry because you have not appeared, but he's agreed to reconsider firing you if you get there before noon. I explained to him it must be a misunderstanding and that you are very reliable."

Pearl stood up and retrieved her hat from the rack in the corner. "But what about lunch? And why were you in such earnest conversation with the town doctor?"

"Lunch can wait. And I talked to the doctor because I work there, too." Enid led the way out the door, into the searing heat. She hurried along as though she did not find the scorching sun the least bit oppressive. "Because of the emergency, Papa and I decided I could do more good at a place like the hospital than accompanying him on his visitations—except for visitations to widows and other unattached ladies, of course. I'll go with him then. But mostly, I'm going to work at the hospital now. I applied this morning and was accepted immediately." Not catching Pearl's scowl, she went on.

"Papa and I agree that one can serve the Lord in many ways—and the ministry proper is only one of them." She fell in beside Pearl. "Pearl, it's so exciting, isn't it?"

"Very. So tell me, how does the good doctor propose to treat patients now that he's sitting in an ash heap?"

"The fire started in a separate summer kitchen, so the volunteers were able to get all the patients and some of the equipment out. We're setting up in the old brewery." She smiled. "Ironic, isn't it? The brewery, which once produced the grog that has ruined so many lives, is now the site for saving them."

"Yair—yes." Pearl hated that local affirmative, yet here she was picking it up unconsciously, so she quickly changed it.

They passed the tree beside the railway station where shearers and other sympathetic strikers had first met to plan strategy six years ago. There were the acacia trees—they had grown some, she noted. She'd seen Marty only once since the riot—a couple months after the strike fell apart.

Why that should bother her, she didn't know. Skinny little runt. And his cousin Jason was even skinnier. What a pair they were! Rich, though. Money counts for something, she guessed.

Four stories high, the abandoned brewery cut quite an imposing figure. Knowing how the locals loved their beer, Pearl had asked once why the brewery had closed. "'Cuz its beer tasted like a scorched bandicoot," she was told. "Ain't easy to ruin beer, but they done it." As far as Pearl was concerned, all beer tasted like that. She had no idea why so many men liked it.

Enid led the way through the front doors and down the dusty halls. "Dr. Symes sees patients in the engine room now," Enid explained. "The floors below and above are being turned into wards."

The engine room. This whole scene brought new dimensions to the word "primitive." Examination tables had been set up on either side of a huge flywheel. Bandages and bottles lined the top of a gauge box, and a stethoscope hung over a big painted cast-iron pipe. At the far end, two huge industrial doors stood wide open, letting in a slow, torrid summer breeze.

Dr. Symes bent over his current patient—a coarse-looking fellow in sweaty, stained work clothes. Obediently he held up his arm as the doctor wrapped it in a massive bandage. *Probably one of the workmen putting this miserable hole into some kind of order.*

The doctor stood erect and shouted at no one in particular, "So where are my scissors? Don't tell me they all burnt up, too!"

Enid leaped into action. "Scissors!" She pawed through a crate filled haphazardly with salvaged hospital paraphernalia. "Here!" She hurried to him with a pair of stubby little scissors.

Dr. Symes stopped long enough to study Pearl for a moment. "Oversleep?"

"No, sir. I was up before dawn watching the fire, along with most of the town."

He snorted. "Eh? Well, I didn't see you helping." He turned his attentions back to his work. "Enid, empty that crate out and line everything up somewhere so we can find what we need without a shovel."

Pearl was surprised when Enid turned and left the room. She had expected her little sister to dive right into the job—she was that sort of ingratiating person. Should Pearl do it? And if so, how? She was still standing there, uncertainly, when Enid returned with a dusty little knee-high table. Enid set it in front of the flywheel between the two examination tables, then dumped the contents of the crate onto a blanket. Turning the crate on its side, she set it on the table. Presto. A perfect instrument table. She draped a large towel to serve both as a mat on top and curtain over the open side. The patient, having received the necessary care, left, and Dr. Symes disappeared down a side hall.

Still uncertain as to what to do, Pearl picked at the pile of unfamiliar objects. Here were scissors that weren't scissors and a vicious-looking stainless steel object. "How are you arranging them?" she asked. How could Enid look as though she knew what she was doing? She was as new at this as Pearl.

"By size," Enid answered. "When Dr. Symes asks for something by name, unless it's scissors, I'm not likely to know what it is at first. And most of these strange things are hard to describe. But he can easily say how big."

Disgustingly logical.

Out by the big open double doors a bell clanged so loudly Pearl jumped in fright.

Enid's eyes bulged. "An emergency!"

An emergency? Pearl followed Enid at a jog toward the doors. She could hear running feet behind her; Dr. Symes was coming.

At the loading ramp outside the double doors, a small, wiry, dark-haired young man had just pulled up in a station cart. The cart horse, blowing and lathered, looked ready to drop. In the back of the cart a tall, lithe fellow was bent over, trying to scoop an aborigine up in his arms.

"Leave him there." Dr. Symes jumped off the ramp and down beside the wagon. *He's remarkably agile for his age,* Pearl thought. "We don't have the time for charity work."

"This one's paid for." That voice! It was a deep baritone or perhaps bass, smooth and easy on the ear. "Horse stomped him." Pearl's heart leaped when she realized who he was.

"I believe it." Dr. Symes stepped back from his cursory examination and waved an arm. "Right, then. Drive it right on up and in, lad. Enid, show these gentlemen to the examination table." The doctor hopped back up onto the loading ramp, and paused beside Pearl. With a finger he tipped her chin up to close her gaping mouth, then disappeared into the gloom as the cart made a tight circle and came rattling up the ramp behind him.

Suddenly Pearl felt very foolish that the doctor had noticed her reaction. Of course those boys would have grown. For all practical purposes they were men now. She gathered up her skirts and ran inside, most unsophisticated. She paused only long enough to arrange herself and pat any stray strands of hair up into place. She straightened her back, lifted her head and joined the group, a lady again.

The lathered horse and its cart were parked not four feet from the examination tables. The lads had transferred the patient to the table and Dr. Symes was cutting off the torn clothing. The patient, a young black man, lay curled on his side, groaning when anyone attempted to straighten him out. Already Enid had tucked a pillow under the aborigine's head and had begun wiping off the dried blood, a basin of water at her elbow. The flies had found the mess already. They buzzed in clouds.

Two sisters in white aprons came running in from a side door labeled "stairs." Deftly they stepped in beside the boys and took over. Sisters. Englishmen called them nurses. Americans called them nurses. Why did the locals call them sisters?

Pearl's cheeks flushed hot. Here they were in the company of two young men their own age. And Dr. Symes was cutting off *all* the injured man's clothes. Pearl grabbed a towel from the linen pile and stood ready to restore modesty as soon as possible.

Jason and Marty were falling all over themselves explaining to the doctor how the accident had occurred. This fellow—Gimpy Jack, they called him—had tried to hold a renegade brumbie, getting kicked and stomped in the process. They described how pale he had become . . . *Pure foolishness. A black man, pale?* The doctor nodded as if he understood. He said something about bleeding inside and operating right now. He used the words "carbolic" and "chloral something." He instructed Enid on what to look for as she cleaned the man's scalp. Then he told the boys they could leave.

With three women doing his bidding, it didn't seem as if the doctor needed her help anymore, Pearl thought. She followed Marty and Jason as they walked outside, leading the horse behind them.

Marty removed his battered hat, grinning. "Almost didn't recognize you there, Miss Fowkes. G'day!" His shoulders had filled out. He seemed so different, so . . . so . . . *manly*. He towered more than a head taller than Pearl. She had to look up to see his deep-set brown eyes. They were even more remarkable than she had remembered.

She curtsied. "I didn't know you at first, either." She turned. "And Jason. You've certainly grown."

He grinned impishly. "Not as much as Marty. That's 'cuz he eats more. You're looking, uh, grown-up. And Enid. I sure wouldn't have recognized her being your little sister if the doc hadn't called her by name. She's *really* grown! She, uh, she got a gentleman?"

"No. Neither of us does." Time to change the subject. "So why did you come to Barcaldine after all these years?"

The broad shoulders shrugged. For all his growth, Marty still reminded her of a little boy in some ways. "We were helping out a neighbor, northeast of Ilfracombe there. Some temporary pens above Saltern Creek. When this happened we decided here was closest, and it's a good hospital." He grinned. "Well, it was till this morning, I guess."

"You'll have to see the remains. Quite a mess, and still smoking."

"Saw it. Stopped there first." Jase nodded. "We smelt it coming in; 'course, we didn't know what we were smelling till we got there."

After chatting for some time, Marty glanced at the sun. "Just about noon," he said. "Soon as they can spare Enid, let's all four go over to the Commercial for lunch. Haven't eaten there for years. They still good?"

"As good as any, yes. That would be delightful." Pearl had suffered a lot of heckling about not being courted, mostly from elderly women who chided her for being too choosy. Wait until the biddies saw her walk through the door with this pair!

The boys wandered out under a tree to wait and Pearl went back inside. If they had operated at all they must have done it in a hurry. Enid was cleaning up equipment, one of the sisters had disappeared, and Dr. Symes was washing his hands. The other sister rolled a bed in, and Pearl took the feet, the sister the middle, and Enid the head as they shifted Gimpy Jack onto the wheeled cot. Pearl felt a bit miffed that the doctor, the strongest one among them, didn't bother to help.

Pearl cleared her throat. "Doctor? The two young men out there—Gimpy Jack's companions—are old and valued friends of ours. They asked that Enid and I accompany them to lunch. By your leave, sir."

Enid caught her breath. "I may not be able . . . I mean . . ."

Dr. Symes's voice rolled smooth as glass. "Enid, you did a splendid job there. You made yourself useful, anticipating ways that you could help, and you follow orders well. This was a difficult case and you deserve the break. Of course, go to lunch with the young men, and I'll see you back here this afternoon." He turned to Pearl. "And you, young lady, are fired." Giving her no chance to respond, he marched briskly out of the room.

Pearl stared after him. "Of all the . . ."

Enid bit her lip as she pulled her soiled apron off. "He needed you, Pearl. You should have—" She stopped. "Well, it's over. Let's go to lunch."

The waiter at the Commercial Hotel did not recognize the boys. The bartender did. Enid seemed not quite herself. Probably she was just a bit nervous, being in the company of men and women a little older than she. They talked and laughed as they waited for their order. When their food arrived—beef stew all around—they wasted no time.

Marty ate the potatoes out of his stew. "Jase, after lunch let's go down to the dry goods store and buy some cloth for a shirt for Jack. Something really loud."

"*Really* loud!" Jason laughed. "Jack, he does like colors. You seen the shirt we cut off him. White with big red roses all over it. The cook made it for him out of curtain chintz. If they ever make a color that glows in the dark, he'll be first cab off the stand to get a shirt from it."

Soberly, Marty looked at Enid. "Something is bothering you."

She forced a smile. "Shame on me for spoiling this happy luncheon."

"You're not. Just a feeling I got."

She laid down her fork. "Your friend is very close to death. Dr. Symes went in—surgically, I mean—and repaired some damage inside, but he had to get in and out quickly because the young man is so weak. That's how he phrased it. No anstha—no anesthetic. And that's the first time I . . . I mean,

I'm just new there. And . . . it was unsettling." Her eyes glistened.

For a moment, Pearl was concerned for her sister. Concern turned into embarrassment. *What a fool she's making of herself.* Pearl couldn't bear to look around and see who might be watching.

Marty put down his own fork. "Gimpy Jack's been working off and on for Pop for six years, ever since that business with Turk Moran. He's the same age as me. He started with Mr. Sheldon and then came to our place. He's . . . well . . . a friend. A real friend. This morning . . ."

His eyes flitted from the ceiling to the walls. "I was sure we lost him. Couple times, I was so sure. Tried to pray and couldn't. Finally get here and there's the hospital burnt down. I was so scared. Until we drove the buggy up into the brewery there and you started working on his head. All of a sudden I knew he was safe. I don't know how I knew, but I felt it." Marty spread his hands. "I know it's rough on you, but I hope you realize how much it meant when . . . ah, gum. I don't know how to say it."

"You sure don't." Jason hadn't slowed down eating a bit. "What he's trying to say is, soon as you and the doc and the sisters jumped in there, we knew you could save him. And he's worth saving. Don't matter that he's black."

Despite the tears, a broad, bright smile spread across Enid's face. "My father and I both felt God wanted me to work there. What you've just said confirms it. Working in the hospital will give me an opportunity to help people . . . and that makes the horrible side of it worthwhile. Thank you!" With that, she got back to work on her stew.

Jason studied her. "You really wanna work there, huh?"

"Yes, I do."

He looked at Pearl. "You work there, too?"

"Now and then."

Enid didn't even glance at her.

Jason jabbed Marty's arm. "You see? That's how I *don't* feel. I really don't wanna be there. The station's real nice if you like to sit around and watch grass grow. Everything's always the same. We muster in October. Why? Because you *always* muster in October, that's why. Move this mob from here to there. Now move that mob from there to here. Build this fence, tear that one down. As exciting as canned peaches."

Marty started eating the onions in his dish. "Since I already heard this here litany of woe, he must be reciting it for your benefit. So listen up."

Enid giggled.

With grand gestures, Jason waxed eloquent. "Life is meant to be savored—its nuances, its thrills and surprises. Like a delicious stew. Now if you have to work the whole time, you might as well be working at something you can enjoy. Like you, Enid. You seem to have found your place. It's rewarding for you. I'm still hunting mine."

"Jase?" All Marty had left now was the meat. "What's a nuance?"

"Aha! So you *were* listening! It's a word I found in one of Henry Lawson's newspaper columns. I plan to work 'egregious' into the conversation, too, somewhere."

Pearl tried to limit her laughter to a ladylike titter. Impossible. "What line of work do you suppose might provide the nuances you crave?"

"Mining."

The way Marty started, Pearl could tell this was new to him. She frowned. "Isn't that terribly dirty work? What sort of mining?"

"Gemstones. I've been thinking of packing up and going to Anakie down the line there. Dig sapphires, diamonds. Crikey. There's a nice living to be made in the semiprecious stones, like smoky quartz. I don't want a lot of money—though I won't refuse it if it comes my way, of course. But I want excitement. I want to live!"

Pearl looked at Marty. "But you like it right where you are. You're a pastoralist—a squatter."

"Suits me."

Suits me. These people all knew what they wanted,

whether they actually got it or not. Pearl hadn't a clue what she wanted.

Marty broke a ten-pound note to pay the check without batting an eye. They returned to the hospital, Enid to go back to work and the other three to sit with Gimpy Jack awhile.

What did Pearl want, exactly? To get away from her mother's constant complaining and her father's religious fanaticism. To marry well. Most importantly, to live in a comfortable city—with the amenities of city life—far away from Barcaldine.

Later that afternoon she was struck by an idea. It was so simple! She would return to Brisbane—perhaps even to Sydney. And not eventually. She would do it now. She would become reacquainted with her old set; that is, if her parents would let her. She would pursue marriage prospects that preferred living in big cities. Already she had wasted far too much time in this forsaken pit.

True, most backblockers were a decent sort, and many of the squatters were quite well-to-do, like the Frobels. But they all lived out beyond the black stump, beyond nowhere. Enough is enough; Pearl was tired of being nowhere. Jason would seek his gems in Anakie. Pearl would pursue hers in Brisbane.

CHAPTER SIX

FLOWERS OF BAIAME

"After Baiame the Creator left this world and went back home, the flowers he had made withered, and eventually they died. The only bees around lived in three sacred trees. And though the children cried for honey, the wise old men would not permit anyone to approach the sacred trees.

"A spirit reported to Baiame how the people would not raid his trees, even though they yearned for honey, and their devotion pleased him. So he sent white sugar on some gum leaves and sugary sap that hardened on some gum-tree trunks, to satisfy their sweet tooth. The children were happy.

"Ah, but there still were no flowers. Three wise old men set out to find Baiame and plead for flowers. After many hard trials they reached him atop his mountain and begged him to help them. The god whisked them into the heavens, where flowers never fade, a place of countless beautiful blooms, and told them to gather as many blossoms as they could. Overcome, the wise old men picked as much as they could carry and returned to their home, scattering their precious flowers on the wind. The bees came back, and every season the flowers bloom, wherever the wind had carried them."

Indirri could almost hear Storyteller's voice now as the boy sat pondering the many meanings of this age-old story while watching a honeybee work the drift of fuzzy yellow flowers all around him. The wise old man had been instructed by wiser, older men before him. They knew which places were sacred, which were to be avoided in order to please gods and spirits. And they had the power within their clans to enforce the taboos. When they needed something—flowers, in this case—they knew where to seek and to find. They knew one had to scatter the flowers to make more. Because they knew all this, they served not just their own generation but the whole world. What wonderful power that is, to be able to serve and to make the world better!

Indirri yearned, desperately, to serve like that. But he never would. He had no wise man, no voice from the past to guide him. He hadn't the slightest notion where to begin.

The bee lifted away and Indirri leaped up to follow. It paused at another small drift for a few moments, then struck out across open grassland. A bee flies much faster than a man can run. Indirri soon lost it, so he kept running toward the next patch of brigalow. He searched for an hour, but found no honey trove. Apparently the bee had changed course somewhere in its journey.

It was dark when he returned, virtually empty-handed, to Mungkala. He tossed the day's catch, two dead lizards, to his companion. "Woman food."

"Food." Mungkala corrected. He didn't bother with a fire. He peeled skin back and began to eat.

Indirri flopped down beside him, suddenly very weary. "You find much today?"

"Not much. Time to move on. This place is about used up."

Indirri nodded absently and watched the colors change in the western sky.

"You're thinking again. So say it out loud. What about?"

"Flowers and bees. Remember Baiame?"

"Yes. And?"

"And I agree we should move on. To the north. We should never have left the land we know best. We must find a clan who will make us part of them. It won't be our clan, but there will never be our clan. And any clan is better than none at all."

"You know what they all say, even the ones out of our father's moiety. You. But not me. I slow them down." Mungkala tossed lizard bones aside. "Time we separated. I know why you're seeking other clans. You want to become a sage. I don't. So I go where I want; you go where you want."

"You can't live without me. You can't hunt. And our mothers were sisters. No. Perhaps when you're stronger. Not now."

"It's been five wets since the whitefellers fell upon us. Coming six. I'm as healed as I'll ever get. The way you see me now is the way I'll always be. No good. You go. Don't worry 'bout me."

Same argument. No matter how it started, whether from flowers or kangaroos, this was how it always ended. With a sigh, Indirri stretched out on his back and watched the sky darken overhead. He could appreciate the joy those wise men must have felt when they found themselves surrounded by beauty. He understood the horror of watching his clan die senselessly. What he could not appreciate or understand was emptiness. He was empty now; no gladness, no sorrow, no anger. The rage was dead. Vivid emotions he could deal with, but how to handle nothingness? He didn't want to continue living—yet he didn't want to die. He wished the Storyteller had taken time to advise him on this point.

Dawn came with the kookaburra's call. Indirri awakened cold and stiff; still, he knew Mungkala was colder and stiffer. He stretched himself, then patiently tugged at Mungkala's right leg and arm until they would move. Once the elbow and knee could bend, it was a simple matter to haul Mungkala to his feet and set him on his way, his stout walking stick in his hand and his spear thrower under his arm. No spear—Mungkala could no longer hold a spear very well. He used the broad, flat surface of the spear thrower to gather seeds and roots, like a woman.

A mile or so of walking would loosen Mungkala up enough that he would be able to get down and stand up again with the aid of his stick. Indirri jogged a hundred yards and turned to watch his cousin totter northward. The crooked right arm hung at his side, nearly useless. The short right leg worked more like a trunk than a limb. And the great jagged scar on his side only emphasized the strange concavity in his ribs. Men their age should display the marks and scars of manhood; Mungkala carried only the scars of inhumanity.

Indirri had not hunted this broad basin for a long time. He paused to scan the area, determining where kangaroos and wallabies would most likely be spending the heat of the day. Roots and flowers, grubs and lizards were all right if there were nothing else, but he hungered for some meat. Real meat. He guessed at three or four promising thickets and began with the closest one.

He must have been daydreaming. That was the only explanation for his mistake. You must never daydream when hunting. A wallaby squirted straight out of the thicket before his spear was ready. It took two long bounds toward Indirri and reversed directions in one mad hop. Away it went. Indirri flung his spear; he missed.

Fffwit. The wallaby jerked mid-leap and landed heavily. It thrashed, the hind legs kicking uselessly, trying to get away. Indirri ran to his spear, grabbed it and started for the fallen animal. He stopped cold.

She stood rigid and tense, halfway between the thicket and the struggling wallaby. A lubra. Her age? Young, yet adult, like Indirri. Her skin was lighter than usual; whitefellers lurked in her ancestry. And her eyes. Even from this distance Indirri was riveted by those eyes sunk so deep in the brown velvet face. Blue eyes. Eyes like the overhead sky.

She carried a weapon like no other Indirri had ever seen. It was made of wood bent into an arch by a cord. A thin stick fit into it crossway, sort of. And she was pointing it at him. She said something he could not understand.

He squatted down and laid his spear aside. If he didn't know what she said, she wouldn't know what he was saying, either. So he said nothing. He smiled.

She scowled and lowered her curious weapon. Her dazzling blue eyes flitted about, scanning everywhere. She moved quickly to the wallaby and laid a foot on it. Her message was clear. *This is my kill and I'm not sharing.*

He pointed to her weapon and gestured with his hands. *What is that thing, anyway?*

She made no hostile sign; she didn't point it at him again, so he stood up and walked casually to the wallaby. A long thin stick with feathers at one end, just like the one that fitted crosswise in her weapon, was sticking out of the roo high behind the shoulders. The wallaby's eyes were glassing over, its movements diminishing. The thin stick didn't kill instantly, but it did the job. That amazed Indirri, for the stick was much smaller than even a child's toy spear.

He glanced at her face. She was studying him, top to bottom. What were those blue eyes looking for? She reached out, poked his arm and frowned. Next she jabbed at his ribs and wagged her head. She said something to him, and her words sounded like a question, but he couldn't begin to guess at what she meant. He smiled harder.

She turned and walked back into the thicket. Minutes later she returned with her dilly bag and woman's bowl. From the dilly bag she brought out a loaf of some sort. Half a loaf, actually. Half of the strangest loaf he had ever seen. How did she ever grind seeds so fine or bake it so smoothly brown? What made it fluff up like that? And the loaf's texture—so soft and even. She plopped it into his hand and drew from the bag a whitefeller's weapon.

His heart almost stopped but he held his place and tried not to let concern show. It was a big shiny metal cutting blade—like the kind of metal that whitefellers' fences were made of. Dropping to her knees, she gutted the wallaby with a few deft slashes. She hacked and sliced, then flipped the animal, stepped on it and broke the spine with an expert yank and twist. She literally cut it in two. She handed the back haunches and tail—the best part—to Indirri and stuffed the front end in her dilly bag.

He stared, dumbfounded. Apparently she believed he needed fattening. Certainly he was thin; it's hard to find plenty of food when you're in one place a long time, and Mungkala moved neither well nor far. But he wasn't a charity case—at least not yet. On the other hand, he was very hungry.

He looked at the loaf in one hand and the meat in the other. She wouldn't understand, but he spoke anyway in the only language he knew. "I am grateful. I'll take this to my friend. He's ill. I'll tell him about you."

Now she was staring, just as dumbfounded. She said in words he could understand, "Your clan comes from the north. Not Iningai country."

His mind lurched and stumbled in a fruitless search for words. Politeness and convention required him to establish their clan relationship immediately, so they would know how to address each other. But he couldn't think. "We came south five wets ago, raiding for lu—" *Come on! Think!* "Because the initiated men thought we should."

She relaxed, her arms hanging and fingers laced together, and her slight smile said quite plainly: *You're as transparent as the east wind, and you are very nervous and I am not.* But her voice spoke, "Do you have a friend, really? Or did you speak from embarrassment because a lubra brought your game down?" Her dialect was that of clans living west of Indirri's ancestral lands, and she framed the words as if she were not accustomed to using that language.

"Come meet my friend."

Without the slightest hesitation she fell in beside him and they began to walk. Indirri had to admit her strong and well-nourished body appeared in better health than his. The lilt in her graceful stride told him she was happy; the sparkle in those amazing blue eyes told him she was intelligent.

They found Mungkala at midday. It wasn't difficult—he hadn't traveled very far. The woman was not nearly the surprise to Mungkala that she had been to Indirri, for he had seen them coming three miles before they reached him. Fortunately he remembered the correct manner of determining relationships. He quickly learned her name was Goonur; her father was a whitefeller of the scots clan and her mother was from the honey-ant totem. They were, as regards ancestry, total strangers.

Not that it mattered now. If this had been a full clan gathering, she would have waited outside camp while they determined her relationship to them. Then they would have greeted her accordingly—warmly or distantly, as the occasion required. They would have waited until the close of day to prepare and eat their food. Somehow, none of that applied now. Neither Indirri nor Mungkala was initiated, she lived as much in the whitefeller world as theirs, and both her clan and theirs were gone forever. Three orphans sat down around a fire in the afternoon sun to eat the wallaby and the strange-tasting loaf.

Indirri gestured toward Goonur's curious weapon. "That thing. Tell me about it."

She smiled. "When I started working cattle at 'Lizbeth Down, all the other drovers carried guns. Pistols on their belts, rifles in their scabbards. So I got brave and I asked the boss cocky, 'Give me a gun, too.' He just laughed. But the other drovers, the men, got nervous. They were afraid I'd shoot them 'cause I'm black or shoot them 'cause I'm a woman and can't shoot straight."

Mungkala's eyes were huge. "You're a drover? You ride on a whitefeller horse?"

"Can't do it walking. By'm by the boss cocky's son came along and heard this. He laughed and said, 'Let's give her my old bow and arrows. Only bow and arrows in Queensland. Then if we find an arrow sticking out of a man or a cow, we know who pulled the trigger.' So they gave me this and I practiced until I can hit 'most anything with it. As good as a gun and a lot quieter."

"As good as a gun." Indirri felt a shiver of envy run through him. If he had owned this bow and arrows when his clan was attacked, the bones of the evil man in the vivid breast cover would be rotting beside his mother's now.

She cut herself another chunk of wallaby meat. "The boss cocky's son and his cousin did Otch Ree, he said. But now they're grown up, they're too busy to do Otch Ree. Don't need bows and arrows anymore."

"What's Otch Ree?"

Goonur shrugged. "I don't know." She stared at Mungkala awhile. It wasn't a rude stare or a fearful one. She simply seemed to be assessing the degree of damage, as it were. "No clan'll let you in, right? My mother's wouldn't, I know."

He shrugged with exaggerated casualness.

"Come work on the station. They find you something to do; you get enough good tucker that you aren't all bones like this. Most blackfellers come and go. Time for corroborree, time for ceremonies, time for hunting up north, they leave. Boss cocky used to get really angry about that. Called them lazy. They aren't lazy. Just have other things to do. Besides, they can mostly live off the land. You, though. You would stay there year-round because you don't have anyplace else to go. 'Dependable' the boss cocky calls it. And a good place for you because you don't fit into blackfeller life."

Mungkala was so shaken he was sweating. "Don't fit into whitefeller life even worse."

"Isn't that hard. Learning their yabba is the only hard part. It wasn't hard for me because of my father. I grew up speaking some of both. I'd help you some."

Mungkala's eyes flicked wildly toward Indirri, like a hunted animal's. Indirri sat thinking. If Mungkala found a niche in the whitefellers' world or near it, Indirri would be free to seek out his own destiny as a sage and elder. No longer would he be his cousin's sole means of survival. How many times had Mungkala said, "You go your way and I'll go mine." Now for the first time Mungkala had the possibility of a way to go. A possible choice.

Indirri said what wise men always say about a new idea. "We will consider it."

It took them two and a half days to walk to the station called 'Lizbeth Down, ample time in which to consider. Indirri felt ripped in two. Every fiber of his body shouted, "You are going with the enemy! The murderers!" And even as guilt and anger screamed, a small voice in his heart whispered, "It is your only chance to become what you have always dreamt of being."

There was the station, within view. Mungkala stopped stubbornly. "Maybe no. Not a good idea."

"How do you know? You haven't tried it." Indirri wanted

to sound casual, but he was solidly convinced now. This was the way.

Goonur pulled a wad of cotton cloth out of her dilly bag and slipped it over her head. It was a whitefeller's woman dress, very plain and sleeveless, reaching from neck to knee.

"See? I don't have clothes. No good." Mungkala was sweating again.

"They give you some. Boss cocky doesn't like anyone running around natural. You get used to it." Goonur walked forward a few strides and turned. "You coming or not?"

Indirri drew a deep breath, trying to slow his pounding heart. "I'm coming."

Mungkala had no choice. He lagged, but he came.

Utter terror wrenched Indirri's breastbone. The enemy camp. The heart of the murderers' lair. And he was walking right into it.

How he envied Goonur! She strode along, relaxed. With a simple piece of cloth she had transformed herself. A moment before she had been a perfect fit in Indirri's world. Now she was fitting quite as perfectly into this one. And why not? The blood of both worlds coursed in her veins. But Indirri was not half and half. Never would he fit here.

And yet, as they approached he realized with a start how many blacks here had made the leap from world to world. Of five men mending a rail fence over there, three were black. A black girl was suspending pieces of cloth from a long rope by the largest building. A black baby played at her feet.

Strong, pervasive smells covered the gentle scent of human beings. Cows, sheep, horses . . . two camels munched at dry grass behind a distant fence. Talk about a smell. Indirri's nose would never forgive him the pounding intensity of these alien odors.

Mungkala looked ready to collapse. All color had drained from his lips and fingernails. Sweat ran down his face and neck.

"Sit here and wait," said Goonur.

They sat and waited, on the edge of the camp, while she went into the largest building. At least this much was familiar and comfortable, but Indirri already knew what his relationship was to these people. No blood relation. Enemy.

Someone beyond some trees shouted. Someone else closer to the largest building yelled and the black girl with the baby ran inside. Indirri leaped to his feet and helped Mungkala up.

From among the trees a horse came pulling a wheeled box up the track. Two young white men sat on a seat and a black man sat in back. The black man wore brilliantly colored clothes on top. Everyone was smiling brightly. People of all sorts came pouring out from everywhere to greet the three.

It appeared to be a joyous occasion, with much laughter and happy-sounding yabba. The two whites hopped down out of the box. Carefully they helped the black with the amazing clothes out the back of it. More expressions of joy and pleasure. Indirri watched carefully for any sign of trouble, but he didn't see the slightest hint of a problem. He and Mungkala were being completely ignored.

Finally he saw Goonur separate herself from the crowd and come striding over to them. She paused beside them. "As soon as the excitement is over the manager will take you on. He asked me if you were dependable and I said yes."

"What is the yabba?"

"The man with brown hair there is the boss cocky's son and the other one is his sister's son. The black's name is Gimpy Jack and he's been here about six wets, come and go. Those three and some others were working at another station down south of here when Gimpy Jack got hurt bad. Everyone thought he would die. But these two wouldn't let him—took him in a hurry to a whitefeller's doctor 'way south."

"They blackfeller's friends?"

"If they make you a friend, you're a friend. We never thought we'd see Gimpy Jack again and there he is. The doctor was about thirty miles from where the accident happened. A day's walk and some, but the horse and cart's a lot faster, of course. And it's almost two hundred miles from here."

Indirri listened as she spoke with admiration for the boss cocky and his son. She spoke with warmth and with gladness for the survival of this Gimpy Jack. There was a kind of clanship here. Gimpy Jack was being led into the largest building. And look! He walked with a limp! These people, black and white, cared for a limping man. Mungkala's chances of survival without Indirri were looking better and better by the minute.

Indirri found himself not just listening to Goonur but watching her as well. The velvet skin. And those eyes. The rest of the world probably saw nothing more than a half-caste girl in a plain dress. Indirri saw one of Baiame's brightest flowers.

CHAPTER SEVEN

THE RUINS OF FIRE

The pastor was up at Aramac today doing a double wedding and a funeral, so Papa was preaching for the service. That suited Pearl. She felt quite important as she sat in the front pew watching her father do what he loved best. He was very good, too, for a lay assistant.

Prayer, benediction, amens. Over.

Mum was already at the door beside Papa, all smiles, greeting the parishioners as they left. For a woman who would rather be home right now, she was very good, too.

A squat little lady with thinning gray hair cornered Pearl to tell her about a new selector up the road a piece toward Ilfracombe. The selector had a wife and five children to support on his parcel, but he also had a brother. And that brother was not only unmarried, he was just Pearl's age. Wasn't that *interesting*?

If Mum could keep the smile pasted on, so could Pearl. Therefore, Pearl remained a model of politeness on the outside, pushing her angry annoyance at the old busybody inside, safely out of sight—though not out of mind. The old biddy.

Pearl spotted the two sisters who worked at the hospital as they went out the door, smiling and shaking Papa's hand. And there, over by the south wall . . . Pearl excused herself, neatly avoiding two other ladies who were descending upon her, and made her way across the church toward the south wall. Marty Frobel was all gussied up in a suit and tie, talking to a small, square-built man in sweeping muttonchop whiskers.

Pearl put on her most genuine smile and extended her hand. "Mr. Frobel. All the way down from Torrens Creek. We're honored."

"Miss Fowkes. Edward Frobel, Pearl Fowkes, daughter of the presiding minister today. My Uncle Edward, Pearl."

His gold watch chain and a diamond tie pin had already impressed Pearl, but Edward Frobel poured on the charm anyway. He turned a marvelous derby hat over and over in his hands as he spoke in warm tones as deep as Marty's. Pearl made small talk on the outside, but inside, her head was abuzz. Did Marty come clear down here to court, or for some other reason? And if that was the case, what would she do about it? She really didn't want to consider marrying this far from real civilization, pinned down forever in the desolate outback with a pack of children. But he certainly was good-looking, and quite well off to boot.

The three of them worked their way to the door, the last in line, smiling and shaking hands as they went. When they were outside, Pearl noted with satisfaction that the gray-haired biddies looked fit to burst.

"So how is Jason? Doing well, I trust."

"Yair. Guess so. He's down in Anakie. Packed up and moved off the station to dig jewels." Marty licked his lips. "Keeps telling me to come down and help him; says he's got a good claim started, but he needs another set of hands."

"The lad's dreamin'." Uncle Edward grumbled. "The sooner he comes to his senses, the better."

Pearl twirled her parasol. "Sounds like hard work."

"There's work and there's work," Marty shrugged. "Station isn't doing so well, really. Those two dry spells, one right on the heels of the other, reduced the grazing so bad we had to sell stock off for less than cost. Then—"

"Freeze 'em!" boomed in Uncle Edward. "I tell you, lad, the secret is freezing. Freeze the meat here and sell it all over the world. Tap a whole globe of markets."

"They put in a freezing plant in Townsville and it loses money, Uncle Ed."

" 'Cause they're not doing it right. Done right, it's a surefire moneymaker. Gunner make that a top priority in my editorial column. Local freezer plant."

"Your editorial column?" Pearl craned her neck to look at him better. "You have a newspaper?"

"Going to start one, right here in Barcaldine."

"But we already have one. The *Western Champion*. It's been here half of forever."

"I'm aware of that, young lady, and I'm acutely aware of the paper's quality. I believe I can do better. Much better. Marty, you said something about pointing out a William Campbell somewhere."

"He's usually at the Commercial having tea about now. We're headed that way." There was a tightness to Marty's voice that Pearl hadn't heard before.

Pearl felt a discomfort here between the three of them and she couldn't be sure she wasn't causing it. And yet, Marty seemed at ease with her. His Uncle Edward was most gracious. Curious. They paused at the Commercial only long enough for Marty to step inside, introduce his uncle to Mr. Campbell and excuse himself.

He escorted Pearl back outside and drew a deep, relieved breath. "Uncle Edward figures all he has to do is dive into something and it'll work right for him. He doesn't know the first thing about the newspaper business. A month ago he was a clerk supervisor at a bank in Brisbane."

"I heard the *Western Champion* is a rather good one, as newspapers go."

"It is. Fair. Unbiased. Gives you the drum. Doesn't lean toward Uncle Edward's political way of thinking, though. If you see the picture."

She saw the picture, although she didn't really care one way or the other about it. "So Jason is digging for jewels."

"Just as well. He certainly wasn't interested in being a stockman. Thought the work was too hard, the pay not so good."

"Are you going to go down with him?"

"I was thinking about it maybe. I, uh, was kind of expecting Enid would be in church, too."

"She gets her church on Saturday night, listening to Papa practice his lay readings and sermons and offering suggestions. Then she works at the hospital on Sunday morning so that the sisters and ward men can attend service. Believe me, Sunday morning is better than Papa's Saturday night practice. Doesn't take as long, either."

The mysterious tightness was gone from Marty's voice. "That must be a real sacrifice for Enid. I know she enjoys church; she's said so a couple times."

That was true, though Pearl hadn't thought of it that way before. "She'll be home shortly. Would you and your uncle join us for luncheon?"

"I think Uncle Edward had other plans for the day. But I'd be pleased to."

Good! Perhaps Marty's reason for being in Barcaldine would become clear at lunch. And she knew Mum would be pleased to entertain the son of a prominent pastoralist for a change instead of the stragglers Papa usually brought to the house.

They strolled about a little longer, seeing and being seen, and then headed home. Mum, bless her, had tidied up; the place looked picture perfect. Papa shook hands and reintroduced himself. His quiet reserve contrasted sharply with the cheerful way he'd pumped everybody's arm at the church door. Mum greeted Marty effusively, expressed her disappointment at his uncle's absence, and ushered Marty to the parlor. The day was going perfectly. Very elegant.

Then Enid came bursting in, flying through the front door and into the parlor so wildly that Marty nearly knocked his chair over trying to stand up in time.

"Papa!" She flung her arms around Papa's neck. "Sister Ellen—you know, the taller one?—committed her life to Christ not ten minutes ago! Your message touched her and I was able to answer her questions. It was so beautiful! Thank you, Papa!"

Mum looked dreadfully embarrassed—nearly as embarrassed as Pearl felt. Marty appeared mildly confused.

But Papa, so rigid a moment before, loosened up instantly with a boyish laugh of pure joy. "How splendid! Your mum and I will call on her as soon as she comes off work. Does she have a Bible, do you know?"

"I loaned her mine until we buy her one tomorrow." For the first time Enid noticed Marty. She acted not the slightest bit embarrassed or hesitant about her previous outburst as she went to him and gripped both his hands in hers. "What a lovely surprise! You can stay for luncheon, I hope."

Mum broke in. "Would you excuse Pearl and me, please? We must complete luncheon preparations." And she whisked herself off to the kitchen.

Pearl set the table mechanically, five places, and strained her ears to listen to the conversation in the other room. She could just hear the three of them in the parlor discussing religious topics—Enid's voice all bubbly, Papa's voice jubilant, Marty's rumble, barely audible, asking questions. She wished she could hear him better, to decide if what she had seen in his eyes corresponded to what she heard. Because what she had seen—and there was no way she could talk herself out of this—was puppy love!

Marty had a full-scale crush on Enid. His comment at church about missing Enid there made sense now. The admiration in his voice when he learned she sacrificed her Sunday mornings became instantly obvious; how did Pearl miss it before? And his face when her sister walked in. . . . Enid was the one he had come to see. She was the reason he was in Barcaldine. His Uncle Edward was merely the excuse.

Pearl absolutely burned. She was furious with her plain little sister for embarrassing her so badly just now. She was furious with Mum for sticking her out here in the dining room. Marty was her guest—*her* guest!—and here she was doing scullery chores. The day was rotten—rotten to the core.

How Pearl managed to get clear through lunch without losing her pasted-on smile she would never know. Now that she knew, she read it in every glance, every move Marty made. And look at Mum, being so painfully gracious toward him! And why not? It didn't matter to Mum which daughter married the prominent pastoralist so long as he was interested in one of them.

By the time Marty left that afternoon, after tea in the parlor, Pearl had formulated a plan. This turn of events was a blessing in disguise. She had nearly fallen for the prospect of accepting a local swain out of convenience, condemning herself to an impoverished life in the outback. This close call had brought her to her senses. She would return to the city and find a more suitable match. She wanted an urbane, sophisticated gentleman. As handsome and polite as Marty might be—in a rough-hewn way—urbane he was not. Yes might possibly be pronounced *yas*, but never *yair*.

She waited until after supper before broaching the subject. Papa was in the sitting room, reading a book about the gospel in the stars. Enid was writing letters at Papa's little desk in the corner, and Mum was sewing buttons back on shirts, a free service she provided her better laundry customers. The hubbub of the day had long since died down. Pearl got out her embroidery (the cross-stitched napkins she'd been working on for a year) and settled into the rocker.

Silence. Peace.

"Papa? I've been considering my prospects here, and I've decided to move back to Brisbane." She hesitated, expecting the world to blow up. Mum blanched, then denounced the idea. "Rubbish, child!" Papa never flinched.

He laid his book in his lap and looked at her mildly. "Oh, you have now. And how will you support yourself in Brisbane?"

"I was hoping for a small advance against wages just to get me started."

"An advance. Look about the room here. What do you see?"

"A very simple but tasteful arrangement of furnishings. Three happy and contented persons." Obviously that wasn't the answer he had been looking for. She kept trying. "A warm and loving family. A Christian atmosphere." Just what *was* he looking for?

"Simple furnishings, you say. Quite elegant furnishings

compared with most of the local homes where I call. Pearl, you are surrounded by what would otherwise be a bank account. As it is, your mother's earnings as a laundress go to the upkeep of this elegant home, and I earn not a farthing spare. We have no funds with which to offer you an advance. Even if you found a job the day you arrived, your first pay would be several weeks coming. And how would you live until then?" He raised his book again. "I suggest you remain here at home until you've built up some savings with which to keep yourself in the city."

"You're making sport of me!"

"Not at all. I'm reminding you of the realities of life." And he went back to reading.

Mum sputtered, "You really should consider carefully before taking so drastic a step, dear. There's much to—"

"Tell me, Mother, how long did Papa consider before yanking us up by the roots and dragging us out to this fried and forsaken strip of nothing? I was too young then to resist. I had to come. But I'm not a little girl anymore. I can make my own choices now. And I have chosen to be done with this wretched place."

"I never realized you were so unhappy here, darling," Mum remonstrated. "I'll admit it's certainly not the city, but it has its few good points."

Pearl closed her eyes and used one of Mum's favorite ploys. "I've made up my mind and that's the end of it. I'll not discuss it any further."

Papa's voice came over and around his book, which he continued to read. "You are under your father's protection until you marry. There will be no discussion on that, either."

Silence. But the peace had fled.

The dream became an obsession. Within a week Pearl had quit her job as a clerk at Meacham and Leyland builders to become an assistant to the advertising editor of the *Western Champion*. The rate of pay was the same—minuscule—but she could put in longer hours.

In September Dr. Symes left town amid scandalous rumors involving someone's wife. No matter how hard Pearl pressed Enid for more details—for she was right there on the inside—Enid refused to comment. She simply quoted some passage in Proverbs about tale-bearing and remained silent. Honestly! Surely it isn't gossip when it's your own sister.

In October, under the guidance of the new physician, Dr. Neilsen, the examining tables were at last removed from the engine room, and the instruments were tossed back into their crate and transported to Barcaldine's spacious new hospital. It had cost over fifteen hundred pounds to rebuild it. Had Pearl remained with Meacham and Leyland, who had built the structure, she could have attended the opening ceremonies, for all their employees had been invited. As a hospital aide Enid was there, looking as proud and happy as if she owned the whole place, shiny new kitchen and all.

By Christmas, Pearl had salted away enough to support herself for two months in Brisbane, if she lived frugally. Or she could work in Sydney for five weeks. Sydney was looking ever better. If she were going back to the city, why not the biggest and the best?

She kept her money not in the Queensland National Bank branch in Willow Street but in the little Barcaldine Building Society in Oak Street. Barcaldine was growing so rapidly, with new buildings going up constantly, that she could earn 2.25-percent interest there instead of the mere 2 percent the bank offered.

The Monday after Christmas began like any other summer Monday, filled with shimmering heat. Pearl went to work early that she might garner in an extra hour's wage. She was never allowed to write copy. She could not compose, set type, or prepare correspondence. She proofread—all day.

The girl who had held the job previously claimed that ads are easier to proof than more interesting pieces. "You get so involved in fun-to-read pieces that you forget to search out errors." Pearl longed for a chance to find out, for advertisements were so boring, so petty. She continued to work through the lunch hour—that gave her another hour's wage.

WHEEEEEE! Pearl found herself standing out in the street, every nerve and hair root on edge, her pencil still in her hand. The steam whistle on the roof of the printing company continued to shriek. But who had set it off?

"Fire!" someone yelled, and beyond the roofs she could see the smoke—over in Oak Street, it appeared. At least it wasn't the new hospital. George, the city editor, came running out with a notebook and with Mr. Campbell himself right behind him. George pointed at Pearl. "You! Come with me!" and off he went. There would be no more ad proofing today. She followed them down the street at a run.

Smoke was pouring out of every window of the Railway Hotel. A rumble and roar inside told her the first floor had just collapsed into the ground floor. Moments later the tin sheets on the roof began to pop; smoke and flame shot skyward.

George ripped his notebook in two and stuffed half into her hand. "Write down everything you see and get as many names as you can—don't forget to note what the person's doing. I'm going over to the bore—be back in five minutes. You're my eyes and ears here, understand?"

She understood, but she had no idea how to go about it. She began jotting things willy-nilly, mentioning people she knew. She failed to recognize most of the faces. When she saw Mr. Campbell writing feverishly on a big foolscap pad, she sort of gave up. He'd record it all a lot more thoroughly than she could.

The buildings on either side of the hotel were literally turning black. All the curtains in the windows of the little rooming house to the west caught on fire; then its wall dissolved in flames. Now the building on the east side was afire, too.

The man responsible for the artesian bore that supplied most of the town's water came running upstreet. Pearl scribbled down his last name—she couldn't remember his first name. He was shouting about cutting off the rest of the town's water and diverting the full force of the bore into the Oak Street main. There went Mum's laundry.

The fire was now so hot that the crowd had to move back half a block. People were rushing in and out of the Black house two doors up from the fire. Screaming wildly, Mrs. Black threw something out the upstairs window. It hit the street and sprayed pieces all over—a clock! She threw a jewelry case out the window as two husky men came out the front door carefully carrying a mattress and bedstead.

In the little pub across from Pearl, two fellows struggled in the doorway with a barrel. They broke its spigot off getting it out the door. Down the street they ran with the barrel spilling rum by the gallon. Finally the firemen arrived with hoses. The hotel was already gutted, so they turned their efforts to the adjacent buildings, spraying them down, trying to limit the fire to what it had already consumed.

Within ten minutes the fire had spread to two more stores, voraciously engulfing the structures and filling the sky with acrid smoke, nearly roasting the eyes of anyone brave enough to watch—which was just about the whole town. Water didn't slow the fire down. The flames licked in every direction, seemingly unstoppable. The violent, howling furnace of destruction appeared to have a power all its own.

The Barcaldine Building Society ignited next. Adjacent to that building was an unoccupied shop, which a small army of townsmen stormed against, trying to tear it down with the meager tools available. It worked. The fire reached that point and smoldered. Workers on the other side tore down an occupied one-story building, and another, and in their enthusiasm, still another. One would have done it.

As the sun set that night twelve buildings lay in ruins, gnawed by fire or ripped apart by frantic hands. Pearl's notebook had but two pages of illegible scribbling. It was nearly nine when the excitement finally died down and people drifted away. She returned to the office and flopped into her chair, rubbing her burning, aching eyes. She must try to make some sense of her notes. George would want them shortly.

This disaster convinced her. Instead of the smoothly concerted efforts such as one saw in a city fire brigade, she had witnessed the frenzied antics of panicked country bumpkins. She was not going to stay here another week. Not another day. Tomorrow she would pack and escape this madness. Oh, how she hated this dinky cow town!

A sudden thought chilled her. She picked up her notebook and trudged out into the dark of night for a personal interview and hoped against hope that she'd find the man she wanted to see.

He was there. The manager of the Barcaldine Building Society was still at his former place of business, poking dejectedly through the ruins. In the light of the flickering flames stood the big safe gaping open, the smoldering ledgers ruined.

Yes, every page of business records had gone up in smoke. No records of loans existed other than copies of agreements held by the recipients themselves. The loan recipient need only tear up his agreement and his debt was cancelled. The depositors? Of course they had their passbooks and could prove how much they had invested. But the passbooks were just as useless, for not a penny of the assets had been insured.

CHAPTER EIGHT

THE START OF A BUSINESS

"Will you quit fidgeting?" Pearl watched Enid's slim little fingers dance on her lap. Her fingers stilled by sheer force of will. Pearl sighed. "I'm sorry you're coming. It was a bad decision. You should get off at the next stop and turn in your ticket on a return fare. Go back home now while it's still easy to do, before this train carries you all the way to Brisbane." She turned her attention to the hills and trees zipping past the window. It looked the same now as it had when she and her family had taken this train in the other direction a long, long time ago.

Enid tipped her head back and closed her eyes. "I don't think it was a bad decision. I feel very strongly led to do this. Besides, this train won't take us to Brisbane. We have to change trains at Rockhampton."

"When *I* feel strongly led, you say it's impulse. When *you* feel strongly led, you say it's God. Precious little difference that I can see."

"Pearl." Enid's voice took on that irritatingly condescending tone. "Pearl, you get an idea in your head and it becomes a compulsion. You worked long and hard hours for months and months when, quite frankly, hard work is not your normal lifestyle."

"Thank you."

"No offense intended. The difference is this: I hadn't the slightest intention in the world of leaving Barcaldine. I enjoyed my job. I loved the church. I liked the town, even with half of Oak Street in ashes. When you lost your savings—almost at the very moment the building was burning—I was seized with an intense feeling that I should leave Barcaldine with you. Even if I could explain it better, you couldn't understand—"

"Now don't start that again!"

"Pearl, you do not have eternal life. Neither do you know the joy of serving Jesus Christ. You don't know the pleasure of having a Master who deserves all the worship and service you can give Him. There are so many things in life to lure our desires. Only God is worthy of all our efforts. I'm happy. I'm so very happy. And I want you to be happy, too."

"Correction. You *used* to be happy. Because of me you don't have your job, or your church people, or even that town. Because of me all your happiness is behind you. Don't think I haven't thought about that a thousand times."

Enid twisted around to talk to her more intently. Pearl hated when Enid did that. "Pearl, please don't say that, because it's not true. My happiness doesn't come from the outside. Not the church or the job or anything. It comes from the inside. The church and job and all are gifts the Lord gave me, ways I can serve Him that give me pleasure, but they're not the source of happiness. They're a product. Do you see the difference between the source and the result?"

Pearl looked her little sister right in the eye, stared straight into that earnest face, and said quite sincerely, "I think you're crazy."

Enid abruptly sat back in the seat. Pearl bit her tongue. She didn't apologize, but she knew she shouldn't have said that. She owed Enid a great deal. When Pearl had announced her intention to leave Barcaldine with or without savings, Enid had brought out her Queensland National Bank passbook with her own savings. Enid didn't just offer her money. She insisted Pearl use it.

When Enid explained to Papa how strongly she felt she should go also, he accepted her wild compulsion unquestioningly as the will of God. Papa had been so adamantly opposed when Pearl had wanted to leave. Now he had changed his mind—almost instantly. Now it was the will of God. For Pearl, maybe, but why Enid? She fit into small-town life. She wasn't half the city person Pearl was. These last three days were very confusing.

Now here they sat, their trunks in the baggage car, and their tickets to Brisbane in their handbags.

Enid's fingers began their dance again.

"If you're so cocksure, why are you nervous?"

"I'm not nervous!" Enid bit her tongue, cutting off whatever else she might have snapped out. "This is God's plan."

Pearl stared at her, and stared at her. Sometimes that worked, just staring at Enid.

Enid glanced guiltily at her sister. "All right, so I overstated things a little. Do you remember when we first started working at the hospital and Jason and Marty took us to lunch?"

"Vividly."

"And Jason made this elaborate speech about how I had found what I wanted to do?"

"I remember."

"It was all rubbish. That hospital thing was a straw to grasp at. I figured if I was very good at that, Papa would be pleased. It's a job that's very . . . very . . . self-sacrificing. You know?"

"What do you mean, Papa would be pleased?"

"When is the last time he called you by name?"

"When he got mad at me just before we left."

"And when did he speak my name?"

"He never gets mad at you. He—" Pearl stopped. "What do you mean, Enid?"

"At least he gets mad at you. He never says a bad thing to me or a good thing, either. Nothing I did in Barcaldine—nothing at all—pleased him or displeased him. I went calling with him, I helped him with his bookkeeping, I did everything I could. And he's never spoken my name."

"Yes, but he loves you. You know that."

"Does he? He loves chocolate desserts, too. I already tried being wonderful in Barcaldine. Now I'm going to try being wonderful in Sydney. Sooner or later he's going to have to notice me."

What do you say to something like that? Pearl held her peace. Enid was wrong. She was surely wrong. Papa preferred her; Pearl was certain. Here was just one more confusing detail to add to the confusing trip.

Sydney. Soon. City.

After yearning so long for this moment, Pearl felt a rush of reluctance. "Enid? Say we reach Brisbane, not Sydney. Sydney's too far, too expensive. If we go to Brisbane, we have enough money—your money—to live for a week or two. No more. Then what?"

"I trust the Lord will supply what we need."

"Right. Just like that." She snapped her fingers. "To attract a man of means, you have to dress well and circulate in the right society. I seriously doubt God is going to supply all that."

"I have no intention of attracting a man, with or without means. I'll become a sister or an attendant at some hospital or infirmary. There are always ready jobs of that sort. I don't need fancy clothes."

"Well, I do. That's why this seems somewhat ill-considered. What we really ought to do is build a purse—a kitty, if you will—before we reach Brisbane."

"How?"

"Well, uh, you can get work as a sister with some doctor, and I can be a newspaper employee or something."

"I thought that George What's-his-name fired you for not taking adequate notes."

"I wouldn't use him as a reference. But I know a little bit of the business now. We'll build a nest egg first, maybe in Rockhampton. Yes—Rockhampton. That way we will be able to outfit ourselves as soon as we have enough money. Then we won't look like country bumpkins when we reach the city."

"I don't mind looking like a country girl. I am one."

"Oh, never mind, Enid." Pearl glanced out the window. It all looked so mundane out there. "What's the last town we passed, do you remember?"

"Jericho. No. Alpha."

"And what's the next town?" Pearl couldn't find her timetable, but Enid pulled hers out.

Enid's eyes got big. "Anakie. That's where Jason James went gem mining! And unless he changed his mind, Marty Frobel will be there by now, too."

"How big is Anakie? Do you remember from the last time we went this way?"

"No. I was only nine or ten. I don't remember hearing anything about it. All I recall is the lady who got on the train to sell gems. I'll bet it doesn't have a newspaper, though. Bet it doesn't even have a doctor."

Pearl smiled. The answer was shaping itself in her mind, clear as crystal. "Think of all the jobs I've had—the soap factory, the boot factory, the clerk position at Meacham and Leyland's. Now add up all the time I spent between them, all the times I was unemployed; do you know what I've done more of than anything else?"

"Look for work."

"Laundry. Mum always had work for me at home. I've done more laundry than anything else. Now. Who gets dirtier than a miner?"

"Who cares less about getting dirty than a miner? I don't think you'll have a very eager clientele. Certainly no silk shirts."

"Plenty of shirts with buttons missing, though. If they have a lot of Chinese, they'll have a laundry already. But if they don't, Enid, the town is mine!"

Enid cocked her head. "And if they do, we simply move on to the next town. Actually, that's not too bad a plan—at least to try."

Aha! Pearl had her! "I thought God told you to go to Brisbane."

"No. Leave Barcaldine with you. Nothing about Brisbane at all."

Pearl sniffed. Enid and Papa. Everything in life revolved around religion, and they were always so certain about everything. The thing they were most certain about—which irritated Pearl most—was that she was not a Christian. She was not "saved." That was why she had no joy, they'd say. What kind of gloom is that to preach to your own daughter and sister?

Pearl would love to find some joy in anything—anything at all. She was nearly convinced joy was just an illusion. About the best one can hope for is to minimize one's misery.

"Next stop, Anakie." The conductor staggered from car to car with his call. You'd think he'd be used to walking through these lurching cars.

Pearl held up a hand to stop him on his way. "Do you know if there is a laundry in Anakie?"

"Laundry." He frowned. "Sorry, mum, don't remember. You'll have thirty minutes if you want to ask. We're loading cattle and some things."

"Thirty minutes. Splendid. Thank you."

Screeching and swaying and clanging its bell, the train lumbered to a halt. Enid walked down to the baggage car to watch and wait, while Pearl took off at a smart clip. Anakie. This little settlement lay under the summer sun even more desolate and insignificant than Pearl remembered.

She didn't even have to ask about a barber shop. There it was, a rather crooked homemade pole with red stripes winding down it, attached to the front of what looked like a pig shed. Pearl stepped inside hurriedly. She had no time to hesitate.

The barber was snipping and trimming at a very rough-looking fellow. They looked at her and stared, their mouths agape.

She smiled. "I must learn quickly if there is a laundry around here, and I thought the town barber would probably know. Can you advise me?"

"A laundry." The bald-headed little barber leaned one elbow on the chair his customer was sitting in and tapped his chin with a comb. "Used to have one. Mrs. Potter down by the creek took in wash, but then her husband decided to try his luck down to Lightning Ridge and they left. And there was this Chinese who did it for a while until some hotheads from Clermont decided Chinese weren't welcome. Scared the pudding out of him and he left. Back to China, I s'pose. Couple of the women might do some for you if you're friends with them. They don't work at it."

"Mrs. Harris over on the ridge," the customer volunteered.

"When she ain't in the sauce. Launders all right, I s'pose, but she drinks so much that her ironing ain't too impressive."

"Thank you, gentlemen!" This was perfect! Pearl could barely contain her glee. "I am an experienced laundress, and I cordially invite you to patronize my brand new laundry services here in town. And if you would, spread the word."

"Surely so." The bald head nodded.

Pearl headed for the door in a haze of delight. This was going better than she had hoped.

"Wait!" called the barber. "Where are you located?"

"I haven't the slightest idea." She hurried out the door and up the dusty street as fast as decorum would allow. Half a block this side of the railway station, she waved vigorously to Enid. By the time she reached the train, a porter was digging their trunks out of the baggage car as per Enid's directions. They had arrived.

The town of Anakie—if you could call it a town—clustered about the railway depot, spreading out in all directions. A haphazard knot of nondurable buildings comprised its center. As the space between buildings widened around the edges of the settlement, the structures themselves became smaller and smaller, more and more ramshackle.

Farther out, houses and living quarters were mostly tents or mere shade frames, wall-less against the wind. Pale mullock piles, the refuse of countless claims, speckled the ragged hills for miles about. Some had shacks and camps, some not. Compared to Anakie, Barcaldine looked like the court at Versailles.

Although any business entrepreneur will tell you that you must have ample basic capital with which to begin an enterprise, Pearl knew better. Her mother had started with nothing; it couldn't be that hard—even here.

After scouting around for a while, the two girls found a nearby creek, which was seasonal, and a spring not too far off. It seemed like a good spot. Then Pearl spied an abandoned claim near the spring. "Let's try this house—if you can call it that."

"What if the owner returns?" asked Enid.

"We'll promise he may have all the jewels we find," replied Pearl, "and we'll sew his buttons on."

What a ramshackle dump! The building was constructed of corrugated metal sheets set on slabs of bark and rough-hewn lumber. There was a makeshift verandah attached to the house, but no windows relieved the gloom inside. It probably leaked in rain, for Pearl could look up at the roof and see dots of light. But no rain fell in this drought, so the question was academic. She needed a good lock for the door. Silly. Anyone could break down the wall as easily as open the door.

Washtubs? She'd sweet-talk the local smith into cutting a discarded oil drum in half for her. Then if she scrubbed the inside sufficiently with sand, she'd have two adequate tubs. She'd get some scrub boards, and buy about a hundred feet of stout cord from the general mercantile to provide enough clothesline to start with.

The girls found someone to bring their trunks. The next few days were spent in making the "house" livable and in gathering the needed supplies. Pearl knew she couldn't whittle clothespins, so she had to pay an exorbitant fee to the general mercantile proprietor to have some clothespins shipped out from Rockhampton. With the purchase of all the yellow soap the proprietor had in stock, they were in business.

"Business" was an exaggeration, of course. Surely nobody wanted to carry his laundry nearly half a mile; but neither did the girls care to carry all their water from the spring to some location closer the main settlement. Around town they put up some signs, complete with a map of their location, and then waited for their first customers.

They received two the first week, one of them the barber with his white tunics. How much should she charge? Pearl quoted a price two shillings above Mum's and a shilling extra for all-wool garments. She expected resistance to the inflated price, but with only two customers the girls had to make a living. Both customers looked at her with mild surprise. "Is that all?"

Two customers in a week. This would never do.

"Very well," announced Pearl the following Monday morning, "it is time for the mountain to move to Muhammad." From her trunk she dug out the elegant calling cards she would have used in Brisbane. She drew a sketchy map on the back of each and on the front wrote "laundry expertly done." While Enid minded the laundry shop, Pearl walked from hovel to hovel, from rickety shop to false-front bank, distributing her cards and shaking hands and making pleasantries as she had learned to do beside her papa at the church door.

The afternoon brought twenty-six customers. Pearl and Enid were elated. The business was taking off!

Twenty-three showed up the next afternoon.

Late Tuesday they hired a local aboriginal girl to help. She didn't last long—only until she had earned enough money to buy her father some tobacco and booze. They put up a help-wanted sign and toiled on.

By Wednesday another seventeen customers had come.

On Thursday they bought out all the mother-of-pearl buttons the mercantile had and ordered more. Pearl also bought four more flatirons, but she had to put them on account; she had not been paid yet. They had to use the irons without seasoning them properly, so the ironing took twice as long as it would ordinarily.

On Friday they opened a bank account. It contained four pounds and eight shillings more than they had when they arrived.

On Saturday they finished the last of the shirts.

On Sunday they rested—gratefully.

Customers were fewer the next week. Apparently the gem miners felt no need to be spotless *every* week. Pearl purchased a ledger and notebooks and worked out a more efficient way of keeping track of bundles.

The next Sunday Enid learned of a man over in Quartz Gully who was sick with the ague. She prepared some vegetable soup and took it to him. There she heard about an epidemic of dysentery around the Nullywog dig. She suggested they carefully boil all cooking and drinking water at least ten minutes. When the dysentery abated within a week, Enid became a folk heroine.

Word continued to spread. Sister Enid, they called her, though she was certainly not a trained sister. The next week she reluctantly set a broken arm, for her medical skills were rudimentary. Before long she found herself elevated to virtual sainthood.

Pearl did not enjoy a similar position of distinction in the community, and while she was properly happy for her little sister, she distinctly felt the snub. Pearl was the blond beauty who did as fine a job on the shirts as any laundry in Brisbane. And yet the only commendation she received was from the lewd comments of the men who didn't realize she had heard them. The boors. The only thing that kept her in Anakie all that first month and the months that followed was, quite frankly, the money. The business cycled up and down from week to week. Even the slow weeks were pretty good weeks, and the good weeks were profitable far beyond her expectations.

But what about Marty and Jason? Pearl swore to herself she would not be first to mention them. So she waited and waited for Enid to bring up the subject. If Enid returned Marty's puppy love at all, she hid her feelings perfectly, and Pearl knew that hiding feelings was not Enid's way. And why didn't the boys come around? By now they surely must have heard about the girls. Everyone in Anakie knew of the Fowkes girls and their laundry.

Summer faded into autumn subtly, gently, as seasons on the Tropic do. Easter fell late this year, April 18. Enid traveled back to Barcaldine to spend the holiday with Mum and Papa and her church friends. Pearl missed Mum and Papa, of course, but she felt no desire to see that town again—not that she particularly enjoyed Anakie, either, which was entirely another matter. She temporarily hired a strong, stocky woman named Mave Hurley, whose background she did not care to investigate, and continued making money.

Pearl spent a quiet Easter, embroidering on that final napkin and trying to recuperate from exhaustion. She thought back to the days when she wished she could work like Mum and stay home from church and rest on Sunday. What an utter fool she had been! Now it hardly seemed like a fair trade.

Monday morning Mave arrived at ten—with a hangover. In disgust Pearl sent her home. That day Pearl worked until dusk, finishing up all but one batch. If Enid caught the train in time, she would be here tomorrow, Pearl thought. Let her take over some of the work. She sprinkled tomorrow's ironing as she steeped a pot of tea, then built a cozy fire in the little stone fireplace for it was becoming chilly outside. She poured a cuppa tea and put her feet up. The day was done—at last.

Or was it? Who would be knocking on the door so late? It was nearly dark. And how did they plan to leave again, to negotiate the crooked path from this door to what passed for civilization in Anakie, when the moon wouldn't be up for an hour yet? She mustn't be impatient. Another customer, another quid. She was in this blasted settlement to make money, and the knock at the door meant more money. Stifling her impulse to tell them to come back next May, she answered the knock.

"G'day, luv." They loomed in the semidarkness with toothy smiles glowing in the light of her fireplace. She intensely disliked this form of address, but it was the common manner in Anakie.

"Mr. Sark. Mr. Riley. Good evening. What can I do for you?"

Mr. Sark stepped forward unbidden. "For starters, call us Pete and Rob. Mister's too formal." He held out a shirt. "The button you put on this came right off again; thought I'd bring it by."

She did not step back to invite them in any farther. She distrusted the tall, gangly Mr. Stark and trusted the robust, bumbling Mr. Riley even less. Besides, he stuttered. She glanced at the shirttail. "Mr. Sark, I did not launder this shirt. I always put my mark where the button band meets the hem." She stuffed it back in his hand. "I dislike ruse. Good night, and have a safe walk back the way you came."

Unmasking his lie didn't put him off at all. "Come, luv. Be hospitable. Invite us to tea, eh?"

As Mr. Riley stepped in beside him, the cold hand of fear gripped her heart, squeezing it. No time now to weigh the foolhardiness of choosing a place so far from other human ears and voices. She was alone. Her voice said, "I think not—good night," as her mind feverishly sifted options. She must reach the door somehow and run outside. She surely knew the path better than they did; it was nearly dark now and she was wearing a black dress. If she could just make it to the Kookaburra claim . . . three hundred yards down the draw in darkness . . . Charlie should be there—

"Ah, right here's the pot, Rob, and all hot and waiting. Told ye she's a good sort once she warms up a little." Sark strode over to the table on his stilt legs. He dumped her teacup out on the floor and poured himself a cup. He leered. "Lump of sugar, Sugar?"

She crossed her arms and tried to look relaxed. "You, Mr. Riley. Do you and he always go everywhere together? Do everything together?"

"M-m-m-mosta the time, yair."

"Hmph. I should think you'd do better on your own, a strapping, handsome man like you."

Sark looked instantly suspicious, but Riley absorbed it like a cotton towel. Bashfulness is unbecoming to a man that size. He shuffled, and in the shuffling moved aside more. She had nearly a clear shot at the door.

She looked right at Riley and pointed over his shoulder. "Sugar's up in that cupboard. Would you get some for your chum there?"

Sark started to say something, but like an oaf Riley turned his back on her and headed for the cupboard. This was insane. Even if she made it through the door, she could never outrun them—but it was her only chance! She bolted. Riley yelled. Sark bellowed at Riley. She heard her teacup smash. Her hand was on the latch. Riley grabbed at her shoulder, and she felt a few buttons pop on the back of her dress. She swung the door wide open . . .

. . . and cried out for joy.

"Marty!"

His arm was up, his knuckles poised to knock. Without missing a beat, he seized her arm and with a hefty yank dragged her around behind him into the cool darkness.

Jason was there, too; silent as a cat he flattened himself out against the wall beside the door. Cautiously, soundlessly, he unsnapped the holster at his side and drew out the pistol.

She was safe.

Sark started explaining in truculent tones how this was certainly none of some stranger's affair, and Riley added his protest, stuttering angrily.

"Is Enid safe?" Marty asked.

"Yes. Out of town."

With a nod he backed out of the doorway, keeping her behind him. He motioned but once, briefly, for the men to leave. Pearl cowered behind Marty's broad shoulders and was startled—yet reassured—by the radiating warmth.

She couldn't see well and didn't want to. She knew the two were coming out. Marty moved aside farther. Jason stood like a statue against the wall, unnoticed.

Sark was abreast them now, glowering, his narrowed eyes looking down at Marty because he was nearly a head shorter. A sudden movement from Sark caused Marty to explode into motion; Sark swore, groaned, and doubled over—all at once. As Sark went down, Jason yelled. Riley wheeled around to stare down the barrel of the cold steel pistol.

"Reconsider," Jason said, his voice edged with warning.

Marty kicked aside the big skinning knife by Sark's hand and picked it up. He wiggled it. "Thanks. I always wanted one."

Riley and Sark needed no play script to know the next move. Riley gave his partner a helping hand, but the gangling miner scuffed away, bent over in pain. They disappeared into the gathering darkness.

Jason looked at Marty and Marty looked at Jason and they wagged their heads. It was over. Pearl need fear no more. She must be a refined and sophisticated adult about this. After all, it's the way of the world, these things happen, and one must accept it and carry on. She never even got a chance to look at those dark, deepset eyes before she latched on to Marty, wrapping herself so tightly around him she couldn't breathe. No matter; she was sobbing too hard to breathe right anyway.

Marty finally reached up and released himself from her stranglehold. Taking her by the arm, he led her inside. Jason followed right behind, closed the door, locked it, and jammed the ladderback chair under the latch for good measure. Marty seated Pearl in the chair, and she tried to pull herself together again. For nearly four months she and Enid had advertised their business, had made themselves known in this dinky settlement. These two fellows had had a hundred days in which to hear of the Fowkes sisters and look them up. She finally composed herself sufficiently that she could speak without blathering.

At last she could look steadily into those melted-chocolate eyes as she asked, "What took you so long?"

CHAPTER NINE

GEMS OF ANAKIE

"A toast! To the gems of Anakie!" Jason flourished his teacup.

Marty raised his too. "To the gems of Anakie; both of whom sit before us."

Pearl giggled as the cups clinked. Why did she feel a tinge of naughtiness about a perfectly proper afternoon tea on the verandah of their little hut? The reference to toasts, no doubt. Enid blushed.

There was a strangeness about it all, too. Marty and Jason in their bush clothes, shirts open at the neck, and sleeves rolled to the elbows, sipping tea from china cups like city folk. Enid was still wearing her traveling dress, for less than an hour ago Pearl and the boys had greeted her as she stepped onto the Anakie railway platform.

Pearl ran the scene through her mind for the hundredth time, trying to read the memory of Enid's face as she alighted from the train. What were her little sister's real feelings? Weariness? Joy? Enid was absolutely delighted to see both boys. But did she favor one over the other? Not then, that Pearl could see. Nor did she now.

Enid met either boy squarely eye to eye. No coy glances, no shy averting of the eyes. She laughed with the same enjoyment at Jason's outrageous comedy and Marty's sly and gentle humor. She listened wide-eyed, obviously horrified, as they described the encounter with Sark and Riley. In short, she was purely Enid, and she put on no show for one colonial lad over the other. Either Marty's puppy love was unrequited or this could be an interesting triangle of affection.

Triangle—Enid, Jason, and Marty. Not a rectangle. Somehow, again Pearl was the odd one. She could feel it even now, in this loose camaraderie among friends drawn together in the common bond of having come from elsewhere. Plain—even mousy—Enid was once again the focus. *Why?*

Pearl listened to the conclusion of the Sark/Riley narrative. "Marty, how could you see him pull the knife? It was almost dark."

The boyish face grinned. "As I recall, the first time I spoke to you, I said something about having good night vision."

"You remember that? Six years ago!"

"Every detail, right down to Ross Sheldon accusing me of doing dastardly things to you." He chuckled. "I wasn't quite fourteen yet, and still dumb about life; know what I mean? I thought the dirtiest thing you could do to a girl was spit on her."

Enid shook her head. "The Lord's timing. I never cease to be amazed by the wonderful way He does things. Like bringing you two to the door at the moment Pearl needed you. We never had trouble of that sort before. We never even thought about it once we got settled."

"We explained to Pearl last night." Jason poured himself another cup of tea. "We just got back to Anakie late yesterday, and came by an hour after we heard about you."

"Where were you? I thought you were going to dig for gems here," Pearl said.

"The livestock business is so bad with this drought that half of Queensland is here digging. It's hard to find a decent place to look, and then you can't relax your guard against claim jumpers."

"We had no trouble finding this place. Someone just abandoned it." Pearl started another kettle for tea.

"Because it's a bad site. Too much overlying rock. The quartz seam surfaces a quarter mile away."

"Charlie's Kookaburra Mine is three hundred yards down the track."

Jason nodded. "And he's on the fringe. Whoever built this place didn't know where to look. Anyway, we decided to try our luck over at Quilpie. Opals there—at Opalton, too. We heard things were better here and came over to see for ourselves. Appears it's about the same all over. Anyhow, we're back. Ta daaaah!" He spread his hands and bowed.

"*Jase* is back," Marty corrected. "I think I'll go over to Opalton again. Try to get enough together to return to doing what I know best—cattle and sheep."

"With your father." Pearl sprinkled loose tea into the pot and tried to hide her disappointment. She didn't want him to leave.

"No. You can't believe how bad this drought is. Pop lost half his cattle to thirst and more'n half his sheep. The Torrens Creek boiling-down plant is the only place buying, with the tick quarantine and all. A lot of pastoralists are turning bottom up. Some big runs have gone under. Jase and I had some luck over at Opalton. If I can do as well these next couple years, I can put a hefty payment down on a nice place. In fact, we stopped to look at it on our way over from Opalton."

"Oh. So this is more definite than just dream-spinning." Pearl felt her conflicting emotions well up. She fought them back. Bitterness. Elation. The first four months, when the boys hadn't appeared, she had felt . . . well, irritated—at least partly. Now that they had come (admittedly, the moment they heard), she was no longer irritated. Instead, she had to contend with a whole different set of feelings. Feelings that she could not describe any better now than she could then. Life is so . . . so . . . so inexplicable.

Jason laughed. "Yeah, he's buying the L in 'Queensland.' I know, 'cause I saw the map."

"You don't buy it," Marty smiled. "You sign a lease on a run and pay the government a rental fee. All you actually buy is a couple square miles around the main station."

Enid didn't seem to mind his leaving. Her voice was as light as ever. "Can't you just buy it all outright? Eventually, I should think . . ."

"The government keeps title. If the population grows in

the district, they open your run to selection, and there's nothing you can do about it. But when these small farmers—the selectors—come in and settle on their parcels, they provide a new market for wool and meat. So it's not a hundred percent bad. And I don't think this run will be opened to selection for a good many years. It's a fine opportunity for me."

"And I suppose you have a name for it and everything. All ready to go." Pearl couldn't believe he'd give up digging if he made money at it.

"Pinjarra."

"The master of Pinjarra. A pastoral tenant of the crown." Jason slapped Marty's shoulder. "Ladies, you're looking at the newest member of the landed aristocracy here—the squattocracy. Gunner be a powerful man. Squatters throw a lot of political muscle around."

Enid smiled. "I can't picture you as a political bigwig, Marty. What is it you used to call such people? Silvertails?"

"Better'n having no power at all." He grinned, throwing Pearl's feelings into further confusion. This wasn't quite the Marty she remembered.

They were interrupted by someone shouting from down the track. Here came Charlie lumbering over at sort of a gallop. Charlie had to be in his sixties, but day after day he forced a twenty-year-old's amount of work out of his aging body. And day after day he promised everyone that his Kookaburra Mining Company would shortly produce the world's finest emerald. Or sapphire. Or whatever gemstone he had happened to see minute quantities of that week.

Charlie arrived at the verandah huffing and puffing, totally worn out. He plopped down and leaned against the roof support. After he got his breath somewhat, he blurted out in gasps, "Jenkins come running to my place—says there's a big problem down at the Dijirru claim. Tol' me to come up here an' pray Mizz Fowkes was back; some people are hurt—"

"Dijirru!" Pearl stared at Enid. Sark and Riley! "Did he say who?"

Charlie shook his head. "They went back to help dig. You two lads might go along; they're needing strong backs."

Marty and Jason were already off the verandah. They both had their horses loosed and were vaulting into the saddle before Pearl could gather her skirts and follow them. In unison the two boys kicked free of a stirrup and reached a hand out . . .

To Enid, of course.

She grabbed the closest—Jason's—stuffed her foot in his stirrup and swung up behind him, her dress all scrunched up.

Pearl gripped Marty's warm hand and pulled herself up behind, and they were off. They rode wildly, dangerously. Pearl wrapped her arms around Marty's waist tightly enough to pass for a mustard plaster. Even so, she kept getting jolted to one side or the other, and all the while she marveled at how firmly Marty stayed in the saddle. A few times during her girlhood she had conceded to riding a horse at a gentle walk. This was another universe of experience altogether.

Of necessity they ate Jason's dust the full mile and a half; Pearl knew in general where the Dijirru was, but Enid knew precisely. The well-used lane was covered with powdery dust a foot deep. Pearl pressed the side of her face against Marty's back and squeezed her eyes shut, choking on the dirt.

As they neared Dijirru, they heard cheering up ahead. Marty dragged his horse to a halt. Pearl raised her head to see Enid being helped from Jason's horse by half a dozen willing hands, and escorted into a dense cloud of orange dust on the shallow hillside. Pearl slid off Marty's horse by herself, aided only by the hand Marty offered her.

Unlike more elaborate workings, this dig was merely a crude, open gash extending two rods back into the hillside, reinforced here and there with posts. At the far end, though, either the posts had given way or they had not been placed in time. Here at the shallow entry end, the walls were crisp-edged and perhaps two feet high. At the far end, where half a dozen grimy miners toiled, the walls had probably been six feet high before they had collapsed into the dig.

Marty got there just ahead of Enid. Tall, gangly Pete Sark was not one of the victims. He stood in the ruins of his own dig and stared at Marty. Marty said simply, "I want to help."

Sark turned away and began digging again with his shovel. Marty took it as a tacit yes and began to dig the loose dirt beside him. Pearl wanted to help, too, but there were so many men already digging that she couldn't see any place for one more person.

Enid's frail back, surrounded by broad backs, bent over the very middle of the dust-ridden mess. Her voice came through strong and clear, though. "He's dead. There's still hope for the other. Leave this one and dig there!"

Pearl could see, just barely, the cavity in the loose dirt where Enid a moment before had been hunched.

Jason and Marty slaved in the middle of it. A coat of dark, ugly dust caked their perspiring faces. Flies and more flies—millions of flies—swarmed around the sweaty men. As confused and disorderly as the operation looked, there was a method to it. Six men became human posts. By sheer muscle power they held timbers and boards in place, keeping the passage open wide enough for the diggers.

"Get her down there!" Sark shouted. Pearl maneuvered in closer. He was talking about Enid, and they were forcing a way for Enid down into the bottom of their frantically dug hole. Had Enid been Queen Victoria these men would not—could not—have treated her more respectfully.

"He's still alive!" Enid crowed triumphantly. "Be careful with that timber; it's crushing against his chest." She disappeared into the mass of churning dust and scrambling miners.

Marty and Jason had plunged in, boots and all. Amid cries of jubilation and Enid's warnings to be careful, a score of filthy hands lifted the second victim out of the choking cloud. Riley.

Jason called out, "Don't stop yet, mates; let's dig the body out before this collapses for good." Three or four men joined him in the gruesome task. Pearl turned her back on the dusty pit. She did not care to see the soil-crusted death mask.

Enid was so dirty you could no longer determine the color of her dress. Blood and sweat streaked her face, and dirt cast into her eyes had brought tears. Yet her cheerful voice directed hands and kept men busy. They fetched some water from a jug, brought a towel, held this, supported that. Whatever she requested.

A disorganized cheer went up when Riley began coughing and sputtering. Then his stuttering voice babbled about death and God. And now he was sobbing—not the least bit manly.

Enid's voice dropped from a bark to a purr, and Pearl recognized the sound of it. Even as she washed his bloodied arm and wrapped it firmly in a towel, Enid was delivering the gospel to Riley just as she had explained it a score of times to Pearl—regardless of how much or how loudly Pearl had objected. Incredulous, and with some disdain, she heard her sister reiterate that same message: Jesus Christ is the only sure way to eternal life. Couldn't the girl think of *anything* else at a time like this? Apparently not. Next came Enid's assurance that God loved Riley so much He was waiting eagerly for Riley to confess that he was a sinner, to accept the fact that Jesus had paid for all that sin with His death, and to let Christ's Spirit enter him and give him a brand new heart.

To Pearl's amazement, Riley was agreeing. In stuttering explosions of speech he made his peace with God as Enid coached him on, prayer of repentance and all. And why not? She had just saved his life, probably more than once in the last fifteen minutes. She was selflessly ministering to him now, even though she knew all about him—and his visit to their hut. He owed her a great deal. The least he could do would be to say whatever she asked him to say. Pearl glanced over at Sark. Someone must have kicked gravel into Sark's eyes, because tears streamed down his dirty face as well.

While Enid was busy with Riley, some of the men brought out the deceased man from the deathtrap. The men removed their caps in respect. Then the men who held the loose dirt at bay with their boards and timbers backed out. With a massive column of dust that spread for yards around, those lethal walls caved in behind the men.

The dead man's mates wrapped him in a blanket and gently carried him away. Willing workers lifted the injured man onto a stretcher the men had devised, then helped Sark trundle him over to their shack nearby. With gratefulness, every man there either shook Enid's hand or kissed it.

By degrees the dust dissipated, and voices faded into the distance. Only the heat and the buzz of a million flies remained. The crisis was past, the emergency over.

Aside from her ruined dress and a small cut on her hand, Enid was none the worse for wear. With a flourish Marty whipped out his handkerchief. "I remember doing this once before." He glanced knowingly at Pearl and smiled as he wrapped it around the palm of Enid's left hand.

"Except that mine bled a lot more. All over my favorite dress." Pearl felt a tug of pleasure that he remembered those little details.

"I poked a nail through my palm just before we reached him." Enid was glowing. "Mr. Riley prayed the sinner's prayer! Did you hear him, Pearl?"

"Yes, I heard him."

Surely Enid didn't think all that confession and conversion was genuine. It was a product of the moment, an emotional and grisly moment. Still, it obviously meant a great deal to her.

Jason brought the horses down and without so much as a by-your-leave, Marty gripped Enid by the waist and hoisted her up into his saddle. He climbed up behind her. Fighting back a pang of jealousy, Pearl took the hand Jason offered her and pulled herself up behind him. Riding back to the laundry, the boys deposited the girls at the door and rode away.

A bath. Ah, a bath. Both girls instantly agreed they were too dirty to take turns washing in the same tubful as they usually did, so they filled two washtubs instead. My, such luxury. They soaked and splashed in the middle of the floor, their backs to each other, as the dust and the heat and the horror of the day fell away.

"I know we're washerwomen, Enid, but how will we ever

get your traveling dress clean?"

"Who cares? Mr. Riley's clean. That's all that's important."

"So you think Riley's a Christian. Enid, you didn't see his face that night, or hear the coarse suggestion in Sark's voice. You have elevated a sinner to saint status, believe me."

"God promised His word won't return void. Besides, it's all I have."

"What?" Pearl twisted in the tub to see Enid's face, but Enid's back was turned.

"I'm frightened, Pearl. What if all this that I learned from Papa isn't really true?"

"You mean the Gospel?"

"I guess, sort of. I get these horrid doubts. And they're coming oftener and oftener."

"No wonder, the way you claim the part-time preacher here doesn't know his theology."

"I suppose that doesn't help. I'm not being fed the way I was at home. But it's deeper than that. What if Saint Paul isn't exactly right and you have to do good deeds to get to Heaven?"

"Then you of all people should be standing at the front of the queue when those gates swing open."

"Not inside. I have these terrible thoughts about—well, they're terrible, anyway. I'm afraid they'll keep me out of heaven. So I set broken arms when I've no training to do it, and I carry more and more soup around, visiting."

"Terrible thoughts about what!"

"You wouldn't understand."

"Don't give me that spiritual insight business again."

"Not that. Something else. Men always look at you and drool, so to speak. I'm plain. But that doesn't mean I don't get thoughts about . . . That I don't dream about . . . Oh, forget it."

"What? You talking about men? Getting married and that?"

Suddenly the voice behind her brightened, lightened. "Depressing thoughts are a thing of the past. Let us enjoy this luxury!"

To complete the luxury, they didn't even share the same towel. After they had dried off, Enid washed her hair. Pearl considered doing so and decided it was too much effort. Instead she'd brush it thoroughly.

In the middle of brushing out the tangles in her hair, she heard a knock at the door. The boys must have cleaned up somewhere. Now, here they were back. In all the confusion, Pearl and Enid had forgotten to invite them to dinner. Thank goodness they had assumed the invitation, and rightly so. With a smile Pearl swung the door open.

The smile fell. "Mr. Sark!"

The gangling miner studied her a moment with the oddest mix of consternation and determination on his face. With a clunk he dropped to his knees on the verandah. He dragged his hat off his head and scrunched it in both hands. "Miss Fowkes, I most deeply and humbly apologize for last night. Riley and me, we very nearly violated one of God's own, and it woulda been to our eternal damnation. Riley and me, we agree that God sent them two larrikins to keep us from sin, and we're grateful to Him for that. Miss Fowkes, I'm so sorry, and I extend Riley's apologies as well."

Pearl was flabbergasted. What does one reply to a penitent miner?

Enid stepped beside her, her hair wrapped in a towel. "Mr. Sark, Mr. Riley is guaranteed eternal life. Are you?"

"Yes'm, but not before this afternoon." Mr. Sark lurched to his feet. "Pa drank, but my mum was a God-fearing woman. She raised me Christian, but I turned away from God till just today. And now"—he nodded courteously toward Pearl—"there's others I must make amends to. God wouldn't have it no other way."

"God bless you, Mr. Sark," and Enid sounded as if she meant it. She beamed like the sun itself.

"God bless *you*, mum." He nodded, he bowed, he did everything but tug his forelock. He backed down off the verandah and turned to leave, his hat still scrunched in his lanky paws.

Just then the boys came up the track. When they saw

Sark, Marty stiffened and Jason laid his hand on his holster.

"God bless you, lads," Mr. Sark bellowed. He paused beside Marty. "You don't still happen to have that knife, do you?"

"Threw it away in the bush. Didn't want you accidentally sticking it into someone who wasn't armed."

"Too right! I'm dangerous." And away he hurried down the track.

Marty and Jason gaped as they rode up and dismounted. Pearl tried to match the Sark of last night to the Sark of tonight, and the absurdity of it exploded out of her as laughter.

Enid laughed delightedly. She sobered. "There! You see the fruit of preaching in season and out of season? You never know where the word will fall. Isn't it beautiful?" And the gem of Anakie turned and went inside to commence dinner.

CHAPTER TEN

THE LOSS OF A GEM

Deep inside Pearl, life had somehow turned upside down. One moment everything was normal, more or less. Then the next, everything felt slightly atilt, like a sailboat in a stiff breeze, and she couldn't say when the change came. Nor could she describe the change. The feeling in her evaded any possible definition. Gloom? Not quite. Foreboding? Perhaps—but foreboding of what? She couldn't guess.

Perhaps it was simply the absurdity of watching Mr. Sark (a man of such recently dishonorable intentions) hustling down the hot, dusty track blessing every person he passed. That alone was enough to cause her to feel askew, all topsy-turvy.

This sense of instability wasn't helped a bit the evening following the accident at the mine, when Marty invited Enid out for a walk after supper. Pearl could tell that Jason was hurt too, though he tried to pretend he wasn't sulking as he helped her with the dishes. The next day Pearl returned from town to find Marty's horse hitched to the verandah post—and Marty and Enid engaging in rapt and earnest conversation inside.

By Thursday the workload was so heavy Pearl decided to give Mave Hurley one more chance and hired her as pick-up labor. Mave snickered off and on the whole day at some private little joke. At dusk Enid went out to hang the colored wash and Mave prepared to leave.

Pearl could contain herself no longer. "Mave, whatever have you been snickering about all day?"

Mave glanced out the door toward Enid and giggled again. "Eh, Mizz Fowkes. Down by the creek track, old Charlie caught that larrikin stealing a kiss from your sister. It's all over town. Hot romance."

Pearl felt her cheeks flush. "Yes, Marty has something of a crush on her. Puppy love."

"Marty. He's the brown-haired one, eh?" Mave shook her head. "Nah, this was the other one, the black-haired one, who stole the kiss." She wished Pearl a good night and waddled off down the track with her day's pay in hand, leaving Pearl fuming on the doorstep.

Frankly, it was time to move on to Brisbane. Well past time, in fact. They now had enough money in the bank to set themselves up attractively in the city. Besides, Marty was leaving here to earn the money to take up a new life as a political basher, of all things. Out in the middle of nowhere. Yes, indeed, it was time to go. They could sell off the tubs and equipment and be out and gone in two weeks.

Should she mention to Enid the word that had spread all over town? No. The less said the better. And what Enid or Jason volunteered, accidentally or on purpose, concerning that kiss might be instructive. She let it go.

All the same, it ate at her.

Saturday morning Enid woke up grouchy, something Enid had never done before. Pearl's world, already atilt, yawed crazily. By evening Enid complained of a ferocious headache—Enid, who *never* complained. She declined to eat because, she said, it was too hard to swallow.

Marty and Jason came by after dinner, but Enid excused herself and went to bed early. Pearl and the fellows sat on the verandah for a few minutes talking, but a dismal pall hung over them all and the lads left early, looking worried.

Pearl retired that night arguing with herself. Enid was as human as anyone and subject to ups and downs. If for once in her life she chose to act like a normal human being, let her have her whimsy. On the other hand, if she felt ill enough to complain about it, she must be sick indeed and perhaps she ought be put on the train to Barcaldine immediately.

Early next morning—very early—Mave Hurley knocked on the door.

Pearl herself was just barely out and Enid was still asleep. Her hair still tumbling around her shoulders, Pearl opened the door and scowled.

"G'day, mum!" Her eyes at half-mast, Mave looked more asleep than Pearl felt. "I know you're usually up and about early, and I was hoping to pick up a day's casual work. Need the money."

"We don't work on Sunday. Day of rest. You know that."

Undaunted, Mave waved at two bundles by her feet. "Here, mum; I brought along a couple batches I happened to gather on the way. Cyril and Mr. Mentges. Cyril will be by on Tuesday, he says. Mr. Mentges's I said I'd take to him."

"No. No laundry today. Enid doesn't feel well and I always rest on the Sabbath. Come back tomorrow."

From Enid's corner of the hut came a strangled sound Pearl had never heard before. Enid! She quickly lit a lamp so she could see her, and as she turned around, she heard Mave cry out. The girl's eyes popped open wide. She gasped God's name and crossed herself. It was a prayer, not a blasphemy. Charging into the house unbidden, Mave had hastened to the corner. Now staring down at Enid, she moaned "Oh, no!" more to herself than to Pearl.

"What is it? What do you see?" With Mave's back toward Pearl, she was unable to see the girl's face, and discern her expression. She could see Enid's though. Her sister's face and neck were tightly drawn, her body quivering.

Mave stood erect, her lips a firm, thin line, muttering to herself, "I'll run down to the boys' place. They have horses. One of them can go for the doctor in Emerald. He's a quack and a booze artist but he'll have morphine. The lad can be back by nightfall. And tomorrow we'll put her on the train to Barcaldine. Hospital there."

Pearl grabbed the woman's arm to keep her from leaving. "*What do you see?*"

"Lockjaw, mum. You ain't seen lockjaw?" The voice trembled. "My own lad died of it. Eleven years old he was. James. He was only eleven." She tore herself from Pearl's grasp and ran out the door.

Obviously it couldn't be that. The woman couldn't possibly know what she was talking about. At any rate, who would be foolish enough to accept the diagnosis of a broken-down old floozy? It certainly wasn't a fatal illness. Enid hadn't been sick a day in her life. Well, very few days. Even when typhoid moved through the area and she worked at the hospital, she remained healthy. And the ague? Everyone but Enid got it. No. The woman was obviously overreacting.

About a quarter century later, or perhaps only twenty minutes, Marty arrived literally in a cloud of dust. He had not taken time to slap a saddle on his horse; the barebacked animal was sweaty already and he was camped less than a mile away. Pearl watched him from the doorway, too numb to be gracious.

He dropped his horse's reins where it stopped and bounded up onto the verandah. "Jase is on his way to Emerald. Mave will be by later. Says she wants to cry awhile first so she won't be weepy around here."

"Marty, she's surely wrong. She's coarse-bred and—"

"May I see her?" He wasn't talking about Mave.

"Of course."

Marty slipped into the house and hurried over to the bed. Pearl was the stricken girl's sister, her only sister. And yet Marty didn't bother with a kind word or a hug. His only thought was Enid. It never occurred to him that Pearl might need comforting, too. Men!

The morning turned into a nightmare. Mave arrived with some sort of homemade remedy. Pearl didn't want her around, but what could she say? The remedy remedied nothing. Enid began to get waves of rigid spasms throughout her body. Mave bathed her with warm towels, trying to relax the muscles. By evening the spasms triggered convulsions every few minutes. Marty did not leave her bedside. That rich, low baritone talked to her about silly, aimless things that would have made her smile had all her facial muscles not been so tightly clenched.

Mave mentioned that opium sometimes relieves the spasms and convulsions by relaxing the muscles. Marty promised to return in an hour and hurried out into the evening light. He was back before dark with some mysterious coarse-grained stuff. Pearl didn't ask any questions about it. With towels and a pie tin of coals from the stove, Marty built a tent around Enid's head, the kind of steam tent one puts over an asthmatic child to help him breathe more easily. He sprinkled some water on the coals to make the steam, then dropped pinches of the remedy on the coals. "Inhale deeply," he told Enid, but Enid was having trouble breathing at all. For a short time it looked as if the powder would work, but after a few minutes of rest Enid convulsed worse than ever.

At dark Jason arrived, winded and on foot. The doctor wouldn't come this far, but he had sent morphine. Mave and the boys put their heads together and between them did a creditable job of administering the drug. Pearl stood by helplessly because she had no idea how to help.

She answered a loud knock on the door. It was Mr. Sark and Mr. Riley.

"We don't want to come in. Just want to sit on the verandah, case we can do something for Miss Enid."

"How did you know she was ill?" Pearl asked.

"Jason told us when his horse fell down dead of exhaustion right by the Dijirru."

More men came. The word had spread. Pearl hung some lanterns on the verandah posts when she realized most of Anakie was holding vigil there. She and Marty took turns resting and watching, but Pearl couldn't sleep. At five-thirty Monday morning, the morphine ran out. It was supposed to be a three-day supply.

Enid seemed neither better nor worse without morphine.

Some of the miners set up a fire in the dooryard and cooked a breakfast of bacon and eggs. Jason ate with them. But neither Marty nor Pearl was hungry. They sat on the floor leaning against the foot of Enid's bed as Mave ministered at the head of it.

Perhaps this was not the time or place, but Pearl could not stand it any longer. "Marty? What makes Enid so attractive?"

"I don't know." He sat silent a few minutes. "I think . . . I think it's because when she's talking to you, you know she's truly interested in you. There's no one more important in the world than you. She genuinely cares; it shows." He frowned. "Know what I mean?"

"I think so." Yes, Enid did care. It was no sham.

"There's a . . . an inner beauty to her," Marty continued. "A sweetness. Whatever she's doing she seems happy, including when she's talking to you. It feels really good when someone is so obviously happy to talk to you."

Pearl nodded. "Beautiful on the inside."

"Yair." He sighed. "Sad, isn't it? If someone who didn't know her came up to her now, they wouldn't be able to see her beauty. This lockjaw has her face and body so tensed up and twisted that the beauty's all driven down so deep inside you can't see it."

"But it's still there."

"Yair, 'cause it's a part of her. It makes her Enid."

Finally it was nearly time to put Enid on the train to Barcaldine. Scores of willing helpers offered to carry her to the railway depot. They moved her as tenderly as they could, bed and all, but even the slightest jostling caused horrible spasms. Enid's spine arched backward, rigid. Her delicate face froze into a hideous grimace. She turned blue because she could not breathe well.

The bright sunlight evidently bothered her. Someone said he had read about lockjaw in an old medical book and that anyone with lockjaw, or tetanus, as it was properly termed, should be in a darkened room. Darkened room? How could they do that at the railway station? Three miners had an idea and ripped the door off a locked, windowless baggage shed so that Enid could lie in partial darkness.

Pearl stood about shifting from foot to foot. Jason walked down the track toward Emerald. She had never seen him sit still for more than a minute or two, except when he was eating.

"Marty? How did you find that opium?" Pearl asked.

"A lot of pastoralists and miners hire aborigines for menial jobs. They pay them off in beef, grog, tobacco and opium; they say the blacks won't work if they don't get it. So I got a box of candy sticks from Mr. Gleason, took them out to the aboriginal camp beyond the creek and traded them for some opium. The blacks have a real soft spot for their children. I figured candy for the kids was about the only thing they'd trade for."

She studied the warm and sun-drenched face and considered the tone of his voice. "You sound as though you like blacks."

He shrugged. "Some of the rottenest people I ever met are black. And some of the truest and noblest."

The train was late. At two o'clock that afternoon, it still had not arrived. Men milled about restlessly, muttering angry threats against the president of the line. At two-thirty the threats grew darker and darker, so that by three they were discussing dismantling both engine and engineer when the train finally arrived. Seized with an idea, men took off in both directions along the railway, seeking a handcar. Unless the train arrived soon, they would put Enid on a handcar and pump her to Jericho or Emerald.

Pearl sat in the semidarkness beside Enid and watched hope fade along with the waning sun. Was Enid's mind lucid yet, or was it as warped and twisted as her body?

In any case, Pearl spoke more to herself than to Enid. "The train is usually late about half the time. It fails to make it at all at least once a month, so I don't know why I should be surprised by this. But you're God's servant. More than anyone in the whole world, you actually enjoy doing things for Him. So if God has any power at all, why does He permit the train to delay? You belong to Him! He should be taking care of you. Not this . . . not this way. This should never have happened to you in the first place. Me, maybe. I could understand that. But not you."

A taut, uncoordinated hand poked her. She gasped. The hand drew her close, motioning her to bend down to listen.

Pearl translated as from a foreign language the tortured hisses and moans from behind clenched teeth.

"God's will, Pearl. Always good. Best. When He gives good things, I thank Him. He gives me this, I thank Him because I know good things will come from it." Enid paused as a wrenching convulsion shook her. The spasms subsided. "I am His and He'll take care of me."

"He's not taking care of you! He's torturing you!" Pearl exploded.

Marty was standing in the doorway. He moved in closer.

"He promised me heaven. He won't break His promise. I will be so alive, Pearl!" The twitching hand touched Pearl's. "Pearl. Good things will come of this. Look for them. Write them down so you don't forget them. And please . . . please come to Jesus."

Outside, the miners stood about in silence or in hushed conversation. Another seizure racked her, a long one this time. Every muscle contracted so tightly that for a minute at a time she could not breathe. She said something else and Pearl and Marty both bowed low to hear. Seizure halted the speech. Pearl straightened a bit to catch Marty's eye. He frowned and shook his head. He couldn't translate either.

Something good of this? Something *good*!

Pearl propped her elbows on her knees and covered her face with her hands. She was so bitterly weary. She listened to the labored gasps and the frightful silences when Enid could draw no breath at all. As tired as Pearl was, Enid was far more exhausted, for the constant spasms and convulsions prevented her from resting even a moment.

Quiet people moved in and out of the dark, stuffy shed. One of them was Jason; Pearl heard him speaking to Marty, but she didn't listen or care about what was said. She wanted the train to come. She wanted the nightmare to end. She wished someone else could somehow take over her hideous burden of waiting, powerless to help.

By measured degrees Pearl became aware of the silence. Ominous, mocking silence. Silence outside and in. She forced herself to raise her head enough to turn and look.

At first she thought the disease had lifted. The cruel arch of Enid's back had relaxed into a casual line of repose. That grotesque grimace had softened to a smile. No longer forced down into the depths of her mind and heart by the wracking illness, her inner beauty rose again to the surface, free at last. Enid's body looked like Enid again. God had reclaimed His gem.

With billows of smoke and a deafening roar, the train arrived.

CHAPTER ELEVEN

THE BIRTH OF DREAMS

Pinjarra and the Commonwealth of Australia were born within hours of each other. On a summer Tuesday in Sydney's Centennial Park, the Earl of Hopetown proclaimed the colonies to be federated states. In the ensuing celebration, the brand-new nation temporarily forgot everything else—even the tumultuous news that Clean Sweep had won the Melbourne Cup two short months before.

On that same hot dry Tuesday in Longreach, Martin Frobel Junior assumed the lease, at five shillings per square mile, on the pastoral run that simultaneously made his dream a reality and made him the best catch of all the bachelors on the Barcoo. During the celebration of this event, his cousin lost his head, momentarily forgetting that one doesn't approach the town bully's girlfriend—no matter who his cousin is. That small error in judgement netted Jason a black eye.

Marty did not neglect to dress for the momentous occasion. As dignitaries in Sydney sported the height of fashion, Marty wore the stiff-collared shirt he detested and the tie his mum had made with "Pinjarra" delicately embroidered in its silk. Gimpy Jack, lover of color, gave him a top hat and a vest of bright blue satin. The man beamed, immensely proud of the gift. Marty wore the vest—his coat mostly covered it—but he insisted Gimpy Jack must also dress appropriately for the occasion and gave him back the hat. The flashy attire with the rigid collar would have been a lot more tolerable had

Marty not forgotten his change of bush clothes in the hotel room.

Just as well that he stayed looking flash, for Pop had rented the funeral director's great open brougham coach with its matching black six-up. Sheer elegance. Mum and Pop, Marty and Jason and Gimpy Jack rode home together to Pinjarra—the whole hundred plus miles—in grand style. And Gimpy Jack wore his new top hat all the way.

Home. His home. When they arrived in the dooryard, Marty assisted his mum to alight from the brougham. Pastoral tenant of the Crown, master of Pinjarra—not a bad thing a few weeks short of being twenty-four. He offered the driver dinner, but he declined graciously, saying he could make it into Muttaburra not much past nightfall if he got on the track right away.

Marty watched the brougham roll out onto the southbound track. "You know, Pop, we really did look pretty elegant in that thing."

Jason spread his hands. "So true, folks, but the master of Pinjarra won't let elegance go to his head. No need to embarrass him by kissing his boots—a simple genuflection will suffice."

Marty snorted. "I can tell right now I'm gunner have trouble with you. When you going back to your dirt and jewels?"

"Don't rush me. Tomorrow I return to Opalton and make my fortune. Today I make merry. What's for dinner?"

"Whatever Rosella killed, I suppose." Marty started in the door, then stopped and turned. "Pop? You look upset."

"Not with you. Something else. When I give a simple order, I expect it to be followed. What's in your front paddock?"

"Take the roan with the blaze face. He needs exercise anyway."

Pop was halfway across the dooryard when Mum called, "Martin? I see dust to the north. I think they're coming."

It didn't take a soaring intellect to figure out that Pop's surprise present had been slow to arrive. Arrive it did—in a parade to match any pageant Sydney could produce. A couple of Pop's station blacks orchestrated the extravaganza, with

Mungkala driving the dray and Goonur bringing up the rear. Marty could see in the half dozen yearling seed bulls the broad chest of Pop's prize-winning stud bull, Goodtime Jack. The horse dray and four of Pop's best bred horses brought Mum's old oak table and chairs.

"Hot ding!" cried Jason. "Now we don't have to eat on the floor anymore!"

"Pop, this really isn't necessary; you don't have to count me as charity."

"You know what I taught you all your life: Never ask for a handout if you're not willing to work for it. This is not charity. You didn't ask for it, but I can see you have your work cut out for you."

And the gray mare. Silently Goonur slid out of the saddle and handed the reins to Marty. She looked unusually sober, even sad. She knew a good horse, and she was sorry to give up this mare.

Marty turned to Pop. "You sure you want to give me this?"

"Remember that colt I sold for three hundred pounds a couple years ago? By Heartbreaker out of this mare right here. Well, she's in a family way again, by Heartbreaker. She should throw you a dandy."

Marty wanted more than anything else to hug Pop, but the man had never been that affectionate with his son and never would; it wasn't his way. Instead, Marty swung aboard the mare without touching the stirrups and rode out of the dooryard, up the rise, across the north paddock.

How do you measure happiness? If you add happiness to happiness, is the sum greater than its parts? Marty pondered the mathematics of joy, but not for long. He let the magic of the mare's fluid motion set him afloat in glorious non-thought. A squatter's life is difficult at best, an impossible burden at worst. Pinjarra had once been another man's dream, a man who had built the house and barn, fences and sheds, and then had had to walk away. Marty could well go under as that man had. He faced long, hard work in his immediate future, and probably a few tears—inside if not outside. But today there would be no tears or hard work. Today was unbridled joy.

The sun chided him as he rode into the barnyard; low in the sky, it told him he'd been out over two hours. For shame, leaving his guests like that! They must all be in the house; he saw no one outside. He slid off the mare and led her into the barn.

He froze.

A shadow . . . that's all—a dark and ominous movement beyond the box stalls. The back of Marty's neck prickled. The shadow said "hostile black," but there weren't any hostile blacks within a thousand miles—not anymore. As his head fumed "ridiculous!" his senses warned "beware!"

Silently he moved to the wall. He lifted a hayfork off its pegs. Keeping the gray mare between him and the box stalls, he stalked forward . . . pausing . . . listening. He kept an eye out behind, to the side. This was silly; he was going to look so foolish when he learned it was a dark coat on a hook or something.

Suddenly, a woman screamed, a man yelled, and Marty yelped in terror. Marty was facing a hostile black, all right, a slim young man wearing absolutely nothing. The blackfeller's spear was poised by his ear, ready to plunge forward into Marty's heart. And Marty's hayfork was poised at belt level, ready to plunge forward into the fellow's belly. Goonur cried out again and came running from the doorway. Fearlessly she lunged between them and grabbed the black's spear.

"Indirri! What the blazes . . . !" Marty didn't lower the fork, though; he had no idea what imaginings drove this half-wild man.

Indirri surrendered to the girl simply by letting go of the spear. He jabbered to her.

Goonur turned to Marty. "He is very sorry. He didn't see you good; he saw you just a little bit, from far, and he thought you were someone else." She looked near tears. "He is very sorry."

"He speaks English. I want to hear it from him."

"Much sorry. Much, much sorry. Him look maybe enemy; I see him wrong. Much sorry." He bore no scars, no cicatrices, wore no paint. Usually young males off on walkabout came back with fresh scars.

Marty looked from face to face and lowered the fork. He knew aborigines are very good at reading emotion in others and at masking their own feelings. Intense emotions boiled here, and he couldn't begin to tell what they were. "You work for Pop. Does he know what's going on here?"

Goonur licked her lips. "We work here now. Your Pop said, 'Marty needs good workers. You take these stuff to him, bull calves, gray mare, that stuff, and you work for him awhile.' Mungkala and me, we came. Indirri went bush and he didn't hear we changed. Now he's back. He can work here . . ." Her voice faltered. "If you let him. Eh?"

"Enemy. Whitefeller enemy?" Marty watched Indirri's face.

He nodded. "Much old, much wets. Old enemy. Whitefeller, yair."

"You almost killed just now, or got killed. Are you going to make another mistake like this one and kill an innocent whitefeller while you're working for me?"

"Mistake. Inns—?" He looked at Goonur and got a translation. He shook his head. "Mistake, no. Never again mistake. Next time, see good first."

Marty nodded. "Then you're on. Goonur, find out what's happening. If you people are working here, I want to know." He left the mare for her to put up and walked to the house. Indirri's error plagued Marty. A whitefeller enemy—by inference—a whitefeller who looked much like Marty. That meant, probably, about the same size and coloring, similar age. Possibly on a gray horse. But there weren't any other horses in the district like that mare. It was important to get to the bottom of this, though. Personnel problems might well become stickier wickets than drought and cattle ticks.

Indirri sat cross-legged before his little fire and fed more sticks into it. He smarted. His very soul smarted from embarrassment. What a horrible mistake to make! He was in the bush, more than a mile away from young Marty and five miles from Pinjarra, when he saw that bright blue breast cover. He should not have gone directly to the barn to lie in wait. He should have moved in first for a closer identification. Besides, he should have known that more than one whitefeller might wear a vivid breast cover.

But there was the thrill, too. He thought about how his whole body sang when he saw that brilliant breast cover in the distance. The rage and hatred he had thought were dead had sprung to life instantly. They weren't dead at all—just sleeping—and now they ate at his soul just as persistently as if the massacre had happened yesterday.

Across from him sat Mungkala with his leg stuck out in that special way of his. The man looked as glum as Indirri felt.

Goonur sat beside Indirri, morose and silent. She already knew about his clan and the raid, but he had never mentioned that bright breast cover to her. Should he now? Young Marty knew every whitefeller in the district, and he was a powerful man. He might be able to help Indirri find his enemy. But he might also warn the enemy about Indirri, or—worse—prevent Indirri from ever finding him. No. He must not mention the breast cover.

Goonur poked at the fire with a stick. "Before you went, I wanted to tell you, but I didn't. Maybe I should have. I wanted to tell you I didn't want you to go. Now you went and you came back. So I'm telling you I'm glad you're back. I missed you."

Indirri paused even his breathing a moment. Was it possible? She had special feelings for him? He admired her in many ways, but . . . No, it could never be.

Goonur asked idly, "Where did you go on walkabout? Places I know?"

"North. West. Mostly north."

"What did you find?"

"Nothing. A few clans. Station blacks. No wise old men who will initiate me and bring me into my dreaming."

"It's a whitefeller world now."

"Everything is gone." In the old days Indirri would never reveal his thoughts to a lubra. These were the new days, the bleak days, and it didn't matter anymore. "I feel like just lying down and going to sleep. My life is useless."

"Listen to you talk!" Mungkala spat on the ground, a distinctly whitefeller gesture of contempt. "I talk like that, you say 'nonsense!' I suppose when you talk like that it's wisdom? I do all the things nobody wants to do. Woman stuff. Little stuff. Sit-in-a-lump-all-day stuff. And you moan about your life."

Goonur rubbed against Indirri. "You're young and healthy. Mungkala might say that. Not you."

"Young and healthy and forever a child. No marriage, no power."

Goonur's blue eyes picked up points of orange light from the fire. Lovely eyes. "Young Marty, he's your age. His mum keeps saying, 'Marty will marry one of these days.' That tells me he's able, even though whitefellers don't carry scars. Find out how they become men. Maybe you can do it that way."

What a stupid idea, the sort of thing you'd expect of a lubra.

The next morning Indirri was sitting on the verandah step when young Marty came out of the big house. He smiled, "G'day."

"G'day." Young Marty started to step off the verandah, then stopped. He studied Indirri. "Need something? Look, no worries about yesterday. It's all right. Goonur explained about your clan and the massacre, and Mungkala being crippled."

"Need something, yair. Need talk-to."

Marty stood a moment thinking. He flopped down on the verandah and leaned back against the porch post. "All right. About what?"

"Blackfeller go from lad to man, uh . . . old men do things, say things; blackfeller do things, say things. Pain. Scars." He raised a hand. "Then man. How whitefeller is man?"

"Well, you learn to read and write, and . . . No. Wait. I see what you mean. An initiation." The man's face softened. "I see. Is that where you were, on walkabout? Trying to get initiated?"

"No old men, no old ways."

The deep-set brown eyes studied Indirri and looked at his shirt where scars would be, if he had any. Young Marty understood. He saw. And just the fact that this whitefeller knew and understood made Indirri's burden a bit lighter—a most curious feeling.

"That Goonur, she's a beautiful girl. Good with horses. Smart. Ever think about marrying her?"

"Man marry. Lad don't marry."

A broad smile spread across Marty's face. "Whitefellers, they say if a lad marries, fathers children, and takes good care of them, that's one of the things that make him a man. A lad can't do all that and do it right. If he can do it, he proves he's a man."

Indirri pointed to Marty. "Him man. No marry, him man."

"When I find a girl, I'll get married. And I'll take good care of her. Her and the little ones."

Indirri took a deep breath and risked everything. "Marry Goonur."

"Whitefellers like best to marry a woman they love. I don't love Goonur. Nice girl, but I don't love her."

Did young Marty hear Indirri's heart beating? Almost certainly. "How whitefellers marry?"

"Couple ways. Best way is go to a church, ask the priest or minister to perform a marriage service. Say things, do things. No pain. No scars." Marty had a relaxed, pleasant look on his face, but Indirri could hear no mocking tone.

Like sunshine after a thunderstorm, hope burst bright upon Indirri's soul. He had but to follow whitefeller ways. Lack of manhood was not a bar to marrying Goonur—Goonur was the key to manhood!

Young Marty grinned effusively as he stood up. "You go talk to Goonur. If you two decide to get married, I'll tell you about another whitefeller custom. It's called a honeymoon."

Indirri stood up, too. A sudden thought struck him. Here he was on the brink of great happiness and Mungkala was still so hopelessly sad, so empty. Indirri fell in beside Marty; they strode toward the barn. "Mungkala feel bad. No man job.

Just lubra job. Any man job him do?"

"Yair. Clear out some of the dingoes and roos from the east paddock. It's getting overrun."

Indirri frowned. Surely Marty knew this: "Him need gun. Horse."

"Then we'll put him on a horse."

One of the attributes of manhood is to lead and make decisions. Indirri saw without doubt that, married or not, young Marty was a man; he fired orders all around, orders meant to be followed. He sent for Mungkala to come from the kitchen. He told Goonur to bring in the gaudy little skewbald gelding. He dusted off the small stockman's saddle, the one with the deep seat. To the one stirrup he attached another by half an arm's length of strap.

Indirri understood young Marty's intent, but there was not a chance in sky or earth that it could happen. Mungkala on a horse? Never! And when Mungkala learned why he had been summoned, every fiber of his being told Indirri that he agreed. Mungkala turned white with fear. He stood propped on his stick, shaking.

"Oh, yair. The stick." From the tack room Marty carried out a scabbard, the leather pouch in which whitefellers carry rifle weapons. He clipped it onto the saddle.

The elder Marty was here now, and his wife. Jason came wandering out and stood nearby watching. In a flaming red shirt Gimpy Jack appeared from beyond the barn. The whole world was about to see Mungkala be shamed. This was Indirri's fault. He ought never have mentioned it.

Goonur bridled the little gelding and slipped the loop of rein over its neck as young Marty saddled it. Marty waved a finger at Mungkala. "Up you go."

Wild-eyed, Mungkala stood there, immobile. Jason seized his arm and hauled him bodily to the horse. He yanked the stick out from under him and stuffed it into the scabbard.

Marty slapped Mungkala's bad leg. "That one goes in the lower stirrup. Like that. Right. Now use your good arm to haul yourself up until you can get your left foot in the upper stirrup. Your other left. That's it."

It took Mungkala three tries. Once he settled in the saddle, Marty and Goonur adjusted his stirrups.

Marty stepped back. "Goonur, walk along beside him and teach him how to ride. After lunch Jase'll give him shooting lessons."

Goonur talked the whole time as they moved out across the dooryard. Indirri could hear her even though he could no longer distinguish her words. The horse stopped and Goonur stepped aside. The horse turned. Mungkala urged it forward and stopped it. He turned it around. He backed it up. Goonur nodded and they continued on their way down the south track.

Indirri hurried into the barn and left by the back. He didn't want anyone to see the tears in his eyes.

The next morning Mungkala rode out into the east paddock to clear it of roos and dingoes.

CHAPTER TWELVE

ROGUE OF THE RED RIVER

With a nasal drone, two flies circled Marty's inkpot. One moment they were in full flight and the next moment they were perched motionless on the lip of the pot. How do flies manage to do that—to switch from go to stop to go so instantly? Two more flies joined them. And another.

Marty closed his books. When watching flies was more fun than balancing accounts, he'd better do something else awhile.

Rosella appeared in the doorway. In fact, she filled the doorway and then some. Like Goonur, she had half of one race and half another in her. Unlike Goonur, who blended the races into a striking beauty, Rosella lined them up side by side; she had to be as wide as she was high. And every inch brimmed with regal composure. Queen Victoria herself could have taken dignity lessons from this lady.

Rosella smiled. "Your lunch is in five minutes, Mr. Marty."

"Thank you. I'll go tell Jack, see how he's coming." He walked out the back door into the brilliant heat, past the summer kitchen and carriage shed, to the hole in the ground. It was close to six feet deep now; Gimpy Jack's head bobbed well below ground level. Marty was somewhat surprised to see the bright yellow shirt and top hat hanging on a nearby fence post. On second thought, he wasn't all that surprised.

Jack stood erect and grinned, bathed in sweat. " 'Bout there, eh?"

"Lunchtime." Marty reached down and gripped the hot,

slippery hand. With a grunt and a lunge Jack was back on the surface. Marty waited while the wiry black washed up by the back door.

Jack poured from the ewer to the basin. "Some stations, they have toilets indoors, like in the cities. Wouldn't have to dig 'em out back if we had it inside." He dived in, splashing.

"You know how those things work?"

"Naw."

"Gotta put a tank on the roof to get some water pressure. Then you pump till you're blue in the face to get the water up there. Then you install this water closet next to the ceiling with a chain. Build a whole new room for it all. And you should see the size of the holes you dig for the septic tanks, not to mention ditches for all the pipes. By the time you do all that work, you could've dug a dozen dunnies. Besides, if we got civilized out here, it would take away all the country charm."

Jack stood erect, grinning. "Not how your mum says. She's gunner civilize us all. For months up at 'Lizbeth Downs, she been telling your pop how the place needs a full-time preacher. She says the squatters can support him and put him on a circuit from station to station."

"So that's what she was talking about at the wedding yesterday."

"Your pop's spread the word among the squatters." Jack reached for his shirt. " 'Course, don' know what we need a preacher for. They hold church down at Winton and on down to Longreach. And once a month at Muttaburra. But you know when your mum gets an idea like that, your pop don't say no for long."

"Too right. The fellow's probably on his way right now."

The dark face softened. "Might not be bad if the preacher had religion like that Mizz Enid did. She was real Jesus."

"To the very end."

So Jack thought about her, too. So did Marty, frequently. Thought about Pearl, too. Marty remembered clearly Enid's last words, that final stricken message for Pearl. Enid was so convinced that God was taking care of her that she didn't mind dying in such an awful way. She trusted God.

Trust. The kind of trust a child has in his father, even as the father is spanking him. And love. The kind of love that makes a child want to obey his father all the more once the spanking is over. But what did Enid do to deserve spanking? Did it matter? To Enid, who lived her life every day in an effort to please God, certainly. It didn't matter to Marty, because he didn't have that kind of complete trust in God. Nor did he have Enid's kind of love for Him. The lesson was lost on him.

Sometimes he wished he could trust God like that. It would make life so much simpler. It was certainly what Enid would have wanted. Even though she had been gone for years, Marty felt a strong desire to do what would have pleased her. Enid. God. Jesus Christ. The three churned about in his thoughts almost as if they were one and the same.

Jack perched his top hat on his head. Suddenly he paused, listening. "Company for lunch, sounds like."

Marty heard nothing. Wait . . . now he did. "Tell Rosella." He walked around to the front.

Ross Sheldon on a big bay Waler entered the dooryard. He rode in shirt sleeves, his coat over his pommel. It afforded Marty the unparalleled opportunity to find out if his vests were brocade in the front only, or front and back. Sheldon swung down off his horse. Front and back both. No scrimping on cost or quality here.

Marty extended his hand. "Welcome to Pinjarra. You just made it in time for lunch."

"Thank you. I was in Muttaburra anyway, so I thought I'd come out and say hello to the new squatter. I heard your father's down here and I was hoping to say hello to him, too."

"Sorry. Mum and Pop left yesterday after the wedding. Two of our blacks married. Now Goonur and Indirri are off in the bush on their honeymoon. Come on in."

Gimpy Jack appeared, resplendent in yellow, and followed them inside. Out of hospitality Marty offered Sheldon a drink. He declined. He hung his own hat on the peg beside the top hat and sat down at Mum's oak table.

Sheldon watched with undisguised distaste as Gimpy Jack took his place. The visitor's attitude rankled Marty.

Marty sat back as Rosella served the soup. "Jack's my station manager. Pop sort of loaned him to me until I hire one. Wish I could keep him, but Pop said forget that. Jack's the best."

"Anyone in mind for the job?"

"Not yet." Marty smiled. Rosella made the world's best soup. "Being the son of a pastoralist gives me an advantage, though. I know nearly all the managers and bosses in the district. Who drinks, who makes smart decisions, who works, who doesn't. Who I can trust."

"I'll keep an eye out. Maybe I'll hear of someone good."

"Appreciate it." Now what should Marty say? Why was this man here, anyway?

Rosella served the bread and cold sliced meat with a sort of disdain Marty had not seen in her before. She didn't seem to like Sheldon much either. Probably his bigotry against blacks was rubbing her. Blackfellers are sensitive to that.

Sheldon dabbed at his mouth with his napkin and started building a sandwich. "One of the reasons I came by was to assure you and your father that I bear no hard feelings, politically speaking. Difference of opinion is what makes horse races, and politics is no exception. Our differences are limited to the political arena; in business and social matters, I trust we're still friends." Marty held him eye to eye, more to confirm the man's honesty than to be polite. "Thank you. The mailbag comes through tomorrow and I'll be sending a letter up to Pop. I'll make sure he knows of your visit here today."

"Good-oh. Next best thing to speaking with him face to face." Sheldon ate in silence a few minutes. He drained his water glass and Rosella refilled it. "Tell me. Whatever possessed you to sink your money into this run? Drought, ticks. It's the worst of times to get into the business."

Marty assembled a second sandwich. Working on the books all morning makes one hungry. "I've been thinking it's the best of times for someone like me to deal into the game. Pinjarra is a fine run, one of the nicest in the district. I was able to make a good deal with the former squatter."

"Who went under."

"Since I'm just getting started, my lease fees are only a third what his were, or what yours and Pop's are, for that matter. I have seven years of low rental to help me get going."

"What stock do you plan to run?"

"Pop gave me some fine yearling seed bulls out of his Goodtime Jack line. The bull is half the mob. And you know cattle are cheap now, especially above the tick line here. I can buy more and better stock today than if prices were what they were yesterday."

Sheldon wagged his head. "Drought's no time to build a mob."

"Drought won't last forever. When the rains come, I'll be set and ready. And I'll have better shipping facilities than you and Pop had in the past. The railway's right in Longreach, and Winton's had its own line for a couple years now, down from Hughenden. It's a coming district."

"You'll learn, lad, that the real source of power in the outback, political and otherwise, is water. Trains need water to operate. Barcaldine's artesian bores make it an important railhead. You can spit in a barrel and have as much water as Winton. Put your money where the power is."

Marty grinned. "What money?"

"Indeed. We all can ask the same."

Mr. Sheldon sat on the verandah for tea afterward, just long enough to be polite, and rode off south again.

Gimpy Jack watched the rider get smaller and smaller. "What's this politics, that he rides clear up here?"

"He'd be the Member from Barcoo in the new federal government right now if it weren't for Pop and me. We favored Ian McHenry, and worked to get him elected over Sheldon. I'd guess Sheldon's mending bridges just in case he decides to stand for office again."

Jack wagged his top-hatted head. "Always gunner be a mystery to me, your whitefeller politics. Sheldon's a squatter.

Thought you squatters all stuck together."

"Oh, he's ruthless about defending squatters' interests, all right. But Ian sees the full picture better—everybody working together for the best interests of the whole area. That and a couple other things about Sheldon are what put us behind Ian."

"Mmm." Jack unbuttoned his shirt. "Back to the hole. When you gunner hire lots of blacks for me to boss around so I don't have to dig?"

Marty grinned. "On my way." But by the time he got the books caught up and put a new damper in the flue of Rosella's cookstove and made out the supply list, it was dark.

Next morning he rode down to Muttaburra to look around, possibly to hire. Nothing. He continued south and spent three days in Longreach. Casual labor was available and to spare, but men of responsibility and integrity—that was another matter. The difficulties of being a pastoral tenant of the Crown were beginning to weigh heavily. He wasn't doing anything here. Time to go home empty-handed. He saddled up very early in the morning and headed north.

The sun said ten-thirty, but his belly was screaming "noon." He should have brought more lunch fixings. The road wound along a shallow ridge here. To either side, a scattering of scraggly trees opened out into sparse, dry paddocks. The track coasted downhill the next couple miles. Good. He might urge a little more speed from his horse, put distance behind him a little faster that way. Marty topped the ridge and leaned forward in the saddle.

His gelding shook its head and shifted into a smooth, casual jog. Marty gave it a gentle kick and it broke into its rocking-horse canter. This old bay wasn't much to look at as horses go, ewe-necked and too long in the loins, but it surely covered ground nicely.

Marty vaguely heard voices ahead even before he came around the big dogleg at the base of the ridge. Not a hundred yards ahead, there were two men on horseback in the middle of the track, arguing earnestly with a young man on foot. Both horsemen wheeled their mounts toward Marty. One of them raised his hand and pointed at Marty's bay gelding. The hand had a pistol in it.

The man on the ground literally leaped in the air. He grabbed both gun and hand, and with a mighty yank and twist pulled the fellow off his horse. Two to one? Not good odds. Marty whacked his reins down across the gelding's shoulder. The horse bolted forward.

The second rider carried a satchel in his free hand. He tried to draw his horse off the track, but Marty's gelding was too quick. Marty rode nearly abreast, then reined the old bay aside, bowling full tilt into the fellow's frightened horse. The horse squealed and staggered as its rider swung that satchel. The bag slammed Marty's arm and nearly knocked him off his horse.

Behind him, the gun fired. Every nerve in him leaped and shrieked. The bay didn't like guns much better than Marty did. It jumped and shied. By the time Marty had both the horse and himself under control and had wheeled his horse to face the fray, those two riders were turning tail. The young man knelt hands-and-knees on the ground, his head drooped low, as that other rider vaulted back into the saddle.

Both horsemen took off down through the trees, one with his gun in hand again and the other with the satchel. Should Marty chase them? Good heavens, what would be the point? He kept his dancing bay in place beside the luckless traveler.

The young man twisted around and sat down in the bull-dust, so Marty stayed astride. He could keep an eye on those two longer from up here, watching them and their dust cloud travel southeast through the scattered trees.

The traveler, a stranger probably no older than Marty, must have spent most of his last few years, at least, indoors. His skin was white like the legs of a man who wore nothing but long pants. He looked as gangly as Gimpy Jack, but he had to be taller than Marty—six feet at least. His bush of white-blond hair suggested that maybe his skin never would tan.

He looked a little dazed. "A gun! That jackanapes actually pulled a gun!" He looked up at Marty. "Does this sort of thing go on around here all the time?"

"Not all the time. Even they have to sleep sometime." Marty watched the two riders disappear into the trees. "You all right?"

"Bruised pride, lost valise. Physically, quite fine, thank you." He lurched to his feet and ineffectually slapped at himself. The dust rose in little puffs from his inexpensive wool serge suit.

"Lost valise. That was your bag they stole?"

The young man nodded and dabbed at his bloody nose.

"What do you keep in it? Bricks?"

The fellow grinned, and with the grin looked five years younger. "Books. Bible, reference books. A change of clothes. Not worth going clear back to town just to file a complaint. Obviously nothing those ruffians will be interested in. In fact, it might do them some good. No real damage done."

"How much money'd they get?"

"I have no money for them to steal. It seems they wanted to discourage me from continuing north. Threatened, cajoled, insisted I should go back."

"Back to Longreach?"

"Back to Canada."

"Canada. That explains the accent." Marty kicked free of a stirrup and extended a hand. "This road goes through Muttaburra to Hughenden. I guess you're headed for Muttaburra, since there's nothing in Hughenden worth walking a hundred and fifty miles for."

The young man stuffed his foot in Marty's stirrup, grabbed the proffered hand and hauled himself aboard. He knew his way around horses. He settled in behind Marty's saddle. "Hughenden's that bad, huh?"

"Worse." Marty twisted in the saddle and held his hand around almost behind him. "Marty Frobel."

"Really! I thought you'd be much older." The young man shook with a warm, firm grip.

"One of us is. I'm Martin Junior."

"Ah! Then your mother is Grace. I'm Lucas Vinson."

The name meant nothing, nor did the fact the man was

from Canada. But the mention of the Bible suddenly registered in Marty's head. "You a religion student?"

"Just completed seminary. Your mother and father wanted a seminary-trained man, the letter said."

Mum's circuit rider had arrived. Marty kept the nervous bay at a walk. "You fight pretty well for a seminary student. You get bailed up; you don't just stand around and accept it. Preachers as a rule have this reputation for being meek and ready to inherit the earth."

The fellow roared with laughter. "You're talking to the Rogue of the Red River. I raised quite a bit of Old Nick when I was young. Out of practice, though. That cretin shouldn't have been able to best me."

"On behalf of the district I apologize for the cretin. We haven't had any troubles like that for years. Sorry it happened to you." Just then it hit him—there was something amiss here. "You said they wanted you to turn around and go home. Like they knew who you were?"

"Yes. In fact, I thought when they first pulled up beside me that they were a welcoming committee of some sort, perhaps to give me a ride up to Elizabeth Downs. They soon proved otherwise, of course. Ruffians."

"Yair. Well, welcome anyhow."

Who knew this man was coming? Every squatter in the whole district if Pop had put the word out as Gimpy Jack had predicted. Who would resist his coming? No one. No squatter would send out bushrangers to waylay a visiting preacher. Marty bought the Rogue of the Red River dinner in Muttaburra and took him home to Pinjarra.

Three miles short of home he found all his fences had been cut. Funny business was afoot—and no reason for it that Marty could think of.

Next morning the minister insisted on blessing Pinjarra and praying with Marty before continuing up to the Downs. It made Marty very uncomfortable. Most of all, it reminded him of Enid and how easily prayer used to come to her. He would never be like that, or like this Luke Vinson, either.

God was going to have to get along without him.

CHAPTER THIRTEEN

THE SPAN OF TIME

"In the beginning there was a terrible drought, the first and worst drought ever. Grass was gone, trees and kangaroos dying. The young men complained, 'Why are the old men not making rain? That's their job.' They didn't understand that this drought was so fierce the old men were powerless.

"All but one, Wirinun, the wisest of them. He had power. For three days he made his magic at the only water hole left in the land. Then he told the young men to build bark humpies against the rain. The young men laughed behind his back, but they did as he said. He worked more magic. Then as the young people slept inside their new humpies, he and other elders marched around the outside of camp, carrying all they owned.

"The clouds gathered. Lightning struck the ground and thunder roared like it had never roared before. The young people hid in their humpies, terrified. The wise old Wirinun, though, stood in front of the camp and with his magic prevented the lightning from harming the people. He began to sing. The lightning ceased. It started to rain. And rain. And rain. The people praised his power, but he remembered when they laughed at him. So he took them to a great claypan. He made rain fall on the claypan until it became a huge lake.

" 'Go,' he said. 'Go out and spread your nets and fish.'

"The young men laughed again. This was a rain lake not even a day old. Fish could not live there. But they did what he said because they feared his power. They cast their nets and drew them in full of fish! They caught fish enough for all the tribes and the dogs as well. And thus with rain did the old man prove his power.

Indirri sat back, his tale complete. Were his audience children, he would have included details of the magic, such as the two secret stones and the stick fitted with white cockatoo feathers, and the song Wirinun sang. But these were adults, none except Mungkala from his own clan, and two of them whitefellers. He would certainly never reveal a detail of magic within hearing of a whitefeller. Whitefellers wielded too much power already.

Because Indirri's whitefeller yabba was none too good yet, Goonur translated for him during pauses. So careful was she to get the meaning exactly right that she asked him twice to clarify some item. Those glorious blue eyes were the door to a splendid heart.

One of the whitefellers, Lucas Vinson, sat cross-legged across the fire from Indirri. His pallid face registered the most amazing expression of pure wonder, as if he were a child of six wets. He spoke only whitefeller yabba (also a speech called French, which nobody else in the world speaks), so Goonur would insert a word of translation here or there whenever she saw Indirri look confused.

Vinson shook his head. "Amazing parallels between your story and the Bible! For example, on at least two occasions, Jesus told Peter to go out and catch fish, using nets, of course. Both times, Peter had already been fishing a long time and caught nothing; there should have been no fish there. And both times his nets were drawn in completely full. And there was Joshua, who marched his army around the walls of Jericho. Even the detail about carrying all they owned—that is, their armor. 'Joshua' is a variation of 'Jesus.' Moses stood between the Israelites and the wrath of God. And more than once Jesus demonstrated His power over storms and water."

Indirri frowned. Never had he heard of a Jesus. Perhaps it was a whitefeller name for one of the people of the dreamtime. The names of such people frequently changed from tribe to tribe.

"What was his name again? The old man?" Casper Mays shifted uneasily. A huge man with massive hands and feet, he didn't fold well when sitting on the ground. He ran his fingers through his shock of yellowish-brown hair. Dingo-colored hair.

"Wirinun," Indirri answered. With Gimpy Jack long gone back to Elizabeth Downs, Mr. Mays was the boss cocky of Pinjarra, just below Marty, who was the most boss. Indirri much preferred the aboriginal system of initiation. You underwent purification and certain rites, were tattooed and scarred accordingly, and took your place in the heirarchy of gods, demigods and men. These whitefellers paid no attention to initiation. They ranked men however they pleased, and changed the rankings pretty much on whim. They didn't even mark their leaders in any way; all looked alike. How was one supposed to discern clan and rank when there was no sign?

"Any chance we can get Wirinun to call down some rain here?" The boss cocky leered. His voice mocked the story. Indirri understood both his words and their meaning.

Goonur pretended she was translating. "Maybe in your dreaming you can get Wirinun to call down lightning on this dingo."

Vinson jammed some more sticks on the fire. "Indirri. Goonur here says you know many stories. How did you learn them? How do your people pass the stories from generation to generation?" He glanced at Indirri's face and rephrased. "From old to young?"

Indirri could hear and understand much better than he could choose words in sequence and speak. "The elders. The old men. Him tell us, we much little children. More and more stories. When we grow, young men are; him tell us more. New stories, more about the old stories. Initiation. Lad is man. Then we learn the things that are secrets from women and children. We learn the—the deep things, real things. How to do them. Take all him days don' learn everything. Very much wise man, all him days every day learn."

"We have more in common than you know, friend. 'Great

is the Lord, and greatly to be praised. And his greatness is unsearchable. One generation shall praise thy works to another, and shall declare thy mighty acts.' From Psalm one hundred and forty-five."

Goonur translated. She paused. "Who is 'thy'?"

"The supreme God. The Lord. The psalm is a song of praise to God. There's more to the psalm than just that, of course."

Goonur cocked her head. "You can say it all?"

"Psalm one hundred and forty-five? Yes. I've memorized the praise psalms and now I'm starting on the hundred and nineteenth." He began his litany. Indirri understood some of it. He didn't need Goonur's thoughtful help to understand "the Lord is good to all." What god can make that claim? Baiame, perhaps. Or was this God and Baiame one and the same?

They shall speak of the glory of thy kingdom, and talk of thy power. Indeed this God came from the first dreaming, for the psalm insisted that His power was absolute. Baiame? Baiame created, then returned to his own realm. This God stayed close to His creations: *nigh unto all of them.* Apparently no one had to undergo difficult trials and climb a sacred mountain to reach Him. He remained near His own, and He paid attention. What a wonderful thing for a powerful God to do for His creation!

Indirri listened with rapt attention to the cadence of the recital. Even through Goonur's halting and sometimes rough translation, he could hear the magnificence of the language in this elegy of praise. His respect for this Lucas Vinson rose immensely; although he bore no tattoos or cicatrices, and white men hardly ever do, the man was obviously initiated into his religion. He knew exactly, word by word, the tenets of his God. Some of the Storyteller's tales Indirri had heard were repeated several times. And every recital had been precisely the same, word for word. A truly wise man treated every word with equal gravity. This man appeared so young to have absorbed the deeper realities of his God.

It was very clear that Mr. Mays scorned Vinson's God as

much as Indirri's. Indifferently he climbed to his feet. "Getting late. Going to bed. Vinson, if you're riding with us tomorrow, you best retire, too. We leave by first light." And he faded into the darkness.

"Thank you." The gangling young man whipsawed to his feet. He looked at Indirri. "Would you come to my quarters for a few minutes? I'd like to ask you more about how you transfer lore and information. It's interesting and important to me. We can share a pot of tea."

"You got sugar him tea?"

"Lumps this big," and he made a fist, grinning.

Indirri smiled. Most whitefellers he had seen treated blackfellers like children. They were spoken to as children and snubbed as children. But not Vinson. Vinson accepted Indirri with the same grace and enthusiasm that he accepted Mr. Mays or Marty. He was very much like young Marty that way.

Goonur hopped up and fell in beside Indirri. Casually she wrapped an arm across his back and hooked her finger in his belt loop. He enjoyed her closeness more than was reasonable, Indirri thought.

Luke led the way to his own little stringy-bark shack south of the house. "Basically, I want to learn more about local blacks; quite frankly, I hope to use that knowledge to tell others about the true God." He paused in his doorway. "Indirri, can you tell me why you turned your back on the old ways?" And they went inside.

No, Indirri could not. In part, his whitefeller yabba wasn't good enough. More to the point, how could he explain about Mungkala and Goonur, and the lack of old men and all the forces he was powerless to resist?

How could he explain the way he enjoyed whitefellers' horses, and how he loved the feeling of power they gave him? And speed! Sometimes, when the bosses weren't around, he'd drive his mount forward at a dead run just to feel the intense pleasure of speed. He loved horses' many textures—the soft, soft nose, the solid shoulder and whithers, the sleek, firm hide, the strange wooden feet. Nothing like that existed in the blackfeller world.

No, he could explain none of that. "Tucker's good," he conceded. And with that, he sat down at Vinson's little slab table for tea.

Excellent move, you made, Pearl. Shrewd. Pearl stood for a moment in the back doorway of her restaurant. Two months ago she had workmen build the kitchen out separate from the restaurant dining room, causing the temperature in the dining room to drop ten degrees. Now, most of the year it was quite comfortable in here. She stepped aside as her waitress brought in vegetable soup to the patrons in the corner.

Vegetable soup. It had once been Enid's specialty, the thing she took to newlyweds, ailing miners—her universal gift. Pearl made certain the cooks followed Enid's recipe to the letter; she became very unpleasant if so much as a clove of garlic was changed. And that soup was now Pearl's, the specialty of the house that had helped to make her restaurant the best on the Central Line.

She stepped forward to greet the patrons coming in. Pete Sark, a newspaper under one arm and his wife on the other, strode in the door. "Good evening, Reverend! Mrs. Sark." Pearl extended a hand to the lady.

"Honestly! When is it going to be 'Pete and Mave?' " Mave Hurley Sark gave Pearl's hand a squeeze. "Join us for a moment if you've time."

"Thank you. I'd love it. Your usual table is available if you like." Pearl led them to the four-seater by the front window. She sat down as Pete held Mave's chair. "How are you doing?"

Mave looked at least fifteen years younger. Marriage had done wonders for her. "We've been down on the Darling; just got back. Pete's considering taking a church at Wilcannia. They seem to like him, and we like the area. They get a bit more rain there than we do."

"Any rain at all is more rain than we're getting." Pearl sobered. "So many stations going under, people on the brink of starvation. I never dreamed it could be so bad." And Marty flashed through her mind.

She could still recite Mum's letter practically word for word. Dated the first week of January in 1901 (*almost four years ago! Time slipped by so quickly*), it told how Marty had just leased his own run; how he and his father had become a political force to be reckoned with because the other squatters respected them so; how Pearl was an utter fool not to have encouraged Marty's interest more; what a splendid husband he would have made her; and how lonely Mum was in a town of country folk, even if Barcaldine did consider itself the Garden City.

Marty was surely married by now. Four years is a long time when you're young and ready for love. Pearl the spinster snorted. Who should know better than she?

Pete was shaking his newspaper open. "This is the first paper I've seen in weeks. Eh, and it's not strictly fresh. November 30, 1904. Ah, only a week old. Fish last three days; papers don't spoil so fast."

Pearl perched her chin in her hand and smiled at Mave. *He's changed so much in a few years, eh?* their eyes said to each other.

"Let's see," Pete mused. "No more bubonic plague reported in Sydney since September. That's good news. 'Sir Hugh Nelson announced on November 4 that . . . ' So what?" He turned the page to another item. "Recruiting of Kanakas has ceased. That's good." His eyes flitted about. "And Acrasia won the Cup."

Pearl interrupted. "In three minutes, twenty-eight and a half seconds, exactly the same time Newhaven ran it in 1896, half a second less than Clean Sweep in 1900 and . . . shall I go on? The Melbourne Cup is the primary topic of conversation in this place from the month before it's run to the month after. I'm an authority on horse racing by default." She saw a customer enter. "Excuse me. Enjoy your meal."

She rose to meet a lanky young man with pale skin and a shock of blond hair. "Welcome. Any seat in particular you'd like?"

"Anywhere is fine. Afterward, I wonder if you could direct me to Pearl Fowkes's laundry? The train will be here for a bit over three hours, the conductor said, which should give me time."

"Certainly. May I ask why?" Pearl led him to a corner table.

"A man named Martin Frobel Junior asked me to look her up."

Pearl wheeled and stared. She hastily composed herself. "Pearl still owns the laundry, but she also owns this restaurant. I am Pearl."

"I should have known." The man held out his hand. "He described you as being very beautiful. Couldn't be two women this lovely in Anakie. My name is Lucas Vinson."

"How is he doing?"

"Would you kindly join me for lunch—that is, if restaurateurs eat their own food. I'll tell you all about him . . . and please call me Luke."

Pearl allowed him to seat her as her heart sang. Marty not only remembered her, but he felt obliged to send this emissary. And what a charming fellow he was, too, so lighthearted and friendly. She ordered for both of them because he wouldn't know that Mabel was cooking today. Mabel made the world's best fried chicken.

For an hour she listened to a tale of struggle. Drought was hard on miners, but it was disastrous for stockmen. Luke described how Marty, gambling that the drought would persist, purchased several hundred bullocks. For three years he fought to keep them alive through the worst drought Queensland had ever seen.

An old bullocky himself, he yoked and trained them. Then he sold them for a tidy sum, because they were the only bullocks in the district; everyone else had let their bullocks die in order to save the breeding stock.

Now he had two hundred breeding cows, purchased from his father at a pound a head, from which he hoped to build a mob of beef cattle, with perhaps a few milkers for cheese. And he still had all but one of the original seed bulls his father had given him four years ago.

Cows, cows, cows. I wonder if he's married! "And how is he doing . . . how is his family?"

"Oh, well enough. One of his blacks, named Indirri, has a perfect angel of a little boy, and Marty loves playing uncle to it. He works too hard, frankly. He fired his manager, a Mr. Mays. Now he takes on both jobs, owner and manager. Wanted me to stay on, as did his parents, but I feel led elsewhere."

"Ah. You worked for him."

"Circuit preacher up and down Torrens Creek there. Served all the squatters." He smiled. "Communal property."

"And now you're moving on." So was Pete Sark. Men of the cloth seemed to lead as nomadic an existence as shearers.

Luke leaned both elbows on the table—an excusable breach of manners—and sighed. "Marty told me about your sister in glowing terms. I'm very sorry to hear of her death. How long ago was it? He was unclear."

"Seven years and some."

"Seven." He shook his head. "Her faith sounded exemplary. And yet, Marty himself stubbornly resists the Holy Spirit in his own life. Seems to think he can never be close to God like Enid was; he even set *me* on a pedestal for a while. He persistently refuses to commit himself to Jesus Christ."

Pearl felt the old anger rise in her. "Marty is one of the most Christian men I've ever met."

"No. Extremely moral. Honest. Helpful. Enlightened. But not Christian. And his is a common attitude, an attitude I can't crack no matter how I preach and persuade. I feel as if I'm butting my head against a brick wall. But that's neither here nor there. The end is, I'm traveling up to Mossman to a little chapel."

"Mossman! Sugar cane country."

"You're aware of the Kanaka problem."

"Black labor brought in to work the sugar fields. They've recently passed laws against indenturing them. There's a problem?"

"Much work to be done there." He rubbed his chin. "I don't know how to explain this. The attitude I see here toward the blacks is, by and large, much the same as I remember from my childhood in Canada on the Red River. Mixed-blood Indians called the Metis resisted what they felt was encroachment by white settlers. Louis Riel led the movement. The trouble lasted nearly two decades, resulting in untold anguish for both red and white. In a way, I grew up seeing the race problems—and possible solutions to those problems. I believe I can be of great service to both whites and blacks in Mossman."

Pearl cocked her head and propped her chin on her knuckles. "Mr. Vinson, are you out to undo wrongs or to tilt at windmills?"

He looked at her a long time, then said, "I hope to undo wrongs. Preaching the gospel is my primary concern, of course, but I can preach it there as well as here. And perhaps to more receptive ears. I want to put the heart of the gospel—service to man—to practical use."

"Godspeed, Lucas Vinson."

He grinned like a ten-year-old. "Thank you, Pearl Fowkes."

With profuse praise he exclaimed over the food and with profuse thanks insisted on paying for it. She sidestepped that easily enough simply by telling her employees to refuse his money. She walked him to the train, learned further details of life on Pinjarra, and satisfied herself that no wife as yet existed. Lucas Vinson would surely have mentioned one by this time.

The train left only twenty minutes later than promised. She waved to him, watched the train disappear, and sat down on the bench by the little shed. That shed.

Pearl, please come to Jesus.

No, Marty is not a Christian. Could Luke be right? His words echoed Papa's own:

Pearl, you're not a Christian.

Neither was Mum, by these people's standard, and no more unhappy and lonely person existed in Queensland. Pearl herself couldn't say she enjoyed life—though she'd always assumed this would change once she left the area. How unfortunate it was, really, that she was making too much money to leave.

How can a Christian not be a Christian?

Come to Jesus. This Lucas Vinson wore his faith comfortably, like an old flannel shirt. The gospel drove him to serve, and he seemed happy. He looked forward to Mossman eagerly, just as Enid had anticipated good things when she left Barcaldine. Enid served here and derived joy. Like Luke, she reached within her for her happiness, to the Christ that dwelled within.

Pearl reached inside and found nothing.

To Enid and this Luke, Jesus was a personal friend. To Pearl He was an excuse to rest on Sunday.

Enid reflected Jesus. Luke reflected Jesus. Papa reflected Jesus. If Pearl reflected anyone at all, it was Mum. Oh, God!

Eternal life probably should mean more to her than it actually did. After all, you're talking about forever. But forever was too distant to hold any attraction for Pearl. She wanted something now, she yearned for something, and she didn't know what.

Please come to Jesus, Pearl, the tortured mouth locked tightly shut.

The tears came, hot and burning, and she let them come. For an hour she sat in the sun on the bench and let tears flood her sorrow. Enid.

Seven years. The span of time, of her resistance, had stretched out far enough. Too far. She was tired of being empty. As the sun beat relentlessly upon her, she admitted to God her sins, most particularly her sin of stubbornness. She begged Him to forgive her, and dwelt a moment on the memory of Enid's voice, the many times Enid promised that God does indeed forgive. *Please come, Lord Jesus. I'm ready. Fill me. Please.*

For the first time in seven years, the memory of the horror in that railway shed subsided. No longer weighted down by that one terrible memory, other memories welled up. Welcome thoughts. Happy thoughts. Visions of Enid bubbling and laughing, earnestly explaining the gospel "in season and out of season," as she was so fond to say. Her profession of joy in doing things Jesus liked and asked of her.

For the first time in her life, Pearl realized what Enid had been talking about.

She heard the words as for the first time. She understood her sister, truly understood her, for the first time.

Enid joyfully belonged to God—then and at this very moment.

And now, at last, so did Pearl.

CHAPTER FOURTEEN

CATTLE OF PINJARRA

Few trees, none of them higher than a man's up-stretched arm. No buildings taller than one story. Streets wide enough to drive a mob of sheep, with room to spare. The endless, shimmering brilliance of an overhead sun unveiled by mist or moisture. Blue sky, yellow dust, weathered buildings—all lined up in sharp, clear lines, all broader than high, with the level line between earth and heaven lying horizontal as far as the eye can see. All dragging the imagination wide from side to side—a brief sketch of infinity drawn in bulldust.

Marty rode down the wide, empty main street of Cloncurry, the only human being left in the universe, as far as he could tell. There on the far side, standing in front of the ubiquitous corner pub, were four horses, tails switching vigorously. No, five. Except for two horses over by the barber shop and a brindled dog asleep in the cobbler's door, those five horses were the only living things Marty saw. He rode his gray mare in beside them and tied her to the rail.

Inside, infinity collapsed into dark, stuffy closeness. A dozen men lolled, some draped over the bar and some sprawled in the chairs at tables along the wall. The conversation rose and fell in lazy tones to match the buzz of flies.

Marty saw no one here he knew—not surprising, for he was nearly three hundred miles from home. He approached the bartender. " 'Scuse me. A John Conlin anywhere about?"

The bartender pointed. "Johnny. Young gent here wants you."

John Conlin was not a big man, though he carried himself in such a way to make you think he was. His face hung in wads, his jowls and cheeks shifted about when he spoke. His skin was the crinkled brown of a man born in the saddle, and his stained and ragged drover's hat stayed together only because it dared not let down the man who had spent a lifetime under it. He perched both elbows on the bar and turned that massive pie face toward Marty.

Sizing Marty up and down, he said, "Looking for work, eh?"

Marty hesitated only a second, weighing this interesting new prospect. He smiled. "Perhaps. I hear you're lifting a mob by Julia Creek."

"That is so. Twelve hundred mixed stock and a hundred bullocks. Overlanding them to a place above Muttaburra. On the track two months. Done much droving?"

"Not much, no, sir."

"New-chum, hmm? Eight a day and a pound bonus when we deliver. You jack up once, you're done. Agreed?"

Marty grinned and extended his hand. "Agreed, sir." The hulking paw that engulfed his hand felt warm and calloused, and as strong as fencing wire.

"What's your name?"

"Marty, sir. Uh, Martin James."

"Coincidence. We're delivering to a Martin. Martin Frobel." He twisted around to point. "Over there's the lads you'll be working with. There's Alf, and Bill, and Clive and Cut'emup."

Alf, a wizened little man, nodded sagely. Bill and Clive, both burly, looked like they ought to be brothers. And Cut'emup, an aborigine, appeared as tall as Marty, with a round, happy face atop a lanky body. They acknowledged Marty with the barest of nods.

Marty settled in beside Conlin. "Two months, you say."

The boss drover lit another cigarette. "Good fat stock you can push ten or twelve miles a day. This drought, though, ain't no fat stock. Even Cobb and Company's stage horses look poorly. Five or six miles a day is the best you'll do with the cattle 'round here. And there's precious little water along the route. We'll have to go outta our way now and again to water. Two months at least."

Marty nodded, pleased. When he entered this place to talk to John Conlin, it had been as the new owner of the stock to be overlanded. Now the questions he would have asked of his new drover could be answered on the journey. Work as a drover for the drover he had hired by mail? Why not? It would not have occurred to him, but since Conlin had mistaken him as a drifter seeking employment, so be it. In fact, it might be fun to begin at this end as journeyman drover and to finish at that end as the owner.

He had cemented the deal just last week, buying the mixed mob of Herefords, devons and a smattering of poleys from a going-broke squatter by Julia Creek. It was a bold front, a desperate move. Marty was one step short of bankruptcy. Less—half a step. On the brink. Either the drought would break and he would turn a profit on this mob he had just purchased, or the continuing drought would kill them all, and his dreams as well. The hundred bullocks that had been added to the deal, he'd whip into shape and try to sell as draught animals; it had worked once before.

And what if Mr. Conlin didn't know who he really was? Being a squatter, dressing primly and properly, wielding power, making vital decisions and shouldering heavy responsibilities—Marty was sick of it. He'd been doing that now for four and a half years. That could, for once, wait for tomorrow. Opportunity knocked here—and a chance for a temporary fling at carefree childhood. For a brief spell he would enjoy what he loved best—working cattle with no responsibility involved. He sent a letter home explaining this turn of events.

When Mr. Conlin took delivery, Marty kept his hat pulled low and made certain he was nowhere near anyone who might recognize him as the young buyer, son of a well-known squatter. He turned his gray mare in with the drover's mob and rode an inconspicuous bay gelding.

And they were on their way.

Marty marveled at how quickly life on the track settled to

a routine, and how easily both drovers and cattle fell into it. Each morning the cook and horse tailer put the wagon—the plant—on its way, along with thirty-some spare horses. The drovers strung the cattle out loosely across half a mile, ambling at a most leisurely pace across the flat vastness.

At midday the point riders would circle the cattle until they lay down. Marty would sit in the shade of a scrubby tree or, lacking trees, in the shade of his horse, to eat lunch—whatever had been left over from breakfast. When the cattle caught up to the plant in the evening, the cook would already have a tarp stretched over a ridge pole—wasn't much, but it was home. His fire would be built, the damper started. Boiled kangaroo or boiled beef and damper. There was a routine to the menu, too.

Being Jacky Raw, the new boy on the block, put Marty at the bottom of the pile. He rode all day at the very back, urging the stragglers forward. Dust—constant dense bulldust. No need to complain; that's where the new boy rode. He saved his gray mare for night work, keeping her saddled and tied close to wherever he slept. He trusted her beneath him when complete darkness robbed even his good night vision. Besides, he knew how the old girl hated breathing dust.

Maybe he was city-soft. Frankly, he missed not sleeping in a bed at all. Working on Pinjarra, he'd roll out his swag for days at a time under a tree or under the stars. Weeks at a time, though, it got to be a bit much. It could be worse, he knew. A lot of drovers didn't even provide a tarp to sleep under.

With no watch or calendar, he lost track of days—enjoying every bit of it. It was a luxury he would not be able to indulge in for long. He let day slip into day as July flowed by and melted unnoticed into August.

Night. This one began like the others with one delightful exception: Cut'emup would keep watch until Alf relieved him; Marty got to sleep the night through for once. He tied the mare close by and folded his blanket double on top before he rolled into it; the clear air was extra crisp tonight.

At dusk a flock of white cockatoos had settled into the

thicket near camp. Now they gabbled and griped to each other, rustling and shifting in the trees, ruffling the silence of the winter night.

Suddenly the air was filled with yelling, screams and thunder. Marty sat bolt upright and was scrambling for his horse even before he was fully awake. Clive and Mr. Conlin swore as they groped for their boots. Marty didn't bother with boots; he vaulted onto the mare barefooted. He heard the rush, though he could not see it. The mob had bolted, startled by some unknown thing of the night. They were angling southeast, pouring uncontainably among the sparse trees, crashing through thickets, running senselessly. Marty turned the mare southeast in hot pursuit.

The third-quarter moon was just now climbing. It provided a bit more light than did the stars. The dust cloud loomed ahead, a silver haze in the darkness. Caught up in the thrill of the chase, the mare extended her neck and stretched out into her jubilant gallop. She was so exciting to ride when she plunged her heart and soul into a hard run like this! Marty was abreast the stragglers already. Vague cow forms ran beside him, and then fell behind. The haze grew thicker.

The theory was simple: ride alongside the herd, try to reach the leaders, and with your whip and the sheer weight of your lunging horse turn them aside; turn them, turn them until the mob milled in a tightening circle and settled to a halt. Marty had never tried to ring a mob before.

He could make out now, however dimly, the general mass of the herd, a churning ocean of horns and backs and dust. Their brute power pulled a tree down ahead, toppling it into the silver dust. He should be on the wing of the mob, out along the edge; instead, he was in its midst far too deeply. He did not like to think what would happen to him should his horse stumble in the darkness. He must turn his mare aside, get out of this extreme danger. And he remembered that other rush of years ago when he rode amid plunging cattle just like this . . .

He broke into a cold sweat as he saw in his mind's eye

. . . Turk Moran spiraling away, his eyeglasses flying off his nose as he was struck down by the bullet from Marty's gun . . . Turk Moran's own gun roaring harmlessly as cattle thundered past . . . and the churning dust. . . .

The gray mare squealed and disappeared from under him. Marty sailed into the air like an eagle at top speed, then slammed into bushes and hard ground. He was sure to be trampled now; the rampaging cattle right behind him would stomp him into the dust and never even feel him underfoot. He tried to curl up, to protect his head, but he couldn't move. Cloven hooves dug into the dirt inches away; the dust boiled so thick he couldn't breathe.

Except for loud and confused lowing, the noise faded. The hoofbeats moved on. Some of the dust lifted, but it was still difficult to breathe. His right side was clamped in a painful vise; his right shoulder hurt even more. He had bunged himself up once before, but he'd really messed himself up this time. It took many minutes to fight his way to his feet and start looking for the mare.

There she was, not ten feet away. And here was the reason Marty had not been trampled. He had been shielded by, quite literally, a wall of cows. Squirming, kicking, mooing, all legs and horns, they were still trying to disentangle themselves from each other in the darkness. A cow would roll and fight loose of the crazy pile and limp away. Then another would somehow lurch to her feet. A few squirmed helplessly, pinned beneath dead beasts.

Bathed in slippery sweat, the mare lay on her side. She would raise her head, fighting, struggling, then fall back again. Marty's left hand and arm were busy holding his right arm tightly against his body, for any movement shot wracking pain clear through him. He had no hand to spare, and he couldn't see well enough to assess the horse's problem.

So he sat down by her mane and laid his body flat across her neck, pinning her head down. Her body heat and her smell and her slimy, resinous sweat penetrated his shirt. He felt her neck muscles bunch and pulse. And he waited.

Hours later—years later, it seemed—a muffled voice called

out in the darkness. Marty cried out. Silence. The voice called again, nearer. Marty shouted "Here! Over here!" again and again. From the south came the sound of a horse on the trampled ground, and from the east another. Clive on horseback loomed above him and dismounted. He let go a string of words Marty hadn't heard since he drove bullocks for August Miles.

Mr. Conlin rode up beside the tangle of cows. The richness of his vocabulary more than matched his drover's. He studied the mess a minute. "Lad, it's God alone saved you. Built a wall around you."

Why didn't He build a wall around sweet Enid? What on earth made Marty think of her now? Simple. He had seen God so clearly in Enid that he just naturally associated the two, that's why.

They rolled two dead cows aside to free the two still alive. The pile was all untangled now, with only two losses.

"Eh, here's what happened, Mr. Conlin." Clive stood erect. "The mob took down this boundary fence. The fence came flying back on itself here and tangled Marty's horse's legs, see? Also tangled a couple cows. They went down. The other beasts couldn't swerve and they stumbled onto the top of 'em. Not half a pile-up. Musta been one bonzer smash, eh?"

"What spooked them; do we know?" Marty listened to the click and snap of wire cutters. Mr. Conlin was freeing his mare's legs.

"Yair. That flock of cockatoos in the gum tree. Something started them bunging on quite an act, squawking and chattering around. That's 'bout all we can figger. Let her up, lad. Let's see what she can do."

Marty twisted around and pulled himself off the mare's neck. "Good mare." He sat in the cool night dirt. "Only got two foals out of her, both fillies, and neither looks like her."

The mare paused a moment, lurched, and then flung herself up on her belly. Another pause and she lunged awkwardly to her feet. Instantly she crashed to the ground, her legs folding uselessly beneath her.

"Here, lad, now let's see how you're doing. Clive, put him

up aboard there and take him back to the bait layer." Mr. Conlin shoved Marty rather too roughly over to Clive. They boosted him onto Clive's horse and Clive swung up behind. The burly drover wrapped an arm around Marty not just to hold him on but to hold him. They hadn't ridden a hundred yards when the gun blasted behind them.

His mare . . . his faithful old gray mare . . . that gun . . . Turk Moran . . . Enid. A confusion of thoughts, sorrows most recent and far past, all swarmed in his brain, forming a pile just as tangled and dense as that mix-up of cattle that had saved him. But if God chose thus to save him, why not simply keep his mare on her feet in the first place? If God had power to do one, He must have power to do the other.

It was sunup and Marty lay half-dozing in his swag when a thought struck him: If God had power to do as He willed, and this happened, then God must have a message in mind. It wasn't too hard to figure out what it might be. After all, He had sent two messengers—Enid and Luke. And their message? Jesus. Always Jesus.

Then Marty thought better of it. Nonsense. Things like this happen, that's all. It could have been worse. It certainly could have been better. Still the notion persisted in Marty's thoughts and would not be pushed aside.

Marty got off light, the drover claimed. A horse, a couple broken ribs and a dislocated shoulder were a small price to pay for one's life being saved miraculously. That philosophical thought did nothing to ease the pain of either the ribs or the loss of that fine old mare. With the cook's help Mr. Conlin popped Marty's shoulder back in. He nodded sagely when Marty mentioned his previous problem with it. "Eh, yair. Had a cousin once with a trick shoulder just like that."

For a week Marty rode in the plant as cook's helper until he could use his stiff arm. Then he was back in the saddle, droving. But there was a difference. Now and then he was assigned to riding wing, in rotation with the others. He received his turn on point, too—the very front with no dust and no stragglers. He had arrived: a full mate in this solidarity of proud and independent men.

As they drew closer to Pinjarra, Marty watched with growing admiration as Mr. Conlin put native intelligence and years of experience to the task of bringing the Frobel mob safely home to paddock. Marty was impressed with the man's skill and ingenuity. Every day Mr. Conlin used more brains than some city businessmen even own.

Let some city drongo find water for thirteen hundred cattle when the gilgais were all dried up. Or feed. Mr. Conlin would look across a distance identical to the distances they had just covered, then announce, "There's grass over that way." And there always was. Each day posed unique problems. Each stage brought them closer home.

Home. He should think more about finding a good woman to share it with. Then his mind would shift to Enid, and the pain stabbed deep all over again. Nine years ago. As splendid a girl as Enid was, that's a ridiculously long time to mourn a lost love. And Pearl. What was Pearl doing now? Surely married. And that thought shot a pang of jealousy through him. Silly galah, Frobel. That was years ago.

Pearl. True, Pearl had been cranky at times. She put on airs. But she was also a good friend. Marty felt comfortable with her, comfortable and easy. She loved cities and city ways. Did enjoying her company mean Marty was a city lad at heart? Here in the middle of nowhere, droving a mob under broiling sun, he couldn't believe that. This land was a part of him.

Still, it was curious the way he and city-bred Pearl got along so well—a mateship, in the best sense of the word.

The land flowed in familiar patterns now. Nearly home. How should he break the news of his identity to this old drover? How about: *Sir, you know how God owns all the cattle on a thousand hills? Well, I own the thousand cattle on this hill.* No. Mr. Conlin wasn't a religious man. He probably wouldn't get it.

Or, *I've been meaning to mention this earlier, but my name isn't really James. It's Frobel.* Direct, but disappointing somehow.

How about: *My pop says he's sending another thousand*

head down from Elizabeth Downs. Can you take on another job? Yair, that's the ticket.

They were less than three miles from Pinjarra now and headed straight for it. Half a day—then home. The excitement built inside his chest and made his breastbone tickle. He saddled the scraggly bay because it hadn't been used for several days and took his place riding point this morning. The plant rolled away over the rise and out of sight.

Soon.

Marty looked up to see a lone horseman at a dead run, appearing from where the plant had disappeared. As he approached, the plant came back over the rise, its four harness horses rocketing along at a disorganized canter. Mr. Conlin muttered something bullocky and galloped ahead to meet the rider.

Marty recognized the battered hat and the black face beneath it, but most of all he recognized the vivid blue shirt. He rode ahead, too. He pulled alongside Mr. Conlin and the rider. "Gimpy Jack! What're you doing out here?"

"Marty!" The whites of Jack's eyes glowed. "We got trouble, Marty. For a month now, raiders been plaguing your place. Stealing things, killing chooks, being a nuisance. Before 'twas by night but they're here now—in broad daylight."

"That's mad! Ridiculous! Why would anyone want to—"

"They're shooting guns and trying to fire the buildings."

"*Right now?* Pop know about this?"

"Didn't tell him. He got troubles of his own."

The boss drover studied Marty a moment and burst into a raucous laugh. "Kinda suspected. Frobel, hey? Now what's this about trouble?"

"It's not your problem. Don't risk yourself or your drovers."

Mr. Conlin's eyes narrowed in the baggy face. "I'll take on whatever problems I choose to and no young squirt's gunner tell me what fights I can or can't take up. Now I promised delivery on this mob and it's gunner happen. Right to your front paddock. I know how to pull a trigger if need be."

"Mr. Conlin, you don't—"

"My professional pride's at stake. Besides, I admire you, young feller. You took orders well, and you pulled your weight. You're a dinkum cobber and willing to work. And cheerful. All that's hard to find, 'specially among the squattocracy. We're gunner help you."

Marty twisted in the saddle. The mob was nearly upon them now, slogging along in its casual way. He looked at Mr. Conlin.

The mob! Here was power beyond comprehension, power Marty himself had experienced firsthand a few short weeks ago. Of course! And no trigger to pull.

He nodded toward the mob. "Let's rush 'em."

A smile as wide as a saltpan spread across the pudgy face. Cheeks and jowls shifted all over. "That oughta scrub the yards clean, hey?"

It didn't take but a minute to set the mob off; a few shotgun blasts at the rear did it. Five thousand two hundred cloven feet charged recklessly forward up the dry slope, plunging the land ahead into danger, mindlessly escaping no danger at all. They filled the crest of the rise with dust and churning confusion.

Marty tried to stay on the wing, to keep them pointed true toward the house. He knew the drovers were where they ought to be, struggling to keep this uncontrollable mob moving right, but he could see nothing but dust and horns and razorbacks.

There was the house—*his* house—in plain sight now. It sat among its outbuildings in lovely isolation in the midst of its broad, sweeping valley. It loomed closer. There were riders, half a dozen of them, and two men on foot carrying torches. Even at this distance you could see the moment the men on foot realized the danger. As the riders paused in Marty's very dooryard, their horses dancing, the men afoot dropped their torches and scrambled madly for their mounts. The riders bolted even as the first of the mob hit the hospital-paddock fence and took it down.

Marty wanted to get close enough to see faces, to identify the scoundrels, but they were too far ahead and leaving in too much of a hurry.

Dust obscured the station now and rose in a churning cloud halfway to heaven. Unable to turn aside for the crush of cattle, three bullocks slammed into Luke's abandoned stringybark hut on the south side. The shed leaned, folded, and disappeared under rushing feet. Cows took out the verandah rail on the north side of the main house. The whole south side verandah collapsed.

A part of Marty sorely wanted to pursue those riders, to try to overtake them, but a wiser part of him warned him otherwise. Too dangerous. Abreast the main house, he veered his horse south as the last of the mob swept by. He rode a wide circle and came in behind the cattle through the choking cloud, up to the front door.

An eerie silence hung on the pall of dust. Marty shouted cooee and swung down off his lathered horse. From inside came a wild and most familiar cackle.

Jase came charging out the front door with his smoking gun still in his hand. "Halloo, Cuz! Welcome home!"

CHAPTER FIFTEEN

FOR THE SON OF AN OLD FRIEND

The golden light of evening bathed the mild little rise ahead, gilding the white trunks of the gums and setting the acacia trees aglow. The land stretched its bosom toward infinity untrammeled, for the fences were all down. A pleasant breeze stirred the air, and the flies were finally calling it quits for the day. The perfect hour was upon him, the sedate cap to a most amazing and frightening day.

Marty settled deeper into this wicker armchair and stretched his legs out across his front verandah. They nearly reached the rail. He drew a deep, contented breath. He was master of all this, a pastoral tenant of the Crown. He was home.

Beside him in the upholstered pine chair, Mr. Conlin chuckled. "Wisht I was close enough to see the look on their faces as that blasted mob come over the hill at 'em. Coo, what a sight! You got some fence building to do, lad. I don't think your cows left you a single section still standing."

"Not to mention the side verandahs and that breezeway out back. Could've lost a lot more. A lot more."

"Too right, lad. Too right. Eh, here they come."

Jase and Gimpy Jack came striding in across the churned-up dooryard, Jase with his swagger and Jack with his waddling limp. Jack sat down and leaned back against the verandah post. Jase grabbed a ladderback chair, swung it around and straddled it backward.

He folded his arms across its back. "You missed most of the fun, Cuz. While you were out playing games with cows, we were holding off who-knows-who. And we don't know who, either. They're imported, I can tell you that much. Never seen them around here before. Four whites, all with beards, and four blacks."

"Raiders! Why me?"

"Don't get too swelled up over it. They've been to your pop's, too. And Cyrus Bickett's. So you're not alone. But why they're pestering local pastoralists nobody knows." Jase grinned. "Hey, that sounds poetic."

"If you're a poet, I'm a brain surgeon. What's the constable got to say?"

Jason shrugged. "Big district, two men—him and his assistant. Comes out now and then to investigate the cause of our complaints, but what can he do? Never here when anything happens."

Occasionally, Marty's brain would work out the perfect solution while he slept or while he was concentrating on other things. But he couldn't count on it. He surely wished it would surprise him with some answers now, though.

Mr. Conlin stood up and stretched. "You nippers can ride all day and carouse all night, but not this old duffer. Gunner call it a day. Get the plant started north tomorrow and lift that thousand head at your papa's."

"You're welcome to my bed in there, Mr. Conlin. Be comfortable once."

Mr. Conlin scowled at Marty, but his eyes twinkled. "Ain't *that* old! Neh, your haymow will do me just fine." He dropped down off the porch and strode out across the dooryard, moving with a sprightly snap that belied his age.

Jason pulled the upholstered pine chair closer to Marty, settled into it, and stretched his legs out across the verandah, too. He chewed a couple fingernails as they watched the gold turn to pink to old rose to gray. His voice dropped from enthusiastic to contemplative. "Nice place, Cuz."

"Ta. Glad you were here." Marty looked at him. "Why *are* you here, anyway? Last I knew, you were over at Opalton getting dirt under your fingernails."

"Got bored. Thought of going up to Anakie, but that place hurts too much. Too many memories." He sighed and wagged his head. "How long ago was that?"

"Not long enough."

Jason was nodding. "Pearl, she's the flashy one, with those curls. You put her on your arm, and when you walk down the street you're saying, 'Lookit what I got!' But Enid, she was flashy inside. No, not flashy. Real. A real light inside. Made you feel special, not just look special." He studied Marty a moment. "You were pretty warm toward Enid there yourself, weren't you?"

"Yair." Marty didn't want to talk about her. And yet he did.

"Ever put the hard word on her?"

"Enid? Never! She was sweet and innocent. Wouldn't in a million years think of—you know. I heard you kissed her, though."

Jason cackled but it wasn't a mirthful laugh. "Yair, just expressing my opinion to her. I was thinking some of getting married then. I can see now it was a crook idea. Don't know what I was thinking of. I wasn't ready for that. Still not. I want to get out and do things. I have places to see yet before I have to tie down to one job and a family and all that."

"Yair, well, I'm ready."

It wasn't a cackle; it was a guffaw, bursting on the quiet air of dusk. "Marty, Cuz, don't come the raw prawn on me! A bunch of little Frobels running around here? And a school, right? Then we gotta have the ladies' sewing circle and the afternoon tea. And a church so's we can have church socials. That's what marrying is."

"Unless you're Indirri," Gimpy Jack chuckled. "Goonur's idea of a good time is go off on walkabout and club a wallaby. Now that's the way it oughta be." He stood up. "Want me to take first watch?"

Marty would have answered but Jase cut in. "Naw. Go to sleep. I'll stay up late and come get you before I turn in. Then you wake me up at dawn."

"Better yet, wake *me* up at dawn to take a turn," Marty corrected.

"No, me." Jason grinned impishly. "We can't have the big boss cocky here losing sleep."

"Break it down, Jase! Hooroo, Jack."

"Hooroo." Grinning, Jack ambled out across the dooryard. That vivid blue shirt faded into the gathering darkness. He had adopted whitefellers' dress and work habits and most of the mannerisms. But when he walked away from you, you could see the depths of his aboriginal roots in the way he moved.

Boss cocky indeed. On the other hand, Marty had better start figuring out options and taking responsibility. "Why's Jack here?"

"We sent you a letter. You must not've gotten it. That Albert Samson outta Ilfracombe, that you hired as manager? Your pop decided to pay a surprise visit here while you were gone. Brought Jack along. Asked to see the books and log. Samson wouldn't let him. Said it was none of his business."

"He was right, actually."

"Yair, but he acted funny. Uncle Martin insisted. Samson said he needed a court order to do that, and he wasn't gunner get one. So your pop pulled his court order outta his holster and set Samson down in the office with Jack sitting on him and went through the log. Paid Samson off with his own check and gave him an hour to get out."

"It was that bad? Samson had the best of references."

"He was bleeding you dry, and you weren't that wet to start with. Anyway, you got Jack now."

"Not for good. Sooner or later Pop's gunner need him back again. Gotta hire someone." Marty wagged his head. "That Casper Mays was a loser, and now this Albert Samson turns out to be a no-hoper. I'm not building much of a record for hiring."

"You'll get better with practice. Seven or eight managers from now, you oughta have it down."

Marty grimaced. The stars were coming out now, winking into their ordained places. "Anybody heard from Luke lately?"

"Luke! Wait'll I tell you! Up around the sugar field, behind . . . behind . . . where'd Luke go?"

"Mossman."

"That's it. Apparently Luke found out about some green cane that blew down. So he loaded I forget how many carloads of downed cane and brought it out on the railway to your pop's siding. Uncle Martin says that wet cane saved that whole mob he was running on his north end."

"Wacko. The lad lives what he preaches."

"Don't he!"

Silence.

Marty studied the darkness. "Jase, if this drought doesn't break in a couple months, Pinjarra's dead. These cows are my last hope of staying afloat. I'm in debt as bad as I can be. Even if rain comes through in time, I might not make it."

"That's sorta what your pop thinks from looking at your books. And Samson buried you worse. Really hurt you."

"I'll take one big swing around, see who's available. Won't spend much time looking. Leave tomorrow, be gone a week."

"Hire someone who knows how to build fences."

The next day, still saddle-weary from that overland trek, Marty rode down to Muttaburra to look around. Nothing. He could have gone on south to Longreach. Instead, on impulse he traveled down to Aramac. He didn't expect to find anything there, and wasn't disappointed; he continued into Barcaldine. He would have paid his respects to Enid's parents, but he lost his nerve. Next day he took the train west to Longreach, having talked to only a few people—none of them named Fowkes.

Conscience got the better of him. He spent forty minutes in Longreach, arguing with himself on the railway platform. He rode the train back to Barcaldine, much to the conductor's amusement.

Ash Street. He paused there a minute, at the storefront where the strike headquarters had been. Strikes were still a fact of life throughout the country, but not around Barcaldine anymore. The attention had shifted to other places and other workers' causes. He recalled walking with Pearl up this street, and her fearful amazement at the torchlight parades.

Oak Street. Pearl had described for him in massive detail the great fire that had leveled blocks of Oak Street along the railroad here. No signs of it remained. Everything was built up again and bustling. Progress. Barcaldine considered itself the leading edge of progress in the outback. Ask any city councilman.

He had stalled as much as he could. Reluctantly, he rode over to the Fowkeses' cottage and knocked. No one home. With immense relief he continued upstreet to the Commercial and turned his horse into the hotel's paddock.

Although transients and widowers formed the bulk of its clientele, the Commercial Hotel at the beginning of the dinner hour also entertained a few locals, and for good reason. They served the best two-shilling plate of roast beef in the district. Marty bought his dinner—roast beef and dark gravy, potatoes with onions, carrots and yeast rolls—and sat down in a corner to partake of food a good sight better than boiled kangaroo and damper.

A hand pressed his shoulder. Vivid vest and all, Ross Sheldon stood beside him. "Marty! Heard you were in town."

Marty grabbed the napkin in his lap and stood up. He waved a hand. "Welcome to join me."

To Marty's mild surprise, the pastoralist accepted his invitation. Sheldon made some sort of signal to someone elsewhere and sat down in the chair across. "Go ahead and eat before it gets cold. I've had dinner, but I'll keep you company."

Marty sat down again and started in on the potatoes. "Town's looking good. New buildings, some fresh faces." He saw now what the signal had been. Sheldon's station manager brought his boss a cup of coffee and, like a butler, silently left. Pastoral tenant of the Crown or not, Marty would never order his people around as if they were slaves, like Sheldon did.

"No flies on this town. Despite the fact that the rail line moved on to Longreach, we've held our own as a progressive community. Next Member from Barcoo will come out of here, perhaps one day the governor."

"Maybe so." Marty finished his potatoes. Politics was one thing he certainly did not want to discuss. Let Pop argue Sheldon down. Marty hated to.

"I hear your father's considering standing for public office. You have a similar ambition?"

"Naw, not for a few years yet. Actually, Pop isn't all that warm to it either, but he sees some good he can do, he says. Me, I have my hands full with the run."

"Ah, yes. I heard you bought some cattle. Julia Creek?"

Marty nodded and started his carrots.

Sheldon wagged his head gravely. "Tick country up there. Heavily infested. I don't think I'd want to bring any animals in from the Cloncurry district. Too sickly. Tick-blown."

"These are clean. I checked them over. Drought wore them down a little, but it's the same for everybody's stock. A good rainy season and they'll be fat and saucy."

"You're inexperienced. You actually trust your own judgment that much? Your ability to make the right decisions about an essentially worthless run?"

Marty felt his neck hairs prickle. "I been working on a station my whole life, and I have the best man in the business to ask advice of. Besides, Pinjarra is as good as any in the district. Good buildings. Good pasture once the rains come. Fences need work."

"So you raise cattle at a loss to send to the boiling-down works. Is that what you want with your life?"

Marty was ready for the onions. He paused. "Yair. This is what I want with my life. Like Pop. He sweats out the drought and ticks and red water; sometimes he makes a profit and sometimes he doesn't. He sticks with it because there's no better life than the life of a pastoralist. I want the same thing—to have my own run, prove myself, start a family, and take a place in the district where I can do some good for people, too, when my time comes."

The evening sun came pouring through the window into Marty's eyes. It set Mr. Sheldon's brocade vest ablaze.

"Your ambitions are noble. Not practical, but noble. I was once idealistic, like you. But times were easier then. A new run could succeed then. Times have changed." He dropped his voice a notch. "How about saving yourself a lot of grief? I need an overseer for a little run I picked up down on the river. Five hundred pounds a year plus expenses, for starters."

Marty stared. "Thought you doubted my ability to make decisions."

"Not at all; just testing your own confidence in yourself, and I find it refreshingly firm."

His mind sifted frantically through a thick pile of thoughts. He decided he'd analyze Sheldon's motives later. For now, he knew the final answer. "Thank you for considering me, Mr. Sheldon, but no thanks. I'll stay with what I have."

Sheldon looked at him a moment, his face expressionless. "Tell you what, lad. When you discover that it takes money as well as guts to succeed, and your dreams go crook on you, you come to me. The offer will still be open. And I'll try to help recover some of your losses. Least I can do for the son of an old friend. I have to go now, if you'll excuse me."

"Yair, surely." Marty stood up and extended his hand. "I appreciate your interest, sir. Thank you."

"Have a safe trip home, lad." Sheldon shook hands and strode away, out the door.

Marty sat down and absently popped an onion into his mouth. *Son of an old friend?* Old acquaintance, more like it. Old associate, maybe. But not an old friend. Pop didn't really enjoy Sheldon's company any more than Marty did; but when it comes to business, you put aside personal feelings. *Help recover some of your losses.* That was assuming a great deal, and none of the assumptions very positive. Why did Marty find himself bristling at what was obviously a neighborly offer, however clumsily it was presented?

He finished his dinner, dawdled over an extra cup of tea, and went out to do what he had to do—and hated to. The Fowkeses were home now, and they received him graciously. He sipped their tea, nibbled at a scone, made small talk, got the latest news and returned to the hotel, relieved that was over.

So Pearl was still down at Anakie and doing very well. Good. What puzzled Marty was why Pearl wasn't in Brisbane or Sydney by now, living in high society.

He spent two days more in Barcaldine and one in Longreach without finding a satisfactory candidate to manage Pinjarra. He spent part of one fruitless day trying to get a loan extension. Cyril Grosvenor, his banker, had once been so friendly with Pop and him both. But in these days of economic chaos, he had become very cold and distant.

Marty almost took the train down to Anakie, just to look up Pearl for old times' sake. No. They needed him at home, especially if this raider nuisance hadn't let up. He stopped by Constable Edding's office to describe the latest incident. He received in return a litany of complaint from the man: how Brisbane had transferred him out here to the far side of forever, when all he wanted was a promotion to some more responsible position in town. Marty listened politely, signed his complaint and left. He saddled up very early in the morning and headed north.

CHAPTER SIXTEEN

THE POLITICS OF TICKS

If Marty's backside never met a saddle again, it wouldn't be too soon for him. Except for the those brief train rides when his horse rode in the open stockcar in back, he'd been wearing holes in his saddle since before Cloncurry. He rode into his home dooryard late in the afternoon, weary of body and spirit.

"Uncle Marty!" Little Bohra came running across the dusty yard, and three months of weariness fled without a whisper.

Marty reached down and grabbed both tiny hands. He swung the lad up onto the front of his saddle. "You been a good boy while I was gone?"

The dark, blond-streaked head nodded vigorously.

"Think your mum would agree with you?" Marty aimed his horse for the barn, though it probably wasn't necessary.

The little brown shoulders shrugged.

Indirri stepped out of the barn door into the sun. He grinned and lifted Bohra off the saddle. "Him need fresh horse. Bohra bring him, one minute. See Jase, eh?"

What now? Marty walked off to the house, quietly looking forward to the day when Goonur could convince Indirri to master the use of pronouns.

Jase came down off the verandah step without so much as a hello. "The stock you brought down from Julia Creek was clean, right?"

"Yair."

And your pop's thousand head should be, too."

"What's up?"

"I'll show you. Let's go muster some ticky cows."

"I shouldn't have any." Ride some more—just what he needed. His backside would never be the same.

Bohra came running across the dooryard on stubby, chubby legs with Marty's big brown Waler in tow. Proudly the cherub handed the reins to Marty and stepped back while his uncle mounted. Marty reached down and ruffled the boy's hair. And he was off again, further punishing his poor innocent saddle.

They crossed a broad, treeless basin and a claypan. They rode through brigalow for hours. Scattered trees studded the barren ground, and under each tree lay a cow. Most of the cows lurched to their feet as the riders passed. Some simply watched them with huge, vacant eyes.

Marty pointed to a cluster of a dozen beasts. "That one of them?"

"The red one, yair." Jase indicated a particularly droopy looking beast with a ragged coat. "I was out this way looking for billabongs to dig into and happened to notice her."

Marty drew his horse in. "Not Pop's or mine. Too much shorthorn in her."

Jase shook a coiled rope out and rode forward. He bore his horse down upon the cow in question and with a swift flick of the wrist tossed the loop over her horns. Just that quickly Marty rode in behind her and threw his loop as she charged aside, catching up her hind feet. He loved doing this. *Splack* she was down on her side in the dust.

Marty dismounted and stood on the cow's neck. Leaning over, he probed the crook behind her front leg. "Look at her. Ticks stacked on ticks. I checked them over before we cut the deal. They'd just been dipped. This 'un's never been dipped. She's absolutely loaded." He ran his finger across the dense mass of dark sand grains behind her ears.

"Got your brand on her."

"Yair, but I didn't put it there." Marty poked at the mark on her rump. "Not my iron. Look at the uneven lines. And there where a line crossed over. Some ring artist tried hard to make it look good."

Marty remounted and stared at Jase. "Why? Why go to the trouble of . . ." And the truth dawned.

Jase nodded. "Find your raiders and you'll find the ring artist who planted tick-blown cows in your mob to infect the others."

"Bet she's bringing me red water as well as ticks."

"No bet. What I want to know is, who thinks we're so dull-witted that we wouldn't notice she isn't ours? Let's go find some more."

Until nearly nightfall, the bedraggled cow in tow, they sought out other cows with ticks. They amassed a mob of a dozen very sorry shorthorn crossbreeds before waning sunlight ended the operation. They returned home so hungry Marty was sure he could eat his saddle.

As the sun burned red on the edge of the ridge, Jase rode ahead and opened the gate to the hospital paddock. The dispirited cows plodded in without so much as flicking an ear. Jase swung the gate shut and chained it. "Good thing the sun's going down, eh, Cuz? Doesn't leave so much time for more things to go crook."

"Stone the crows." Marty stared, startled and unbelieving, into the distance. From away down the road came a small buggy drawn by a single horse, and in it a driver in derby hat. Even from this distance, a diamond flashed in the orange light. "So you think the day's as bad as it's gunner get, huh? Wrong, Jase-oh. Look who's our houseguest."

Jase appeared to have been stepped on by some huge giant's boot. He stared a moment and deliberately banged his forehead against the fencepost. "Uncle Edward."

"A beautiful young girl was well-known among all the tribes and clans for her graceful dancing. Blowing hot and dry, the North Wind saw her dance and fell in love. He tried to carry her away, but two lake spirits heard her distress and saved her by turning her into a brolga. Today still, the brolga likes to be near lakes. And she dances beautifully."

The brolgas were dancing now. Out on dry, treeless flats a quarter mile away, because there was no lake, a loose company of the stately gray cranes leaped and bobbed. They stamped. They flapped. They dipped their heads forward and arched them back, the long beaks slashing skyward. What exuberance! As Goonur completed her translation of his tale, Indirri watched the dance and smiled, enjoying their unbridled enthusiasm for life.

He felt that same enthusiasm here in Marty and Jase. They weren't dancing, of course, like brolgas. Their enthusiasm was an inner thing, expressed neither in words nor actions. Yet it was there, this joy of living, and it emerged whenever they talked about Pinjarra.

Jase and Marty turned their horses aside and headed home. Indirri did, too. Goonur rode up beside him. The old white mare that hated being separated from Goonur's gelding fell in behind, with Bohra perched on her back. Indirri watched three-year-old Bohra ride with mixed feelings. She was a gentle horse, true, and one that would not likely stray. Still . . .

They copped the rise and rode abreast down into the dooryard of Pinjarra. From this gentle ridge, the land sloped gracefully into a shallow basin and on out flat to the east. The buildings whitefellers treasure so highly sprawled out across the basin in wide variety. There was the elegant main house with its verandahs, some old and some new. A roof on posts connected it with a summer kitchen in back.

Across the dooryard to the north loomed a two-story barn, a monstrous structure. To the east under a large roof were parked drays and wagons. To the southeast behind the house were sheds and lean-to's, Luke's old hut still flattened on the ground.

The five of them rode up to the front door of the main house. Marty swung down and handed his horse off to Bohra. The child beamed.

As Jase turned his roan over to Indirri, Uncle Edward came storming out the door. "Where've you bludgers been?

You're supposed to be tending to business, not wandering through the bush like a flock of galahs." He lowered his blustering voice. "I told you to get rid of those cattle you found. Instead, you go out picking rosebuds, and not attending to business. Now you're gunner wish you had listened to me. You've a man to see you, Marty. Constable Edding."

The exuberance Indirri felt only moments before chilled instantly. Marty studied his uncle as he drew a deep breath. Whatever he would have said he swallowed unspoken. "Indirri, you come along inside. Goonur, take the horses over to the hospital paddock. Don't put them away yet." He went inside.

Indirri tried to act nonchalant as he gave his horses to Goonur. Probably he didn't fool her. For the very first time he was entering a building other than a barn. He paused before he went inside. There was no animal smell in here and no dust. It was brighter, too, for the walls were nearly all windows.

Inside here were even more walls and doors than on the outside. Beyond a door down a narrow passageway Indirri caught sight of a boxlike piece with blankets smoothed across it. That must be the bed Goonur talked about, where whitefellers sleep at night. The woodstove in the kitchen was cold. He looked up and was startled to see the house end so quickly. The flat roof of the room was so low you could almost reach up and touch it. There was no sense of sky here at all.

Here were the pieces of wooden furniture they had brought down from Elizabeth Downs, the table and the chairs. A whitefeller in a thick moustache and black wool tunic stood up at the table as they entered the room.

He nodded to Marty. "Good to see you, lad. Sorry this is business."

Marty reached across the table to shake hands. "I'm not. You saved me a trip to town—I wanted to talk to you about business, too. Glad you came. Sit down."

Marty, Uncle Edward and Jase folded themselves upon chairs across from Constable Edding. Indirri had never sat on a chair before and he had no intention of doing so now.

He stood aside, his back to a cool plaster wall, crossed his arms, and watched.

Uncle Edward's voice rang loudly in the confining space. Insides of houses do strange things to sound. "Constable Edding here is accusing you of cattle duffing, lad. I told him how preposterous that is, but he thinks it's—"

Constable Edding interrupted him. "Mr. Frobel, I've your complete statement here in my notes. Now I must get Marty's statement independently of yours. Standard drill."

"Well, certainly. He's the one found those scraggly strays."

Marty sighed. "He means, Uncle Edward, you should wait outside."

"Nonsense. I'm twice your age and I know about these things."

Jase leaped to his feet. "Uncle Edward, Constable Edding's teacup is empty. Why don't you go make some more."

"That's that black girl's job. Just tell her to—"

Jase gripped Uncle Edward's arm and bodily lifted him out of his chair, and his face was not kind. "Come with me." He guided his uncle toward the door. "While you're helping Rosella make tea, I'm sure you'll notice she isn't a girl. She's a lady your age, and a dignified one." And out the door went Uncle Edward, protesting forcefully.

Marty tried to hide a grin behind his hand and couldn't do it. His eyes crinkled up into telltale creases when he smiled.

The constable frowned. "I'll get hard on to it, Marty. An anonymous tip says some missing cattle are in your paddock where they shouldn't be."

"How anonymous? A note under your door or someone you know?"

"Someone I know."

"You've been through the place here looking, eh?"

"Quick check. I'd like to look around a little more."

"Good, 'cause I want to show you some things." Marty stood up. "Start with the hospital paddock. Uncle Edward's back in the summer kitchen, so let's go out the front door." He led the way. Indirri was powerfully glad to get out of the heavy air in that enclosed space. They strode out across the open, inviting dooryard with the sky stretching forever upward. He jogged along beside Jase.

"Mr. Edding, who besides Cyrus Bickett runs shorthorns?"

"Most people. Manning, Ward, Sealy, Sheldon, Fairburn, Hopkins. That's just the runs south of here with purebred. You get into crossbreeds and anything north of your father's run, you find most everybody does."

"And everybody with tick problems and red water."

"Just about. Inclusive. What you getting at, lad?"

Marty climbed onto the top rail of the hospital paddock and waved a hand. "They've got shorthorn in them and they're not ours."

The constable peered over the rail. "You admit you put your brand on cattle that aren't yours?"

"Not at all, sir. I tried to find any mark on these that would tell me where they're from. Nothing. Clean skin until they were ringmarked."

"That's nonsense, lad. No ring artist would put someone else's brand on a stray cow."

"And no squatter would brand a cow with a makeshift iron when his proper branding irons are a hundred yards away over there. Here's the mob, there's my irons. Goonur. Go run me that red one up into the squeeze pen."

She hurried to her horse. Goonur loved riding even more than Indirri did, if that were possible. Indirri opened the gate and she rode inside. He hopped back up on the rail to watch.

With a practiced flick of her whip she separated the red cow from the mob cowering in a corner and chased it through a small gate. Indirri wouldn't have had the slightest notion how to proceed, but Goonur knew exactly what to do. Jase pulled a long iron stick as Goonur slammed the gate shut from horseback. The cow bawled once and accepted the indignity of being squeezed inside the narrow pen.

Marty and the constable walked over to the confined cow; Indirri followed. The constable gazed up close at the cow's disputed brand mark.

Marty reached through the slats. "Look at her. Wasted. Fevered. Sick enough to die of red water. And the ticks. Pop built himself a dip just before he sent me his thousand head, and the mob I brought down from Julia Creek were dipped before we left. Help me find out whose these are, and we'll know who's behind the harassment out here. It's a moral certainty they're one and the same."

"Or else my informant is correct and you're picking up a few extra head here and there to round out your fine new mob. Perhaps covering up with false tales of raiders." He shook his head. "You buy stock and pay cash on your lease and no real source of money. The evidence is against you."

"Now wait a minute!" Jase exploded. "Some of that money's mine, drafted off the bank in Opalton. You can't say that."

Marty looked perplexed. "Who's been talking to you like that? Nobody local. Everyone around here has known me my whole life, and Pop before me."

"I'm sorry, lad." Constable Edding rubbed his chin a moment. "Based on your uncle's statement, plus this stock in your paddock . . ."

"My uncle's statement! He wasn't even here."

" . . . plus this stock, I'm arresting you in the name of the Crown for cattle duffing. Since you freely admit the stock in question isn't yours, and you're cooperative, I'm sure the magistrate will release you on your own cognizance pending a court date. And I'm gunner take these beasts with me as evidence."

"Mr. Edding . . ." Frustrated, Marty waved a hand helplessly.

Jase stepped in close. "We appreciate the favor: nice of you to take a dozen tick-blown, dying cattle off our hands so we don't have to feed them hay at twenty-two the ton. Got a pencil and paper handy?"

The constable gave him a small stick and a scrap of something thin.

Jase rubbed the stick on the paper and handed them both back to Edding. "This is my lawyer, up in Jericho. When these cows die—and most of them will—you're to deliver the rawhides to him. We'll want them to prove the brands aren't our work. Need a hand droving?"

"I think I can handle my prisoner and a mob of twelve by myself. You can put your statement to writing in town, lad.

"You, young James, had better tell your lawyer what's going on." The constable climbed aboard his horse with its fancy flat saddle and black saddle cloth.

Jase swung the paddock gate open wide. The constable entered, and with a couple whistles and hoots drove the dozen sorry cows out into the dooryard. He was forgetting the cow in the squeeze pen; Indirri poked Jase's arm and pointed. Jase hissed "Sssh!"

From the verandah, Uncle Edward came boiling out across the dooryard, teapot in hand. "What's happening? What's going on?"

"Your nephew's under arrest for—"

"Oh no he's not!" Uncle Edward summarily dropped the teapot. It broke in two, spewing tea. Fumbling in his pocket, he yanked out a short, heavy gun weapon. "Stand aside, sir! I knew this would happen if I weren't present. You'll not commit this gross miscarriage of justice while I still breathe." He waggled the weapon. "Stand aside, I say!" He took a dozen steps forward.

Quietly Jase took Goonur's bullwhip in hand. It lashed out suddenly, snaked around Uncle Edward's arm and jerked it downward. The gun roared aimlessly, sending the cattle bolting away down the track, their tails stiff.

The constable whipped out a set of metal rings and slapped them on Marty's wrists. "Sorry, lad, no release. Resisting arrest demands mandatory incarceration."

Jase exploded, "But it wasn't him! It wasn't him who—"

The wild flurry of arguments that followed came to no avail. The constable and his prisoner clattered away down the road in pursuit of the runaway evidence.

Uncle Edward turned on Jase. "How dare you . . ."

Jase ignored it. He wheeled. "Goonur. Turn that sick cow loose."

She ran back inside, shoved the iron bar up and swatted

the bony rump. Freed of her restraints the cow lurched forward and out into the paddock, looking confused.

Jase locked his dark eyes onto Indirri's. "You're still wild enough to track a flying bird. I want you to study this cow's trail so that you can return to where we found her—backtrack her clear across the continent if need be. Understand?"

Indirri had no notion how far a continent might extend, but he got the general idea. He also saw an opportunity. "I track him like; him take care of Mungkala all day every day." And he tested out a word whitefellers often used. "Deal?"

"You track I like, and I'll take care of Mungkala. Deal."

Jase shook hands with him—a strictly whitefeller gesture—and swung aboard his horse. He dropped a loop over the cow's horns and dragged her out into the dooryard, then walked her, jogged her.

Indirri dropped to his knees in the dirt and bent low. He studied the marks of each cloven hoof in turn. He studied the way they occurred together, both at the walk and at the jog. He studied the exact angle with which the cow put her feet down and the slight scuffs she made as she picked them up. He stood up, held Jase's eye with his own and nodded.

Jase smiled. "Go get 'em."

Indirri understood the challenge, understood that far more than pride of accomplishment hinged on his skills—skills he had not used for a long time. He threw aside the hat. He pulled off the tight, hot boots. He took off his whitefeller shirt and pants. He put behind him the ways whitefellers called "civilized" and set his face toward the ways he knew best. Following the tracks this cow had made six days ago coming in, he set out east from the station.

By and by, Jase caught up. He brought with him two full neck bags of water and a big bag of tucker, food for two days at least. He rode his roan and led a saddled horse for Indirri. He brought the old cow along still on the end of his rope.

This leg of the track was easy. The sickest of the mob, she had trailed at the back; her spoor lay on top of the others. He didn't even have to stoop over yet. With an easy stride Indirri backtracked her to a broad scuff in the dirt.

He pointed. "There him fall down ropes. You and Marty."

Jase cooed in admiration.

"Now comes harder." Indirri rested his eyes a few minutes and set out through the dry, open woodland. Here the cow browsed, and he could tell what she ate. Not much. "Here she him lie down night. See? Possum tracks cross. Possums only at night."

Because the cow lay under trees so much, Indirri tracked her through three days' roaming in just a short time.

"Was she as sick then as she is now?" Jase asked.

"Yair. Passing red water. Very . . . very . . . not strong. Week. No. Him is seven days . . ."

"Weak. That's right."

Indirri wagged his head. Whitefeller yabba.

When darkness robbed him of his sight, they made camp. At first light he was on the way again. Blackfellers don't bother much with breakfast.

Whitefellers do. No matter. Because Indirri was tracking the cow's aimless wandering, he was still within half a mile of their camp when Jase ate a morning meal and rolled up their swags to join him.

The track changed. "No more walkabout. Here him horseman. See? Horses, extra heavy. Mob now, come straight from south."

"How many in the mob?"

That took some sorting. Indirri counted off the fingers of both hands and two more. "She still in back. Easy track now."

"How many horsemen?"

"Three."

They tried turning the cow loose, hoping she'd head for home, wherever home was. She stood there. They took her under tow again.

During the heat of midafternoon the cow fell over groaning. Jase put a bullet through her head. They skinned her. Neither horse liked carrying the hide.

Now, what was this beside a thorn bush? Cautiously Indirri picked up a wad of black hair with strings in it, all stinking with whitefeller sweat. He frowned and handed it to Jase.

Jase crowed, "I don't believe it!" With a happy grin he hung the strings over his ears—a big, thick, black whitefeller beard!

Darkness. Camp. First light. On the way. Indirri would jog a couple miles, then walk to rest the sweaty horses behind him. He had not felt this free, this much at home, for years. His soul sang in harmony with earth and sky.

In the far distance, the railway traced a thin dark line to echo the flat horizon. The mob angled more toward the southeast. Just north of the railway the cattle tracks churned to a confused halt. The mob had been ringed here, held in place. Indirri ranged out and circled the mess. Here, exactly here, was where his cow entered the churned area.

He pointed. "Him jump down train here. All mob jump down."

"Jump down? Or unload down a ramp?" Jase gestured with both hands. "A ramp; a wide board from the railway car to the ground."

Indirri double-checked his first analysis. "Jump. Very jump. No board. No marks. Him jump down. See—feet cut deep."

Jase slumped a bit in his saddle. "Now what? No tracking the train." He brightened momentarily. "Kind of a pun there. The beard's a nice bit for us, but not for the judge. It's in our possession, so the prosecution will only say we invented it. End of track."

Discouraged, Indirri sat down in the burning dust of midday. For all his bush skills, he had failed.

CHAPTER SEVENTEEN

THE OWNER OF THOSE COWS

Indirri observed closely the blackfeller across the street. The man was sitting very loosely, his legs sprawled, on a bench under the verandah of a large building. Indirri eased himself onto the bench, as he had seen Marty do, under a verandah on this side of the street. With a forced casualness, he arranged his legs just so and crossed his arms.

His casual exterior belied a most nervous and uncertain interior. Town. Indirri had on occasion viewed a town from afar—*much* afar—but this was the first he had ever actually been in one. He didn't liked it a bit. Buildings like towering cliffs, bigger even than the barn on Pinjarra, crowded in on all sides. The trees grew much taller than usual. Noises and smells, penned in like Indirri himself, collected in one place or another. Town had all the stuff Indirri recognized as normal, and yet nothing was actually, truly normal here.

The blackfeller across the street tipped a bottle up and drank heavily. Indirri had no bottle. He sat still, concerned that perhaps he would be identified as a Munjong because he had no bottle. Time passed. The feller across the street took another drink and started to sit up. As Indirri watched, slowly, majestically, the blackfeller tipped off balance and rolled off the bench quite literally onto his ear. He curled up where he fell, as a weary child would do, and after a few snuffling adjustments, went to sleep.

Indirri suddenly realized his mistake. He had sat in the middle of the bench; that feller sat on the end. It was easy for the blackfeller to roll off, sitting on the end. Moving slowly, ever so naturally, so as to avoid notice, Indirri wormed his way a bit at a time down toward the end of the bench so that he could roll off similarly. He hoped no one was noticing his error. Several times over, he rehearsed his movements with the pictures in his mind that he might get the complex maneuver right the first time. Obviously, getting off one of these benches takes excellent coordination and a bit of practice.

Whup. Jase flopped down beside him. Jase sat smack in the middle of the bench, so apparently he wasn't intending to get off very soon. "How's your clothes fit?"

"Good-oh! Much easy wear these. More than other whitefeller clothes at Pinjarra. What name him give me clothes?"

"St. Vincent de Paul."

"Ah. Yair."

"When you backtracked that cow, you could tell night from day, right? Most of the time."

"Night, one day, night, next day?"

"Yair. Let's say you got it right within two days. So by counting back I calculated when the train stopped to drop those cattle off, plus or minus two days. Came in here and talked to the stationmaster. Bingo!" He grinned and waved a thin white bark strip. "Here's a copy of the bill of lading for a dozen cattle, loaded at Alpha just down the road. You got the day exactly right. And the stationmaster remembered which engineer. He's on the train today, so now we go over to the railway station and talk to him. Ever been around a railway train up close?"

"Naw. Him don' need it."

Jase laughed. "Well, him needs it now. Come along." And he sprang to his feet, smoothly and quickly.

Should Indirri get off the bench like a blackfeller, or like a whitefeller? Perplexing.

"Come on, will you?"

The blackfeller's intent was to take a nap, and Indirri's was to walk away. Hoping that intent rather than race determined one's actions, Indirri stood up. He glanced around quickly. No one noticed, no one commented. He hurried down the street after Jase.

A dozen whitefellers and a few blacks lolled about the station platform, strolling up and down or sitting on benches. Indirri avoided benches; too many decisions. Jase leaned against the building, so Indirri leaned beside him.

Jase looked casual enough, as he always looked, with a touch of the larrikin about him. But Indirri could sense in the young man an intensity, an urgency. There was a faint smell of anger in him, too.

Here it came. Indirri steeled himself. He told himself there was nothing to fear. Look at all these people—not the least scent of fear in any of them. He arranged his body similarly to Jase's and froze himself deliberately in place.

No amount of preparation equipped him for the enormity of this terrifying monster. Big as a house, black as a starless night, it loomed greater and greater until it filled earth and sky before him. It attacked all his senses at once; smoke and hot iron assailed his nose and his taste, unimaginable shrieking and clanging sounds deafened him, the heat of its great belly roasted him as would a giant fire. Its multifarious parts churned and spewed smoke both black and white from half a dozen places.

Jase turned to him and smirked. "Not bad, Indirri. I wouldn't guess you felt afraid at all, except your eyes are this big and you're covered in a cold sweat. Wanna wait here?"

"Good-oh." His voice croaked.

Jase sauntered over to the thing. He stepped right up to it, close enough to touch. He talked to a whitefeller inside it who stood in an open box with a window. They shook hands before Jase climbed into the monster beside the whitefeller. He leaned against the inside of it talking and nodding. He gave a piece of the white bark to the man. The feller spent time looking at it and doing something with it. By and by they shook hands again and Jase hopped down. He strolled back to Indirri, not in the least anxious to get away from the beast.

Jase laughed, and a bit of the intensity had relaxed. He

headed down into the town again and Indirri stayed close at his side. "We got it, Indirri! The reef. The mother lode. The engineer wrote me a statement here that he unloaded the stock out in the bush just this side of Ilfracombe—exactly where you tracked them to. Met by three riders who drove them north."

"Him know three man, him see him?"

"Nope. Didn't recognize them, but we don't need that. We have the name of the shipper on the bill of lading here. Now we know who those ticky cows belong to."

They continued past the bench of Indirri's recent experience. The blackfeller across the way was still asleep. They continued down to the Commercial Hotel paddock to their horses.

Jase tightened his horse's saddle girth. "Got another job for you, Indirri, but you hafta keep your clothes on for this one. Know that fake beard you found?"

Indirri swung up into his saddle. "Yair."

"Want you to pick me out the gent that wore it. We're gunner start looking with a visit to Ross Sheldon's southside camp. He just happens to keep three drovers there."

They rode half a day at a rather rapid pace. The intensity returned in Jase—in his voice and in his actions. They passed very sorry-looking sheep and even worse-looking cattle. The grass and bush here were in far worse shape than the forage on Pinjarra. Cattle and sheep had gnawed the grass down into the roots and stripped branches off trees. Not even a wallaby would find a good meal here anymore.

"Over there." Jase drew his horse in and pointed to a stringybark hut beside a small paddock, where three men sat on stovewood spools around a flat surface, playing at cards. His snapping black eyes met Indirri's. "Now, remember the drill? What you're supposed to say?"

"Yair."

"And remember you have to be certain. You sniff the gents over. If you can't get a clear match—a definite yes—we'll go look elsewhere. Understand?"

As Jase pulled that wad of black hair out of his saddlebag,

Indirri uncorked his waterbag. He splashed water up into his nose and snorted a few times. Jase handed the beard across. Indirri buried his face in it, inhaled both with mouth open and mouth closed, memorizing the nuance of odor. He handed it back, nodding, and Jase put it away.

Jase grimaced. He unsnapped the cover on his holster and loosened the gun there. "Let's give it a burl."

They rode forward into the camp. The three men stood up, watching Jase and Indirri as the station cat watches mice in the hayloft. With a friendly smile Jase introduced himself. The three men mentioned their names. Indirri smelled fear and anger here.

Jase's voice cooed like a pigeon's. "Now this sounds silly as a goose at a tea party, but I'm hoping you gents will do me a big favor. I have a bet on with some bludgers down in Ilfracombe that Indirri here can tell what station a bloke works for just by the smell of him. Would you be so kind as to let Indirri take a whiff of you?" His hand rested easily on his holster.

They looked at each other. They looked at Indirri. They looked at Jase. "Yair," said one of them cautiously. "Why not?"

Jase nodded. Indirri stepped up to the closest, a pot-bellied fellow, and sniffed around the man's neck and ear. No.

He tried the second, a man with a jagged white scar above his right eye. Yes. This was the one who had worn the beard.

He sniffed the third. No. He stepped back. As they had rehearsed, he announced, "Sheldon man, all three."

Jase cocked his head. "That true? You Ross Sheldon's stockmen?"

"Yair. He can really do that by smelling?"

Jase shrugged. "The straight oil. Never woulda guessed it myself. Looks like I'm losing a bet." he backed up. "Well, ta, gentlemen."

They rode away with one eye out behind, so to speak.

She owned this. She owned all this. Pearl looked out her

office window, across from the hotel on the corner. It would be hers in February if she decided to close the deal. Next to it stood the general store. She owned that, too, now. The laundry had generated enough money to buy the restaurant, which had in turn produced the capital to purchase the general store—where once she had purchased flatirons on account because she didn't have enough money to pay cash. The sunlight danced on the fruits of her ambition.

She turned her attention back to the mail on her desk. A few bills. A carefully lettered envelope from a gentleman—probably a marriage proposal. A letter from Mum. She laid her hand on the little pile of envelopes. Here in a microcosm was her whole life: bills, a man she didn't know asking for something she didn't want, and word from a person she'd been distancing herself from. What an empty mailbox.

Knuckles rapped on the office door. It swung open. "Your tea, mum. The scone is fresh." With quick, slim fingers, Louise set up tea on the corner of Pearl's desk. Louise was perhaps twenty-five at most—just a very few years younger than Pearl herself—but how old she acted and sounded! Elderly dowagers were not so cold and reserved as this tall, skinny, somber girl. "Will that be all, mum?"

"Thank you."

Louise curtsied and swept out on silent feet.

Suddenly tea held no interest at all. Pearl stood up and watched at the window a few moments. She stuffed the unopened mail in her bag, plucked her hat off the rack and adjusted it on the way out.

Where was she going? She knew exactly where, even as she pretended to be strolling at random in Anakie's dusty streets. Anakie had been in decline for some time now, but until recently the decline had been subtle. Nothing subtle about it now. Buildings stood vacant. Collapsed tents lay abandoned in vacant lots. She owned the store because she was the only one who would buy it from the retiring proprietor. It would supply her other investments at wholesale, even if its over-the-counter sales dropped. She held option on the hotel for the same reason: she was the only one interested in its purchase. On the surface, Anakie did not appear to be the best of investments.

Pearl smiled to herself. Phooey on appearances. The laundry was still turning a quid for her, the restaurant with its reputation as the best eatery around was doing very well, and the general store was the only place in Anakie selling mining tools and hardware. For every miner and gem seeker going under, two others came pouring in to try their luck. And they all needed supplies.

She came out into the wide railway yard and walked the length of the platform. Her feet had not crossed these boards since she set Luke Vinson on his way to Mossman to tilt at windmills.

Here was that shed where Enid had lain and she had sat that terrible day. She had little dreamed that she would ever know God as Enid did. Well, she still didn't, exactly. Enid had walked hand in hand with Him. Pearl always walked ten paces behind, it seemed.

Marty. He had been there, too, on that day. How was he doing? She thought about his chocolate eyes, and those strong shoulders that had once shielded her from harm. Now *there* was a man. No posturing, no false boasting, no need to prove anything. She smiled at his memory.

She sat down on the bench beside the ticket office. She could purchase a ticket to Brisbane this very moment if she wished. She could purchase the whole train, probably. She remembered the fire that once burned in her heart, the desire to travel to the city and marry well. So long ago, that was. Without Enid to share it the dream simply faded to nothing. Gone.

Now here she sat, a spinster—a wealthy spinster, the object of many men's affections and proposals. And propositions. If you have taste and scruples, it's very lonely being a good-looking woman in a mining town.

The shed. Enid had asked another thing of Pearl besides her accepting Jesus as her Savior. A list. Enid had wanted Pearl to keep track of all the good things that had come out of that tragedy. Until this moment, Pearl had forgotten Enid's list.

She pulled the letters out of her bag. She opened Mum's, scanned its three pages and folded it up. Every letter from Mum was the same. She let her hands fall in her lap. Then she riffled through her bag, produced a pencil and began to write on the back of the envelope.

What good things had come of Enid's travail? *Pete Sark.* That reprobate was now the Rev. Peter Sark, serving well and joyously. Considering what the man used to be, that alone might be looked upon as a miracle of sorts. *Robert Riley,* ambassador for Christ, without portfolio. He still stuttered, and since the accident his arm hadn't worked right, but every Sunday he held Bible school for the ragamuffins living in the area. He loved children and they loved him, and every week he preached Jesus to them.

The *Enid Fowkes Library.* Nearly every man (and most of the women, including the shady ones) felt the urge to give money for something, somehow, in Enid's name. Anakie would never have obtained its extensive four-room library any other way. It was now patronized respectfully and constantly by lonely men from the mines.

Most of the people here in town who had known Enid still went to church. A surprising number of them loudly proclaimed Jesus as Savior to anyone who would listen. Large numbers of people, though, had since moved on to other places. Pearl had no idea where they were or what they were doing. She wrote *Fruit, in and out of season* on the list.

Anakie had a doctor now who had saved a number of lives over the years. The miners wouldn't have united in their efforts to obtain medical service, and then supported it by subscription, had Enid not died for lack of it. *Effective medical aid.*

She paused. To these people, the educated and the uneducated, Enid had represented Jesus Christ.

The train was due soon, for here came the paper boy hawking the latest news. He always hit the platform around train time. The lad presented her with a choice: she could continue to reflect upon the past or she could escape into the trivia of the present.

"Here, lad." Her smallest coin was a shilling. "Keep the change."

She snapped the paper open. On the front page they were still arguing over whether to install sewer lines by the creek. Disposition of cases recently on the docket filled most of page two. The constable's report took a very small column. Even crime was in decline. On page three—

Page three shouted at her. The memories of the past united in a feverish dance with the headline today. She hopped to her feet and marched quickly to the ticket window.

CHAPTER EIGHTEEN

THE RESCUE OF A DREAM

Longreach was a nice enough town, Marty mused, sprawled across the flats beside the dry bed misnamed the Thomson River. Somehow, it lacked the atmosphere of Barcaldine, though. The unpretentious cow town was simple, practical, good for a laugh on Saturday night. By contrast, Barcaldine was entertaining in its very puffery as it strove with its population of two thousand to be the Melbourne of the north. Looking back, Barcaldine lay claim to history with its shearers' strike of '91. Looking forward, it courted new businesses and public service facilities. Barcaldine's deep artesian bores made it the Garden City, the cultural center of the outback.

Marty was stuck here in Longreach—for a long time to come, considering how high his bail was set. Either the judge or the constable was in somebody's pocket. Outside his barred window, a chattering flock of honeyeaters attacked the berries on a gum tree, free as birds. Inside this encompassing little cell, the hot air hung close and still. Confined. Confining.

"Martin Frobel Junior, cattle theft?"

Marty sat up on his pallet and looked toward the tiny barred window in the door. "There's two people in this jail right now, and the town drunk's the other one. You have to ask who I am?"

"According to the law, when addressing a prisoner I must confirm his identity and the charges against him. I operate by the law. You have a visitor." Constable Edding, for all his freedom, was bound by bars and chains more cumbersome than Marty's.

Marty stood up. He knew who the visitor was. Jase. And he knew the news Jase was bringing: Pinjarra existed no longer. His dream had withered on the vine. Back to digging, or droving, or perhaps a future of begging in the streets. But Jase's ever-cheery face did not appear at the window. Instead, the door clanked, scraped and opened. "Bring your hat, Mr. Frobel."

My hat?

In blind obedience, Marty stepped into the dismal passageway and preceded the constable through the cellblock door from gloom into brightness. Then he stopped so suddenly the constable ran into him.

She rose from the bench by the door, and the broadest, loveliest smile graced her pretty face. She crossed to him, extending a hand. "Mr. Frobel."

"Miss Fowkes." He could do no less than take that graceful hand in his and kiss its soft, white knuckles. This was definitely not the hand of a washerwoman. "Despite the circumstances, I'm delighted. Overwhelmed. You look beautiful."

"And you look absolutely terrible. Four days' growth does nothing for those handsome, weatherworn cheeks of yours."

"The constable was afraid I'd fling shaving cream in his eye."

Constable Edding actually started to protest, so slow was he to catch the joke. Abashed, he marched to his desk to leaf through paperwork.

"Ah! Here's the lad." Pearl turned as a boy in knickers came hustling through the door with a fistful of papers. He glanced at Marty and looked a bit disappointed. Apparently Marty didn't appear quite as dangerous as a felon ought. The court page laid the papers before the constable and stepped aside, his big brown eyes ever on Marty.

"Miss Fowkes, you sign here and here. Mr. Frobel, there. Also these copies. Miss Fowkes, you understand the responsibility you're assuming if he fails to appear in court. I believe you are aware he resisted arrest."

"Yes, and I can hardly wait to hear about that." With a

flourish she struck an ornate *Pearl Annalee Fowkes* across first one, then another official-looking form.

Someone better read these papers first. Marty scanned the sheets as she passed them to him. He stared at her. "Pearl, do you realize how much my bail is? You can't afford this!"

She straightened and drew herself to full height. Her eyes came just to his nose, but somehow she seemed as tall as he. "Martin Frobel, don't you presume to tell me what I can and cannot afford. For years I've . . ." She drew a deep breath. "I'll explain later." She blipped the tip of his nose with her finger. "For now, just assume you're worth it. Sign them." And she stuffed the final form into his hand.

Marty signed.

He stood erect. Now what? For the first time since he had stepped out from under Mum's roof, a woman was calling the shots. He felt uncomfortable with it. Constable Edding handed him a slip of paper, a permit releasing his horse from the police department stable. The august officer launched into the final duty, reciting by rote a litany of do's and don'ts for prisoners out on bail. Marty wasn't really listening. It was mostly common sense anyway. He was trying to sort this confusion out, and nothing was falling into place.

With a clap, Pearl rubbed her hands. "You're a free man. I've hired a buggy and bought a picnic supper. As soon as we've stopped by the bank, let's enjoy blue skies and freedom."

"Shouldn't I shave first?"

She pondered that a moment. "I think not. You want to play on the banker's sympathy—as if he had any—and you don't want to look too spiffy. Not like a no-hoper, of course, but more like a man in dire straits."

"A man in dire straits. That won't be hard. But why do I want to impress a banker?" He held the door for her as they stepped out into the sunshine. His eyes would definitely have to get used to direct sunlight again.

"Manipulating bankers is always a good thing. I do it all the time."

He eyed the slim figure, the dark golden curls. "No worries for you—you have the tools."

They crossed Swan Street to the bank and went in the

front door. Mr. Grosvenor rose from his desk as if he had been expecting them. Marty took part in the required pleasantries, all the while watching Pearl with growing admiration as she handled this imperious financial icon. Clearly Marty was there to observe, not to negotiate.

She charmed. She baffled. She promised nothing, and yet the promise was there somehow, implicit in her very being. With a smile and a firm voice she accomplished what all Marty's trips to town had not. Half an hour later—thanks to a hefty draft on Pearl's bank—Pinjarra was safely shoved back an inch or two from the brink of ruin.

More pleasantries, more smiles, more shaking of hands, and Pearl and Marty were whisked out into the sunshine. The doors closed behind them, the end of the business day.

"What's next?" Marty squinted against the brightness and scratched an itchy shoulder. "Do I get to shave soon? A bath wouldn't be a bad idea, either. And flea powder, or maybe paris green. They should have a law in that jail against anything smaller than a rabbit."

She stepped back to study him. "No bath. I think I prefer to watch you suffer." She marched up to the corner and turned right onto Emu Street.

He fell in beside her. *All right, be that way, your Highness. Throw your weight around. You have a wad that would choke a wombat and you've decided to buy me with it—probably Pinjarra as well. And there's no way to prevent you. I'm all yours, courtesy the power of the almighty British pound sterling.*

"I need to get my horse at the police station. Where are we going?"

"We'll stop there first."

After retrieving his horse, Marty and Pearl walked down the street into Duck Street, where she veered suddenly off the curb and climbed into the seat of a dusty buggy. Marty tied his horse to the back and then untied the buggy's lackadaisical old hack, arranged the lines and hauled himself up to the seat. At least she was letting him drive. A picnic hamper sat at their feet and she gave no specific directions as to destination, so he turned the little horse off Duck Street into

Eagle Street and headed north out of town.

The exquisite heat of afternoon was just now beginning to wane. Land and sky dipped gently to the west, and beyond the dip rolled away endlessly. A patch of lacy trees here, a low rise there softened the level line between stolid earth and soaring heaven. From the roadside a mob of noisy galahs rose up, a churning cloud of gray and vivid pink.

And Marty's spirit rose with them. His heart sang as the unpleasant memories of that oppressive jail and intimidating banker gathered behind them in the dust. The sheer infinity of the land and the sky beguiled him and burst his bonds of care. He didn't even mind anymore that this beautiful woman beside him had him tightly wrapped in her purse strings.

Beautiful? Yes. Beautiful indeed. "Flash," Jase called her, and flash she was. In addition, there was a new firmness about her, a comfortable new self-confidence that Marty found most appealing.

Three miles out of town, the road climbed over a shallow ridge and swooped down through an open grove of gum trees. Marty turned the horse aside and drove back among them. He chose a huge gnarled patriarch of a gum tree primarily because of the generous shade it cast and tied the horse to a nearby sapling.

"This good enough?" He hopped down even before she replied, "Delightful." He gave her a hand out of the buggy and scooped up the picnic basket. Either there was enough food here to feed a shearing crew or she had purchased a hod of bricks by mistake.

She spread a carriage robe under the tree as he lugged the hamper over. When he had set it down, Pearl reached into the basket and began to unpack it: china dishes, a quart pot full of water and a two-cup teapot. *So that's why the thing was so heavy.* As she set out plates and food, he built a fire to boil the quart pot, but he had to ask her for matches. Felons aren't allowed to have matches in jail, lest they burn down the iron, brick and stone structure.

It was a simple supper of bread, meat, cheese and apples, topped off with fresh-steeped tea. With the rustle of gum leaves overhead and the fresh breeze of evening, the supper tasted infinitely better than jail food. They dawdled over the meal, laughing, and playing a back-and-forth game of "do you remember. . . ?"

The sun was angling low enough now that their shade would soon yank itself right out from under their picnic. Marty watched the light of evening ripen from white to gold.

With admiration he studied the interesting things the yellow sun did to those golden curls. "Why are you here?"

She considered for a moment, apparently deciding on an answer, or perhaps simply deciding on the phrasing. "Rescuing dreams."

"That doesn't tell me much. Or don't you want to let me in on your mysterious motives?"

She giggled, a bit nervously. " 'Mysterious motives.' I like that. They're so mysterious I'm not sure I know what they are. I miss Enid, Marty. I miss her so much."

"Yair. Every time something religious comes up—anything at all— she comes to mind. And you. Sometimes I think of you with no reminder at all. Those were good times, those days. Footloose. Good friends. You and Enid. You were our best friends."

"All I could think about was making money and more money so I could hit the big city in grand style. You know what? I really dreaded having to take Enid along. She was such a bother sometimes. A millstone around my neck, I thought. Suddenly she was gone and I was free of the bother. Pretty soon I had the money. But without Enid . . ." She shrugged helplessly. "She didn't figure in my plans at all. She wouldn't know how to dazzle a sophisticated city man; in fact, she probably wouldn't want to. And now I didn't want to go without her. Isn't that silly?"

"So you stayed in Anakie and made more money."

"Wasn't anything else to do. I was so empty. But I didn't know what to . . ." Her voice trailed off. She sighed. "I won't get into all that. When your friend Luke came through, I finally saw the light about Jesus Christ. I suppose I thought that would instantly cure everything. It changed things. I take part in a church service now, instead of just sitting there, and it has infinitely deeper meaning. It's fun to read the Bible, and meaningful. But it's still not the same as Enid's faith. Or your friend's."

"We haven't had contact for years. What possessed you to come today? How did you know?"

She smiled. "I saw a piece about you in the local paper. Cattle theft, falsifying complaints, I don't know what else. Jail—I read that and it hit me in the stomach as if they'd accused *me* of those things. As always, I acted first and thought about it later. I was on the train and headed this way before I worked out what was going on inside me."

"Then you're way ahead of me. I don't have a clue what's going on inside me."

"I know this much. I left for Brisbane to realize my dream—to marry well. But what's well? A man with money? I don't need one. I have my own money. A man who will take care of me? You find those all over. Big city? Nice, but it has very much lost its luster. I've come to understand this country and the people in it. You might say it's rather grown on me."

"I can't picture you being content in Anakie."

She giggled again, like music. "Neither can I." She sobered. "My mother writes frequently. Every letter's the same. She hates Barcaldine because it's so provincial. No one influential lives so far outback. Her life is so hard. She can't buy nice things. She has no friends because there are no women in such a small town that she'd want to have for a friend. She wants me to come home and live with them, as if I were still sixteen. And on and on."

"Maybe she's a city lady like you."

"That's it exactly. She yearns for the city, same as I did, and she's absolutely miserable. But you know what? When she lived in Sydney and in Brisbane she was miserable then, too. Never content, never close to anyone. Sydney or Barcaldine—it didn't make any difference."

What could he say? "I'm sorry your mum's not happy."

"She wants me to keep her company so she has a shoulder to cry on. But she's not content to seek happiness where she is. Marty, I almost became that woman myself."

He watched the earnest, lovely face a moment. "Are you answering my question? I asked why you're here."

"Yes. I'm here because I don't want to become like my mother, lonely and discontent. I don't know anyone in Brisbane anymore. If I move there I'll have to start all over building friendships and evaluating business associates. I wouldn't know whom to trust. I hate trying to figure out whom to trust.

"Then I realized something: I already have friends, who accept me just as I am. Certainly it's a dumpy little town. But it has very nice people in and around it, and one of them is in trouble. I can go off looking for friends that couldn't possibly be any nicer than the ones I already know well, or I can help an old and valued friend out when he needs it."

He stared at her the longest time. She was not at all the shallow Pearl he remembered, and the new depth in her amazed him. "That's very beautiful."

"It's very selfish. I'm trying desperately to avoid unhappiness."

"Aren't we all. So you're rescuing a dream. Am I a dream?"

"You're part of it because you're such a good friend. My dream is happiness, ultimately. You know what? If you hadn't gotten into trouble like this, I'd still be in Anakie wondering what to do with myself. Wondering what God wants. I might never have figured out these things about Mum and friendship and all; you never know. Your problem here has been most unpleasant for you, I realize, but it's been life-changing for me."

He watched the light play across her face. Do you kiss an old and valued friend? More important, would kissing that friend wreck the friendship? He looked into those wonderful eyes, more beautiful now than when he first saw them so many years ago. They told him very clearly: *Give it a burl, mate—it's well worth the risk.*

He kissed her softly, the barest touch of lips. She didn't back away. He kissed her properly, firmly, gently, as a beautiful woman ought to be kissed (he supposed; he had precious little experience in that arena). And he learned what he might have known all along, had he thought about it. Kissing an old and valued friend is infinitely better than dreaming the most wonderful dream in the world.

CHAPTER NINETEEN

JUST A TASTE OF SERENITY

Pearl Fowkes prided herself on her business know-how. When she bought that restaurant she had personally inspected every inch of it, including the crawl spaces. She had known the general store's exact inventory before she ever signed the papers. Now here she was—contrary to everything she knew to be wise—up to her ears in the finances of a cattle station, sight unseen.

Until this moment. And now that she laid eyes on it for the first time, she had absolutely no idea what she was looking at. Was this a superior station or a miserable one? Were the buildings commendable or deplorable? What was the standard and how did this place compare?

Marty turned slightly in the buggy seat beside her, smiling. "Welcome to Pinjarra."

"Thank you. Forgive me, but somehow I imagined a couple of stringybark shacks. This is actually quite, er, civilized. Lovely home. Big barn."

"One of the better ones. You should see Elizabeth Downs, though. There's the best of the lot." He drove up to the front door. From out by the barn a young black girl, half-caste with pretty blue eyes, came striding across the dooryard.

She grinned as she took the buggy horse's bridle. "Indirri's back; he got big good news for you! Him and Jason." She giggled. "You should hear the stories he tells 'bout town. First time in a town. And see a train . . ." She rolled her eyes in delight.

Marty laughed. "You'll have to translate them for me; his five-word vocabulary probably wouldn't do these stories justice. Where's Jase?"

"Inna house. You need your horse anymore?"

"No. You can put him up."

She nodded. Pearl expected her to leave the horse where it was, tied to the back of the buggy, and lead the buggy to the barn. No. The girl untied the horse, vaulted into the saddle and led the other horse and buggy to the barn.

Marty laid a hand on Pearl's elbow to escort her inside. "Goonur doesn't like to do anything unless it's from the back of a horse." He paused inside the front door. "Hallo!"

"What's this I hear?" A familiar voice cackled from off to the right. Jason came bounding out with red jam all over his mouth. He froze. He gaped. He stared at Pearl, at Marty, at Pearl again. What a broad, bright, irrepressible grin swept across his face! Pearl saw right here the value of sticking with old friends. She was welcomed and loved and cared about. Jase didn't bother with formal handshakes or elegant pleasantries. He scooped her up into a rambunctious hug. "What a glory you are, Miss Fowkes! More beautiful every time I see you!"

He turned to Marty and pumped his hand exuberantly. "Beaut! Now tell me, who's bringing who here?"

"I brought her, and she bought me." Marty swiped a finger across Jason's sticky cheek and licked it. "Raspberry. Where'd you get raspberry?"

"Your mum sent it down. She and your pop are on their way shortly. Come on! Indirri and I are raiding the bread and jam to keep us going till dinner." He led the way through the far door.

A guest would be entertained in the parlor. Pearl was immediately ushered into the kitchen, like a member of the family. That pleased her immensely. Marty held her chair. She settled into it and removed her hat. The slim young black Marty introduced as Indirri nodded cheerfully to her and went directly back to work on a big chunk of bread and jam.

"Rosella in the summer kitchen?" Marty asked. "How about some tea?"

"Yair!" Indirri hopped up. He paused. "Much glad him home again, Marty!" A score of white teeth, all outlined in red jam, flashed in a happy smile. He disappeared out back.

Jason grinned smugly. "Indirri there tracked our sorry red cow clear down to the railroad. Amazing piece of work! Then we went into town and I turned detective. Had a glorious time!" The smile turned grim. "Your ticky cattle were shipped from Alpha personally by Mr. Ross Sheldon. The engineer remembers what a scraggly bunch they were; couldn't understand why someone would pay good money to move them that short distance when they weren't worth the freight cost. I mailed our lawyer the engineer's written statement. Incidentally, the dates match exactly with Indirri's tracking."

"Ross Sheldon." Marty closed his eyes briefly. "Great piece of work, Jase."

"I'm not done. On the way Indirri came across a fake beard. Big black beard. It definitely belongs to Harry Bagley, the guy with the scar over his eye. At the moment he's one of three monkey-dodgers working Sheldon's southside camp."

"You're sure?"

"Got it on the best authority. Indirri's nose." Jason raised a finger. "I'm still not done. That Albert Samson you hired with all the beaut references? Forged. He was a manager on one of Sheldon's holdings on the Thomson. Sheldon planted him."

"Sheldon!" Pearl looked from face to face. "Why would he do these things? We're talking about terrible things. Illegal. Immoral."

"Yair." Marty looked at Jason. "Why?"

"Pick up this run cheap, is one good guess. Or at the very least, run his stock onto it and then say, 'Oops—the fence musta broke.' His is so overgrazed and so underwatered that his stock are dropping right and left. He needs this land, needs it bad; I might even say he needs it just to stay in business.

"Politics would be my other guess. Your pop and you have Bickett and the others behind you. You're the major barriers between him and his march to the prime minister's seat—or whatever ambitions he has. If he can damage your pop's reputation by ruining yours, that's two ducks down, and he's got one foot in the door at Brisbane already."

Marty leaned both elbows on the table. "You say Pop's on his way?"

"Soon's he clears up some odds and ends at the Downs."

Indirri came flowing like water through the door with a pot of tea. The man was extraordinarily graceful.

"He's gotta know about this. Sheldon's on his hammer, too, it looks like."

"Yair." Jason jabbed Indirri's arm. "You know what a holiday is?"

"Naw."

"Walkabout, no work. You earned yourself a bonzer day off. How about you take Goonur and your boy and a dilly bag full of tucker and go enjoy the country awhile? Ask Goonur to explain a day off. Come back by and by?"

The black face shone. "Good-oh. Take Goonur, take lad out, tell him about honey-ant people. Honey ant him clan Goonur side."

"Yair. Don't forget. Take lotsa tucker."

The black eyes twinkled. "This maybe? Goonur, lad, him much like." He hefted the jam jar.

Marty laughed and his rich baritone rumbled. "Sure, why not?"

Indirri disappeared like smoke on the wind.

They finished their tea presently, amid the happy chatter of friends too long apart. Then they moved to the verandah, where it was much cooler and breezier. Pearl might not know a good station from a bad one, but she could certainly tell a pleasant view when she saw it. She settled into the wicker chair offered her and gazed out beyond the dooryard to a gently sloping tree-studded ridge.

Jason sprawled by the verandah step and leaned back against the roof post. He closed his eyes, a contented man.

Marty scrunched down on his spine in the pine chair beside Pearl's and stretched his feet out. "I can't tell you how good it is to be here. Pearl, I can't thank you enough."

"Thanks are unnecessary, now that I've seen Pinjarra. I can understand your love for it, at least a little." She let the peace and beauty of the place drain the tension from her body. Serenity is potent medicine.

Out across the dooryard, Indirri and the half-caste girl waved enthusiastically. They each carried weapons and large dilly bags. A small child gamboled at their side. With long, flowing strides they walked up the hill and disappeared into the trees.

"So he could smell that beard and tell who wore it," Marty mused. "You know, he's getting so civilized he's not going to be able to do that sort of thing much longer."

"I'm not so sure." Jason opened his eyes. "He's never gunner be just another station black. Even when he's scared spitless, you can see dignity in him. I think there's a lot going on in that head we'll never know about."

"That's a moral certainty, unless his English improves considerably."

"Now what's this?" Jason sat up, squinting. His hand darted to his holster; Pearl heard the snap click open.

She looked down the track toward the south. A brilliant waistcoat seized her eye. Ross Sheldon.

Two men accompanied the squatter: Mr. Edding the constable and a rough-looking stockman. They came riding up to the door in a choking cloud of dust. The stockman and constable remained astride their horses. Mr. Sheldon dismounted.

The constable removed his hat and bowed from the saddle. "G'day, Miss Fowkes. Mr. Frobel, this is Mr. Harry Bagley, an experienced stockman who is assisting me. Standard procedure requires that I check for strange cattle now that you're free on bail. I'll just take a turn around."

"Rubbish!" Pearl snorted. She remembered Jason mentioning a scar over the eye. This Harry Bagley had one.

Her outspokenness startled Constable Edding. He collected himself and he and Bagley rode off toward the barns and paddocks.

Mr. Sheldon extended a hand to Marty. "Marty!"

Marty made no move to shake. "Sheldon."

Jason leaned back again and casually laid his gun in his lap.

If Pearl had not seen it herself she would not have believed the transformation. Instantly Sheldon's face turned from open to black, from friendly to hard and cold. His demeanor frightened her, though she was fully accustomed to hard men.

Marty rumbled, "I hope you didn't ride clear out here for a friendly visit, 'cuz we're not feeling real friendly. You can understand why, I trust."

Sheldon glared at Jason. "I want to know who your abo is, the one you hauled out to my southside camp. I want to talk to him."

"You don't have Buckley's chance of finding him."

Had Pearl thought this place was *serene*? Nothing could be further from reality now. The tension sang like wind in telegraph wires.

Sheldon laughed suddenly, harshly. "An abo's testimony's not worth a brass razoo. You know that."

"Yes, it is." Marty drew his legs in and sat forward. "Hear this, Sheldon. Your game's out in the open. Now that we know where trouble lies, we're ready for your shenanigans. If you're smart, you'll back out of this power play right now and cut your losses."

At that moment the constable and Mr. Bagley came across the dooryard, still astride their horses. Harry Bagley shook his head at Sheldon. "The only one here who's anywhere thin enough and young enough is a scarred-up cripple who can't use his arm and leg right."

Sheldon's eyes dripped malevolence. He swung aboard his horse and reined it viciously away. They clattered off, leaving only their dust.

The tension did not lessen once its source had gone. Pearl took a deep breath and realized she'd been holding it until now. "Jason, you're the expert on enemy tactics. What would he do if he found . . . what's his name?"

"Indirri. I think when Harry reported in, Sheldon added

two and two and realized we'd backtracked him. To do that you need a good blackfeller. And if Harry noticed his beard was missing, he probably added that one up right, too. What Indirri can do and what stories he can tell hasn't got Sheldon half worried, I 'magine."

Pearl frowned. "Might Sheldon do a Herod?"

"A what?"

"You know. When Herod killed all the babies in Bethlehem just to make sure he got the one baby that posed a threat. Might Sheldon kill all the young blacks he can, just to get Indirri?"

Marty's lips formed a tight line. He nodded. "Most men with strong prejudices, like Sheldon, can't tell one black from another. There's a good side to that, though. If Sheldon does come across him somehow—or probably even if Bagley does—they won't know who they're looking at."

"Got another good thing going for us," Jason added. "Indirri doesn't have any reason to go seeking out Sheldon. Sheldon means nothing to him. To Indirri, Sheldon would just be your average whitefeller in a garish brocade vest."

CHAPTER TWENTY

FEAR OF FIREARMS

Golden evening. Marty's favorite time of the day. He settled deeper into the wicker chair and stretched his legs out. On the rise beyond the dooryard, yellow evening light gilded the trees. All the elements were in place; where was the magic?

Beside him in the upholstered pine chair, Pop sighed audibly. "Almost as pretty as the Downs." He raised a finger. "Mind you, son, I said 'almost.' "

"The Downs. No place is as pretty as home." Maybe that was it. Maybe he was just yearning for the old days, when problems that loomed large were actually very simple.

Uncle Edward shifted in the wingback chair beyond the verandah step. "Be a lot better with some sign of civilization. Railway. Smokestacks. Progress, you know."

Mum came out of the house with her carpetbag. Marty leaped up and gave her the wicker chair. He plopped down on the step and leaned back against the post, very weary.

Mum peered a moment into her bag and hauled out the big needlepoint frame. She settled it in her lap and took up the laborious stitching, almost by habit.

Marty closed his burning eyes. "By the time you finish all four of those chair covers, Mum, you and Pop will be ready for the pensioner's cottage and you'll only have room for two chairs."

"Oh, these aren't for us. They're your wedding present."

Marty opened his eyes. "Do you know something I don't?"

Mum smiled slyly. "That Pearl is a lovely girl."

"Who never married yet because she doesn't want a back-blocker. She's said so a million times. She's just an old friend."

Uncle Edward chuckled. "A girl with taste. But you don't know, lad. She might be quite happy at Pinjarra."

"There's not gunner be a Pinjarra."

"Good point." Uncle Edward's chair creaked.

Pop's voice sounded almost bitter. "You giving up, lad?"

"Look what's happened. I sank all the money I ever made into this. You gave me more than you could spare, putting the Downs at risk. Jase lost a wad. Now Pearl's life savings are going down the chute. I buy another hundred bullocks thinking that as the state lifts the tick quarantine, bullock teams will be in demand again. It's not happening. Bullocking's a thing of the past. There's more cattle in Queensland than there are people in Australia, and nobody's gunner eat a cow apiece. This last drought clinches it. I'm in the wrong business making the wrong decisions and losing everybody's money besides my own."

"So you flop over on your back and let Sheldon take over. If you get tonked, boy, it'll be because you let yourself get tonked."

Marty's voice was rising as he answered. He shouldn't be yelling at his own father. "He bought the constable; he's probably bought the judge. He buys anything that'll make him the money to buy more, and everything he owns turns into a money-spinner. He'll buy himself a seat in Brisbane and there's a better'n even chance he'll buy his way clear to the federal level."

"Now that he's shown his true colors, we'll back him down."

"No, we won't." Now Marty was sounding like Uncle Edward and he hated that, mostly because he knew everything his uncle was saying was true. "He has money, and that's power. And you don't have any and all I have is debts. That's *minus* power!" He waved a hand. "You see this big beautiful run in the golden sunshine? All the gold's in the sunshine, Pop. There's no power here. Pinjarra is lovely, but she's weak as a sick cat."

The pine chair groaned as Pop leaned forward. "You been praying about this?"

Marty stared at him. "I thought you let Mum handle the religion stuff."

"Yair. Then before Luke left, he set me down with the Bible. Your mum can't save me by being a Christian; I gotta do that myself. And she shouldn't have to carry it all; it's a man's place to head up the family, religion as well as other things. Some of Luke's notions are bull's wool; but when it comes to religion, he's worth listening to." Pop stopped suddenly and looked beyond Marty.

Goonur stood there, her blue eyes almost black. "Marty."

"That's Mr. Frobel, girl," Uncle Edward fumed.

Marty sat forward. "What do you need?"

"Dunno. There's a problem, bad problem. Indirri and Mungkala went bush."

"Thought Indirri, at least, was more responsible than that. Left without you?"

"No. That ain't the problem. He wanted me to go and I said no, I won't do it."

"What's the problem if that's not it?"

"Remember how he has an enemy? And he been looking for him for years?"

"He found him? The whitefeller?"

She shuddered and nodded. "Couple days after we come back from walkabout, Indirri took Bohra out. Gunner teach him tracking. Took him into the east paddock. Gunner track roos, I suppose. Lots there. And he saw him. He saw the whitefeller."

"He almost made a mistake once. Maybe he—"

"It's him. You'd know if you saw Indirri when he brought Bohra back. He wouldn't come near the whitefeller when Bohra was with him, for fear Bohra'd get hurt. Now he's all over the country gathering up blacks. By 'm by, gunner take fen . . . I forget the word."

"Vengeance?"

"Vengeance, that's it. Gunner wipe 'em all out." And her facade of composure dissolved. Her wailing voice broke.

"Marty, he's gunner get himself and Mungkala and all those others dead is all he gunner do. Even if they kill some of their enemies, the whitefellers gunner hang 'em. Shoot 'em. They gunner be destroyed every one. And he knows that and I can't talk him out of it. I tried an' tried."

"Know about where he's going?"

"Northwest, above Muttaburra. Heard about some blacks there. Left late this morning. Woulda left earlier, but I was arguing with him a long time."

Marty stood up and stretched his back. "Blacks don't like traveling by night, but I don't mind it. Moon's coming full. I'll ride out that way and see if I can catch up to them. Talk to him. With Mungkala along, he won't be moving very fast."

She looked near tears. "They took your horse. He's riding. The skewbald."

"That's horse theft!" Uncle Edward snorted loudly, instantly irate.

"Going out this late's a wee bit dangerous, son." Pop looked grim.

"So's a war between blacks and whites. Besides, I need to get away awhile. Can't just sit here watching Pinjarra die."

Pop stood up and unbuckled his belt. "Take my gun."

"No."

"*Take it!*"

Marty looked at Mum. She stitched away silently, her face sad yet resigned, mirroring the faces of all the women in history who stayed behind—grieving—while their men rode forth to do foolish things. He accepted the holster with its lethal load and ran his own belt through its loop.

He took the roan Indirri usually rode because he knew how well Indirri liked this horse. Every little bit of familiarity, every fond memory, would help now. He angled across country to the northwest, watching everywhere for movement or night fires. When it grew too dark for even his owl eyes, he rested the roan as the moon climbed above the horizon.

He rode to the crest of the only rise left between here and Cameron Downs to the north. If Indirri and Mungkala were in this area at all, he'd see the dull orange dot of their night fire out there somewhere.

Firecrackers. Firecrackers? Surely not. They pop-pop-popped again in the distance off to his right. He reined the roan aside and dug his heels in. In his breast welled the secret dread that the war had started.

If Mungkala were involved here at all, the skewbald's white markings would show up in the rising moonlight. He broke the roan out of its ground-eating jog into a full canter. The broad, open expanse of silver-gray bushes gave way to scattered trees with their towering shadows—black blobs that marred the clean moonlight and obstructed vision. He pulled the roan up; the gelding danced in place, tossing its head and flinging about the foamy sweat on its neck.

There—over there . . . a slight movement beneath a bottle tree . . .

"Indirri!"

"Marty!" Jase's voice! "Down! Duffers!"

Guns exploded, thunder and orange flashed among the trees beyond the bottle tree. On the far left a pair of light-colored trousers ran from a black shadow to a black shadow.

At least now he knew there was an enemy, where it was, and where they were moving to. Marty dragged the roan to comparative safety behind a gum tree. "Jase!" he shouted. "Where's your horse?"

"Dead!" Jase sounded much too far away. "Get back to the Downs and bring help. Don't try to wade in here."

"No time. I'm coming to get you."

"No! I'll come to you." The figure behind the bottle tree darted across a patch of moonlight to the blackness of a gum-tree shadow. He ducked across another open pool of silver. A gun roared from the trees beyond. Bushrangers. Most town constables would have you believe bushrangers no longer existed, except in folklore and history books. Yet here were four of them, big as life—at least four, as near as Marty could tell.

He saw a dim gray shadow bob far to the left: a horse's blaze face. One of the bushrangers was astride and trying to ride around to cut off Jase and Marty's escape. Jase must have seen him, too, for he fired at the man, and the gunshot, much too close, almost shredded Marty's nerves. He wanted desperately to run away, and so did his roan, Marty could tell. He was just as jumpy, lurching and swiveling to escape. *I must stay. Jase is doomed without me!*

He heard Jase's gun click. Suddenly he popped out of the shadow into silver light. Marty lunged the roan forward. He leaned forward and down, his arm out. He almost had him. Jase need only grab his hand and swing up behind; they'd be gone and safe before these dingoes could—

Jase grunted as if someone had slapped him too hard on the back. He slammed forward against Marty's leg. Marty groped wildly, grabbed a big handful of shirt, then wheeled the horse away so his cousin wouldn't be trampled. Jase's right hand clung to Marty's pant leg for a minute, then fell away. He was dead weight in that shirt. The shirt ripped; the weight fell away.

A thousand strident voices shrieked "no!" in Marty's ears. Pop's gun was in his hand even before he dragged the roan to a stop and spun it about. He saw just barely a smoky form in the distance, moving through the gray. The gun in his hand bucked and jerked him back with its kick. The form in the distance cried out, and in his head Marty heard Turk Moran's voice.

Over there, another movement—Marty fired, fired again. He didn't hear Turk this time; he didn't let himself hear anything, not even the roar of this bucking, kicking lethal weapon.

Jase was on his hands and knees at the roan's nervous feet. He reached up and grabbed Marty's boot. Marty shifted his reins to his gun hand and reached down to grab Jase. Together they squirmed and struggled and finally got him up behind the saddle. Marty reined the roan toward home and with a whoop and a shout turned it loose. The terrified horse needed no encouragement. It stretched its neck out and flew. With all his strength Marty clung with both hands to Jase, struggling to keep him aboard. Only when the roan began to stumble badly did Marty gather up the reins and draw him in.

Marty slid off the spent horse and helped Jase scoot forward into the saddle. Then with his cousin sprawled across the roan's neck, Marty jogged off homeward with the horse trotting in tow. Even so, the roan was tottering and ready to drop when they finally copped the rise and staggered into Pinjarra's dooryard.

Marty yelled, and a gladsome wave of relief washed over him as he saw Pop jump down off the verandah; he'd been waiting up! By the time he reached Marty, lanterns were glowing yellow in two windows.

"Starve the bardies! What on earth—" Pop exclaimed as he pushed nearer for a closer look at Jason.

Marty stepped back to let Pop take over. His legs were like rubber. His body shivered, slick wet from top to bottom with a drenching sweat. Not even the night air was cool enough to relieve either him or the horse. Pop led the roan toward the house with Jase still slumped in the saddle.

The kitchen door swung open, spilling yellow light. Mum called, "Martin? What's wrong?" She clapped both hands to her mouth.

"Shove his leg up, son," Pop said as he led the roan up onto the verandah. Marty swung Jase's right leg straight back and up while Pop managed the left, putting the injured man prone on the horse's back as they led it right through the door into the kitchen. The roan's belly scraped both sides of the kitchen doorway. With a sweep of his arm, Pop shoved a basket of apples from the table. "Right here. Easy does it." The apples hadn't stopped rolling before they had Jase flat out on the kitchen table.

Mum, a seasoned squatter's wife, never even blinked at a horse in the kitchen. Whipping out her sewing scissors, she cut away the remains of the torn shirt as Pop applied dish towels to the bleeding chest.

Jase's shirt was stained with a mixture of partly bright red and partly dried brown blood, like blood he had seen before. But this wasn't Turk Moran. Marty had not spilled this blood. Other men, evil men, had done this. And he, Marty, the inveterate coward, had not let his cousin down. He hadn't run. He had stayed and fought. He had pulled the trigger.

Inside him a new and undefined feeling exploded. It wasn't pride. It wasn't the heady thrill of victory. It wasn't rage exactly, but "rage" came as close as any word to describing it. Those duffers had entered his run, his Pinjarra, to attack Jase.

They made a fatal error doing that, for Marty would find them and defeat them and bring them to their knees. He knew he could, he knew he would, for now he had mastered the one enemy that would have kept him from winning—his own fear of guns.

Uncle Edward came waddling into the kitchen, tucking his shirttail into his trousers. He blustered and gasped a few moments. He hovered around, uncertain, then shook his head. "Fatal. Bullet in the lungs is always fatal."

Mum scowled. "Ed, run fetch the feather pillow off my bed. *Now.*"

Pop's hands were smeared with blood halfway to his elbows. He tipped Jase slightly for a better examination as his voice purred, smooth and casual. "Bullet entered from behind, right beside the shoulder blade here—see, Grace? Probably took out a rib here, but nothing serious. Then it broke up and exited here in pieces. Looks like ground beef under your arm, lad. But the lung's not compromised or he'd be coughing bloody foam by now." He straightened. "You got off lucky, Jase. What happened, anyway?"

"I was riding up the creek," Jase explained, "looking for dried-up billabongs that might be wet enough yet to dig down to water. Came on tracks of horses with cattle. Fresh tracks. None of our people moving stock there, and that's about where Marty's seed bulls ought to have been. So I followed them out."

Uncle Edward returned with the feather pillow and stuffed it under Jase's head. "Marty, you should've had someone in the saddle by now, going for a doctor. You're wasting time."

Pop snorted. "This far out? That's rich. Doctor's not going to travel two days to come see this. Sunday's nearly here and this is Father Bill's week at Muttaburra. We'll take him down to St. Joseph's church. Father Bill was a medic in the army. Good as most doctors. Now finish your tale, lad."

"They were lifting Marty's seed bulls, all right. Four of 'em. It was dark, the moon just coming up. I didn't know what to do. I yelled and fired in the air, hoping they'd think they were found out and run. Instead, they turned on me. I never expected cattle duffers would take up murderin' on the side."

Pop nodded. "That's what it'd be—murder. They would have hauled you away or buried you in a claypan, and nobody would ever have known what became of you."

Jase simply lay there breathing awhile before he continued. His face was the color of mashed potatoes. "I almost got away in the dark, but they shot my horse out from under me. Kept them at bay in the trees, but I was running out of shells. Then Marty yelled in the darkness. Nicest sound I ever heard—and the worst. I was afraid they'd get him, too. I didn't know he was carrying a gun. He never did before. I used my last bullet, but he was able to burn our way out of there. He saved me, and that's the truth."

Pop looked across the table at Marty. "Next time you argue with me, son, you're gunner hear about this. Count on it."

"*Every* time I argue, so long as we both shall live. Jase, did you see anything of Indirri or the skewbald?"

"No. Nobody out that way."

Suddenly Marty was too nervous, too keyed up, to stand still. He took up the roan's reins and led it outside before it did unspeakable things to the floor.

Goonur was standing there in the dark by the verandah step, barely discernible. "Did they do this?"

"No. Whitefellers. Cattle duffers."

"Did you find them? Hear of them?"

"No. If these duffers were the enemy he's looking for, he might've come to grief. If they don't mind shooting a whitefeller, they sure won't mind blasting a black."

Gimpy Jack came hobbling toward them. "What's going on?"

"Jase ran into cattle duffers." Marty handed the roan's reins to Goonur. "Put him away, will you?" He thought another moment. "Goonur, you don't have any trouble going bush. You're a good hunter, a good tracker. And Jack, the first time I ever saw you, you were tracking for Sheldon. Tomorrow first light, I want you two to track down the skewbald. Find out what's become of Indirri and Mungkala. If you overtake them, tell them to come back. I need help against my enemies just as they do."

With a bright smile she nodded eagerly and led the roan off toward the barn. Jack watched Marty closely, with a peculiar look on his face.

"Marty!"

Marty wheeled.

There stood Pop in the doorway. He strode down off the verandah, his eyes narrowed, and stood in front of his son. "I heard that. You're not the same man who rode out there this evening. I can feel the change in you. You're about to make a fearful mistake, bringing the blacks in on this. They don't care about the subtleties of English law, nor even what's fair. And they don't—"

"Neither do I anymore. Nobody comes onto my run and shoots to kill. They were closing in on him like a pack of dingoes, Pop. Cold-blooded. Deliberate. They knew who he was."

"The blacks will follow you to a point, but the minute they decide you haven't gone far enough, they'll cut loose without you. They're unstoppable. You'll be unleashing a bloodbath that won't stop with your enemies. Once this thing starts, scores of innocent people will die—black and white, people you grew up with, people who're supposed to be your friends."

"Jase would be dead now except for a twist of luck. The bloodbath has already started, Pop."

Pop glared, spewing anger. "Gimme back my gun."

Marty unbuckled his belt, never taking his eyes off his pop. He dropped his voice a few notches. "Remember that incident with Turk Moran years ago? Back then everybody called me a hero. The brave little boy who stopped him in his tracks. They toasted me in the pub. I wasn't old enough to drink but I got toasted. Even you said you were proud of me.

"Pop, I didn't want to hurt anyone. I didn't even mean to shoot him. It just sort of happened. I was trying to protect Jase and got mixed up. It took Turk a week to die. I know, because

I visited him at the hospital. He cursed me, not for shooting him but for spoiling his dream. They pumped him full of morphine but he suffered horribly anyway, and then he died."

Marty pressed the heavy holster and its pistol into Pop's hand. "I was sure I'd never . . . I mean, even hearing a gun go off . . . Until a couple hours ago, I never thought I'd touch a gun again. You're right, I've changed. I'm ready to fight now. And I'll win any way it takes."

Pop stared at him. "I never guessed. You never said anything." He drew an audible breath and let it out slowly. "You take Jason down to Muttaburra. I'm leaving at first light."

"Back to the Downs?"

"Beyond the Downs to the railroad and up to Mossman. There's one man who maybe can save us from war. I'm bringing him back here."

"Luke Vinson? How?"

"I don't know how. But the man's got a line straight through to God, and that's what we need. The blacks respect him, the whites respect him, and I never met anyone who knows more about what God wants and what He can do."

Pop started to turn back toward the house, then stopped. "My first reaction was 'God help us.' It still is. I figure it's up to me to give the Almighty a hand."

Marty smiled in spite of himself. "Never ask for a handout if you aren't willing to work for it."

Pop studied the dirt at his feet a moment. "Yair," he chuckled. "That's about it, ain't it?" He walked back inside.

Marty didn't bother going all the way around the house. Instead, he climbed in the window to his bedroom. He lit the lantern beside his bed, opened the clothes press, and got down on his knees. He set aside the bootbox, all dusty-smelling, that held his crocodile boots. He got out the other bootbox, the one tied with string. He yanked the string. It broke with a twangy *pung*.

Gently he lifted the lid. So many sordid memories lived in this box. He dug through tissue that had not been disturbed for over fifteen years. Then, with determination and a certain reluctance, he lifted out the gun that had killed Turk Moran.

CHAPTER TWENTY-ONE

THE SOURCE OF POWER

"When Baiame sent the first people out across the land, land that had never felt the press of men's feet before, he did not send them out powerless. He taught important magic to the old men. Then he instructed the old men to pass their wisdom on."

After so many years, after his dream had long since gone dormant like bushes in a drought, Indirri was tasting of that wisdom. The power of a thousand centuries was beginning to seep into him at long last. With absolute joy he sat beside this little fire listening to a storyteller.

The cicatrices on his back burned. They would be sore for weeks yet, for rubbing ashes into them like that slowed the healing process. It also made them welt up and stand out, bold marks that would forever tell the world of Indirri's new status. He glanced across at Mungkala. Mungkala didn't seem nearly so pleased to have become a man at last.

The three other initiated men in this clan appeared in the muted light and settled on their haunches. The elder spoke. "We talked about your story. We considered your idea. Your heart is right. Also you have the old pride, the kind of pride we used to carry in the old days. So many young men, they don't want the old ways anymore. They don't want the pain. They say, 'Why do this when we get no power anyway?' We listen to your heart, and hear wisdom speak."

Indirri's heart thrilled. Never had he been praised so grandly. "When I came to ask your help against an enemy who hates all blackfellers, I didn't know about your old men. I didn't know I could do this. You have made my life full."

"You saw our lubras. We have five ready to marry, and no young men for them. If you become one with us, we will fight for you. But you must marry with us."

"I have a wife and child."

"There is no place for them here."

Indirri glanced across at Mungkala; his cousin's face looked startled, even frightened. Take a whitefeller's crockery bowl and smash it. Now fit the broken shards together into a bowl again. That's how he must piece together his many thoughts.

Goonur. She meant everything to him. Bohra. His future, the part of him that would live even after Indirri had returned to the Ages. What would happen to them if he left them? Nothing much. They would remain at Pinjarra. Goonur would find another man, perhaps a better man. Indeed, if Indirri effectively removed this enemy, Goonur and Bohra would live much safer lives—particularly when on walkabout, for this enemy roamed onto Pinjarra's paddocks.

Another thought occurred to him. As an initiated man, Indirri in his dreaming could cast protective shields around Goonur and Bohra. Yes, the more he thought about it, the more he decided Goonur and Bohra would be better off were he to join this clan. He thought only briefly about the pain of separating himself from them. If he dwelt on that too long, he would surely lose heart and return meekly to Pinjarra. He would never be a man then.

The memories of that massacre boiled up fresh in the pictures of his mind, as if it had happened yesterday. With it came the hatred, fresh and new. The blood of all those innocent people of his clan cried out for vengeance with voices too shrill to be refused. Love and family must stand aside. For years he had yearned for revenge in a vacant way, for he was powerless to do anything about it. Now these other men, strong warriors, were agreeing to help him. He had their dreaming, and he was on his way to developing his own manhood. He couldn't lose.

After all these years, at last he had tapped a source of power.

Marty scooped deep into the basin and splashed a double handful of water on his face. He let his face drip and carried the basin out to the garden. He dumped it on the nearest row—lettuce—and brought it back to the kitchen door. His face was nearly dry now, and much cooler. He gave it a hard rub with the towel and walked inside.

"Eat in half an hour. Corky brought in a cow haunch—not dead long enough to smell bad, so you got beef for dinner." Rosella chopped up what looked like cooked spinach. As little as Marty liked spinach, Rosella's spinach with vinegar and bacon wasn't bad.

"Uncle Edward back yet?"

"Don't think. Didn't hear him. And if you don't hear him, he's not there."

Marty exploded laughing. He chuckled all the way back to the office. He paused in the office door. A buggy was coming—Uncle Edward, no doubt. He backtracked to the front door.

Pearl! She drew her horse to a stop in front of the verandah and was out of the buggy seat before Marty could get down off the step. She studied him coldly. "So where were you?"

"Where was I when?"

"Yesterday. You were supposed to be in court yesterday. We're talking about my bail money, Prince Charming."

Marty's heart thudded. "Somebody wants me in court, they're gunner have to tell me the day before, not the day after."

"Your signature was on the subpoena. You were served."

"I was not."

Those wonderful blue eyes looked into his for the longest time. "Perhaps not. Jase said he didn't think you were."

"You talked to Jase since yesterday? Then you stopped in Muttaburra."

"He's feeling much better, he says. I couldn't talk to him

very long; he was trying to explain to Barton Wiggins that he couldn't possibly have the cattle at the price Uncle Edward had sold them to him. I happened to bump into him when—"

"Stop. Whoa." Marty took her elbow and plunked her into the wicker chair. "Start over. What did you say about Uncle Edward?"

"Your uncle sold a hundred head of cattle to Bart Wiggins. Bart's a restaurant supplier out of Brisbane. I know him, so I was able to help Jason smooth it over. Marty, your uncle's under the delusion that he's in charge of Pinjarra. You've got to talk to him. He's causing you all sorts of problems."

"Why didn't Jase just take the money?"

"At fifteen shillings a head?"

He closed his eyes and sighed. "Seventy-five pounds. How far does Uncle Edward think that'll get us?" He opened his eyes again, letting the harsh sunlight of reality burn them some more. "What about yesterday?"

"I told Jason you forfeited bond. I saw the signature, and I was so sure—and so angry I couldn't think. I just hopped in the buggy and headed up here. I suppose it's a good thing Jason grabbed me, so to speak, and helped me cool off." She smiled wanly. "Of course, driving for two days rather cools you off anyway. Why can't you live closer to town?"

"Jase didn't come back with you?"

"He says he's going to rest another day or so and then take Cobb down to Longreach to see if he can do something about getting my bail money back. I have serious doubts about his chances."

Marty looked up as he saw two horses coming his way. He hoped Rosella had cooked the whole haunch. Goonur and Gimpy Jack entered the dooryard and rode up to the verandah. The looks on their faces told him he might as well prepare for the worst.

Jack swung down off his horse and tipped his top hat to Pearl. "G'day, mum. We woulda been back yesterday, Marty, but we did a little extra tracking. Mungkala and Indirri's safe. They're with other blacks up the creek a ways."

"Then why do you two look so glum?"

Goonur slid out of the saddle. "The black clan—two of them drove us off. We couldn't even get close. They came very near spearing Jack. And the paint—" She stopped.

Gimpy Jack explained more to Pearl than to Marty. "The patterns on their body paint say they're hostile. Ready to make war."

Marty's eyes went shut again. The world was closing in fast. He needed Jase and Jase was gone. He didn't need Uncle Edward, though they could hear his buggy coming a ways off, up the road. He needed Pop and Pop was who-knows-where up on the coast. If he estimated the depth of Indirri's hatred correctly, Marty had now lost two valuable workers—worse, they might now be his enemies as well. *A bloodbath*, Pop called it. And Pearl's money, and this whole out-of-control court business, and Sheldon's monkey business, and the drought and his stock dropping and . . .

"Marty!" Pearl was out of her chair and shaking him. "Are you all right?"

His eyes popped open. "Yair." He was master of Pinjarra. As such, he must now make more decisions, possibly life-or-death decisions. "Goonur, would you go help Rosella? Extra mouths to feed mean extra work. Jack, put the horses up. Pearl's, too. She'll stay here tonight. We'll set up a watch, since we don't know what's happening out in the bush there."

Gimpy Jack nodded grimly. Goonur started into the house, looking terribly dejected.

"Goonur?" Marty reached out and touched her arm. "None of this is your doing. Indirri made his own decision. You and Bohra eat with us tonight."

She flashed a false smile and brushed past him into the house.

Uncle Edward's cart came rattling up to the door. Jack grabbed the horse the moment it stopped, untied its harness, and with a whack on its rump sent it on its own toward the barn.

"*Now* what's going on?" Uncle Edward tipped his derby to Pearl perfunctorily and glared at Marty.

"Black troubles. Uncle Edward, what's this about—"

"Because you're too lenient with them! If you'd put your foot down right from the first, the way you're supposed to do, you wouldn't have these constant troubles. You don't even gain their respect. How do you think you're going to control them? Lollipops and a pat on the head?"

"What's this about trying to sell at fifteen per?"

Uncle Edward waved a finger in his face. "Seventy-five pounds on account with the store will get you supplies for another month, maybe two months. Right now your credit is flat. They're not extending you another farthing. No flour, no sugar, no nothing."

"*Fifteen a head!*"

"I was trying to get you something for nothing, lad!" Uncle Edward hissed. "It's more than they're worth. Ragged bags of soup bones."

"Unless it rains soon."

"You can't count on that. You have to be businesslike about this. You must assume it won't."

Pearl stood up and swept down the step. With motion as fluid as windswept leaves she walked away, out across the dooryard.

Uncle Edward lowered his voice. "Marty . . ." He took a breath and started over, even lower. "Marty, dreams are beaut. I know; I've had a few myself. But there comes a time to lay the dream aside and be practical. Sensible. Holding out for rain now is simply not going to work. You're dragging everyone you love down with you."

"What do you suggest?" Marty didn't really want to know.

"Sell out for whatever you can and repay as much on the pound as possible. Your creditors will understand. You tried. It didn't work. Now close the books."

Close the books on a dream. Just like that. Easy for Uncle Edward to say—it wasn't his dream. But then, the very fact it wasn't his dream might mean he could see the picture with eyes unclouded by dream-smoke. If he were right . . . and he'd been around long enough to know . . .

Marty leaped up and jogged down off the verandah. It didn't take more than a few fast strides to catch up to Pearl.

He slowed down beside her and matched her stride for stride. "Uncle Edward says I should give it all to the knackerman. What do you say?"

"I don't know." She shook her head and tears filled her eyes. "I really don't know. It's all so messed up. Not just you, but me, too. All of it."

He wrapped an arm across her shoulders and drew her in tight against him. It felt good. It felt so good. "I'm sorry you got sucked into this."

"It's not just that—not the money, I mean. It's all of it." She snuggled in closer still and put an arm around his back.

"All of what?" Even in the depths of his despond, her presence there exhilarated him.

"Remember Enid asking me to come to Jesus? And remember also when we were on that picnic, I told you I finally did. Right after Luke Vinson looked me up. Less than two years ago, isn't it?"

"Something like that." They stopped because they had arrived at the front paddock fence.

"Enid derived such joy from serving God. She seemed to know exactly where God wanted her. She had"—the lovely hand waved helplessly—"direction. She did something and saw the good results almost right away. I try to do something and I don't see anything. I can't tell if I did the right or wrong thing. Pinjarra is just one example of many."

"Maybe it comes with time."

She shook her head. The golden curls bobbed. "I need black and white answers—right or wrong. Remember when you two brought Jack into the hospital? You said something to Enid that confirmed in her mind that she was doing the right thing. I forget the details."

"I sorta remember."

"I can't hear those confirmations. I don't . . ." Her voice trailed off. She laid her head against his shoulder. "Marty, help me."

He wrapped both arms around her and pulled her in tight, and the weight on her heart bowed his down just as heavily. "I don't know how."

They set a watch that night but nothing stirred. Uncle Edward went through Marty's books listing assets, estimating the probable return on them. The very thought of him doing that—and worse, possibly being justified in doing it—tore Marty apart.

The next day over the dinner table, they made plans for the night. As evening waned Marty saddled the roan and rode out north, aimlessly, for no other reason than to be doing something. He carried the revolver along, just in case.

Here was part of the mob Pop sold him. He still owed Pop that thousand pounds. If he managed to sell them all at the price Uncle Edward found, he would be able to pay Pop seven hundred and fifty of it. No. *Please, God . . .*

But why appeal to God now? What did God have to do with the likes of him? The God who snatched Enid away certainly wouldn't smile benevolently on a doubter's lost dream.

He watched his cattle awhile and had to agree with Uncle Edward. They were so gaunt they weren't worth a pound apiece. They stood about listlessly or lay folded up, as cows do. None of them chewed a cud. None moved as he rode near. They stared off at infinity, awaiting death with a stoic patience cows alone can summon.

The promise of Pinjarra had evaporated into blue and cloudless skies.

Well, not quite cloudless. Marty could see a faint dust cloud rising just beyond the trees. He moved the roan farther away from the track. Blacks didn't travel by road—but black-bearded raiders well might.

With relief, Marty saw it was Pop's open six-seater with four persons inside it. He and Mum must be moving in; a fully loaded wagon followed a quarter mile behind. Marty rode out onto the track, waved and pulled alongside.

No greeting, no ritual pleasantries. Pop growled, "When's the last time these cows had water?"

"We dug them a hole beyond the rise there, but it's likely

dried up now. It was the last we could find. Hallo, Mum!" She was too far away to hug or kiss so he reached an arm out.

She reached a hand out to touch his. "Hallo, Marty." She couldn't take her eyes off the revolver on his belt. She looked frightened.

"They need twelve gallons a day each to thrive, eight minimum."

"Hush, Pop. You're sounding like Uncle Edward."

"So be it. Tomorrow we're gunner move your stock down to that south paddock. Muster ought be quick and easy, as feeble as they are. No runabouts trying to avoid us."

Marty turned his attention to the other two travelers. With the first lift his spirit had felt in days, he gripped Lucas Vinson's hand. "Welcome back!"

Luke grinned. "I wish to introduce the former Margaret Connolly, now Margaret Vinson. Meg, this is Marty Frobel."

"Crikey, Luke! I turn my back for just a second or two and look what you've done!" And old Luke had done a great deal. Marty doffed his hat. She was a beauty, pure and simple, with glowing reddish-brown hair and soft, misty gray-green eyes that looked deep enough to dive into.

She leaned forward to reach Marty for a handshake. "Sure'n I've heard an earful about ye, and all of it fine. Me pleasure, Marty."

Irish. Right off the boat Irish.

The wagon had caught up. Mum gestured toward it. "Luke and Meg have a few things, so we thought they might keep them at your place awhile. And I brought you a crate of chooks. You must be sick of beef."

Marty tied the roan to the back of the carriage and hopped in beside Mum. He wrapped an arm around her, not so much a gesture of affection as to feel the comfort only Mum could offer. The carriage lurched forward, building its dust cloud behind.

"Anything I should know about?" Pop asked.

"Lots of things. They can all wait till we get there. Too fine an evening to rot it up with business."

"Rot it up."

Marty glanced at him. "Far as we know, Jase is in town somewhere, doing all right. Gimpy Jack's got a watch set at night; the trouble could be black or white. Uncle Edward's planning Pinjarra's wake. Other'n that, not much on."

Luke snorted. "I thought surely by now you and Pearl would be married. I can't be the only one who gets these notions."

"You've been talking to Mum." Marty gave her shoulders a squeeze.

"No, talking to Pearl, on my way to Mossman. She glowed like Christmas all the while we discussed you. Does she ever visit?"

"She's here now. She was going to go back to Anakie tomorrow, but with you two here, she may want to stay awhile."

Pearl glowed when she talked about Marty? Luke must be misreading her. She was a friend, an old and valued friend. She wasn't someone Marty would think of courting. They knew each other much too well to go through the artificial motions of courtship.

He watched Luke and Meg, very proper and yet very intimate. Talk about a glow. They both shone. A stupid, insane, unjust jealousy swept over Marty. Luke had a working relationship with God. He had a solid faith in Jesus Christ. And now he had the perfect wife. He had it all.

And all Marty had was a dried-up, shriveling dream.

CHAPTER TWENTY-TWO

TWIST OF FATE

It wasn't a pleasant lunch, exactly—thanks to Marty's Uncle Edward, mused Pearl. Things started out all right, with cute little Meg all big-eyed with wonder over her first muster. Frankly, Pearl couldn't see the romance in moving a mob of sluggish, half-starved cows from the north end to the south end. But Meg, in her role as driver of the plant and assistant cook, bubbled with delight.

Then Edward started in. "The beginning of ruin in this state," he declared, "was giving women the power of the vote last year. Women do not—they cannot—concern themselves with weighty matters, particularly matters of state. Disastrous." It sounded as if Ross Sheldon had been talking to Uncle Edward.

Pearl adjusted her voice enough to freeze the water in the glasses. "I have on my own built up an estate worth five figures. I have chosen managers for my enterprises who are good enough that I can absent myself for periods of time without loss of revenue. Yet I am unable to address weighty matters?"

"You are a notable exception. Most women . . ."

Pretty Meg, bless her, chimed in. "Meself, sir, less than two years in this fair land, has found me precious Savior, and me precious man. We walk hand in hand, the three of us, and me husband avers I'm a worthy helpmeet, privy to his deepest needs and concerns. Nor am I chary of attemptin' and succeedin' at anything new, such as our adventure yesterday. Ye cannae do that if y're brainless."

"You're exceptional, of course, Mrs. Vinson. Most—"

Marty's father fumed. "Grace here managed the run all by herself those two years when my back was out. She handles my business when I'm away and does it as well as I can. You ready to tell me, Ed, that Grace is too dizzy to vote?"

Marty's mum eyed his Uncle Edward with a smug, absolutely haughty "chew on that, ratbag" look.

"Hardly, Mart. You're misreading me."

Even Marty added his bit. "Amazing place we have here. Three ladies in the room and every one of them is exceptional. Not a normal female in the mob. Uncle Edward, one of the lesser reasons we opposed Ross Sheldon was that he opposed the move for women's suffrage. We respect our women." He folded his napkin. "I'm off. Pearl, you're staying?"

"Yes, please. Drop me a line at this address if you need bailing out again."

Marty grimaced. "That bothers me. I do need bail again, and higher bail this time. I'm a bail jumper. Constable Edding should have been here by now to scoop me up. Can't understand why he hasn't appeared. Or Jase, either."

Gimpy Jack cleared his throat. "Uh, you don't ever wear that blue vest much."

"Haven't had occasion to. I'll wear it now, since I just might land in court." Marty grinned. "Dazzle the magistrate, eh?"

Marty walked out into the hall. Pearl got up and followed him back to his room. She leaned against the jamb of his open door and cleared her throat.

He shot her a smile as he dug into the nether recesses of his clothes press. "Sure I plan to wear it. Gimpy Jack's as true and faithful a friend as I'll ever have." He hauled out a flash of blazing blue.

Pearl giggled. "Pure Gimpy Jack, all right. My, that's something!" She sobered. "I've changed my mind. You will need cash, if they let you go free at all. I'll go along."

He slipped into the vivid blue atrocity. "Naw. Stay here with Mum and Meg. I'll do fine." He reached for his coat and glanced at himself in the mirror.

And he froze.

From the doorway Pearl could see his reflection in the mirror. Startled, she watched his eyes grow bigger and bigger. His face loosened and lit up, as if some stupendous revelation had hit.

"That's it!" he cried. "Of course!"

"*What's* it?"

"This was what I was wearing when Indirri mistook me for his enemy. It wasn't my size or age—it was this vest!" He grabbed his hat and almost trampled Pearl getting out the door. "Pop! Indirri's enemy is Ross Sheldon. He's out to kill Ross Sheldon! Come on!"

Martin bolted to his feet, and Luke was right behind him. "How do you know?"

"I know!"

Marty was already halfway out the front door. He screeched to a halt and reversed himself. "Jack! Remember fifteen years ago or so when Sheldon said he was attacked by a black raiding party and old Hosteen got speared? It was the other way around. He and his crew massacred a whole clan. Mungkala and Indirri are the only surviving eyewitnesses; it was their family. He'll never be brought to the docket for that one if we can't get their testimony. You and Goonur *must* reach Indirri and Mungkala."

Jack's dark face changed expression from bewilderment to sudden determination. "We'll do it." He raised a warning finger. "You take off that vest, hear? Don't want Indirri spearing the wrong man." And he hurried out the door.

"Right." Marty stripped off the vest.

Marty's father paused in the doorway. "I'll take the Muttaburra road down to Longreach. You go the Aramac way to Sheldon's place. Better for me to go into Longreach than you."

Marty weighed thoughts a moment and nodded. "Uncle Edward, you defend the fort here. I don't think they'd attack this place, but we don't know that for sure." He hastened outside.

Pearl ran out after him. "Marty? What are you going to do?"

He stopped and turned. "Try to reach Sheldon in time to warn him. Then find Jase's lawyer and see what kind of legal smoke we can bung up—maybe even file against Sheldon for murder. Probably have to go through the Rockhampton courts; Sheldon's bought these out here. If we can get Sheldon out of the area, in jail or otherwise, the situation might simmer down."

She ought to let him go. Instead she grabbed his hand and pulled him closer. "I'm afraid. I have such a bad feeling . . ."

"Yair. Me, too. Here I was fretting about that cattle duffing charge and now that's the least of our troubles. This whole district will dissolve in blood if Indirri feels revengeful enough to really cut loose." He shook his head. "And he's just about our only chance to stop Sheldon legally."

"Marty . . ." She could feel tears starting, and she didn't know precisely why. He looked so vulnerable, so easy to hurt. And so many hurtful things loomed large.

He pulled her against him in a strong hug. "It's going to work out fine. If you don't believe me, ask Luke." His voice softened. "I really believe it will, Pearl. We finally know what we're up against."

She shuddered. "What can I do?"

"Both Pop and Luke will tell you to pray. Maybe that's the best thing you can do."

"I want to go with you."

"Can't. I'll be riding cross-country where the buggy can't go. And don't try to return to town alone. The road's too dangerous."

Horses clattered behind her. Marty released her and took his roan's reins from Jack.

Jack dipped his head toward the barn. "Goonur's sending Bohra up to the house here to get some stuff. Then we'll leave. We'll find Indirri."

Marty nodded grimly. He put a hand on his saddle and paused. His long arm reached out and gathered Pearl in, and he kissed her. A kiss full of promise. Turning aside, Marty vaulted onto his horse and wrenched its head away. She watched them clatter across the dooryard and down the southbound track, shrinking ever smaller. Finally all she could see was the dust.

She ought be embarrassed by that blatant display of affection, but she was too grateful. A soft, fragile hand took hers. Meg stood beside her watching the dust cloud also.

Goonur rode up beside them, with horses in tow. Marty's father grabbed one and rode away down the track. Little Bohra came running, fearlessly leading a horse that dwarfed him in both size and weight. *The child has no concept of fear*, Pearl observed. As Luke took the horse, Marty's mum scooped the little one into her arms. In vain Pearl tried to picture her own mother lovingly cuddling an aboriginal child—or any child, for that matter. Bohra called out, but Goonur and Jack were away, galloping off to the north.

Luke paused beside Marty's mum, his horse dancing in place. "We're splitting up. They'll pick up the track from where they last saw the band, and I'm going southeast toward where we think Indirri spotted Sheldon. Tell Marty and them when they get back." When his horse's hoofbeats faded, the last sounds went with them. Silence.

Pearl took a deep breath. "Now what?"

"Now we pray." Meg sounded so matter of fact. "I trust ye'll join us."

The hot tears were threatening again. "I wish I could, with some assurance I'd be heard."

"Eh, lass," soothed Meg, "I hear y'r plaint, for 'twas me own not too long ago." She drew Pearl's hand toward the verandah. "Come. 'Tis purely amazed y'll be, at the wonders prayer works. It wrought a miracle at Sugarlea, I tell ye." She draped her delicate arm around Pearl's shoulder. "When this is all done and over, meself has a tale to curl y'r hair. Just wait'll ye hear what God did at Sugarlea."

Marty's mum rubbed Bohra's head. "You, too, scamp. We need your prayers as well. In fact, as I understand, God is going to listen to yours first."

They were so confident, these women. Their confidence buoyed Pearl in spite of herself. She allowed eager, energetic Meg to lead her into the house to pray—an exercise she had never excelled in. Ironically, the power of prayer was the only power she had to influence what would happen next. *All the money in the world would do them no good now.*

Martin Frobel Sr. cracked hardy on the outside. The world saw a powerful and commanding pastoralist—unshakable in extremity, generous in plenty. On the inside, though, he feared. He feared for young Marty so beset with troubles. He feared for the blacks and the whites as well. He had never voiced his fears, not even to Grace. But he expressed them now to God, with lips that moved without uttering a sound. Surely God, a Father in His own right, would understand. His was not a formal prayer, resplendent with thee's and thou's. He simply told God what was on his mind and beseeched help in no uncertain terms.

He got to Longreach in midafternoon and rode directly to the constable's office. Edding was out on his verandah having a cup of tea. Martin waggled a finger at him and strode into the office.

Constable Edding darkened the door, but he stood cautiously in the middle of the room, wary as a rock wallaby.

Martin perched one hip on the corner of Edding's desk. "I hear you're in Sheldon's pocket."

Edding drew himself up. "That is slanderous, sir!"

"I also hear you're on the outs with the home office for sticking you out here in the bush when you'd rather be in Brisbane."

"What is your game, Frobel?"

Martin kept his tone low and even. Much depended now upon the tone of voice. "I have eyewitness testimony that about fifteen years ago Sheldon and his monkey-dodgers massacred a family group of aborigines. You know me well enough to know how that sort of thing sits with me. I'll see Sheldon pay for it, and we have a good run at turning this cattle duffing thing around. He might just pay for that, too."

"Now you're multiplying your slander."

"I said proof—or weren't you listening? Listen. You're in the wrong pocket, Edding. Sheldon is about to be brought low. He has no power now to help you, and life is gunner get worse for him in a hurry. You can be his lap dog, as you have been, or you can get smart. And unless you get smart, you don't have Buckley's chance of ever seeing Brisbane again."

He stood up; the desk creaked in relief. "I suggest you look up the incident in question. A man named Hosteen was speared. Sheldon's version is a matter of public record. See if it mentions defenseless women and children. Hear this, too: two survivors of that massacre are out to destroy Sheldon—sheer retaliation. We get to either Sheldon or the blacks in time or Sheldon's dead." He started for the door.

"What makes you think I know Sheldon's whereabouts?"

"I'm telling you what's happening. And you tell me: who is gunner be held responsible if the blacks decide to avenge themselves on the general white population?" He paused beside the perspiring man in the wool tunic. "You're a clever fellow. Work it out."

Martin walked out into the slanting sunshine. That portion of his mission had gone smoothly. Now he stopped at various pubs, asking for either Sheldon or Jason or both. Jason had left on the train hours after he had first arrived, several days ago. Sheldon? Out on his run, most likely. Not here.

Martin toyed with the idea of keeping quiet, but decided against it. Taking a few key friends aside, he explained why he needed to find Sheldon. He took an extra couple hours to write a detailed letter to a friend in Rockhampton and post it. Then he was on his way again.

The euro's tracks led across a dusty glade and up into the rocks beyond those gums. Indirri followed, not that they needed the euro; they needed water. Mungkala's skewbald gelding was a mixed blessing. On it Mungkala could go nearly anywhere everyone else went. But it drank gallons of water every day. So far the old men were patient with Mungkala, but it was obvious to Indirri that their patience was running low.

He stood still, listening for flies. Silence, except for a crow in the trees beyond. He moved another hundred strides in a likely direction and listened again. Over there. He signalled to a flash of white in the distant trees and walked toward the buzz.

Through the trees came Mungkala, that extra stirrup swinging back and forth beneath his skewbald's belly. He wrinkled up his nose. "There's not enough water here."

"Better than no water." Indirri scooped the gilgai out, clearing it as much as he could of green slime and mud. The thirsty horse drank it up anyway, slurping it dry, gunk and all.

Off in the northwest, a nightjar cawed and gobbled. Mungkala pulled his horse's head up and rode quickly out around the ledges, headed southeast. Indirri made himself very straight and rigid, as if he were just another tree, and waited. Here came two old men through the trees. He watched them and watched behind them. Satisfied, he stepped out as they came near.

The very old Djirra motioned with his head. "Your wife is persistent. She comes this way, on a horse, and with her that fellow in the bright whitefeller shirt."

No woman could be a good enough tracker to so quickly follow trained warriors cross-country. And Gimpy Jack? Too long a station black to have kept any skills he once possessed. Indirri grimaced. "She's following the horse."

Djirra nodded.

What would happen to Mungkala if Indirri left him behind? Nothing—the same as Goonur and Bohra. Had not Jason himself promised that Mungkala would always have a home and tucker? Jason was a noble man, though he was young. Indeed, the whole reason Indirri set foot on a station in the first place was to find a life for Mungkala. Mungkala was secure now; he didn't need Indirri anymore.

Indirri nodded, too. "Let them have the horse. If we stay on the ledges they cannot follow us."

Djirra smiled. The old men glided away, two dark shadows moving up across the rocky outcrop. The euro leaped from hiding and bounded off, unmolested. Indirri waited. He must let his eyes watch her one more time. There they were just coming into sight through the trees, riding about twenty feet apart, studying the ground. He watched the tree-filtered sun dapple her warm brown skin and he imagined the velvet touch of it. Her head twisted, looking around, and with his mind's pictures he gazed into those wonderful blue eyes. Every fiber of her being, body and spirit, called to him. *Come to me. Come again to be father and lover. Please.*

And little Bohra . . .

With the mightiest of efforts, Indirri ripped himself away from the vision and the memory. Silently he slipped off into the rocks.

Marty wasn't exactly like Daniel in the lions' den. Daniel was thrown in; Marty was riding in voluntarily—riding into a war zone. The scene here reminded him of the Crimean battlefields he had read about in his old history book—full of bomb craters and ragged snags. He guided his horse through the debris of dead trees and branches, left here probably by starving beasts looking for food. Roos and sheep had eaten the grass and scrub to below ground level, churning the dirt to reach the roots. Even when it rained, if it ever would, this pasturage would not come back. Marty's paddocks were in bad shape, but rain would turn them green again. Sheldon's paddocks would not support any living thing again for many years to come.

He began to pass dead stock with increasing frequency. These sheep and cattle, and more than a few kangaroos, had not died very recently. The flesh had long since rotted and dried up, parched hides wrapped tightly around their skeletons. Everywhere amid the snags here, there hung in the dusty heat that pervasive, penetrating musty smell of naturally formed mummies.

At last Sheldon's main station loomed on the horizon, buried within its desolation. Marty was feeling extremely depressed at his surroundings by this time. He would warn Sheldon of the danger. If Sheldon weren't home, he'd tell whoever was around and continue on south to Barcaldine. From there he would catch the train to Jericho and find Jason's lawyer. Surely some legal way existed to foil Sheldon's high-binding schemes and call him to account for that massacre.

Half a dozen riders were gathered in the dooryard. Sheldon couldn't be starting an early muster; by the looks of it he had nothing left to muster. Two riders out by the front paddock looked toward Marty as he approached. They pointed wildly at him and shouted to the men in the yard. One of them yanked out a pistol even as the other was pulling a rifle from his scabbard. The pistol wielder aimed with both hands, his head disappearing behind the puff of blue smoke.

Marty didn't wait to assess the rifleman's intentions. He twisted the roan around and dug his heels in. He slammed his reins across the roan's neck, then—in desperation—against the other side. This was futile. His horse was nearly spent from two days under saddle, and these fellows were probably on fresh mounts. He'd never win this race, let alone learn why he'd had to run it.

Gunfire opened behind him—the rifle and a couple pistols. So far he was out of range. As his roan raced across an open glade, he glanced back; they were gaining on him! He wouldn't stay out of range much longer. His horse stumbled. He was in trouble.

Harry Bagley was an employee any boss would be proud of. He did what he was told. If something didn't ring quite true, he told the boss about it right away. The boss would never have known about that stinking abo and the tracking and the beard if Harry hadn't taken it upon himself to go tell him. Now he was assuming another responsibility for himself.

The boss had said, "Take care of Frobel's place once for all. I can't afford to wait any longer." By a sudden and unexplained twist of fate, here was the Frobel kid himself walking right in. Harry would take care of him exactly as instructed. The outback would swallow him and no one would ever know what had become of him. The boss had been happy with Harry before—big bonus and everything. He was sure the boss would be ecstatic at this one.

The kid was a good rider, but they were closing on him. His horse was starting to falter—and no wonder, if he'd just ridden clear down from Pinjarra. Chet and Morry got a few shots off but they were out of range. Frobel's roan stumbled badly. Another mile or two and they'd have him.

They lost him around a turn and a rise, but no worries. There was no place he could go. His dust cloud drifted through the trees, betraying his passing. Like English huntsmen after a fox, Harry's crew rode out through the trees, whooping.

There went the dust. Frobel had shortcutted the bend and was back on the road. They had the roan in sight now, but wait! It was flopping in the dirt, then struggling clumsily to its feet. Quickly the horse lurched forward, nose and tail high, and cantered off northward, riderless.

Riders churned in place in wild confusion.

"He's gotta be close! There ain't no place to hide. Chet, you sweep around through there. Morry, swing out that way. When you see him fire once, whether you get a good shot at him or not." Harry got a second thought. "And watch up in the trees! He mighta climbed a tree!" He watched his crew break up and spread out for the search.

Then silence. Where was that gunshot? Harry looked at the road all around, but a score of hooves had churned it up so badly no mark or sign was left. Harry couldn't even see where the horse had fallen.

He started calculating. Sure as shootin', the kid wasn't here. That means when his horse stumbled, Frobel hit the ground running and just kept running. A good runner can go ten, twelve miles an hour. That's half a mile in the time they were wasting here. He was half a mile away at least, and here they stayed, milling around like sheep in a paddock. Half a mile on his way back to Aramac and home.

Harry Bagley cursed—at himself and at the Frobel bucko. He fired one shot into the air to call in his crew. They would fan out and start searching between here and Pinjarra. The Frobel kid was smart, but not that smart. He couldn't get far afoot. Harry would find him. Harry Bagley, if nothing else, was a valuable employee.

CHAPTER TWENTY-THREE

THE BEST OF PLANS

There is an awesome magnificence to the Red River Valley of Canada, a sweeping grandeur. There's a sense of history about it, too. Studded among the fine modern farms are sheds and buildings and abandoned homesteads of an earlier era. Here along a hedgerow you see a broken, grey wooden plough, long ago supplanted by a steel-share two-bottom wonder of engineering. Threshing machines perform the labor of many even as Sal Pierre-LeGrand on his hundred-acre lot painstakingly scythes his wheat each summer and threshes it by hand.

There was an awesome magnificence to this Queensland country also. In fact, when it came to sweeping grandeur, this open outback took the prize over any place Luke Vinson had ever been. But there was no sense of history here, no weatherworn link with the past. There was only the present—intense and biting. Stay alive now. Make a life for yourself now. Seize now, because yesterday is gone—what there was of it—and tomorrow is so terribly uncertain.

He paused his horse to rest it, admiring anew this wonderful country. These lacy, gangling trees would never pass muster in an arboretum next to a good, solid eastern black oak. Still, they stood about here and there and pretended they were a forest. That was one thing this stretch of Australia lacked: a true forest, packed with big, honest, compact trees—trees so dense that rain didn't reach the ground beneath them.

Luke smiled to himself. Rain didn't reach the ground beneath these trees either, but not because of the foliage. He glanced to the north and east. There was haze there, and mares' tails. Possibly this horrific drought would break. The rain certainly wasn't holding back for want of prayer.

Off to the west—what was that? Half a dozen riders had spread themselves wide across the land as if they were seeking something. Luke felt the strongest urge to avoid them. Silly. They didn't look particularly dangerous, but in an inexplicable way, they did. Luke had been a very practical person in his youth, and his major training had been in the sciences, physics especially. It had taken him a long, long time to learn to shed the scientific explanation for everything and listen to his inner voice. But he had learned. He listened now, and quietly drew his horse aside and away through the trees.

He continued south, the sun at his back. He knew Aramac was behind him somewhere and that Barcaldine, or perhaps Ilfracombe, lay somewhere ahead. Other than that, he was lost. Continuing south, he would bump into the Central Line sooner or later, and then he wouldn't be lost anymore. He would simply follow the railway west and end up in Barcaldine. Or Ilfracombe. Or Longreach. Or perhaps Alpha, depending on how lost he was now.

That body of men had safely passed. Luke tried again. "Indirri! I need you!" He had called at intervals throughout this last day and a half. No response. He tried once more, just to be certain.

Was that a human voice he had heard? Or an eagle-hawk crying? He urged his weary horse forward a quarter mile and called again. The answer came again, to his right. He found him! At last he had found Indirri. Now they could all breathe easier!

His own breath caught in his throat. That wasn't Indirri. It looked a lot like Marty, the hat especially. He whipped his startled horse into a run.

The moment he saw that he was seen, Marty sat down in the dirt and simply waited. With his left hand he clutched his right arm rigidly at his side. Luke bolted off his horse before it had stopped and dropped down beside this bedraggled tenant of the Crown.

He took one breath and literally fell back. "How you stink! What is that?"

"Long story. Sure glad you showed up." Marty struggled to his feet, but he couldn't get there without a hand. "Let's ride double-dink; I'll tell you about it on the way."

Luke made a face, but gave Marty a boost into the saddle and swung up behind. "This is a sacrifice for friendship I wouldn't make for just anybody. What *is* that smell? It's familiar."

"I was coming up on Sheldon's government house when six riders fell on me, shot at me, and chased me. The roan was too tired to keep the pace. He went down and I landed on my shoulder. Popped it out. That's happened before."

"It doesn't look disjointed now."

"I think it popped back in when I squirmed under the cow, but it hurts too much to move it. I crawled three feet and dug into loose dirt under a sun-dried cow carcass that had fallen by the track." He shuddered. "Luke, you'd never guess how many thousands of bugs live under a dead cow. Not just flies and maggots. Big beetles with scratchy feet."

"Indeed. Six apiece, in fact." Luke listened a moment to the labored breathing. He must get this man some help quickly.

"They were right there on top of me, not a yard distant—the men, I mean. I expected them to find me any minute. Longest hour I ever waited in my life. I knew if they found me they'd kill me. And those bugs . . ."

"Why kill you? That's rather drastic—not to mention illegal."

"I knew it, that's all. When I was certain they'd moved on, I came out and started walking north behind them. I figured so long as I stayed behind them, I'd be all right. They wouldn't be expecting me back there—they'd already checked the basin pretty thoroughly."

"I saw them. They would have killed you, all right—put me off—and I was a mile away." Luke had better make some plans here. "Where to? Aramac?"

"No. Sheldon's people will get there before we do. They'll

post at least one of their own in town to watch for me. We gotta get home."

"That's a long way off, even if you know where you're going, which I don't. And you can't ride that far in the shape you're in. Besides, I doubt my horse would make it with two."

"Cy Bickett keeps a dozen horses at a camp near a little seep to the northeast. It's out of our way, but not too far. If any of his stockmen are there, we can recruit them—at least tell them about the possible war."

"Not the best of plans, particularly if you decide to pass out on me. You alone know our way around this wasteland. A seep, huh? Suppose there's enough water in it to wash some of that smell off you?"

Meg tried curling up on her other side. That didn't work either. She sat up on the floor and tried to see something. Anything. This was the darkest night she'd been in for ages. Marty's mum and Pearl were asleep on top of Marty's bed. That narrow pallet couldn't be much more comfortable than the floor here. Meg got up and stretched. Oh, she was stiff. She was fully dressed—they all were (battle-ready, Marty's Uncle Edward called it)—so she groped her way down the hall to the front door.

Edward's voice barked a very military "Who goes?"

"Meg Con—Vinson. It's me."

"Not you. Them."

"Halloo!" A familiar and most welcome voice called from the distance of the east paddock.

"Luke!" Meg's prayers were answered, her day complete, and it wasn't near sunup yet.

"Are you certain?" Edward sounded suspicious.

"I'm certain." She hurried out into the dooryard.

A horse without saddle or bridle came clattering into the yard and right past them toward the barn. A minute behind it came two more horses. Luke slid off a bareback horse Meg didn't remember seeing before. With a happy grin, he wrapped both arms around her and kissed her soundly.

He turned to the other rider. "Your turn. Go find Pearl."

"Break it down, mate." Marty! His right arm was bound firmly to his body with a sling and swathe. He carefully disengaged himself from his saddle and slipped to the ground. He was controlling his horse with a length of rope over its nose.

"What happened to ye? And why the . . . and why are ye two together?" Meg looked from face to face. "And what in heaven's name is that smell?"

Marty grimaced. "Gully Joe's clothes and a bath and I still smell like that cow. Gunner stink for a month. Meg, how about rousting out Rosella for at least ten pounds of breakfast? We're starved."

"I'll tell her." Edward disappeared in the dense gloom.

A lamp filled a window with an orange glow as Luke pulled the bridle off his horse and whacked it lightly across the rump. It trotted off into the blackness toward the barn. Marty took the rope off his horse and let it follow the other.

There was light in the kitchen now as they went inside.

We could be sitting out in the pleasant dining room at a lovely oak dining set, Meg idly observed; *yet everyone seems to prefer crowding into the kitchen with its roughhewn slab table and stools.* Luke did bring an oak chair from the dining room so that Marty could sit and lean back.

Rosella had already lit the little coal oil cookstove. She started a big pot of porridge. "Steak and eggs coming up. We wouldn't have the eggs except for your mum's chooks, Marty. They're good layers and yours went on strike."

"Thanks, Mum." Marty waved to his mother as she entered the kitchen.

She looked at him in shocked consternation, studied the sling a moment and sighed. "Silly goose, I am. I thought after we raised you and kicked you out on your own, we'd be done with worrying and fretting about you. Doesn't work that way, I guess."

Meg would have started coffee, but Rosella was already throwing grounds into a pot. At that moment Pearl entered the kitchen. Meg watched her face with some amusement; here was a woman who loved, though she was not necessarily "in love" in the romantic sense. Pearl crossed to Marty, leaned against the wall beside his chair and put a hand on his good shoulder.

Here, too, was a man who loved. He let his head rest against her and idly laid his left hand on hers. He looked drawn and intensely weary.

Luke hovered over the coffeepot in eager anticipation, a mug in his hand. "I found him down below Aramac yesterday afternoon. If you think he smells bad now, you should have smelt him then. We rode up to a Galilee Spring where we borrowed two fresh horses and a change of clothes and tidied him up a bit. Rode all night to get here."

"Cy's horses, eh? They don't know their way here. How did you manage?" Marty's mum flopped wearily onto a stool. "It's blacker than the inside of a cow out there."

"Please, Mum, don't mention insides of cows." Marty glanced at Luke. "Rode by starlight until the overcast blotted them out. By then we were close enough that Luke's horse had his ears up. So we turned him loose and followed him in."

The porridge was starting to bubble. Meg set out flatware and dishes and listened to the talk. Marty described his hairsbreadth escape and Luke described finding him. Both men fit comfortably in a wide open land that intimidated Meg. She was used to the close dampness of her native Erin, or even the encompassing gloom of the rain forest behind Mossman. Marty's mum was just like them. She understood instinctively not just the lads but their horses as well, and what the land itself permitted and forbade and . . . and, well, all of it.

Luke got his coffee at last and sat down. He looked not much less weary than Marty. Meg settled herself near him and he wrapped his long arm around her shoulders. Would Meg ever develop the easygoing oneness with this vast brown wilderness that her Luke and the others enjoyed? For that matter, did she want to? Wanting to didn't matter; she'd better. Outside the window behind her the sky was getting light at last. The terrors of the night slipped away. What terrors would the day bring?

Harry Bagley chewed nervously on the bumper of an unlighted cigar and watched out the window. Here he came at last, riding up the dusty little street of Aramac. Sheldon wasn't nearly as imposing when he was dressed normally, without one of his awful brocade vests. He looked less set apart, more like one of the boys. The early morning light didn't have anything to bounce off of. He tied his horse out front of the cafe and came striding in.

Before Sheldon entered, the room held only Harry and three of the lads; but when he came in, his presence filled the room. He nodded toward the little Chinese lady in the kitchen door and plopped into a chair beside Harry. "Get it done?"

"Not yet."

"Why not? I told you I can't wait any longer! I accomplished quite a lot at the meeting last night, but there's another scheduled for the first of the week. If the Frobels show up at that one, I could still lose."

"I thought that redistricting scheme was home on the pig's back."

"I thought so, too, but some of them balked. If they get Frobel on their side, it's dead. And I told you already, we've got to redistrict if I'm going to get enough political pull to get what we need. And the bore on the east side dried up completely two days ago. Until I can drill deeper, I got nothing. I need Pinjarra's south paddocks now."

"The Frobel kid showed up. Right outta nowhere. We chased him but we lost him. He's got one fast horse, y'know. I figured we better wait for you. There has to be some reason he'd come down right to your door."

"From the south or the north?"

"North."

"And you couldn't outrun him?" The door squealed open. Whatever Mr. Sheldon would have said next had to wait. He twisted to see who was coming in.

Constable Edding's scrawny assistant, Walker Hayes, slunk through the door; he seemed somehow swallowed up by the room. Edding's shortcomings—both as a man and as a constable—were reflected on an even grander scale in his assistant. Hayes' tunic, cut small to begin with, hung out over his shoulders and bagged at the sides. He pulled his cap off thinning mouse-brown hair and grimaced a greeting smile to Sheldon.

"Ah. They said you'd be here. I've important business with you, sir. Two matters, in fact."

"Sit down."

Hayes dragged a chair from another table and perched on the edge of it, facing Sheldon. "About the redistricting meeting you attended last night: first let me compliment your forceful and splendid presentation."

"Thank you. What about it?"

"You left immediately thereafter, on other business, I presume. At that time there was some question as to why the Frobels were not present, since they so utterly oppose your redistricting scheme. There is rumor of funny business on your part. It's a fence you would do well to mend in the near future."

"And the other business?"

"Fifteen years ago. An incident in which a man named Hosteen was speared."

"Attacked by savages. It's a painful episode I'd rather forget."

"Some say not. They've opened an investigation of it. There's a possibility you may be held culpable. Eyewitnesses—surviving abos."

"The abos filed a complaint fifteen years after the fact? Turn it up, Hayes."

"Not the abos. Whites representing them. The abos are out on Pinjarra."

"How many?"

"Two, I think. Their names were recorded, but I don't remember them."

"What's Edding doing about it?"

"I don't know. He's out of town."

"Right when I need him he goes on holiday, the drongo." He stared at Hayes a moment. "Wait outside."

Like a well-trained house pet, Hayes got up and left.

Harry spat out a stray shred of tobacco. "I coulda swore on a stack of Bibles there weren't any eyewitnesses."

"Maybe there aren't. You heard him—these so-called witnesses are on Pinjarra. Maybe it's just some lark that Frobel's dreamed up to put me off."

Harry leaned forward. "I for one ain't about to take that chance. If they can really put the finger on you, then it's on me, too. I was the one killed that gin. We all had a hand in it, which means we'd all swing together."

"Not for a couple wild abos. You're dropping your bundle, Harry. Relax. Get yourself together."

"Wild abos, maybe not—maybe just a prison sentence. But station blacks? That speak English?" Harry sat back. "This day and age, that's murder. You gotta get rid of them."

"No, Harry. You."

Harry studied his boss. Until now, Sheldon's orders, while not exactly legitimate, were easy to carry out. Fun, even. Had Harry put the Frobel kid away, no one would be the wiser; it was done in a corner, and scant chance he'd ever be prosecuted. But now, Sheldon wasn't just talking about firing a barn or scaring a few station hands. He was telling Harry to stick his neck out like a turtle on the run. Harry stood a good chance of losing on this one, while Sheldon's neck was still tucked safely in his shell.

"No." Harry felt a strange mix of dread and exhilaration as he stood up to his boss for the first time ever. "No, Mr. Sheldon, you wear a beard, too, on this one."

Sheldon glanced around the room as Harry prayed to heaven the lads would back him on this. It was their necks, too. Sheldon pressed his lips down to a tight white line. "All right. All of us. Best plan is to surprise them. Hit fast and hard, torch the barn and house, kill every black on the place. All of 'em, understand? Big ones, little ones. That means we hang around long enough to make sure none go running out of the burning buildings and get away."

"You're asking a lot. Bonus in this?"

"If it goes right."

"It'll go right." Harry would do most anything on bonus, as would the other lads. If nothing else could be said for the man, Mr. S. was generous with bonuses. And now, Harry had a vested interest in this raid. If there really were abo witnesses to that thing so long ago, Harry's very life depended on this raid. "It'll go too right, Mr. Sheldon."

CHAPTER TWENTY-FOUR

INTO THE MIDDLE OF IT

Meg was impressed with how seriously Marty's Uncle Edward was taking his role as protector. He sat up on the flat top of the barn's gambrel roof—his crow's nest, he called it. From there, he could see in all directions. Into the haylift she hooked the basket holding the quart pot full of stew and the pot of freshly steeped tea.

She hauled away. "All's quiet, aye?" she asked, despite the creak of the pulley.

"So far. So far. Thank you, Mrs. Vinson."

He eased down and leaned over the side to retrieve his basket of dinner. He clambered back up to his perch. Meg noted that this crow's nest was aptly named, for it came replete with the birds. Several were alighting at the far end of the barn. They were settling unusually early this evening. But then, the Frobels and their guests were eating an early dinner also.

Rosella was serving in the dining room when Meg came back into the house. She took her place by Luke and he asked a blessing. Strangely, the conversation was much lighter and happier with Edward on the barn roof.

Meg found herself staring at Marty and quickly averted her eyes. He was painstakingly picking through his dish, his fork in his clumsy left hand, eating the potatoes first.

Marty's mum smiled at her as she cut up little Bohra's meat. "He's always done that. The correct order is potatoes, turnips, carrots, beans, peas, onions, meat. I put barley in the stew once just to see what he'd do. He stared at it the longest time. Then he took an hour and a half to eat dinner, picking out all those little grains. Incidentally, barley ranks between potatoes and turnips."

"You're poking borak at me." Marty gaped at her, then said, "No . . . you're not making fun of me; you're serious, aren't you!"

"I only did it once. I have a heart when it comes to my boy."

Meg laughed. "For contrast, there was me brother Edan, six years me senior. 'Edan' means a consuming flame; ye should've seen the lad consume. Set him in front of a fine stew like this and he'd eat whatever his fork reached first, no matter the size of it. And be back for seconds before y'r own fork touched meat."

Marty's mum looked at her. "Was?" she asked gently.

"Murdered by Brits during partisan troubles on the Auld Sod, as was me former beau, Sean Morley. There be nae peace in the world. Nae here, and nae a world away."

"Mum's back!" Bohra shrieked. He hopped down and ran for the door. From atop the barn roof the dinner triangle clanged.

Meg stared at Luke.

Luke shook his head. "I've seen it often. They have a sixth sense. Perhaps you ought to stay inside until we know what we have."

Meg followed him to the front door. But Marty's mum and Pearl and even tiny Bohra were out on the verandah. Meg ignored Luke's suggestion this time and went out, too. Cross-country from the southeast came three riders. Meg knew the one by his top hat and vivid shirt. She could barely make out the small rider who would be Goonur. And between them rode a blackfeller on a gaudy little horse splashed in white and brown.

They rode up to the door and Goonur jumped off her horse, sweeping Bohra into her arms. Her face was wreathed in smiles as she held her son.

Bohra hugged quite as tightly. "Where's Papa?"

Her face sobered. "Gone bush yet."

The three were escorted into the house as Luke walked over to the barn to talk to Edward.

Rosella scowled at Mungkala, then turned to Marty. "I suppose you're feeding this duffer."

"He's back in the fold. Bring us some stools from the kitchen, eh?" Marty sat again at his place.

Goonur sat at Bohra's place and settled him into her lap. Her eyes were downcast. "I'm sorry we couldn't find Indirri."

"Mungkala is very important. You did well." Marty looked at the shame-faced black. "Mungkala, do you know what it means to give testimony as a witness in court?"

"Naw."

"You stand in a special box. Some men will ask you questions and you tell what you know. That's what a witness is: a person who tells what he's seen and heard." Marty hesitated to let it sink in. "You're a witness, Mungkala. We want you to go into a court and tell those men about that attack fifteen years ago that crippled you."

"Why?"

"If you do, the court will condemn the man who did it. We know who he is now, the man in the bright vest. With your help we can bring him to trial and he'll pay for the attack."

"Pay how?" Mungkala looked not at Marty but at Luke.

Luke put his hand around his own throat and gagged. Mungkala was not impressed.

"Indirri gunner do him that. Don' need no coat do it."

Luke leaned forward and locked Mungkala eye to eye. "Listen. If Indirri kills that man out of vengeance, the law—that is, the court Marty talks about—will hang Indirri just the same as it would hang that man. The law does not allow revenge. The law makes men who kill other men pay, black or white, revenge or not."

"Goonur and Jack, him talk lots to me. I see."

Marty looked at Gimpy Jack. "You explained about bringing Ross Sheldon to account?"

Jack nodded, too busy eating to spend much time in lengthy discourse.

Goonur nodded also. "He understands. He's ready to do it the law's way. He's ready to be a witness in law court. But Indirri, don' know. Couldn't talk to him. Couldn't find him."

Luke smiled at Marty. "Half a loaf is as good as a whole one in this case."

"The whole loaf would be better. Lots better."

After dinner Goonur and Luke retired with Mungkala to take down a written statement. Marty's Mum and Pearl took Bohra along to retrieve Edward's dishes. Jack went off to put the horses away. Marty sat staring at the wall as he nursed the last of his tea. He looked overwhelmed, dejected, as spent as those sorry cows they had moved from north to south. Meg hefted the pot. Half a pot left. Unbidden, she refilled his cup.

"Ta." He gave her a wan smile.

Where should she start? "I appreciate y'r hospitality very much. These are delightful people, all of them. Y'r mum's a jewel, and . . ."

"She really did that with the barley, you know."

"And a jewel all the more because of it, aye. And Pearl. What a lovely girl. Uncertain in her Christian walk, but eager to grow. And she speaks so warmly of ye."

The corners of his mouth turned up, but it wasn't exactly a smile. "When I was young I had the hardest time talking to girls, especially the pretty ones. Still do, some. All bashful and tied up. But never with Pearl, which is amazing; she's so beautiful." He chuckled. "Maybe seeing her trip over that axle and sprawl in the mud took some of the mystery away. She's always been different to me. A mate, a chum. Someone to talk to."

"Y're saying there'll never be another lass like her."

"That's the drum! Dead set!"

She let his thoughts steep in silence a few minutes. Then, "Y'r mum and pop have both come to depend on the Lord. Pearl has turned to Christ, as have Luke and meself. Do ye nae feel uncomfortable being the odd man out?"

His head snapped around, his deep-set chocolate eyes latched onto hers. "Now, isn't that a crook way to make one of Luke's religious pitches!"

"Whatever works. And it be nae Luke's. 'Tis me own. It hurts me to see ye suffer so. Y'r mum says that somewhere ye seized the notion that money is power and water is power and Pinjarra has precious little of either." She leaned forward. "Tell me, Marty—how do ye think wealth and water will stand up against the wrath of God?"

"What?"

"The Bible says God is jealous for His own. 'Vengeance is mine,' saith the Lord, over and over. He fights for His own; ye know that. Ye think Indirri's vengeful? He can't hold a candle to God's vengeance. There's y'r power. That's the real power of Pinjarra—not wealth or water—and y've ought but to tap into it."

He shook his head and looked past her. She twisted around. Luke was standing behind her with Mungkala at his side. Goonur pushed past them and went outside.

Wonderful! Meg had been a Christian such a short time that she didn't have the wealth of Bible wisdom Luke tapped into so readily. Now that he was here, Luke could supply the Scripture they needed, the solid word that would speak much more eloquently to Marty's spirit than the opinion of a humble Irish lass.

Luke squeezed her shoulders and sat down beside her. "She's right; I hadn't thought of it that way. Absolutely right. I believe God will prevail regardless whether you commit yourself to His Christ. 'Where two or three are gathered, there will I be,' said Jesus. By that standard, we're an army—your folks and us. But we so deeply desire you to come to know the Lord, as we do. He loves you, Marty."

Marty licked his lips. "I've seen that loving God of yours destroy one of His choicest servants by a slow, torturous death. It was pointless. Cruel. And I couldn't help. I couldn't do anything."

"You're talking about Enid. Marty, have you ever wondered how good can come from bad? How an unspeakably hideous event can trigger immeasurable good? In First Corinthians, the second chapter, Paul is talking about the crucifixion of Jesus. You know Jesus sacrificed himself for us.

But Paul was convinced that if Satan's minions had understood God's plan, they would never have crucified Christ."

"You didn't see Enid die!"

"You've never seen a crucifixion, and it was God's own Son!" Luke lowered his voice. "From the worst possible atrocity that could be committed came the grandest possible gift and blessing mankind could ever have. If Christ hadn't died, our sins wouldn't be paid for. Don't you try to second-guess what God is doing, because you haven't a clue. We accept that He knows what He's doing. We believe Romans eight twenty-eight: all things turn out for the good for His own. And that, my friend, is exactly what faith is. Trusting God to do His job."

Like a trapped fox, Marty looked from face to face. He paused to stare at Mungkala. *Surely Mungkala didn't hold to this. The poor blackfeller had suffered too much.*

But Mungkala was no help. "Indirri and me, much little lad. Storyteller ask a—a puzzle. Question. 'Bout two friends from Dreamtime, Mirram and Wareen. But never him answer. Today, now Luke him answer. God take bad thing make to good. Now I see."

"Mungkala sees. Do you see?"

"Enid said the same thing. I forgot till now. She was happy to go because she said good would come from it. She was so certain."

"Marty, if Pinjarra is lost, if Ross Sheldon wins, if the world falls apart—it will all be worth it if it brings you to eternal life. Those are all temporal things, not important when you match them against eternity."

Marty lurched to his feet and walked out.

Meg looked at Luke. He bore the happiest smile on his face, an exultant look of triumph. He knew Marty pretty well; she prayed he was right.

Mungkala was frowning. "Sacker—huh?"

"Sacrifice?"

"Tell 'bout."

This was obviously man to man. Meg excused herself and

walked out into the warm, shifting breeze of this tense and uncertain evening.

Indirri's heart was restless, heavy. He was now so very close to the goal that had driven him, at greater or lesser intensity, his whole life. The man in the bright vest, a vest brighter than Marty's, worked somewhere in this area. This was where Indirri had seen him. What a cruel stroke of fate that Indirri had had Bohra with him then, or this business would be finished. But he had done right in returning to Pinjarra to avoid endangering the boy. And because he had sagely bided his time, he was now initiated, at least in the first stages. That good thing would not have happened had he fallen instantly upon his enemy.

Joy should have been welling up in his breast as his moment approached. But there was no such thing. Thoughts of Goonur haunted him, tormented him with longing. Soon he would have other wives. But they would not be his Goonur.

Sound and vibration told him horses were coming. Indirri and his companions made themselves invisible among the trees nearby. Seven whitefellers came riding through the trees, staring grimly ahead. They all carried guns—short guns and long guns. Behind their saddles were tied rag-and-stick torches reeking with coal oil. One of those stinking black beards hung from the pommel of the nearest rider's saddle.

Indirri thought of the raids on Pinjarra by men in black beards. These were those men. He felt the strongest urge to run ahead of them up to Pinjarra and warn Marty. Marty was a good whitefeller.

No. His mission, the mission shared by his new friends here, was to avenge the murders of blacks by black-hating whites. He would not be deterred. Marty was on his own.

The riders were nearly abreast now. Indirri could see details on their faces. There was that feller with the scar named Harry and the other two Indirri had sniffed. He got a good glance at the face of this big feller in the lead. Indirri's heart stopped. It was his enemy! The man who had worn the bright vest! The face . . . the build . . . yes! Add fifteen years to his features . . . and here rode the enemy not a dozen paces away!

Had Indirri not lived for all those years among whitefellers, he might not have recognized him, for all whitefellers look alike until you get used to them. In fact, were Indirri not so close he would never have identified him because the man had removed his bright vest. Two strokes of fate combined to bring the enemy into Indirri's lap.

He dared not step out and spear him now or Indirri would die in the blaze of half a dozen guns. He couldn't alert his companions; they were scattered round about. Again, for the second time, he must let the enemy pass unharmed. But not for long. The end was near!

The enemy gave an order: "Step it up, you galahs, or it'll be dark before we're done."

The riders urged their horses forward at a quicker pace. Indirri and his companions would be hard-pressed to keep up, let alone overtake them. The moment he could safely move, Indirri chirred like a magpie to call his friends. Soon! Oh, so soon!

Meg so enjoyed outback evenings. This time of day was usually beautiful, with golden light. But there was no gentle light tonight; heavy clouds had gathered—scudding clouds with thick black bottoms. Might the drought be breaking? Or was this one of those brief and sudden thunderstorms that washed over the land and disappeared, leaving the soil as dry as ever?

Out on the line, forgotten laundry flapped as the errant breeze shifted. Meg walked around to the back of the house to take the clothes down, just in case rain should come.

Marty's mum came around the corner and started at the other end of the clothesline. Meg watched the woman surreptitiously. So like her own mum this dignified lady was, with a dollop of humor her own mum lacked. Now they were close enough to converse.

" 'Tis a thing meself be still not accustomed to; the violence of y'r weather. There was a typhoon through Mossman last year, the likes ye could nae imagine. And here y'r heat is so hot, y'r dry so dry. And y'r wind. Sure'n it's like to pull y'r house down."

"Violence. Yes. We like to think we're civilizing the land, but we're not. Civilization here is confined to a coat of paint. Any bit of turmoil, like this dog's breakfast right now, strips the paint away, and all you have left is the raw beginning. Rain, drought, distance."

"Ye think it'll come to bloodshed?"

"Probably. Pitched legal battle at the very least." She snorted. "The men will posture and fire their guns, but it's the women who are the real warriors. We're left with the cleanup afterward."

Goonur came out of the summer kitchen with a water bag and a tucker bag. "Would ye see to Bohra, mum? I'm going back out. And mum, if my horse comes home without me, don't be scared. I'll set him free if the track leads where he can't go."

"You truly think you can find him?"

"Indirri and his friends are too good in the bush. I can't hope to catch them. But maybe if I'm alone, by 'm by I can get close enough to call him and he'll come to me. All I want is to tell him about the law; that his enemy is Marty's, too. That the whitefellers can avenge him if he'll help them. That he doesn't have to kill and then die for it."

"God bless you, Goonur."

"Thank you, mum." She walked quickly away toward the barn.

Meg watched her disappear around the house and shook her head. "Aye and tooroo, y're right. 'Tis we who are the warriors," she murmured. "And the sufferers."

Mum took up the filled wash basket. "I'll go find Bohra." She dipped her head toward the laundry. "A woman picks up a ten-pound bag of flour and a man leaps forward and says, 'Here. Let me do that for you!' But let her pick up a twenty-pound load of wash or a thirty-pound child and nobody notices."

Meg giggled, " 'Tis the way of men!"

Sszzzzffak! Meg jumped a foot as a ragged blue streak ripped through the sky nearly overhead. Resonant drums of thunder followed right on its heels.

They had retrieved the laundry just in time, it appeared. Marty's mum hurried into the kitchen with her load. Edward would be scampering down off the barn roof if he knew what was good for him. Meg ran toward the barn to help him with his precarious rope ladder.

There was Bohra with his uncle Mungkala out across the dooryard. Meg detoured to tell Bohra to run into the house.

From the barn roof the dinner triangle rang furiously. Edward tossed it aside. It clanged its way down the sheet-metal barn roof as he grabbed up his rifle. He flattened out on his belly and took aim.

Meg stopped, paralyzed with shock. She had never seen highwaymen in Ireland, much less bushrangers in this up-side-down country. There they were! Men in thick black beards galloped their horses into the yard from the south, torches ablaze, guns roaring, their wild-eyed mounts lung-ing.

Bohra shrieked as Mungkala fell upon him. Edward's rifle blasted from the barn top. One of the raiders' horses screamed and fell backward, carrying its rider with it. The war had begun. And Meg was smack in the middle of it.

CHAPTER TWENTY-FIVE

THE WRATH OF GOD

Globs of cold water too big to be called raindrops slammed like bullets into the dry dirt; each kicked up a puff of dust. The heavens opened with a vengeance Noah would have appreciated. Cold, drenching rain beat upon Meg's head. Lightning was striking very close, but you couldn't hear the thunder for the roar of the guns.

Lightning again—thunder—more guns.

Without thinking, Meg bolted forward toward Mungkala. Bohra had crawled out from under him. The child was on his feet now, crying. Meg scooped him up and wheeled. With Bohra wrapped tightly against her, she raced for the safety of the barn.

She was almost there when she felt the presence of a horse behind her and the drum of its hooves. Its big brown head appeared beside her; its hard shoulder bowled into her. She sprawled in the dirt, her legs so tangled in her skirts she couldn't get back to her feet. Still gripping Bohra, she rolled to her back, looked up and screamed.

That beard couldn't hide the bright rage in his eyes or the white scar over his right eyebrow. Even as he fought to control his frantic horse, he had straightened out his gun arm, aiming his pistol directly at little Bohra! Meg struggled to disengage her legs enough to roll over. She must protect Bohra!

Fffwit! The man's eyes widened, bulged. Bright rage faded to startled fear. As his gun arm sagged, his pistol discharged harmlessly. The bullet meant for little Bohra kicked up the dirt at the horse's feet. An arrow had materialized from nowhere, piercing the gunman's breast.

Meg's skirt ripped. At last she could roll to her feet. Clutching Bohra, she ran to the barn.

In the barn doorway Goonur dropped her simple archer's bow and reached out. Bohra twisted and leaped from Meg's arms to Goonur's.

From the house, glass shattered. Meg caught sight of the orange flicker in the parlor. How could she possibly reach there in time? The next thing the torch came flying back out through the broken window; then a flurry of motion and out flew a burning window curtain as well. Meg vaguely saw the outline of Marty's mum inside.

Now a torch had been thrown at the barn! Meg ran to an open back wall of a box stall, where smoky orange flames boiled out. Snatching up a horse rug, she beat at the fire from the stall door. She fell back, seized a pitchfork and forked flaming hay out the big open back side into the rain. Her eyes burned, her lungs burned, her nose burned.

The air was clearing a little. She stamped out the few licks of flame that were left. Another torch had landed on the clean-swept barn floor. She grabbed it up, dumped a nearby bucket of water on the smoking charred spot where it had fallen and stuffed the smoldering torch head into the bucket.

She looked up to see Gimpy Jack come from the back of the barn to the front at his waddling, lumbering run. He swung a shotgun up and blasted at the raiders as they rode back and forth.

Marty and Pearl were running toward the barn doorway now, dragging Mungkala between them. Where was Luke? Meg's heart panicked; she kept telling herself that Luke was a wise young man who would keep his head down. The two of them left Mungkala leaning against a stanchion. He still clutched his walking stick tightly. Marty took up a position inside the half-burnt box stall, where he could shoot. Close beside him Pearl curled up with her head below window level and shut her eyes.

Goonur cried out. Meg wheeled to stare.

Indirri. Wearing nothing but paint and raw welts and carrying a spear, he appeared from the south side stall doors. Goonur fell upon him, clutching him fiercely, jabbering nonstop. Mungkala yammered to him rapidly. Bohra wailed. Indirri answered them in syllables just as frenetic. And the thunder and the guns continued. Meg thought she'd lose her mind in this whirling madness.

Out by the paddocks she saw dark shadows—Indirri's friends, no doubt. A spear sailed across the dooryard and struck a rider's leg.

Marty called, "I'm out of shells! Anybody got shells?"

Jack shouted, "And bring me some shotgun shells!"

Suddenly Indirri knocked Goonur onto the floor. He brushed Mungkala aside and positioned himself in the doorway. He raised his spear, watching, waiting for a solid presence in a sea of chaos. His enemy! One of these raiders was his enemy! He was waiting patiently, prepared to avenge himself of his clan's destruction.

"No, Indirri!" Luke cried from over by the hospital paddock. He started running toward them, shouting, "There's a better way! Please trust me! We can get him the whitefeller way!" He was halfway to the barn when a bearded rider came upon him from behind and sent him sprawling, a motionless mass.

Meg's world turned cold. She didn't bother listening to guns; she paid no attention to the flying hooves and men. Luke was all she saw, his silence was all she heard. She ran out across the dooryard, through the driving sheets of rain.

She was nowhere near strong enough to budge this tall and gangling fellow, of course. But that was not important. Only his safety was important. She seized his limp hands and began to drag him through the slimy mud toward the barn.

They were nearly there now, nearly safe. She looked over her shoulder. Gimpy Jack lay groaning, clutching his head with both hands.

And Mungkala. . . ! With a *whock* of his walking stick, he

struck Indirri from behind. The warrior dropped like a stone. Mungkala threw his walking stick aside and snatched up the spear in his only good hand. With lurching half steps he yanked himself out into the rain.

The spear poised itself up beside his ear, wavering. Meg kept tugging. Almost there. A large man, the same rider that had struck Luke, was coming back this way. He saw Mungkala and wheeled his horse. Wild-eyed, the horse skidded, nearly losing its balance in the mud.

Indirri was trying to sit up. He screamed and reached out to his crippled cousin, his friend. The spear arched gracefully through the driving rain and lodged in the horse, causing it to fall on its side, kicking and squealing. The big man went down beside his mount. He jerked himself free. Perched on one knee, he fired again and again into Mungkala.

Meg's legs buckled and she sat down with a thump, too shocked to move. Horror upon horror splashed in waves across her. Marty was at her side now. He clamped his good arm around her and dragged her bodily, still on her knees, into the barn.

"Luke . . ."

But Pearl had Luke by one arm and with dynamic effort was hauling him faster than Meg could have. They were shouting at someone in the dooryard, "Get inside! Get inside!"

From beyond the dooryard, from the southbound track, came thunder on the hoof. Nearly a thousand cows, all that mob from the south paddock, came storming through. They were aimed right at the barn. A brilliant bolt of lightning struck the huge gum tree by the hospital paddock; it exploded in a flash of flame. The mob veered away from the tree.

Indirri was pulling Goonur and Bohra back behind the stanchions by the tack room. Meg ought to do something; but she was too numb to function. Nothing in all her years in Cork prepared her for the incomprehensible violence and horror of this terrifying moment.

The mob was headed in a new direction now, angling to the northeast—straight toward the house! The front verandah shook, then collapsed upon the sea of horns and bony backs. The dooryard was filled end to end now with galloping, wide-eyed, slavering, frenzied cattle.

A few came bucketing into the barn, tore through the length of the structure, and went smashing out the far end. Luke stirred and struggled. Meg wrapped her arms around him and pressed back against the tack-room wall. It was not until several minutes later that she realized how wildly she was sobbing.

Then it was not just her arms around him; his arms were wrapping around her, too, keeping her close and safe. The chaos in the dooryard dissolved into a few spattering hooves. The rhythm of the hoofbeats changed. The cattle had passed. There were horses in the yard now, not cows; the raiders were back!

No, they weren't. It was Marty's father, his cousin Jason, and two strangers. Marty's father, pistol in hand, danced his horse in circles in the middle of the dooryard, gaping in utter disbelief.

Marty stepped out into the rain, and Luke lurched to his feet to follow. Meg was not about to stay behind. Still clinging, she stumbled along beside him.

Marty's father rode over to his son and dismounted. Their eyes met and held. From the intensely emotional expressions on their faces, Meg expected them to fall into a warm embrace. Instead, the father took one last look around and said laconically, "Didn't do your fences much good."

"Yair. All of them, it appears." He walked over to the man who had shot Mungkala. He reached down and ripped away a soaked and bloodied beard. He stood erect and looked at his father, who nodded grimly, confirming the identity. The elder Martin turned away.

Meg caught more of a glance than she would ever want of the man. Scores of cattle hooves had . . . She buried her face in Luke's breast. His hand pressed her head tightly against him. She could feel him breathing, could feel warmth coming through his muddy, rain-soaked shirt. She twisted around to look the other away.

There lay what remained of the man who tried to murder little Bohra. "It's over now, isn't it?" she said, shuddering sobs choking her.

"It's over." Luke's gentle fingers rubbed her temple.

"Mungkala. He knew what was going to happen."

"I never realized when he wanted to talk about sacrifice that he might have this in mind. Yes, he knew."

Marty was shaking his head. He had turned away from the body, and the two strangers were now bent low, examining it. "I don't understand, Pop. He was one of the biggest in the district. What would make him resort to this sort of thing?"

His father shrugged. "Power-hungry. I don't know."

"More than that." Pearl stepped in beside Marty. Absently he put an arm around her and drew her in close. Even rain-bedraggled, she was beautiful. "Didn't you see? He and his people were shooting at the blacks. They were trying to kill all the blacks. He really did try to pull a Herod—kill them all to reach one or two."

Luke sighed. "And Herod died prematurely, a madman."

Marty stared at Pearl. "You're right. They even tried to get Bohra, who couldn't possibly have been a threat. Which says that he and his crew were guilty of that massacre, or they wouldn't have gone to these lengths to remove the witnesses."

His mum and Rosella came running out through the rain. Rosella buried her face in her apron.

Jason stood in the downpour looking all around, his eyes wide. "Crikey. Here I thought I was bringing you some hot news, and we come on this. My news is nothing compared to this."

"Good to see you. Tell me anyway," Marty said.

"Your pop and I bumped into each other in the magistrate's office in Rockhampton. Both had the same notion, so we worked together. Got a writ against Sheldon based on the blackfellers' accusations and got you a stay of arraignment concerning that duffing charge. All sorts of high-powered legal wrangle."

Marty's pop waved an arm. "Detective Inspector Murchison of the Queensland Police and an assistant, Sergeant Melrose. They're here to conduct an independent investigation all around—including malfeasance in the constable's office itself."

Marty shook hands left-handed and introduced everyone. Meg curtsied when mentioned, but her mind was flying.

A few minutes later she was able to draw Marty's father aside. "Please, sir?" she asked. "How did ye make those cows come charging through?"

"We didn't. Lightning spooked them. Jason and I and these two officers were just coming up the track when we saw them take off up ahead. Wasn't half a rush. They were headed right for the station, so we tried to turn them aside." He wagged his head. "Them cows were so weak and feeble, I wouldn't have thought they could walk, let alone run like that. Try as we might, we couldn't catch them. We were behind 'em all the way."

Clouds still blanketed the sky overhead, but the evening sun had slipped beneath them. Soft golden light swam across the ridge to gild the trees and the fresh, stubby grass. What a lovely time of day.

Meg nestled against Luke. Too bad about the verandah. It would be such a pleasant place to sit once Marty rebuilt it. For now they all sat on dining room chairs and kitchen stools where the verandah had once been, beneath a canvas rain fly.

"So once my rifle was empty I simply lay flat on the roof. I knew they'd instantly forget about me. I was safe." Marty's uncle completed his portion of the day's rehearsal.

Pearl came out of the house and settled down beside Marty. "I just looked in on Gimpy Jack. A day or two of rest and he should be fine. He has a hard head. Bullet bounced right off, and I told him so." She leaned back to look at Marty. "You still smell a little funny when you get rained on. Like a dog."

"You'll get used to it."

She giggled.

Meg smiled to herself. Had Marty popped the question yet? It certainly wasn't Meg's business; they'd announce it in due time. Everybody knew, and finally now Marty knew also, that he was going to.

Indirri, Bohra and Goonur came walking across the yard. Fully clothed, he didn't look the least bit savage. He bore the expression of a man who deserved whipping at the post. Now and then Goonur would glance at him almost reprovingly. He arranged himself self-consciously in front of Marty. His eyes darted everywhere.

He muttered to Goonur, who muttered "apologize" back. He grunted and opened his mouth to speak.

Marty cut him off. "You did well this evening, Indirri, giving your statement to Inspector Murchison. Luke says you did it in English start to finish. Your statement and the one Luke wrote down from Mungkala's testimony just about wrapped it all up and put a bow around it. Thank you."

Indirri frowned, speechless. Apparently praise was furthest from what he had anticipated. "I apologize, all the hurt . . ."

"Apology's accepted."

Indirri brightened a bit and shifted his attention to Luke. "Wirinun. Remember Wirinun?"

"No, I . . . yes, I do, too. He's the old man who showed his power by breaking the first and greatest drought. Thunderstorm."

"Big God, same. Him show big power, eh?"

"Big power."

"Him tell me 'bout Mungkala, all him say today." He muttered to Goonur and got an answer. "I thank you. Thank you for tell him all last story. 'Bout Jesus good thing, bad thing. All of Him. Is tell me, much big heart in Luke."

Goonur interrupted. "He's thanking you for telling him about Mungkala's last conversation, including the answer to some sort of puzzle from years ago."

"In my Lord's name, you're welcome. It was my privilege. Mungkala was a noble man."

Marty dipped his head. "Sit down, all of you. Join us. We're just soaking up a little welcomed silence."

Luke leaned forward. "Indirri, tell us a story. You know, like you'd tell to Bohra here."

Indirri's face relaxed. He pursed his lips a moment. "Law, no big thing. Talk English for him law, no big thing. But story. Story much big thing. I not good talk English. Goonur, him give you the drum."

He sat down in the rain and the mud and motioned Bohra to sit before him. As Indirri began speaking, Meg watched him change right before her very eyes. Gone was the uncertainty, the hangdog look. Gone was the reserve and the stiffness, replaced by a gracious new dignity. He was a storyteller now, a privileged position he obviously held very dear. His voice purred in the lovely, lilting cadence of a thousand generations. Goonur watched his face carefully, translating as he spoke.

"I will tell you tonight how the first kangaroo and the first wombat came to be, and how good can come from a bad thing.

"Mirram and Wareen were hunters. They ranged together through the hills to the west of the sacred Oobi Oobi Mountain where hunting is good, and they were friends. . . ."